Touch of Rain

DATE DUE

PRINTED IN U.S.A.

BOOKS BY TEYLA BRANTON

Unbounded Series
The Change
The Cure
The Escape
The Reckoning
The Takeover

Unbounded Novellas
Ava's Revenge
Mortal Brother
Lethal Engagement
Set Ablaze

Imprints Series
Touch of Rain
On The Hunt
Upstaged
Under Fire
Blinded

Colony Six Series
Sketches

Other
Times Nine

UNDER THE NAME RACHEL BRANTON

Finding Home Series
Take Me Home
All That I Love
Then I Found You

Lily's House Series
House Without Lies
Tell Me No Lies
Your Eyes Don't Lie
Hearts Never Lie
Broken Lies
Cowboys Can't Lie

Noble Hearts
Royal Quest
Royal Dance

Picture Books
I Don't Want To Eat
  Bugs
I Don't Want to Have
  Hot Toes

Touch of Rain

TEYLA BRANTON

WHITE STAR PRESS

This is a work of fiction, and the views expressed herein are the sole responsibility of the author. Likewise, certain characters, places, and incidents are the product of the author's imagination, and any resemblance to actual persons, living or dead, or actual events or locales, is entirely coincidental.

Touch of Rain (Imprints Book 1)

Published by White Star Press
P.O. Box 353
American Fork, Utah 84003

Copyright © 2017 by Nunes Entertainment, LLC
Cover design copyright © 2017 by White Star Press
Originally published by the author under another name as *Imprints*.

Printed in the United States of America
ISBN: 978-1-939203-89-2
Year of first printing: 2017

For my family, who puts up with my eccentricities and endlessly cheers me on. Especially my daughter Cátia, for her encouragement and unending support.

Chapter 1

My breath came faster as I stared into the shoe box sitting on the counter at my antiques shop. None of the items inside was exceptionally valuable or remarkable in any way—a kaleidoscope of bric-a-brac and childhood keepsakes that had once made up a young woman's life.

A missing young woman.

I met Mrs. Fullmer's swollen, tear-stained eyes, small and brown inside the fine scattering of wrinkles that were evidence of her suffering. Her hands tightly gripped the edges of the box holding her daughter's possessions, though the box sat on the counter between us and needed no support.

I didn't want to do this. I didn't have to. If I refused, Jake would escort the couple quickly outside and make sure they didn't return. I was very near to fainting as it was, though more with fear of what I would discover than of what the box contained. I'd learned the hard way that some emotions left imprinted on random objects were better off undiscovered.

"You okay, Autumn?" Jake's voice was both worried and curious. He smiled tentatively, his teeth white against his brown skin.

"I'm fine," I said.

A soft snort came from Mr. Fullmer. "Maybe we should be going."

An unbeliever. I didn't blame him. I hadn't believed in psychometry myself when the imprints had begun, and I hadn't told anyone about my strange gift for months after. I'd confessed to Tawnia first, and that my practical sister believed me was a testament to the connection between us—despite our having spent the first thirty-two years of our lives apart.

Jake Ryan was the second person I'd told. Solid, reliable Jake, who was gorgeous despite—or perhaps because of—his chin-length dreadlocks, or locs as he called them. When he was at the counter in my store, women bought more of my antiques just to see him smile or to have an excuse to talk to him. He had increased the sales in the Herb Shoppe considerably since I'd sold Winter's business to him. Winter Rain, my father.

Silently, I met Mr. Fullmer's gaze and saw him notice my mismatched eyes, his mouth opening slightly in surprise. People are always surprised when they look at me long enough to actually see my eyes. I didn't give him credit for seeing, though, as we'd met already once before and because he'd been staring at me for the past five minutes, searching for obvious flaws. He took a step back, which I regarded as defeat.

"If there's any chance Victoria left a clue," Mrs. Fullmer said in her breathless voice, "we have to try. She's been gone for months."

When no one spoke further, I slowly removed the oversized antique rings from my fingers and handed them to Jake, the comforting, pleasant buzz they gave off ceasing the moment I released them. Wearing them wouldn't prevent me from reading other imprints, but it would soften them, and I didn't want that now. I reached for an object. A hairbrush. I held it in one hand, running the fingers of my other hand over the polished length, pushing at the hair-entwined bristles.

A face in a mirror, a narrow, pretty face with long, blond hair. There was a sound at the door and a flash of an angry man staring down at me, words falling from his lips: "You are not going tonight, and that's final!" The urge to throw the brush at his face, an urge at least nine months old.

I shook my head and set the brush back in the box. I'd recognized the girl as Victoria from the picture they'd shown me and the man as Mr. Fullmer, but the scene hadn't told me anything except that once last year Victoria had been angry enough to want to throw the hairbrush at her father. She hadn't done it, though, and the memory was already fading. Mentioning it now wouldn't help them find her. I moved to the next item, passing purposefully over the new-looking socks and worn swimming suit.

I'd learned by touching everything of Winter's after his death that distinct feelings or imprints remained intact only on belongings connected with great emotion. Objects a person treasured most or held while experiencing extreme levels of joy, fear, worry, or sadness. Items that weren't often washed or forgotten.

For Winter that meant the colorful afghan my adoptive mother, Summer, had crocheted, the first vase I'd made on my wheel when I'd gone through my pottery stage, his favorite tea mug with the sad-looking puppy on it, his plain wedding band. And of course, his cherished picture of Summer, the one I'd dropped in shock and surprise on the day of his funeral eleven months ago, causing the glass to shatter. It was the first object that had "spoken" to me.

Other objects gave off a muted sensation, a pleasant low hum, but no clear images or scenes I could relive when the burden of missing Winter became too great. I never found anything among his possessions that contained angry or hateful imprints. He must have long ago come to terms with those feelings. My adoptive father had been an exceptional man.

My hand settled on the journal from the Fullmers' box, but I could tell right away this hadn't been a real journal for the missing girl. No emotional imprints, except perhaps the barest hint of old resentment. If she'd written in the book at all, it hadn't been willingly.

I picked up the prom pictures instead. Victoria was a slim, pretty, vivacious girl, and her date equally attractive, but though he was nice enough, the girl hadn't been attracted to him. The feeling had been strong enough to leave a faint residue of distaste on the picture when she'd held it in her hands as recently as six months earlier, which would have been mid-December, several weeks before her disappearance. I set it down.

The sea shell hinted at the ebb and swell of the ocean, the girl's possession of it not long enough or felt deeply enough to make an imprint. An old compact mirror with jeweled insets radiated a soothing tingle. Most of my antiques were like that, the emotions clinging to them soft and old and comfortable. I believe that feeling is why I went into the antiques business. Perhaps the objects had quietly hummed to me all along, though I hadn't yet understood their language.

Even in the old days there had been attractive items I'd never wanted to bring to my store, and now that I was conscious of my gift, or curse as I sometimes thought of it, I suspected those were the antiques that had fresher, negative imprints, perhaps even violent ones. A cast iron statue at an estate sale last month had flashed a terrifying image of crushing a human skull. No way had I wanted that statue in my shop. I didn't care that my markup would have been phenomenal.

I let my hand glide over several more objects in the Fullmers' shoe box, scanning for emotions that might be clues for Victoria's mother. The letter (contentment long faded), the porcelain figurine of a ballet dancer (sleepy dream of the future), a book of poetry (whisper of an old crush). To tell the truth, I wasn't positive any of these weak impressions were real or if my mind showed me only what I expected to find. These items had obviously been important to the missing girl at one time, though, or she wouldn't have kept them all these years.

Not until I reached the black velvet jewelry box did I feel a jolt. My hand closed over it, my palm covering the small object completely. Even through the box, the emotion was strong— too strong to come from even my active imagination.

"What is it?" Mrs. Fullmer asked. "That's my daughter's—"

She was hushed by her husband, who probably thought I would make something out of whatever information she might let slip. But I didn't need anything from the mother to tell me the girl had loved whatever was inside.

I opened the box and took out a gold chain with two inter-twining heart-shaped pendants, one studded with diamonds. A beautiful piece, one that would never be outdated, and expensive enough to be out of reach for most young girls in their first year of college. I knew Victoria had loved the necklace because it had been her grandparents' high school graduation gift to her mother and then her mother's to her. Yet the overall feeling emanating from the piece was not love but guilt, one emotion overlying the other.

I gently rubbed the hearts between my fingers, my eyes closed. Jewelry often retained the best imprints, which was why I'd saved the velvet box for last. "She wants to take it with her," I said aloud, "but everything she has will become theirs, and she knows it's not right to give them her mother's necklace. It should stay in the family. She thinks you will give it to Stacey when she's gone."

I very clearly felt Victoria replacing the necklace with a sigh. She hadn't wanted to pass it to her younger sister, and that's where the guilt came in. She'd wished there was a way to follow her dream and keep both her family and her necklace. With the guilt came several earlier flashes of memory, rushing like water through my hands to my brain.

A college campus, a park, a man dressed in a flowing, button-down shirt with a wide, pointed collar and elaborate cuffs turned upward, the tails of the shirt untucked. He had kind eyes and longish black hair, and he was surrounded by younger people wearing white T-shirts.

"Yes, I'm going with you," I said to him, my hand going to the pendant at my throat. "But first I have to go home. There's something I have to do."

When I opened my eyes, everyone was staring at me. "She left on her own," I said. "Or at least she was planning to leave with a man in an old-fashioned white shirt. He had blue eyes, black hair down to his collar, a short beard. She wasn't the only one to go with him. Did you ever see her wear a white T-shirt with blue lettering that says 'Only Love Can Overcome Hate'?"

Mr. Fullmer paled noticeably, but Mrs. Fullmer was nodding. "She had one."

"A cult then," Mr. Fullmer sputtered. "That's what you're saying."

I shrugged. "Maybe a commune."

"Same difference," Mr. Fullmer said.

"I can't say for sure. I do know that she believed anything she took with her wouldn't be hers anymore. She wished she didn't have to choose between them and you." Almost as an afterthought, I added, "They were selling Christmas cakes at a park. Near a university, I think. That was when she met them."

"She came home early on break," Mrs. Fullmer whispered. "She'd been having a hard time, but we didn't know until later that she missed all her final exams. She never registered for the next semester."

That explained the despair Victoria had left imprinted on the necklace. "She was more hopeful when she met them," I said, meaning it as a comfort.

"It's not only the colleges these people have targeted," Jake said into the awkward silence that followed my statement. "I've seen a similar group here down by the river, selling things to the crowds who come to watch the bridge reconstruction. In fact, they've been there almost every time I've driven by the past few weeks."

"Stupid child." Mr. Fullmer's gruff voice was tinged with pain. "She should know better than to talk to crazies."

"She could be in danger," Mrs. Fullmer protested. "She's too young to know better."

I didn't respond. I didn't need to. There was nothing more I could give them. I stood back from the counter and waited for them to leave.

Jake handed me my rings. As I slid them on, his warm hand touched the middle of my back, and I was grateful for the support. Last September I'd begun entertaining the thought that we could be more than friends, but our relationship remained mostly linked to business. I didn't mind too much. After my sister, he was my best friend, and since Tawnia had married and was now expecting her first child, her attention was divided. At this point I needed Jake's friendship more than I needed romance.

The Fullmers left, walking together slowly. Mr. Fullmer, his back rigid in his dark suit, carried the box of his daughter's belongings. His sandy hair was thinning in the back. Jake had a natural remedy that would halt the hair loss, but that wasn't why he'd come, so I remained silent. Next to him, Mrs. Fullmer looked shrunken, her shoulders hunched forward, her blond head bowed. She clung to her husband's arm, staggering more than walking. Below her dress I could see a run in the back of her nylons.

Before she reached the door, she paused, stepped away from her husband, and retraced her slow steps to the desk. "Thank you," she whispered. She looked around somewhat frantically before her hand shot out to grab the Chinese thirteenth-century Jun Yao vase that sat in glory next to the cash register. It was wider than it was tall, a dark, glossy red piece with bright blue highlights. The sale price was seven hundred dollars and a steal at that because it was in extremely good condition. I'd found it in a basement in Kansas when I'd sheltered with some people during a tornado.

"I want to buy this," Mrs. Fullmer said.

I arched a brow. I didn't think she really wanted the vase, but business had been slow, and I wasn't going to turn her down. I took it from her, enjoying the pleasant tingle of the thoughts that surrounded the piece. Not an image I could see but nice and comforting. At least one person who'd owned this vase had cared for it lovingly and had lived a life of quiet contentment.

I wrapped the vase as Jake rang up the sale. Mr. Fullmer waited by the door, impassiveness and impatience alternately crossing his stern features.

As I passed the bag with the vase to Mrs. Fullmer, she caught my hand and pressed something into it: the velvet box with the necklace. "Keep it for a little while. Maybe there's something more."

I shook my head. "There's never anything more. I'm sorry." The last words felt ripped from me, not because I didn't mean them, but because I knew they wouldn't help her suffering.

She made no move to take back the box. "Please."

I nodded, sighing internally. Keeping it gave her false hope, and I didn't want that, but I wasn't strong enough to refuse.

She smiled. "Thank you for the vase." She turned and joined her husband.

I didn't feel guilty about the vase because they could obviously afford it, but I did feel bad that she might think buying it could help me see something more.

"That was nice of her," Jake said.

"Nice?"

"Buying the vase. I told her when she called that you didn't accept money, but I did suggest that she might want an antique for her house. This way you earn something for your trouble. That's important, especially if it makes it so you can't work the rest of the day."

As he spoke, he was pushing me onto the tall stool I kept at the counter. Then he disappeared into the back room and returned with a small book of poetry that my parents had written for each other for their wedding. I took it willingly, grateful for the positive emotions that flowed into me. Touching it, I could see them as they held the book in turn and exchanged their flower-child vows in the forest, Summer with a ring of flowers on her head and Winter with his prematurely white hair in a long braid down his back. Though this session hadn't been all that draining, I felt full of life as I witnessed their silent, love-filled exchange. I hoped these feelings would never fade from the pages. Almost, it was like having them with me again.

I kept the book at the store because not all imprints were as easy to stomach as Victoria Fullmer's. Last month I'd been asked to touch the bicycle of a ten-year-old girl named Alice, who had vanished while riding her new birthday present. At first there had been only elation at her new toy—until the dark-haired man had stood in her path and torn her from the bicycle. I'd fainted with her fear. Later my description of the man had allowed the police to make an arrest and had eventually led them to little Alice. Too late. The memory still haunted me sometimes when I was alone. I'd had to sleep with my parents' book for a week—and the picture of Summer as well. I tried not to do that often, afraid my parents' imprints would be overwritten by my own.

Jangling bells told us someone had entered the Herb Shoppe next door. Jake looked at me. "You sure you're okay?"

"I'm fine. Go ahead."

He walked around the counter and sprinted to the double doors that joined the two stores. My father had put in those doors back when Jake had worked for both of us. Jake and I still helped each other out, using a networked computer program to keep track of sales so we could ring people up at either counter. We also shared two part-time employees, Thera Brinker, who worked early afternoons and Saturdays, and Jake's sister, Randa, who came after school and during special weekend sales events. Thera mostly worked for me and Randa for Jake, but they crossed over when either store had a rush of customers. It worked for all of us.

"Jake," I called. Too late, I thought, because he had disappeared, but his dark head popped back in. "I'm going for a walk, okay?"

"No problem. I'll keep an eye on things until Thera gets in."

I knew he would, but to make it easier for him, I locked my outside door on the way out, flipping over the sign that told people to use the Herb Shoppe entrance. That way Jake would be aware of any customers coming to browse my antiques, and they'd have to pass by him to leave. Only a few pieces in my inventory were really expensive, but all together, my inventory added up to my entire future.

The cement felt warm against my bare feet, and I relished the sensation. In my late teens, the only time I'd gone through a shoe phase, my back had ached constantly, and once I'd spent a month in traction because of the pain, so for me it didn't make sense to continue wearing shoes. But then, I liked the feel of the earth under me—or as close as I could get in this cement jungle. There was a better connection with nature that way.

Thankfully, not wearing shoes wasn't against the law, not even while driving, and there were no government health ordinances banning bare feet in public buildings. Only the few years I'd gone to school as a child had I been given any grief about my choice, when each October the principal would threaten to call child services until I brought shoes to school and kept them under my desk. My parents, who I'd called by their first names, had always taught me to celebrate my differences, so Summer would have been happier teaching me at home, rather than see me conform, but I'd wanted the public school experience. Yet I was always glad I had stayed with her that last year, when I was eleven, the year she'd died of breast cancer.

My hand grazed the box in my pants pocket. I felt not the velvet but a flash of emotion. Victoria had loved this necklace, and she'd loved her family. Yet she'd chosen to leave them. A well of bitterness came to my heart. I'd give anything to have Summer and Winter alive and in my life. I could no sooner have left them than I could have cut off my own arm.

What had possessed her? Was there more to her family than I'd seen? Had her father's anger driven her to seek people who might love her unconditionally?

It's none of my business, I thought. My part was over. They knew she'd left of her own will, and they knew where to begin looking. I'd even been compensated for my trouble. In a few days, I'd mail Mrs. Fullmer the necklace so she could eventually give it to her other daughter.

Decision made, I focused on my surroundings. I'd walked long and far, or what most people would consider far these days, and my bare feet had taken a path I should have anticipated, given my reading for the Fullmers and what Jake had said about the group he'd seen.

I'd ended up near the Willamette River, downstream from the Hawthorne Bridge, where the bombing had taken place and where Winter had died. We'd been on the bridge in my car when the explosion collapsed the structure. I had come up from the cold, heavy depths, and he hadn't. Thirty others had also lost their lives in the bombing, and though those responsible had been punished, the holes in the lives of those left by the dead weren't easily filled.

I hadn't been this close to the river since Winter had been

found a week after the bombing, and it was strange to see the rebuilding in reality instead of on television. The construction area was fenced off, so I couldn't go all the way to the riverbank, but I could see the bridge had come a long way in the past six months. The promise to have the bridge ready for traffic in less than three years would probably be kept. Not that I'd ever had any doubts. My brother-in-law, Bret Winn, was the director of the project, and he was conservative in his estimates. In fact, he was conservative in almost everything—that was part of what my sister loved about him.

My tumbling thoughts halted abruptly as I caught sight of a man wearing coarse brown pants and an old-fashioned white shirt that looked all too familiar, though he wasn't the man from Victoria's imprint. He stood in front of the high chain-link fence surrounding the construction site, handing out flyers with his companions—young people of all sizes and shapes. All of them carried baskets and were wearing royal blue T-shirts with white lettering that proclaimed *Love Is the Only Thing That Matters.*

Jake had been right about the group coming to the river, though why I had felt compelled to track them down was another matter altogether. Victoria's college wasn't far away, but that didn't mean this group was connected with her disappearance.

Or maybe they were. How many groups like this could there be in the same town?

I moved toward them purposefully. Questions might not get me very far, but that didn't mean I couldn't find a stray imprint or two. If they were hiding something I was going to find out what.

Chapter 2

At first glance, it was an odd place for street vending, until one noticed how people from the many buildings near the waterfront had made this out-of-the-way construction site a gathering place for the lunch hour. Last year the bridge collapse had brought the people of Portland together, and it seemed their continuing patriotism included personally checking up on the rebuilding of the bridge.

I felt a rush of anger that this white-shirted man would take advantage of people's sentiments this way, but almost immediately I realized that if he truly believed his own teachings, or what I presumed must be his teachings, then what better place to search for lost souls than among the grieving or the hopeless?

I didn't think he was the same man Victoria had left imprinted on the necklace, though his shirt was similar, but to be sure my memory wasn't faulty, I forced open the box in my pocket and let one finger rest on the gold chain.

No, not the same guy at all. The man Victoria had seen was at least in his forties; this man was much younger. Probably not many years older than the eager helpers around him, who also didn't match any of the faces from Victoria's memory. The saying on the T-shirts was also different, though similar in theme, and they weren't the same color as the one Victoria had owned. Could it be another group?

I hadn't expected to see Victoria here, but I felt disappointed anyway. I wished I knew if she was still alive and happy with her choice. I wondered if she missed her parents as much as I missed Summer and Winter.

A girl with long blond hair and a round face devoid of makeup pushed a flyer into my hands. Glancing at it, I saw it didn't contain the group's philosophy as I expected but rather a price list for the hand-knit sweaters, brightly colored bead jewelry, pottery, wooden-faced dolls, T-shirts, and various food items the young people carried in baskets. People from nearby offices and retail stores were buying the breads, muffins, and cookies, talking and laughing together as they pointed out features of the rebuilding. With the coming of mid-June and warm weather, this unlikely place along the riverbank, practically in the shadow of the overhead I-5, had apparently become a bustling place of conversation and commerce. When the novelty died down, the youth would probably have better luck selling their wares at the park across the river. Or maybe they already had another group there. It might be worth driving over later to see if I recognized anyone from the imprint.

No. I needed to leave it alone. This was not my business anymore.

Yet Mrs. Fullmer's desperation remained with me.

The girl who'd given me the flyer stood in front of me, waiting. She glanced at the tips of my bare toes, just visible under my khaki pants. I wore my pants long enough to make my lack of shoes less noticeable, but it was the only thing I habitually did to make others more at ease with my lifestyle choice. My toes were dirty and dusty, but I was accustomed to that. Like every other part of me, they were easily washed.

I smiled at the girl, who looked rather gypsy-like in the colorful skirt that didn't match her blue T-shirt. She smiled back, a beatific smile that held so much hopeful innocence that I wondered if she'd even finished high school or held a job or seen anything of the world before giving her life to this organization.

I watched as the girl drifted toward the man in the white shirt, touching his arm so briefly it must have felt like the brush of a bird's fragile wing. Her mouth moved, and they both looked at me. I wondered what he saw. I was thirty-three, older than he was by three or four years at least, but with my average height, short mop of red and brown hair, slender frame, and myriad of freckles, I knew I looked younger. I'd never regained the weight I'd lost when Winter died, though I ate almost constantly. Tawnia joked that my food was too close to its natural state to stay with me for long.

Because I wanted to talk to the man, I stayed where I was and waited for him to approach. But what would I say? I couldn't exactly ask if he'd seen Victoria Fullmer. Or could I? Even if she was known to him, it was likely he didn't know her real name. They probably called her Flower or Snowflake or Rainbow. I knew from my own experience that people like these shed their real names as easily as they shed clothing. My adoptive father had legally changed his name from Douglas Rayne to Winter Rain when he'd met Summer. His friends had called him Winter for years anyway because his hair had gone completely white in his mid-twenties, and officially changing his name had simply marked his commitment to Summer. A commitment he'd kept, even through the twenty-odd years he'd lived after her death.

The white-shirted man now stood before me, the tails of his crisp shirt occasionally fluttering as they caught a stray breeze. He was broader than my first impression had indicated, and a bit shorter, though still taller than average—a physique that might go easily to flab if he wasn't careful. He had tan skin, slightly receding brown hair pulled back in a five-inch pony-tail, and kind brown eyes that crinkled at the corners when he smiled. When he lifted a hand in greeting, the long, cuffed sleeve of the shirt fell back, revealing a silver timepiece strapped around a hairy, muscled arm.

"Hello," he said. "I think you're looking for me. I'm Korin, director of Harmony Farms. My people call me Director Korin. You have a question, don't you? Please be at ease. We always have room for the weary."

Maybe reading Victoria's imprints had taken more from me than I'd realized. Then I shook myself. No, this was his way of finding converts, of targeting people who fit his criteria of lost souls. Unlike the others around me, I was alone and I wasn't buying food. Plus, I wore no shoes. In fact, that alone must be the reason they had targeted me. Yet he didn't really see me. He hadn't noticed my eyes.

No harm in playing along with his misconception of me. "Your watch," I said. "It reminds me of one my father owned. May I?" The only other thing I might be able to touch would be his shirt, and with a few exceptions like my mother's afghan, clothes weren't good at holding imprints. I didn't know if that was because they were so often washed or because people quickly lost interest in them.

A line of puzzlement creased his wide brow, but he held out

his arm, making sure the sleeve fell back to expose the time-piece. It was probably too much to ask him to take it off for me, so I reached out two fingers, placing one on the glass face and the other on the metal band.

Director Korin stared at me, but he didn't flinch or draw away. The scene came almost instantly.

I was opening a door with a key. A dark, musty room. Light falling on a man's thin, eager face. "You're letting me go?"

"Of course, Inclar. You're my brother. I can't stand to see you hurting."

"They're all your brothers, Korin." Spoken with an under-lying bitterness.

"Not by blood like we are."

The thin man nodded. "Then come away with me. Away from this place."

"No," I/Korin said. "My place is with Founder Gabe now. He needs me to help him run the farm. Where will you go?"

"Back to Portland, of course. To be close to Sarah's grave." The thin man put a hand inside his clothes and brought out the watch. "Take this. To remember me. It's all I have left of Sarah."

"I can't take it. You loved it enough to keep it all these months."

"I want you to have it."

Stunned with this generosity, I accepted the treasured time-piece and watched the man slink into the darkness. The image faded.

"Your brother," I whispered. Apparently they had both been a part of the organization, but Inclar had not remained a true follower.

"What did you say?" Director Korin's face tensed slightly,

but I wasn't sure if that was because of my words or because he'd just noticed my strange eyes.

"I said, 'Thank you, director.' Your watch is very nice, but I guess it really doesn't look like my father's after all."

A smile relaxed his face. "Would you like to hear more about Harmony Farms?"

"I had a friend once who talked about you," I said, making my words soft and distracted. "Victoria Fullmer. At least it might have been you guys. She was a sweet girl. I really liked her, but she went away. Maybe she went with you."

"I haven't heard of a Victoria, but many have joined us." He shuffled the flyers in his hand and came up with another one, this one glossy instead of plain paper. "Our commune is in a beautiful location outside Rome."

"Where?"

"Rome, Oregon. Southeast of Burns. Close to the Oregon-Idaho border."

I nodded. Now that he mentioned it, I recalled something about the name coming from geological formations that reminded people of Roman ruins, but I'd never been there.

"We're always looking for those who wish to live a simple life," Director Korin added.

"What religion are you?"

"We don't subscribe to any religion. We are simply a brotherhood who share common ideals. We serve others, work together, help each other. We value nature. We love everyone."

I smiled a real smile this time. "You sound exactly like my parents. But they didn't go away to some farm. They loved everyone right here in the city. They helped a lot of people."

Korin returned my smile. "Some people are strong enough

to do that, but with all the trouble in the world, it's increasingly difficult to do. Many people these days crave a community around them, a family who lives and believes as they do. We provide that. To you too, if ever you want it."

"Thank you," I said, glad for the memories he'd evoked of Winter and Summer rather than his offer.

"We'll be here for several days, if you want to learn more."

I nodded and walked away.

Another disciple with a basket was emerging from a white van parked some distance away, a young man with ultrashort blond hair. A shock of recognition flooded my body. I slid my fingers over the chain in my pocket. Yes, the face belonged to one of the T-shirted youths in Victoria's imprint. That meant these people were the same ones who had enticed Victoria away from her home and family.

I reached for my cell phone, knowing I had to make the call. Mrs. Fullmer answered. "Hello?"

"It's Autumn Rain," I said. "I'm down by the Hawthorne Bridge. Not the park side. On the side by my store. There's a group selling goods here, and I believe they're the people your daughter left with. I recognized one of the men from the imprints on her necklace."

"I'll be right there!" Her voice had gone from listless to energetic in the space of my few sentences.

"No! I mentioned Victoria's name, but they didn't seem to recognize it. I think you should go through the police. Or a private detective. That would carry more weight with these people. But if you tell the police I identified them because of an imprint—well, I don't know how they'll take that."

Actually, I did know. They'd laugh in her face—or at least most of them would. Shannon Martin, the officer I'd worked with on the bicycle case might listen half-heartedly, if he didn't throw me in jail for fraud, but everyone else would laugh. A private detective, however, might pursue the case just for the money.

"I'll figure out what to do," Mrs. Fullmer said. "But I want to see them for myself."

"Well, I have no idea how long they'll be here, but you can try." I hung up with foreboding. Mrs. Fullmer had been excited to receive the information—too excited. Though I'd emphasized calling for help, she might jump in her car and drive down here, perhaps bringing her stern husband along in the hopes of cowing the disciples into talking about Victoria. I wondered if Mr. Fullmer owned a gun. For the sake of Director Korin and the others, I hoped not.

To make the call, I'd withdrawn from where the youths were pushing their wares, hiding partially behind the pillars that held up the freeway. From where I stood it was clear that the lunch crowd was rapidly dispersing, and already a few of the basket-laden youth were returning to the van with their wares. Within fifteen minutes, only Director Korin was left. He gazed around at the construction, as though considering it.

What was keeping him from joining the others?

Go, I thought. *Before the Fullmers get here.* Though I wanted Victoria to be found, I didn't want to be the cause of trouble. If Korin left soon enough, the Fullmers would be forced to talk to the police and let them handle the situation.

I spied a movement between me and the riverbank, near another pillar. Korin saw it too, and started walking toward it. I ducked behind my pillar and waited a moment.

When I dared looked again, Korin had disappeared. I'd begun to think he'd followed the others to the white van when

I sensed another movement and spotted him farther from the bank, his head bent as he talked intimately with a man who was strangely familiar. Where had I seen him before? Never in person, I was sure.

Wait! He was the thin man imprinted on Korin's watch, the wild-eyed brother who'd left the commune to be near his wife's grave.

They spoke, heads close together. Korin reached into his shirt and withdrew a packet, handing it to his brother. The two embraced, and then Korin strode away, heading toward the white van and the youths who awaited him.

The other man watched until the van pulled away before ambling off in the direction of Clay Street. What to do? I could stay and face the Fullmers when they arrived, with or without the police in tow, or I could do a very stupid thing and follow this man and try to talk to him.

No choice, really. I needed to find out what this surreptitious meeting between the brothers was all about. What had Korin given him?

Or maybe I just didn't want to look into Mrs. Fullmer's sad eyes again.

Chapter 3

The thin man had already begun walking in the direction of Clay Street. Too late, I wondered if he had a car. I hadn't brought the old clunker I'd finally bought before last winter had set in—my previous car having sunk to the bottom of the Willamette during the bridge collapse. If he did have a car, he'd easily outdistance me. Then again, given the tattered condition of his clothing and his general unkempt appearance, it wasn't likely he owned anything more than a bicycle. But even a bicycle would leave me far behind.

He moved like a beaten animal, head tilting forward as though hoping no one would notice him, not looking to the right or to the left. I followed. The sidewalks were almost empty this time of day, though cars whizzed by steadily on the streets. One block, two, three. Finally I lost count. He had a lot of endurance for such a small, thin man. As for me, my feet had been toughened by many years of going without shoes, and I was accustomed to walking long distances. The sun felt good on my face and warmed me so much I was glad I'd worn short sleeves that morning.

At last we reached 12th Avenue. Residential houses sprang

up along the tree-lined street, mixed in with a few squat apartment buildings and businesses. One sign read *Dancing—Beer.* On we went, past more buildings and a muffler shop. Older houses, some tiny bungalows, others still small but with two stories. There was no way to pretend now that I simply had business in the same direction, so I wasn't surprised when he whirled to face me, his narrow face flushed.

"Why are you following me?" He was still bent over slightly, his head tilted to one side. It took me a minute to realize that his right eye didn't meet mine but looked off to the side. Useless. Or perhaps uncontrollable. I guessed him to be around my age, though he acted as if he were a shriveled old man awaiting death.

I lifted one foot and with my finger flicked off a minuscule pebble that had been embedded in my sole for at least a block. He followed the movement but showed no expression at my bare feet.

"I saw you with Director Korin," I said. "I know you're his brother. I just want to ask you something, that's all. I don't mean you any harm."

His left eye narrowed, or maybe he was squinting because of the overhead position of the sun. "Your eyes," he said. "They're different."

So he'd noticed that my left eye was blue and my right hazel, which in my case was a hereditary condition I shared with my twin: heterochromia. Neither we nor our separate adoptive families knew exactly where the anomaly came from. We knew little about our birth mother's family, but her eyes had been a normal blue.

He didn't speak again but stood waiting, so I plunged on. "A girl I know, Victoria Fullmer, was talking with your brother's group. I think she went with them. I want to know if you know her and if she was okay when you last saw her. She left in December, after Christmas. You would have still been there then."

"How do you know that?" Suspicion dripped from his voice. "My brother didn't tell you." Now there was a tinge of insecurity, as if he really wasn't sure about his brother's fealty.

"No. I touched his watch, and I saw that it was you who gave it to him. You left in January. She would have been there."

Every time I read a recent imprint I could tell when it had happened, almost to the week. If it was really fresh, I knew even the day. Older impressions were hard to pinpoint to a decade, much less a year, and only with antiques did that ability come in handy.

His right eye rolled oddly around in its socket, coming to rest on me as though it had been there all along. It was blue like the other, but there was knowing in it. "I can't tell you what you want to know," he said. "I am sworn to secrecy. My very soul depends upon keeping my word."

I hadn't expected him to believe my brief explanation. No one ever did except those close to me or those desperate enough to need hope to cling to. "Why did you leave?"

"Only my body left. It was weak. My spirit is there."

"But not your heart. That's in the grave with Sarah."

His right eye wandered off again, but his left held a sheen of tears. "She died. I wasn't there when it happened, but I felt it. The connection was gone."

He was the first person I'd ever met who talked about connections the way I'd felt them with my parents and still felt them with my sister. "What happened?" I spoke softly and gently, not wanting to startle him into silence.

His eyes shut, and his head began rotating up and around, backward and forward. Seconds stretched into minutes as he stood there silently, his head bobbing with exaggerated, repetitive movements. Then he said, "Don't go there. You might never leave. Some of us are not meant for the truth. We cannot live the law."

"Are you talking about Harmony Farms?"

"I wanted to be strong like Korin, but I'm not."

"What happened?" I begged. I was beginning to think I'd have to go to Rome myself to search for the answers.

"It's hidden. Hidden. Where you think it is, it really isn't."

I clenched my fists in frustration. "I don't understand."

He rotated his head again as though it were the eye in the socket, going around and around. *He's crazy,* I thought.

I decided that was all I'd get from him; already he was sidling away. But he stopped after about ten feet, and his next words shocked me. "You see from objects. I see from here." He tapped the side of his head. "I left because I couldn't stand the crying. The screams. The death."

Chills shuddered up my spine. If he was to be believed, whatever Victoria had gotten herself into was not the benign group of friends it appeared on the outside but rather a cult that exploited youth who were too young to know better and the elderly who were too sick of the world to care.

Or maybe he was completely insane.

"Please,"—I searched my memory to come up with his name—"Inclar. Don't you have any information at all that you can give me?"

He grunted. "Don't use that name. He gave it to me, but I am not worthy." He ducked his head. "I will always belong to them."

"Not to Sarah?"

His head twisted around again, as though fighting an internal demon. "I failed her." He started down the driveway of a small, red brick house.

"What about Victoria!" I shouted after him. "Her parents are worried about her."

"She's already lost," he answered, his words barely reaching me. "Unless you can find her soon. She might be hidden. A few are always hidden."

He scuttled up a set of rickety-looking stairs to what I was sure must be a tiny attic apartment under the steeply sloped roof. Seconds later the door slammed shut, the sound echoing loudly in the quiet neighborhood.

"What a strange little man," I said aloud, thinking he could do with a few choice herbs from Jake's shop. Calming ones, mainly, and something to help his eye and improve his thought processes. Had I learned anything of value from him? I didn't think so. His information was unreliable at best and at worst meant to mislead. Still, he seemed to both fear and worship Harmony Farms. Or someone living there.

Whatever the truth, I was glad he was gone.

I walked briskly back to the shopping district, realizing I'd been away much longer than I'd intended. Both Thera and Randa would be at work by now, helping in the Herb Shoppe and Autumn's Antiques as needed, and I should have been doing books or maybe researching upcoming estate sales, where I always found the best pieces in my inventory. At least with Mrs. Fullmer's purchase, I wouldn't have to worry about the day's profit. I was already ahead.

My store had only one customer, who was with Thera, but Jake and Randa were busy with a rush of people in the Herb

Shoppe. Randa was tall for her sixteen years and slightly on the too-thin side. Her skin was a shade or two darker brown than her brother's because she came from her mother's second marriage, though she shared some of the same facial features—the curve of her nose, the shape of her brown eyes. She wore her hair as she always did, in thick corn rows on the front and sides, ending in the back with a ponytail of black frizz. In all, she was a beautiful girl with a fun personality to go along with her looks. At the moment, she was steadily ringing up people at the register, unconcerned at the line of waiting people.

I went through the double doors to the Herb Shoppe to see what I could do to help. Jake was over by the B vitamins, talking with a frail, old woman, who gestured vivaciously with her hands. He caught my gaze over her head, asking a silent question with a flick of an eyebrow. *Are you okay?*

I nodded and he smiled, looking so beautiful that my breath caught in my throat. I glanced away quickly before any of my thoughts could reach my face.

"Miss," a large man said, "can you help me find flaxseed oil? My wife usually comes to get it, and I haven't any idea where to look."

"Sure. It'll be in the refrigerator over there." I led him to the oil, leaving him to choose the size while I helped Randa ring up customers at the counter.

Fifteen minutes later we had only two customers left, and they were with Jake at the front of the store discussing the healing properties of magnets. "I'm going to check on Thera," I told Randa, heading for the antiques shop. I'd actually rung up a few antiques at the herb counter, so today was turning out better and better for my work.

"I'll be there in a minute to dust the toys," Randa called. "Thera hates doing that."

"Take your time," I returned.

Thera, her white hair swooped up elegantly on her head, was sweeping the floor, as she did every day, though it really didn't need sweeping. She did it from some misguided idea of protecting my bare feet. Afterward, she'd wash the windows and soap down the counter. Her movements stopped when she saw me. As usual, the older woman wore all blue, a calming color that helped her forget the years she'd had to endure a difficult husband. Her favorite multi-strand blue bead necklace lay against her large, soft-looking bosom.

"I sold the Victorian dresser and one of the music boxes!" she exclaimed, a note of triumph in her voice.

"Way to go." The dresser had been an unusual piece and slightly damaged. At only a few hundred dollars, the customer could pay someone to fix it properly and still have a good deal. "Which music box?"

"The one with the pony."

She meant the nineteenth-century Swiss cylinder music box with the inlaid horse.

"Great! I should have guessed." With a price tag of two hundred dollars, it had been the most expensive box in my shop and my favorite. If I hadn't had five other boxes at home that I couldn't bear to part with, I would have kept it.

That was how it went in this business. A flurry of sales and then sometimes a week with almost nothing, and I'd have to either send Thera home or seize the opportunity to go searching for more appealing inventory. I didn't mind living hand-to-mouth, especially now that the money Jake was paying me for

Winter's store, whose inventory had represented nearly all his life's savings, went into an IRA account.

Thera nodded. "Maybe then you can afford shoes, eh?"

I laughed. "I don't think so. Where's my sister?"

I knew Tawnia was nearby. The line of connection that existed between us had grown fat and beckoning as I entered the store. She must have come in while I was busy at the herb counter. Tawnia felt the connection between us as well, though not in such a tangible way. She felt it more like a craving being satiated. Either way, the feelings were stronger at times like today when it had been too long since we'd been together.

Thera didn't show surprise at my comment. We'd grown close over the past nine months she'd worked here, and she was one of the few who knew about both my connection to my sister and my new talent.

"She's in the backroom. Making tea, I think."

"Thanks." I hurried to my narrow back room that ran nearly the entire width of the antiques shop. There was a long worktable where I prepared and ticketed items, a corner that held a bookshelf crammed with texts about antiques, an old electric stove, a mini refrigerator, and a ratty easy chair that I sometimes napped in when business was slow.

Tawnia was nowhere to be seen, but at the far end of the room was a door that led to a bathroom, and she was probably in there. I removed the boiling teapot from the burner and poured ground tea leaves into the infuser.

As if on cue, the door opened and Tawnia emerged. She had my freckled face and upturned nose, my oddly colored eyes, set slightly too far apart for real beauty, and my hair—albeit longer than mine and in our natural brown. Her body had been more or less like mine before her marriage, but now her stomach was distended with seven months of pregnancy. After her marriage last September, she hadn't wasted time getting pregnant, saying her biological clock was already ticking. Tawnia, raised as an only child, as I had been, wanted to fill her house with at least three or four noisy kids.

"How's my niece?" I asked, coming toward her with my arms extended. We hugged tightly.

"You can't know it's a girl. I don't even know."

"I know," I insisted, though I really didn't. I just wanted a niece. My hands were on Tawnia's stomach now, and I put my mouth close to the blue shirt stretching over her stomach. "Hey, you in there, are you almost finished cooking? We're getting anxious out here. You know your mom and I were born before eight months. You might think about hurrying up."

"Stop," my sister said. "It's way too early."

"Just kidding," I said to the baby. "Take your time. Your momma still hasn't decided how she's going to take care of you. So stay put for a bit."

The decision whether or not to leave her job as a creative director at a prestigious ad firm to take care of her child consumed Tawnia's every waking moment.

Tawnia sighed. "That's the truth. I haven't been at my job a whole year yet, and our team's the most talented I've ever worked with. I'd hate to stop working with them. But I also don't want to leave the baby."

"Then go part time. It isn't as if you and Bret need the money."

"If I went part time, I'd probably have to go back to being an art director, or a freelancer."

"So? You miss actual drawing, and you'd still be a member of the team, even if you worked from home most of the time.

I'll watch the baby when you have to go in, or you could take her with you." It seemed a simple choice for me, because I'd gone to work with Winter and Summer at the Herb Shoppe for as long as I could remember.

"Maybe."

I perched on the edge of the table so she could choose between the table chair or the easy chair. "Besides, she'll be spending so much time with me here that you might as well get working on the next baby as soon as she's born."

Tawnia laughed as she settled into the easy chair. I could always make her laugh. "I'm sure you'll have her refusing microwave dinners and hiding her shoes by the time she's two."

Now it was my turn to laugh. Pushing off the table, I poured us each a cup of tea. It was naturally sweet enough for me, but I plopped a bit of raw agave nectar in Tawnia's cup without asking. I'd missed lunch, so I pulled out a container full of my homemade buttermilk biscuits, feeling strangely as though we were making up for all the childhood tea parties we'd missed having together while growing up.

I still had difficulty forgiving the doctor who had separated us at birth after the death of our teenage mother. I'd tried to make peace with the past, though, because I wouldn't trade my growing up years with Summer and Winter for anything, and Tawnia felt the same about her family. At least Bret's investigation into the bridge collapse had finally brought us together. Interviewing me at the bombing site, he'd known at once that I was somehow connected with his old girlfriend, Tawnia. He'd introduced us, landing himself a wife in the process. We had each other now, and that was the important thing.

We sat in companionable silence as we sipped our tea and ate the entire container of biscuits. We heard the ringing of the electronic bell I'd installed at the shop door, deeper than the sound of Jake's real jingle bells, but Thera would take care of it. For now, I was content to be with my sister.

"So what's up?" I asked, when my cup was almost empty.

She shook her head. "I kept thinking about you all day. Did something happen?"

"I did a reading for someone." I shrugged, trying to show it was no big deal. "A missing girl. I think she was taken in by a cult. Her parents will try to get her out, but the mother's devastated."

"How sad." Tawnia studied my face, as though trying to ascertain if I'd told her everything. "Well, finally I gave up trying to work at the office and left early. I wanted to invite you to dinner, but we'll have to stop by the store on the way home because I'm fresh out of anything edible. So, will you come? I'll work back here until you can leave. I brought my laptop."

"Sure, I'd like that." Tawnia wasn't much of a cook, but Bret knew his way around the kitchen, and between the two of us, we'd come up with something both healthy and filling that would please even my junk food-loving sister.

"We could invite Jake." Tawnia's brows rose suggestively.

"He has class on Thursday nights."

"I thought he hated college."

"It's a botany class, and that interests him. He'll be taking two over the summer. But you're right. I never thought I'd see the day he went back to school."

Truth was, last year I'd been afraid he'd get bored and leave Portland, but since selling him the Herb Shoppe, I'd been less worried.

"So, no progress between you two?" Tawnia asked.

I shook my head.

Tawnia leaned as far forward as the bulk of her stomach allowed. "Why don't you push things along? You've always had guys eating out of your hand."

I snorted. "Yeah, right. I haven't had a proper date in a year. Besides, Jake's a friend. I don't want to mess that up."

"A relationship doesn't have to mess up friendship."

"Always has before."

"Jake's different. Like Bret." Tawnia rose from the easy chair and poured herself another cup. "What is this tea, anyway? I couldn't decide which to make."

"African honey bush. Don't worry. No caffeine or anything bad for the baby. It's highly recommended for pregnancy. I threw out any of my herbal teas that might not be good for you and the baby, just in case."

She smiled. "Of course you did." Her eyes watered as they seemed to do far too often these days, what with hormones raging in her changing body. "I love you. You know that, right?" She hugged me, her swollen belly pressing into my stomach.

"Yeah. I love you too."

When we separated, Tawnia sat down at the table in front of her laptop. Only then did I notice the folders and loose sketches spilling out of her briefcase. One caught my attention.

I drew it out. "What's this? Did your art director do this?"

Tawnia snorted. "No, I did. It's a picture that keeps popping into my mind. I think that's part of why I was so distracted this morning."

My body felt suddenly chilled. I scooted myself onto my worktable, drawing my feet up, hugging my legs with my free arm as I studied the picture. It wasn't an exact likeness, but there was no question that the sketch resembled the white-shirted Korin.

"I saw this man less than an hour or two ago," I said, unable to control the shakiness of my voice. "He was down by the riverbank where they're doing construction on the bridge. His group is the one connected to that girl's disappearance."

Tawnia turned to me, her mismatched eyes wide. "I thought you said that was no big deal."

"It wasn't."

"Then why did you track them down?"

"A coincidence. I happened to run into them, that's all." But it wasn't a coincidence, not really. Not after Jake had told me he'd seen them there.

"Well, I wasn't with you—I couldn't have drawn that man."

We stared at each other for a few moments. I saw worry in her eyes that echoed the feeling in my heart.

"The group sells homemade items," I said. "It's been so cold and rainy lately—until the past few weeks. It's natural they'd visit the city now. They probably have groups all over. You could have seen him and not remembered."

"Maybe I saw coverage about them on TV." Tawnia was nodding, relief evident on her face.

Strangely, I felt a stab of unreasonable disappointment, as if a part of me thought it would be nice if my twin had an ability too.

"Well, I'm out of it now." I set my cup firmly on the worktable. "It's not as if I'm a private investigator or anything."

"Promise?"

I smiled at her worry. "I won't do anything dangerous." I jumped off the table. "Now I'd better get out there and take care of a little business before we leave."

I emerged from the back room, feeling better for having seen my sister, but my mood was immediately destroyed by the steady gaze of the man waiting at my counter. He had curly blond hair, barely short enough to maintain a semblance of professionalism. The kind of hair that invited fingers. His eyes were blue, his brows and lashes thick and blond like his hair. A smattering of freckles across his nose and cheeks lent him an air of boyishness, though there was no trace of playfulness in his demeanor now. Not a customer, of that I was sure. Otherwise, Thera would be helping him. Instead, she stood near the windows, her small hazel eyes seeming to drill an angry hole in the back of his head.

"May I help you?" I asked.

"I'm looking for Autumn Rain." He spat the words, as though they tasted bitter.

"I'm Autumn." I kept my face expressionless. Every signal told me I wasn't going to like what he had to say.

"Your employee wouldn't tell you I was here." His mouth formed a thin line of disapproval, and his lean body, nicely clad in a pair of snug jeans and a casual blazer over a T-shirt, exuded an air of impatience that somehow didn't detract from his considerable looks. Still, I didn't like him.

Thera must have felt the same way, because ordinarily she was anxious to have me waiting on attractive men who didn't wear wedding rings.

"I was busy," I said. "But I can help you now. What do you need?"

"I'm Ethan McConnell. I'm a private investigator, and earlier this afternoon I was hired to look into the disappearance of Victoria Fullmer."

I sighed internally, trying to keep the reaction from my face. "I'm glad someone's helping the Fullmers, but I fail to see why you're here. I told them everything I know, and I notified them about the people at the riverbank. I can't tell them anything more."

His blue eyes narrowed. "You're a fraud, and you're playing on the fears of desperate people. I've come to tell you that if you don't back off, I'm going to see you in jail."

Chapter 4

$\mathcal{I}$ laughed. I couldn't help myself. He was so serious and stern but at the same time so wrong that there really wasn't anything else to do. It was either laugh or cry.

"Go ahead," I invited, letting loose another giggle. I lifted my hands out toward him. "Take me to jail." I dropped the levity. "Oh, wait, you're not a policeman, and you can't do that. If you're quite finished with your threats, you can leave now, or *I'll* be the one calling the police."

He blinked, and I knew I'd surprised him. That wasn't a new reaction; from my youth I'd grown accustomed to people thinking I was odd. In fact, I *liked* being that way, and to have startled this particularly annoying man pleased me more than it should have.

"Autumn, what do you think about using a realistic cartoon figure to sell underwear?" Tawnia called from the back room. "I know it's popular these day to see men prancing practically naked on TV, but it seems a little effeminate to me, no matter how many muscles they—" The words broke off as she came into view, her face paling as she caught sight of Ethan. She glanced down at her paper and then back up again. When it slipped between her fingers and floated to the tile, she didn't bother to pick it up.

"Who's this?" she asked. Despite her pallor, her voice was remarkably steady.

"He's someone who is just leaving," I said, giving Ethan a pointed stare.

Ethan looked from Tawnia to me, obviously using his great private detective skills to deduce that we were sisters. Not a rocket scientist by any means.

"I'm here to discourage Miss Rain from inflicting any more damage upon my clients," he said.

"I'm not inflicting anything upon anyone!" I shot back, my anger getting the best of me. I was never as calm and collected as my sister, even at the best of times. "They came to me, remember? For my part, I'd rather not know anything about their missing daughter. I knew I shouldn't have agreed to help them. I *knew* it. If Victoria hated her father enough to throw her brush at him, I should have figured he'd send someone to intimidate me into staying out of the case and away from his wife."

"I thought you *were* out of it," Tawnia said, at the same instant Ethan said, "He made Victoria angry?"

"Of course I'm out of it," I told my sister. To Ethan I added, "It was months ago. At least nine."

"So she confided in you," he said.

"No." How had this guy ever become a private eye? "I never met her. I experienced the imprint on her hairbrush. And on this." I pulled the necklace box from my pocket. "But since you're working for the Fullmers now, maybe you can return it. As I said, there's really nothing more I can tell them."

One side of Ethan's mouth flicked upward in disgust. "You expect me to believe you can read something from this necklace?"

"Of course," Tawnia said. "She does it all the time."

"Then maybe she can tell me what this says." He held out something small on his hand. A ring, a tiny one meant for an infant, with minuscule gold circles interlocking across the front.

Tawnia frowned. "It has to be the right object. It has to be something important to the—"

"Right. I thought as much." Ethan began to withdraw his hand. "And this obviously isn't the right kind of object."

He was wrong. The ring had a definite imprint, a pronounced one whose teasing images danced just out of sight. I willed myself to let him take it away. I didn't *want* to see those images. I didn't care if he thought I was a fraud.

That was a lie. I did care. I wanted to shove my ability in his self-satisfied grin and see him grovel in abject apology. *Let him go,* I told myself, even as I snatched the ring from his hand. Scarcely was the hard little circle between my fingers when a scene blazed to life.

A man in a white coat, holding out the tiny ring. "I'm so sorry. She didn't make it."

Agony pierced my soul.

No, not my soul but whoever had imprinted on the ring.

A wish for oblivion, for a way to escape the horrible, mind-numbing pain. Stumbling from the suddenly tilting room. Ethan's serious face floating toward me.

"Marcie," he said, but that was all I heard. Welcome blackness.

An earlier scene followed on the heels of this one.

Smiling down into the face of an infant, the love in my heart so large I didn't know if I could contain it. No words, just an emotion that grew and filled every part of me, satisfying all the longings I'd ever had for a child.

Or rather, all the longings Marcie had ever experienced. The woman's emotions were so inclusive and wonderful that it was a struggle to keep myself separate from them. They were as filled with joy as the agony I'd just experienced.

The love almost blotted out the sad fact that my baby's father wouldn't be here to see our child grow up. The cancer had come unexpectedly, but now I had this last gift. A part of him forever.

That was all. The doctor's sad face reappeared, as the imprints started to replay. I gasped and dropped the ring onto the counter, unwilling to experience the agony a second time.

"Autumn, are you okay?" My sister's voice.

I nodded, but tears blurred my vision as I met Ethan's gaze. He was suddenly still, the mocking grin vanished.

"I'm sorry," I whispered. With the imprint had come the knowledge that the eight-week-old infant had died a year ago due to a birth defect in her heart, but I couldn't bring myself to say it aloud.

I turned to go, but his hand shot out to grasp my shoulder, though the counter was still between us. "What did you see?"

A bitter half-laugh escaped me. "I can't help you. Now let me go." I wrenched myself from his hold.

"You're a fake, a fraud! An actress who preys upon the sorrows of others."

I whirled. "Just because your niece is dead doesn't mean you have the right to take your anger out on me. I can't help your sister! I'm sorry Marcie's husband died. I know it's not fair. My mother also died of cancer, and my father died in the bridge bombing here last year, so I know what you're going through. The baby—" I broke off. "I'm sorry."

Ethan stared at me, his disbelief and anger slowly becoming amazement. Acceptance. I felt no satisfaction at my triumph; it came with too much attached.

"Please, don't go," he said.

I hesitated in my flight but stood glaring at him with my arms folded, my fury threatening to burst forth and flatten us both.

"Look, I don't know how you know all that, but I'm willing to wait and see."

"Don't do me any favors," I retorted. This guy was something else. "Just do your job. Those people should be back at the river tomorrow. Go talk to them."

"I have. Many times." He leaned forward over the counter, staring at me intently, as though by doing so he could force my cooperation. The pleading expression of his eyes and the underlining of freckles splattered over his nose and cheeks made an appeal I felt helpless to ignore. I wondered if his blond curls were really as thick as they looked.

"They won't talk to me," he continued. "And when I followed them to their factory in Rome, it's really just a front. They have a small warehouse where people—mostly young kids—are baking muffins and breads to take to the cities. They also sell a lot of handmade items there, but the warehouse is too small for everything to be made on site. The faces seem to be different every time I go, though they claim they are regular employees. Only a few of the kids I've seen match those in the cities hawking the muffins and crafts, so I know there are more of them. I think there has to be a separate place where they actually live, raise food, and make the rest of their products."

"What do the police say?" I asked.

"I've gone to the local authorities, but their hands are tied unless there's evidence of a crime. All the kids seem to be over eighteen, or they have a parent with them."

"Back up a minute." Tawnia sat on the stool and leaned her elbows on the counter. "Why have you been tracking these people? I had the impression you were new to this case."

She was right. The Fullmers hadn't yet hired a private investigator when I'd talked to them that morning, though they'd discussed the case with a few over the phone. Leave it to my sister to keep her head. This guy was hiding something.

"Okay, it's true I'm new to the case," Ethan admitted. "Originally the Fullmers were talking to a PI friend of mine about it, but when they called to hire him after talking to you this morning, he referred them to me instead."

"Why?" I'd gathered enough wits to ask that.

"Because of the cult connection." He paused slightly before adding, "And my sister."

"Your sister? You're tracking this case because of your sister?"

He nodded. "The month after Marcie lost her child, she met these Harmony Farms people. She spent hours talking with them. She was vulnerable, you know. I didn't do enough to stop it because I wanted her to have some relief, and she wasn't talking to me much. I even laughed the first time I saw her wearing one of their T-shirts. Then one day she was gone."

His face hardened into the same tough mask he'd worn earlier. "Her clothes and furniture were missing, and her bank accounts had been emptied, including fifty thousand dollars' worth of life insurance. I tracked the clothing and furniture.

Most had been sold to secondhand stores. No trace of the money. So I took a year sabbatical from my job and started searching for her. I have to know she's okay."

"I take it you're not really a private eye." Tawnia smirked at him, and a faint blush tinged his cheeks.

"I am now. I also teach math at Willamette University. I'll have to go back in the fall, but until then I'm going to do anything I can to find my sister."

A math professor turned private eye? That didn't sound at all promising. Didn't most investigators have experience on the police force or something?

Tawnia tilted her head, as if trying for a better view. "You don't look like a math teacher." I knew what she meant; there was something more rugged about him. Exciting, vital, alive. Who knew math could be so exciting?

To my surprise he sighed. "That seems a lifetime ago." He caught my eyes again. "I'd like to show you a few other things my sister left, if you don't mind. Just to confirm what I think I already know about where she went. I feel I've gone as far as I can without more drastic measures. Maybe you can discover something new."

"I doubt it will help. Anything she left behind wouldn't have any information about her current location."

He nodded. "Yeah, but it's still worth a try—if you don't mind."

I did mind because I was feeling shaky from the agony Marcie had imprinted on the baby ring. Yet how could I refuse his need?

Instinctively, my hand found the little poetry book that Jake and I had left on the counter after our session with the

Fullmers. The positive imprints from my parents' wedding steadied me, easing the horror of the little ring. The tiny piece of gold still sat on my counter, but no one would ever be able to convince me to pick it up again.

Shaking my head, I drew myself back to the conversation.

"Okay, then." Tawnia was saying. "We'll expect you around seven."

Ethan nodded. "Thank you. I'll be there." He swept up the ring from the counter and sauntered out the door.

"What just happened?" I asked.

"He's coming to dinner."

"What? Are you crazy?"

Tawnia shrugged. "He's cute. Did you see those freckles? And the poor guy needs fattening up. He's got muscles, but he's far too thin."

"Tawnia, I'm not going out with him." He hadn't even noticed my eyes.

"It's not anything like that. Weren't you listening?"

"Not really. I sort of spaced off for a minute. That ring. It was intense." I stifled a shiver.

My sister's expression became immediately solicitous. "Don't worry. He just wanted to show you those items before he confronts the cult guy tomorrow. I told him you'd be at my house this evening and he could come there. It seemed impolite not to invite him to eat if he was going all that way."

"It's not far from here."

"Yeah, but he lives in Woodburn, near Willamette University. That's a thirty or forty-minute drive. He left his card, though, so I guess we can cancel if you're not feeling up to it."

"No, it's okay. I'd rather get it all behind me, anyway. If I have to do it at all." Exhaustion abruptly fell over my entire body. Reading imprints was like that sometimes.

Tawnia motioned to Thera, who was talking to a customer. Thera said something to the woman and came our way, her hazel eyes questioning.

"I'm taking Autumn home," Tawnia said. "Feed her a little dinner. Do you think you can handle things here?"

"Sure. I'll lock up when I leave."

"Thank you."

Tawnia went to gather her belongings in the back while I emptied the cash drawer of a check, a couple of twenties, and signed charge slips. As I squatted down to remove my bag from a cupboard under the counter, I spied the paper Tawnia had let fall earlier. I picked it up, turning it over. On the front was a rough sketch of the cartoon figure she had considered using for the underwear campaign. The face on the figure was Ethan's.

My jaw dropped, and sudden goose bumps made me shiver. Still squatting on the floor, I looked up as she returned with her briefcase and laptop. A soft sound escaped her mouth when she saw what was in my hand.

I arose. "You never saw him before?"

"No. I got the idea right after you left the back room. Can't you see how rough the sketch is? If I didn't know better, I'd guess I'm drawing things you see."

"Or maybe you're seeing things before they happen. Or as they happen."

Her face paled. "I don't have an ability like you do. It's just our connection, the twin thing. That's all."

I nodded but mostly because I didn't want to make her more upset. That wasn't good for the baby. I stuffed the paper into my bag. "I'd use another face," I said lightly. "I get the feeling Ethan McConnell wouldn't want to be an underwear king, even in cartoon form."

Tawnia laughed. "That's advice I think I'll take."

Before we left, I slipped my parents' poetry book into the bag next to the day's proceeds. I had no idea what other skeletons Ethan had in his closet, and I wanted the book close.

I waved good-bye to Thera and steered my sister into the Herb Shoppe. Familiar smells assailed me, seemingly stronger with her by my side. I felt a sadness that she hadn't grown up as I had, knowing the names of herbs, that she couldn't relate the smells or tastes to the scenes from my gloriously carefree childhood with Winter and Summer. No matter how close we became, there would always be that bittersweet gap of time. Bittersweet for both of us because she also had wonderful childhood memories that didn't include me.

Jake came toward us, smiling a welcome. "Tawnia, I didn't see you come in." He took her hands and kissed one of her cheeks. "You look gorgeous today, as usual."

Which I supposed I could take as a compliment as well, since we were identical twins. But he never said such things to me. Or maybe he was referring to that mysterious glow pregnant women were supposed to radiate.

Tawnia laughed. "Thank you. You were busy, or I would have stopped to say hi when I came in. I'm taking Autumn to my place to eat—and you know what I mean when I say that. Only Autumn can eat as much as me these days. I'd planned to invite you, but she says you have class tonight."

"Ah, but what Autumn doesn't know is that my class was canceled. If the invitation is still open . . ." He looked at us hopefully.

"Consider yourself invited," Tawnia said.

"Great. What time?"

"You can come anytime, but we'll probably eat at seven."

I cleared my throat. "That means come early so you can help me cook."

"Are you going with Tawnia? Because if you are, I can give you a lift home." He made motions with his hands, as though revving the engine on his motorbike. "We'll take the long way. Should be a nice night for a spin."

I pondered his invitation. We lived only a block apart and often gave each other rides to work. In fact, he'd come by for me this morning. Tonight I preferred to drive myself so I could be in control of my unruly feelings toward him, but the opportunity to put my arms around him was too tempting.

"Sure," I agreed. "But that doesn't get you out of helping me with dinner."

"I'll be there as soon as I lock up." Jake winked at me. "I'll double check your door, too, on my way out."

"Great." His wink made me feel as if I'd swallowed a handful of live spiders. It was easier back when that hadn't happened, before the idea of Jake as a possible love interest had wormed its way into my mind.

Tawnia headed toward the door, but Jake stopped me, his strong fingers warm on the bare skin of my arm. "Who was that guy that was here earlier? He didn't look like a customer." His tone had gone serious, and I wondered if he'd seen me arguing with Ethan. No, if he had, he would have come running. But that he'd noticed made me feel both protected and annoyed all at once.

"He's a private investigator hired by the Fullmers, but he's really a math teacher. He became a PI last year when his sister disappeared. He thinks she may be with the same group that took Victoria." I shrugged. "He wants me to read some of her stuff and see if I can learn anything."

"He teaches math and he believes you?"

"He does now." I shuddered, remembering the agony that was too private to share. And yet, only by sharing it could one really come back to the world. I'd found that out the hard way when Winter died. It was too easy to fall into your own space and let the world pass by. Easier, but not at all emotionally healthy.

Being left too much on her own might have been what had attracted Marcie to Harmony Farms in the first place. They would have offered constant love and affirmation without the need to come to terms with anything, no need to live in the real world. With as much money as Marcie had in her assets and accounts, they might be content to let her simply sit in a corner for years, if that was what she wanted.

Jake studied me with his dark eyes, rendering me suddenly self-conscious. His smooth face was already showing signs of new beard growth, darkening his brown skin further in those spots. His locs made him seem tough, and the muscles straining across the front of his short-sleeved polo supported the notion. Yet I had seen Jake tenderly nurse sick animals back to health. I'd seen him spend long minutes helping old ladies who didn't know what herb they were searching for. He'd been more than supportive after my father died, being insistent with me when I needed it or letting me cry on his shoulder when I simply couldn't take any more. He and Tawnia had been my salvation during that terrible time.

"Jake." My voice caught in my throat, coming out all husky.

"Yes?" His face tilted down close to mine to hear me better. I had the sudden urge to kiss him, to feel his lips against mine, to rub my face against his cheeks. "I want to thank you for everything you've done for me since Winter . . . died. I don't know if I ever told you how much that meant to me."

His smiled faded into an enigmatic look more appropriate to my statement. "You have, but you've always given me much more in return. I value your friendship more than I can say."

Friendship. The word was like a slap in the face, and I stepped back quickly before I made a fool of myself. "I'll see you later."

Puzzlement creased his brow, but I certainly wasn't going to explain my behavior. If he had any sense—and I knew he did—he could figure it out. Of course, since it was scientifically proven that men and women are completely different, he might come to an erroneous conclusion.

All the better for me. I didn't want his pity. On the other hand, I did want and need his friendship, even if that was all he could offer.

Chapter 5

*J*ake, Bret, and I slaved in the small kitchen of Bret and Tawnia's rented bungalow, while Tawnia sat contentedly at the round table, her feet up on a chair. As usual, she was sketching something.

"Somehow, when I envisioned having guests over for dinner," Bret told his wife, "that meant we'd feed them, not make them fix us dinner."

Tawnia laughed. "They know I'm no good at cooking. Besides, neither one of them would eat anything I'd make, anyway."

This was not strictly true. My sister had come a long way in the cooking department since our reunion nearly a year ago. Moreover, Jake and I were not as picky as she implied. We ate meat and eggs and milk and cheese like most people, as long as the products came from animals that were fed and housed the way nature intended. As for everything else, there were plenty of wholesome foods that didn't contain preservatives.

"We don't mind," I said. "I need to make sure my niece gets some healthy food before she's born."

Bret snorted. "I can tell you, that's a full-time job."

Normally serious and thoughtful to a fault, my brother-in-law had mellowed over the past months of marriage. He had straight blond hair and blue eyes in an oval face. He was slightly taller than average but leaner than he should be for his height, though he'd gained a few needed pounds lately—not from my sister's cooking, of course. Probably from all the midnight ice cream feasts Tawnia had begun in her fourth month of pregnancy. Bret was handsome in a conservative way, not like the exotic Jake, who could trace his roots to Africa, or even the rugged, unruly-haired Ethan who, math teacher or no, might have missed his calling as a movie star.

"Hey, I can't help myself," Tawnia protested. "This baby's taken control of my taste buds, and he or she loves sweets."

"Especially chocolate milk." Bret dropped a kiss on Tawnia's head. To me he added, "Anything else I can do?"

The pork chops were on the grill, the spinach and blue cheese salad chopped and ready to go, the whole wheat rolls in the oven, and the fruit and vegetable plate ready for munching.

"You could stir this pudding," I said.

Tawnia loved banana pudding over fresh pound cake, but it had taken me a while to discover a recipe that satisfied both my nutritional requirements and her taste buds.

I moved away from the pan, but Bret didn't take the spoon. He was staring down at Tawnia's newest sketch. "Hey, that looks like an engineer I hired today. Nice man. The nose is a little off, though."

Tawnia's hand froze over the picture. Her eyes sought mine, their different colors prominent even from where I stood at the stove.

I smiled encouragingly. "Do you think he'd mind being in an underwear ad?"

"What are you talking about?" Bret asked.

Tawnia and I laughed, but I sensed worry behind her smile. Something odd was going on.

We were saved from further thought on the matter by the doorbell. "That must be Ethan." Tawnia jumped to her feet and grabbed my hand. "Honey, take over on the pudding so Autumn can go with me to the door."

"I'm going too," Jake said.

Bret rolled his eyes. "That's right, the engineer always gets the tough duty."

My hands felt suddenly sweaty. It was show time. I really hoped Ethan would wait until after I had food in my stomach before he started hauling out his sister's possessions. I was still shaky from the little ring.

To my disappointment, Ethan's snug jeans and blazer were gone. He was now dressed similarly to Bret, with slacks and a gray, long-sleeved, button-down shirt. He'd probably bought them by the dozen when he was teaching. I noticed Jake eyeing him with unconcealed mistrust, his hands shoved into the large pockets of his off-white cargo pants.

Besides the dress shirt, Ethan looked the part of a strong, capable, mysterious PI. He was as tall as Jake, which meant slightly shorter than Bret, and leaner than either of the other men. His intense blue eyes gave him the look of a man on the edge.

The edge of what?

I let Tawnia make the introductions, because this was her party, and watched her repeat the process after we joined Bret in the kitchen. He had the pudding off the stove now, and it was perfect. I smiled at him to show I was pleased.

We left the food on the counter, filled our plates, and took them to the small table. It was a squeeze with five people, and I wasn't sure where Tawnia had found a fifth chair. I sat between Jake and Ethan, instinctively shifting closer to Jake, bringing one bare foot up under me as I customarily did. Ethan eyed my foot but said nothing.

"So, you're a math teacher," Jake said as we started eating.

"It was the only thing I was good at," Ethan confessed.

I grinned. "If you were my high school math teacher, I certainly would have paid more attention." So he didn't have a chance to misconstrue my meaning, I added quickly, "Mine was bald and fat, and he took entirely too much pleasure in stumping us with impossible equations."

Everyone laughed, except Jake, who took my words seriously. "Well, you obviously learned enough math to do your books."

"Only because there was this really hot guy behind me who took pity on me. He explained everything."

Tawnia laughed, but the guys didn't seem to find that funny.

"And now you're a private investigator?" Jake asked Ethan.

"Only until I find my sister, and I'm almost certain she's with the Harmony Farms people."

"Speaking of which," I said. "Today a guy from Harmony Farms invited me to join their group."

Tawnia snorted. "As if."

Ethan looked thoughtful. "I've thought about disguising myself and trying to join them. It might be the only way to find my sister." He paused before adding, looking first at me and then at Tawnia, "I just noticed your eyes. They're different colors."

"We were born that way," Tawnia said. She threw me a grin that said, "Ha, he noticed." I smiled back.

"Did you go to school to be a PI?" Jake asked Ethan. "I mean, is there a two-week course or something?"

Knowing Jake as well as I did, I caught the derision. That wasn't like him at all. "Why would you care about school?" I asked. "We're both college dropouts." I turned to Ethan. "We ended up taking only the classes that interested us, and believe me, general education wasn't on the agenda."

Ethan didn't seem to hear me. "I did take several courses," he said to Jake, "but mostly I studied books about how to track people and how to follow a paper or electronic trail. On the whole, PI work is basically a lot of reading and research. I'm good at that. It's methodical—like numbers."

"That counts me out," I said.

It counted Jake out, too, because as smart as he was, he didn't read well, and I knew that was something he worked on privately. He'd dropped out of college because of the required reading, while I, who loved to read, had dropped out strictly from boredom. My parents had been good teachers my entire life, exposing me to people and ideas others my age couldn't begin to fathom. Learning with students my own age had seemed slow and confining compared to what I could do on my own. Not to mention that I had trouble seeing the importance of tests; after all, wasn't the knowledge itself the important thing?

Fortunately, Winter had encouraged me to follow my dream to open Autumn's Antiques. I wouldn't be building a new house any time soon, like my college-educated sister and her husband, and maybe I never would, but I spoke proper English and I knew antiques and herbs better than anyone, even Jake.

"I'm taking a botany class right now," Jake said. "The professor is adequate. Mostly."

Another veiled insult toward our guest, who by profession was linked to the comment. What had come over Jake?

"A teacher can only teach as well as a student is willing to learn," Ethan shot back. "Far too often teaching is like talking to an empty room."

"Only if the teacher is boring, though, right?" Jake's predatory smile belied his casual voice.

"Well," Tawnia said, coming to her feet before Ethan could respond, "I don't know about you guys, but I need another helping of that wonderful brown rice."

"I'll beat you to it." Relieved at the distraction, I leaped up and scooped three large spoonfuls onto my plate, along with a second pork chop, though my first was only half-eaten.

Ethan stared in amazement. "You can eat all that?"

"She's only just beginning." Jake passed me the fruit plate.

So the meal went on, with Tawnia and me competing to see who could eat the most and Jake and Ethan exchanging increasingly barbed comments. Bret, smiling widely, remained silent.

Only when Bret helped me serve the dessert did he quirk an eye in the direction of the table and whisper, "Man, they're at each other's throats. Something tells me you have two admirers."

So I wasn't the only one who'd noticed the tension. "Nothing to do with me," I returned, flushing all the same. "They just didn't hit it off."

What other reason could there be? Jake had confirmed earlier that we were simply good friends, and I didn't know Ethan well enough for anything else. More likely I was a puzzle for his mathematical mind to solve or possibly a way to find his sister.

"Right." Bret's grin was annoying. "If you believe that, I have a bridge in San Francisco you should buy. The Golden Gate Bridge. It's made of pure gold."

"That joke is terrible, especially coming from a guy who builds bridges for a living." I punched him hard in the shoulder, causing him to drop the pan of pudding. Fortunately, only half spilled on the counter, leaving enough for us to slather over the individual slices of homemade wheat pound cake.

"Eat up," I said, carrying two plates to the table for Ethan and Jake. "It's best when it's warm from the oven."

"And we can't warm it up very easily," Tawnia added, "because our microwave mysteriously broke last week." She glared at me as though it were my fault, which it might have been if I'd thought of it. My niece deserved better than food with the vitamins nuked out of it.

"Hey, don't look at me," I said. "It died from overuse, is all."

Jake and Bret guffawed, while Ethan smiled politely with the look of someone who'd been kept out of the family joke. Tawnia tried to keep glaring but was soon laughing with the others.

I felt better than I had in a long time. Laughing just to laugh, not thinking about Winter's death or my gift. Even Jake and Ethan seemed to put away their barbs for the moment.

All too soon, we'd cleared away the dishes and Ethan went to retrieve his duffel bag from the living room couch. I didn't know what to expect, but I was hoping for clothes. *Not jewelry,* I thought. *Please, not more jewelry.*

When he returned to the kitchen, everyone was abruptly still, from Tawnia at the kitchen table with her feet up on a footstool to Bret and Jake at the sink and dishwasher. I almost wished I'd suggested going back to my place so I could do this alone. Apart from Ethan, these were the people I loved most, but now I felt on display. Vulnerable.

Forcing a smile, I indicated that Ethan should sit by me. Jake retrieved the poetry book from my purse on the floor and set it on the table. He didn't sit but stood by my chair in a protective stance. It felt both silly and comforting.

"Bret, would you pass me my sketchbook?" Tawnia said. Bret obliged, and she turned to a drawing of the baby's nursery in the new house. They wouldn't be moving in for at least six months, and already Tawnia had changed the design five times. I felt grateful for her nonchalance and for the way she occasionally asked questions of Bret. It made things easier for me not to have them staring.

Ethan took out a small wedding photograph in an elaborate silver frame. "Marcie has larger pictures of their wedding, but she kept this at the bank where she worked before she came home to care for Rubin and have the baby."

I slid off my three antique rings, setting them on the table, and took the picture. As I expected, there was nothing but a pleasant buzz of pride and love, with only the slightest bit of quiet regret. I shook my head. "She didn't handle this or think about it much after her husband got sick."

He nodded and drew out a pair of gardening gloves. "She did a lot of yard work after the baby died."

"They've been washed." I set my fingertips on them. Nothing but the smell of dirt came to me. I guessed they'd been rinsed under the hose instead of laundered in a washing machine. "Clothes rarely keep good imprints."

We had similar luck with a decorative plate she'd treasured, a new-looking baby bootie, a picture of her parents, a decorative figurine, a basket, a baby pillow. I shook my head with each item, saddened at this minuscule sum of the person she had been.

I glanced at Tawnia and saw that she'd turned the page in her sketchbook. She was working on a new picture with a method I remembered from high school—blackening everything except a figure in the middle of the paper. I couldn't tell what the figure was yet, though it had a vaguely human form.

Ethan looked inside his bag, anticipation mingled with anxiousness. I realized he'd been holding something until the end, which made no sense at all.

"Give the bag to me," I demanded. "Let me find it—if there is anything to find." I reached for the duffel, pulling it from his reluctant grasp.

I put my hands inside and ran them over the remaining objects. Knickknacks, more pictures, a wedding ring. Though it was significant that she had left this particular piece of jewelry behind, I was relieved the vibes emitted were simple like those on the wedding photograph.

So, I'd been right that I couldn't help Ethan any further. I was beginning to relax—until my hand closed over the book. I had to bite my lip to keep from gasping aloud. I felt Jake's hand go to my shoulder, one of his fingers touching the bare skin on my neck, sending an odd tingling throughout my body. The touch was enough to help me blot out a bit of the intensity imprinted on the book.

Thank you, Jake, I thought.

I drew the book out slowly and read the title: *Life After Losing Someone You Love: A Guidebook through the Complex Grieving Process.* Images came to me. Marcie had tried repeatedly to read this book, to comprehend her own despair, but every effort had led to blurred words and a physical sickness.

The first solid imprinted scene—which meant the most recent—was of Marcie placing the book deep under her bed, heartache in every movement. She did so furtively, as if afraid someone would find out. Next to the book was a pile of dusty pills.

An earlier imprint followed. *My/her eyes left the pages of the book and focused on eager young faces. A bearded man in an old-fashioned white shirt came toward me/her. With his black hair and kind eyes, he reminded me of Rubin. Rubin, who I missed desperately.*

"I'm Founder Gabe," the man said. "I think I can help."

I recognized Founder Gabe as the same man from Victoria's imprint. Yet despite her heavy cloak of grief, Marcie's view of the man was more complete than Victoria's, from his age that she pinpointed to around fifty to his charismatic personality that she understood might harbor an ulterior motive. Even so, Marcie had begun to believe the only way to survive was to disappear, to become another person, someone who hadn't experienced loss, and Founder Gabe was her way to do that.

In the final imprint, Marcie was struggling with the book when Ethan approached her, holding her medicine in the palm of his hand.

"Take it," he told me/her. "Please. You have to get well."

Taking it was supposed to keep me afloat, but it made concentration more difficult. Did it really matter? Concentration wouldn't bring back my baby. I put the pill in my mouth and swallowed it down.

Deliberately removing my hand from the book, I met Ethan's gaze. "She met a man named Founder Gabe and planned to go with him. He's the same man Victoria planned to leave with—I'm sure of it. Marcie thought he looked like Rubin, but he doesn't. Not to me."

Ethan's expression crumpled, and he stared down at the table for a moment to regain his composure. I touched his arm. "She couldn't read the book, but she tried very hard. There's a lot of emotion on it."

"Not hard enough."

My jaw clenched so hard it ached. "You don't understand how grief can take control." His parents were dead, I'd learned during dinner, but he hadn't been close to them. Neither had he been close to Marcie's husband, and he hadn't held the baby more than a few brief times. Only the loss of his sister appeared to have affected him deeply, but as far as we knew, she still lived, and that meant there was hope. He had no true understanding of the grief his sister had endured.

"I should have been there for her more," he said. "After Rubin and again after Kayla died."

Kayla. This was the first I'd heard the baby's name. Marcie's feelings for her infant daughter were so much more than a simple name could convey—a soul-felt communication between mother and child.

"So where do you go from here?" Bret voiced my own thought.

Ethan dragged a hand over his face, his jaw hardening. I hated seeing his mask come down again, but I knew it was for self-protection. "I'll stake them out. I've got a friend down at the police department. Maybe if I can somehow convince them that Marcie's disappearance is connected with Victoria Fullmer's, they'll do something on their end."

He turned to me. "Thank you for verifying my suspicions

that she met with the Harmony Farms people. I've questioned their leaders numerous times, and they deny ever seeing her, but I'm more sure than ever that she's with them. Now I'll do what it takes to find my sister." His voice was dry and his face expressionless as he spoke. My heart hurt for him.

I looked to Tawnia for support, but she was staring at her drawing that now portrayed a woman sitting against a large barrel in a dark room. She was holding a bundled blanket as though it were a baby, but there was nothing inside. Her mouth opened in a silent cry.

The darkness caught my attention most. The thin man, Inclar, had mentioned darkness and screaming. Who was the woman in Tawnia's picture?

But I knew, and so did Tawnia. We'd both seen Marcie's wedding photograph. Tawnia finally lifted her head, her eyes searching for mine. I opened my mouth to speak but stopped at the slight shake of her head.

"There's really nothing else I can do," Ethan was saying. "I'll have to keep a close watch on them. Maybe they'll make a mistake and lead me to her." He paused before adding, "Unless you'd be willing to help."

"Me?" I dragged my eyes from my sister's. "How?"

"You said a man invited you to join them. What if you—"

"No way," Jake interrupted. "Anything might happen."

Ethan scowled. "I wouldn't put her in danger. She could pretend to join, and I'd track her to wherever they're staying. Then I'd help her leave before I went in to talk to Marcie."

"What if she couldn't leave?" Jake challenged. "Isn't that what you think happened to your sister?"

"No, I think my sister's sick. I think she needs help, mental help, and somehow this commune is exerting some kind of control over her. If I can find out where she is, I could sneak in and get her. I've already talked to a doctor about her, and he's experienced in this sort of thing."

"What if she's well and happy?" My eyes skittered doubtfully toward Tawnia's drawing. That woman certainly wasn't happy. "What if she doesn't want to leave?"

Ethan took a long breath. "Then I'll leave with the understanding that it's her choice. At least I'll know where she is."

"I'd probably have to be there for a few days," I said. "To find Victoria too." This was something both of my adoptive parents would have done in a heartbeat. They'd spent all their lives looking after others, and a chance to help two women or to prove Harmony Farms harmless would have been irresistible.

"You can't be serious!" Tawnia's face had lost all color. "Autumn, I won't let you do this!"

"Neither will I." Jake had both his hands on my shoulders now. At any other time I would have welcomed his touch, but who was he to tell me what to do, especially with such authority? It wasn't as if he were my brother or my boyfriend.

Only Bret kept quiet. Wise man, my brother-in-law. No wonder I liked him so well.

"Don't you think this is a job for the real authorities?" Jake pressed.

Ethan stood, shaking his head. "I've been working with the so-called real authorities for a year. The bottom line is that without proof Marcie is being held against her will, they've helped me all they can. Even my friend is taking days now to return my calls. Autumn wouldn't have to do anything dangerous. I have the equipment to make sure we're in touch all the time, and if she doesn't contact me regularly, we'll go to the police. It's not as if they could claim she ran away. We're all witnesses here of what she intends."

"Find someone else," Tawnia growled.

"I promise, I won't let anything happen to her," Ethan insisted. "I have a concealed carry permit, I'm trained in martial arts, and I've studied dozens of texts about military operations and criminals. Please, this may be the only chance to find out what happened to my sister."

"Can I talk to Autumn alone for a minute?" Tawnia asked icily. When no one moved, she jumped to her feet almost nimbly, despite the mass of baby at her waist, and headed down the short hall to the only bedroom in the bungalow. I arose more slowly and followed, stopping to pick up Tawnia's sketch book.

The tiny bedroom was dominated by the queen bed. Pictures hung on the wall at regular intervals, and everything was organized and neat. Quite the opposite of my apartment, where my collection of antiques and other belongings crowded every corner.

Tawnia folded her arms above her jutting stomach. "You told me you were out of this."

I sat on the bed and slowly pulled my legs up under me. "I thought I was. But I want to do this." Perhaps the idea had been in the back of my mind since the moment I met Director Korin.

"Why?"

My eyes slid past hers to the small window. "Because of Alice—that little girl with the bicycle, that horrible case I worked on with the police. I couldn't help her, but maybe with Marcie and Victoria it will be different. It might not be too late for them." I didn't add that this was different from the runaway teen or cheating boyfriend cases that usually landed in my path, most of which wrapped up with a single reading. I liked closure, and there was none for anyone in this case. There might never be if I didn't do something more.

Tawnia didn't reply. I could tell she was close to tears, so I stood and put my arms around her. "You drew Marcie," I said softly. "She needs our help."

"It might not be her. I have a great imagination."

I shook my head. "If my ability is something programmed into my DNA, like our brown hair and our weird eyes, then it follows you would also have some kind of ability. One that perhaps took a slightly different path, like with my love of antiques and your talent for art. Everything artists draw comes from what they see or experience or imagine. This is just one more type of seeing."

"But this—it's bad. She's holding that bundle as if it were a real baby, and she's so thin she's not eating much. I think if she doesn't get help, she's going to die."

"That's why I have to help her." Releasing my sister, I returned to the bed for her sketchbook. "But it's possible we're misreading things. She could simply be working after dark on a craft or something. What if you try to draw Victoria?"

Tawnia hesitated a moment before walking over to the dresser and finding a pencil next to another sketchbook. Her brow creased in concentration, but after a few strokes, it was clear she was sketching not Victoria but a large, smiling black woman standing on some sort of stage or porch.

She chuckled ruefully. "Guess that didn't work too well. Does she look like anyone you saw in the imprints?"

"No."

"Then maybe the other drawing means nothing."

I heard the relief in her voice. "You drew the man I saw at the river and the engineer Bret hired," I reminded her.

She shrugged. "Coincidence?"

"Nothing more's coming to you?"

"Sorry." She didn't look sorry.

"Well, if I can help Ethan's sister and Victoria, I think I should do it."

"What if it's dangerous?"

"I don't think it will be. I met them at the river today, remember? They seem sincere."

"Yeah, as if everyone's always exactly what they seem."

"I promise I'll leave if I see even a hint of danger."

"You're just attracted to Ethan," she said with a sniff. "What's wrong with you? Have you forgotten he's a math teacher? Totally not your type."

I laughed. "Hey, looking isn't the same thing as getting involved." I wasn't being totally honest on this, though, because during at least half our dinner I'd been thinking how it might be to go out with him.

Shaking my head at these thoughts, I regarded my sister solemnly. "Are you okay with this, then? Or at least enough to support me?"

She nodded slowly. "All right. But be careful."

I let out a sigh. I wasn't accustomed to being so closely concerned with another person's emotions like this. Though I'd lived with Winter until his death, he had never been one to interfere in my life or respond with alarm to anything I chose to do. Even as a child, I'd been allowed the freedom of an adult. Tawnia said I was lucky to have survived adolescence alive and unhindered by addiction. She was probably right, though I wondered if Summer's dying when I was so young had perhaps made me more responsible.

"We'd better get back to the others." Tawnia ran the tips of her fingers under her right eye, which was still tearing a bit. "Bret's probably fighting to keep those two from killing each other."

We found quite the opposite. In the kitchen, both Bret and Jake were sitting on either side of Ethan, looking for all the world like small, fascinated boys at the wide assortment of gadgets and electronic gizmos that littered the table. The object most prominently on display was the large handgun in Ethan's hand. My stomach churned when I saw the weapon. Even from a distance my nerves tingled with the imprints emanating from the metal.

No way I was going to touch that.

The gun was my first indication that maybe I was in over my head.

Chapter 6

I tore my eyes away from the gun. "I'm in," I told Ethan, ignoring Jake's surprised glare. "What's the plan?" Now that I'd made my decision, I was anxious to get started. Maybe so I couldn't change my mind.

Ethan smiled. "Great. You can start by asking them tomorrow when they'll be leaving town. They'll probably be hoping you'll show up again after your conversation with them today. Once they know you want to join, they'll probably suggest that you make certain preparations to leave. You know, see loved ones for the last time—without telling them you're leaving, of course—collect any valuables, clean out your bank account." His voice had turned from informative to bitter.

"I don't have any money—not that I'm willing to give them, anyway."

"Don't people usually take more time to recruit?" Jake asked. "Are they really going to believe Autumn decided to join in only one day?"

"From what I've seen of this cult over the past year, they'll invite Autumn to meet with them at the hotel where they're staying, introduce her around, and find out her weaknesses so they can exploit them to get her to join. It's all pretty methodical." Ethan ran his finger over the barrel of his gun, which for some reason made my heart beat a little faster—though not from fear. There is something intrinsically powerful about a man holding a gun.

"Most people seem to take a full month or more to join them," Ethan continued, "but I have seen people join after one weekend of meetings. It may not make sense to you or me, because we're emotionally balanced, but for people on the edge, or people who've undergone a recent tragedy or a change in their life, it can make all the sense in the world."

"So basically they're all wackos," Bret said.

Ethan shook his head. "Not really. Cults may attract a lot of desperate and needy people, but a lot of regular people get involved as well. Some experts claim we have more than three thousand cults in the United States alone. Still, it's true they prey upon the emotionally fragile."

Emotionally fragile. I wondered how long it took for a math teacher to become comfortable spouting such phrases.

"Autumn, this isn't funny," Jake growled.

I hadn't realized I was grinning. "I don't think it is." I sank into the chair next to Jake.

"As for the money," Ethan continued as though we hadn't spoken, "I've saved a bit that you can offer them to throw off suspicion. But money won't be their sole objective because they obviously need people to work for them. They must rake in a pretty penny with all those unpaid laborers."

I pulled up my feet onto the chair and wrapped my arms around my legs. "What if you never get the money back? I mean, what if they're exactly what they seem and there's no fraud going on beside underpayment of workers? With three thousand cults around, there have to be some that aren't destructive influences. I'm sure many communes fit the cult description but do only good for their members."

"Not Harmony Farms," Ethan said, shaking his head. "I'm sure they're dirty. They've gone to too many pains to hide their real operation. Besides, the money means nothing compared to finding my sister and getting her the help she needs. I don't care if I get it back as long as we find Marcie."

"I still don't like it," Jake muttered.

I smiled at him confidently. "It'll be okay. I want to do this. My parents were people like these, and I'm sure I can handle myself around them."

Ethan began repacking his equipment into a large black briefcase. "I'd like to go over some things with you before you talk to them," he said to me, "and then again after you tell them you're joining. Once we know when they're pulling out and what their plans are regarding your membership, we can organize a plan of attack. I can give you a lift home tonight so we can talk—unless you drove your own car, of course." His eyes met mine, the intense blue holding a message that had nothing to do with Harmony Farms. He wanted to see me alone. For what purpose, I was willing to find out.

How convenient that I hadn't driven my car. I opened my mouth to accept, but Jake beat me to it. "I'm taking her home. We have plans."

We did? Riding home on his bike wasn't exactly a plan. I glanced at Tawnia for help, but she shrugged, her mouth curved in an amused smile. Good thing someone was getting enjoyment out of this.

Ethan gave a short nod. "Okay, tomorrow morning then. I'll drop by your shop." He finished packing his things and scooped up both the briefcase and the duffel with Marcie's belongings. "Nice to meet everyone."

He met my gaze again for a long moment, while I silently berated Jake for his interference. In the past Jake had always been helpful when I became interested in a new guy. What was his problem now?

When Ethan had gone, I said goodbye to Bret and a still worried Tawnia, grabbed my handbag, and went with Jake to his bike. He pulled on his black leather jacket after first offering it to me. Then he straddled the bike and motioned for me to climb on behind him.

I shook my head. "Why did you tell Ethan I couldn't go with him?"

His jaw hardened. "We had plans to go for a ride, didn't we?"

"Well, yes, but it's not as if . . . I mean, you said yourself that we're only . . . Sheeze, Jake. He's, well, hot. And I like him. I mean, now that he's not being a jerk. I think he likes me too."

"Of course he does," Jake said stiffly. "But you know nothing about him."

"Yes, I do. He's a math teacher turned private eye, whose sister is missing."

"So he says." Jake arched a brow.

That irritated me. After all, I wasn't completely stupid. "I *felt* his sister's loss, and I saw him in her imprint. I know she was planning to join the people at Harmony Farms."

"Look, I know you've seen and experienced a lot," Jake said, his voice strained. "But for all the things you've done in your life and for all the variety of people you've met, you've basically remained untouched by the really bad stuff. I don't know if that was Winter's influence or if your own energy attracts the better sort of people, but Harmony Farms is connected to two missing women, who could be dead or worse, and you don't seem to be taking this seriously."

I wanted to tell him to mind his own business, that I'd spent time with more druggies and criminals than he'd likely glimpsed in his entire lifetime. But the truth was, he was right. For all my odd schooling and the strange characters that had marched in and out of my life over the years, I'd been set apart, untouchable, as Winter's daughter. People had come to him— and Summer when she'd been alive—with broken, seemingly irreparable lives, and he had given them herbs, found them places to stay and a job to do. Most of all he'd loved them, and that love had evoked a deep loyalty.

People still showed up at the Herb Shoppe to repay me for something Winter or Summer had done for them. A new shelf for my antiques, repairs for my car, a knitted sweater, a box of food, pottery, and even jewelry. Of course, some hadn't been able to scrape the pieces of their lives back together, and others had cracked again after Winter's repairs, but none of these had ever dragged me into their dirt, though I'd slept in the same apartment with many of them.

I took a deep breath, filled with both longing and anger at the man who'd been my father—longing for his presence and protection, and anger at his desertion, however unintentional. Tears bubbled from the corners of my eyes, and I looked away from Jake so he wouldn't see.

Too late. He was off his bike and reaching for me. "Autumn?" he asked tentatively.

"I miss Winter," I whispered.

Jake had stopped short of touching me, but now he drew me into his arms. I smelled the leather of his jacket, the faint aroma of cinnamon and comfrey from the store, and a hint of aftershave. Aftershave? He normally only used that when we went dancing at the club.

His strong presence filled me up, sealing all the cracks in my inner walls where the despair had oozed in. The anger at Winter disappeared and the longing faded, not completely but enough. Then I was feeling something else entirely, something that tingled down to my toes and made the world stop turning. For that moment I was completely happy and would have been content to sit down on Tawnia's grass and sleep there all night with Jake's arms around me.

Not possible, of course. I shook myself, remembering who I was with. My *friend* Jake. I stepped back from him and smiled. I'd never been great at hiding my emotions, but Tawnia was good at it—at least when she wasn't pregnant—and I had learned a thing or two from her in the past year.

"Thanks." My voice was little more than a mumble, but it was either that or cry again. Or throw myself at him—and that was out of the question.

Placing my handbag over my head and shoulder so it wouldn't go flying, I silently put on Jake's extra helmet, climbed onto the back of his motorbike, and slid my arms around his waist. The helmet didn't go around my chin, so once I lifted up the visor, I could press the front part of my cheek against the back of his leather jacket. I reveled in his solid form and the warmth of his body.

In the next moment we were off, air beating against my face. Exhilaration quickly replaced the sadness, and I knew Jake had chosen this nearly deserted route home on purpose for the high speed we could achieve. We rode for an hour, until the summer night became cool and I had to tuck my hands under his jacket to keep them warm. He turned in the direction of home.

We pulled up at my apartment, and I eased myself off the bike, my muscles having grown stiff. The night was warm now that we'd stopped, and I flexed my fingers so the cold would leave them more quickly.

"That was great," I told Jake, as we both removed our helmets.

"Better than going with Ethan?" he teased.

"I know you aren't happy about what I want to do, but I have a chance to help those women. Winter would understand."

Jake's lips pursed, and that did funny things to my heart. Jake had great lips, full and generous and inviting. I'd always thought so, even before I'd begun falling for him.

"I understand why," he said, "but I still don't like it. And I don't trust Ethan."

"Why?"

Jake frowned. "I've seen the way he looks at you."

"Oh." This was interesting. "How does he look at me?"

"Like . . . like he wants something."

"I hate to break it to you, but he does want something. He wants me to help find his sister."

He looked ready to say more but finally shook his head and sighed. "I just worry you're getting in over your head, and it's all my fault. I'm the one who brought the Fullmers to see you."

So that was the real story. He felt guilty because none of this would have happened if he hadn't opened the door. "You've always urged me to help people with my ability. What else can I do except look into it?"

"I don't know."

The parking lot light nearest us was burned out so we were

in the dark, close together. I wished I had the nerve to step even closer. He let out the breath he'd been holding, and I could feel a hint of its warmth. Something built inside me, but I wasn't sure what it was.

"Want me to walk you inside?" he asked.

I shook my head. Despite the broken light, this was a relatively safe area. I knew all the neighbors in my apartment building and most of those in the surrounding ones, by sight if not by name. Since Winter's death, everyone had gone out of their way to show me kindness, as though they shared my tragedy. Because I'd survived the bombing, I had become something of an icon to my neighbors, a symbol of hope and survival.

Jake hugged me quickly and got on his bike, though he waited to put on his helmet until I reached the lobby doors. The street light near the building worked, and I used it to find the keys inside my purse. My hand had scarcely closed around them when the door clicked open with a soft buzz. I smiled and waved at the windows above me, though I couldn't see a face in them. Probably old Mrs. Turnbull was watching TV in her bedroom and had called for her husband to release the lobby latch. We all looked out for each other that way.

I shouldered my handbag, keys out now, and slapped on the lobby light with the palm of my hand. Outside, Jake's bike engine revved as he sped away.

I'd gone up the three lobby steps and turned left toward my apartment on the main floor when I realized I wasn't alone. "Hello?" I called.

Out of the corner of my eye I saw a movement. A figure shot toward me from the direction of my door, ramming into me. I barely had time to register fear before my head hit the wall and I crumpled with the pain. For a moment I saw stars.

Before I had time to decide if I was going to live, the figure was on top of me, weighing far too much for his thin, wiry build.

"You should stay away from the farm," hissed the voice. "Far away."

My vision cleared enough to show me Inclar, the man I'd followed from the river. "Maybe I want to join them," I said through gritted teeth.

"You won't leave the same—if you leave at all."

His right eye was rolling like crazy, though his left was steady enough. His hands were at my throat, but they weren't choking me. Yet.

"Get off," I managed.

His hands tightened, and his face came close to mine. I gagged at the sourness of his breath. Gray and brown stubble covered his cheeks, and at this close range I could see each individual hair. I choked as the lobby began to grow dark. Ten feet from my door and safety. Not a pretty way to die. I clawed at him. I could no longer smell his noxious breath because I couldn't breathe. My body screamed for oxygen.

"No," Inclar said, "I don't want to kill her. She's sees."

No one else was in the lobby. Who was he talking to?

"I won't do it." His hands relaxed marginally. The eye still rolled loosely in his head, and his face was pale and frightened. A sob escaped his throat. I tried to move, but his fingers were like small steel rods pinning me in place. "Please don't make me," he whined like a beaten man.

I'd dropped my keys when I fell, but I stretched for them now, hoping to use them as a weapon. Another half inch and I'd be able to reach them.

Inclar contorted his body and kicked the keys away with

his foot. His contortion gave me an idea. With effort, I brought up my legs and managed to curl one foot around him, pushing him away with all the strength I had left. For a moment we held steady, and black patches filled half my sight. Then Inclar yelped and fell back.

At once he scrabbled to a crouched position, hands curled out before him like claws. I drew in a ragged breath, wondering how I was going to defend myself. He launched, but this time his body hurtled past me, down the three steps to the lobby, and out the door into the night.

The world went dark.

Just the light in the lobby going out, but I was shaken enough to huddle on the floor against the wall for a moment to regain my strength. As the cold from the marble floor seeped into my body, I slowly took stock of my limbs. Nothing seemed broken, though my head pounded and my throat was sore. A tiny patch of light from the street light filtered through the glass door in the lobby. I moved, kicking something with a foot. My keys. I crawled to them, and then to my door, fear and pain making me sluggish. I didn't sense anyone in the lobby, but I couldn't be sure Inclar wouldn't return.

Why was I even still alive? He'd seemed intent on killing me. Or at least half of him had.

At last I closed my apartment door behind me, locking it. I sagged against the door, swallowing in relief. My throat hurt less now, and the quiet buzz of my antiques filled the room with comforting images.

I should call the police. I knew where Inclar lived—if he was stupid enough to return there—and they could pick him up and question him.

But if I called the police, Detective Martin would hear

about the attack, and he'd never let it go until I told him every-thing. When we'd worked together on the bicycle case, he'd been almost impossible, alternating between believing me and threatening to throw me in jail for what I seemed to know. If he got involved in the Harmony Farms case, there was no way he'd let me go undercover.

Something white registered in the corner of my vision. Unsteadily, I turned my head to see a business envelope that was partially crumpled from being shoved under my door. SAVE THEM was written across the back of the envelope in unsteady block letters. I reached for the envelope, dragging it toward where I sat. There was something heavy inside. I opened the envelope with shaking fingers, and an old-fashioned brass key fell out on the floor, the metal darkened with use. For the moment I let it stay where it was because there was also a letter-sized piece of paper with a map of the area near Oregon's border, complete with a large X in yellow highlighter. Shaky words at the bottom proclaimed: *They would kill me if they knew you had this.*

What was going on? Inclar had obviously slipped this under my door. How else could it have gotten here? But then why try to kill me? Or had he followed someone else here—perhaps one of the farm's disciples?

No, they didn't even know my name. Come to think of it, how had Inclar known where I lived? Yet as I considered, I realized his finding me wasn't really a mystery. He lived in the area and could have seen me in the shop. Since many of my fellow shop owners knew where I lived, especially following the publicity of Winter's death, anyone could have traced me with a few questions. Yet why give me a map and a key and then try to kill me? He was a psychopath at best and probably schizo-phrenic on top of that.

There was no imprint on either the envelope or the map, which told me this wasn't a treasured object or something that had been touched very often or for long, despite the obvious feeling behind the scrawled words.

I picked up the key. At once intense images shot through my head in a rapid, blurry succession. *Darkness. Pain. Laughter. Evil. A slap on the face. Fingers bleeding from the stab of a needle. Power and conquest. Agony. Triumph. A corpse.*

My fingers opened, and the key slipped back into the envelope. I swallowed hard, my heart pounding erratically. This was the second object I'd come across that held such intense and rapid conflict that my brain couldn't process anything with any degree of intelligence. The first time had been days after Winter's funeral. I'd fainted then.

Rising, I stumbled unsteadily across the room to the couch, falling over the back and sprawling onto the cushions, too tired to go around. I set the envelope on the antique coffee table and the map on top of that. My handbag I let slide to the floor. Pulling Summer's multicolored afghan over me, I basked in the imprint of her memories that washed gently over me like warm, soothing water. They were so gentle and faint that sometimes I wondered if they were only my memories and no longer imprints at all.

After a while, I reached out and took Summer's picture from the coffee table. This imprint was stronger. I felt a rush of love, saw thin, familiar fingers on the frame. Winter's fingers. I'd replaced the glass that had shattered when I dropped it on the day of his funeral, but the imprints on the gold and black frame were unchanged.

Exhaustion lay heavily upon my shoulders, but I knew I should call someone. Jake? No. He'd just be more set against my participation in this whole thing. Too bad, because he was my first choice. He could stay with me all night, sleeping in Winter's room or on the couch. But because the attack was wrapped up with Harmony Farms, I knew I couldn't call him without raising more objections to my plan. Same with Tawnia and Bret. The people in my building and my friends from work couldn't begin to understand what was going on. So far none of them had even a hint about my gift. Better to rest now and figure things out in the morning.

A creaking came from the apartment above me. Or was it coming from my place? Maybe someone was in my kitchen or in one of the two bedrooms. I looked around for something to use as a weapon. Not my antique vase or the ogre statue. They were too valuable.

The sounds stopped, but I found myself clutching Summer's picture, my hands shaking. This was going to be a long night.

I had Ethan's business card out of my purse and was dialing the phone before I realized it.

"Hello?"

"It's Autumn. I'm sorry to bother you this late." My throat ached at the effort to speak, and my voice sounded husky even to my ears.

"It's barely ten."

"Oh." It seemed much later to me.

"Are you all right? You're not having second thoughts?"

"Someone was outside my apartment tonight. That guy I told you all about during dinner, the brother of that leader—not the leader in Marcie's imprint, but the younger one I met today. Anyway, his brother left a map under my door. At least I think it was him."

"A map?" Ethan's voice was eager. "Of what?"

"It's not marked, but there's some cryptic wording about his being killed if they knew I had it, which is sort of stupid since I thought he was going to kill me before I even saw it."

"He hurt you?"

"I must have startled him when I got home. I think he's a little nuts." I explained the attack and how Inclar had debated with himself whether or not to kill me.

"I wondered what was up with your voice," he said. "I wish I had been there."

"Me too."

"What he wrote on the envelope seems to indicate someone needs saving."

"I agree. But who?" I was feeling steadier now that he was on the line. I scooped up an antique vase and checked out the bedrooms. No one there, and the windows were closed. The tiny kitchen was also empty, my tall frame of herbs against the window undisturbed, the familiar smells welcoming me like an old friend. A cup of chamomile tea was what I needed for both my sore throat and my nerves. I set down the vase, and put my teapot on the stove.

"Has to be the rebellious disciples, I'd say," Ethan replied, answering my questions. "Who else would need saving?"

"I thought about going to the police, but I worried that would get in the way of what we were trying to do."

"Maybe it would help."

"Maybe."

"Then again you could be right. If he's obviously crazy and we have him arrested, his brother might come to get him out on bail, or whatever."

"And my chances of joining Harmony Farms would probably be nil."

"Yes, your identity could be compromised. But what if he tries to hurt you again?"

"Well, I'm not going to open the door for him." I took down a mug from the cupboard.

"Don't open it for anyone."

I snorted. "Let's not go overboard."

A loud horn sounded from his end, and I wondered if he lived near a freeway or large road. "Well, just be careful," he said. "So about the map, is it legible?"

I went back to the living room to retrieve it. "Looks like a photocopy—a poor one. I don't recognize any of the land-marks, though there is a main road down at the very bottom. The 95, I think."

"That goes through Rome."

"Just a minute, and I'll check it against my own map."

I plucked my Oregon map from the bookshelf and took it to the kitchen. The water in the teapot was hot, so I added the chamomile. Letting the tea steep, I spread the map onto the table.

"Well?" asked Ethan, who was understandably anxious.

I had to search for a moment. "Yeah, I think it is there. Like I said, the photocopy is kind of poor, and my map doesn't show a lot of details, but I bet we could find it from this."

"Maybe you wouldn't need to join them after all."

"You think you'd be able to find your sister if you watched the place?"

He sighed. "You're right. She might not be in view. Without someone on the inside, it'd be hard to tell if they are what they appear to be. They aren't going to be abusing anyone in the open, even if the place itself is hidden."

I hadn't exactly been implying any of that, but he did

have a point. I didn't mind letting him think I'd come to that conclusion before he did. All was fair in love and war. I smiled, knowing which I hoped this might be. Intelligence, finger-attracting hair, a smile that made my heart beat faster, and a steady job. What more could a girl want?

"I'll make you a copy of the map at work tomorrow," I told Ethan.

"Thank you. I'd like that."

"Well, I guess I'd better let you go."

"I don't like the idea of you being alone. Maybe you should call your sister."

"She'd be freaked out, especially now with all the hormones."

"What about that guy. Jake, was it? I got the feeling you two are, uh, close."

I frowned. "He's like a brother to me." Unfortunately.

"A brother." Ethan sounded glad, and that made me feel better.

More small talk while another idea occurred to me. I turned on the computer I'd crammed in a corner of the kitchen next to the washer piled high with dirty clothes. With a little help, I might be able to find myself a better map. It took me less time than I expected. I'd only finished half a cup of tea before I was able to pinpoint a dark patch of green on the interactive map that I thought might be the location of Harmony Farms.

"It's a lot clearer on the Internet," I told Ethan triumphantly. "I mean, it's just a patch of trees—I can't see any buildings or anything, but that might be because they're hidden or the satel-lite picture is old." I sent the file to my email address, planning to print it at work since I didn't have a printer in the apartment.

"Great. That's really going to help."

Help him, maybe. Because for me being able to find it on a map and in real life were two completely different things. I was hopelessly directionally impaired, another trait I shared with my sister. Without exact coordinates, I wouldn't be able to use my phone's GPS.

I turned off the computer, my eyes heavy. I decided to finish the tea in the living room under my mother's afghan. "Look, thanks for everything, Ethan. We'd better hang up now."

"Not yet," he said. "Go open your door."

"What?"

"Open it."

I went to the door and peered through the peephole. Ethan was standing outside, smiling with his phone at his ear. My gaze flitted to the clock to see that we'd been on the phone more than forty-five minutes. Still, he'd made good time; at normal speeds he lived forty-five minutes from Tawnia's and my apartment was fifteen minutes farther.

"There's a man outside my door," I said. "He might be here to attack me."

"I don't think so. He might actually protect you."

"How did you find me?"

He laughed, a sound I could hear through both the phone and the door. "I'm a private investigator, aren't I?"

I let him in, embarrassed to be so happy to see him and glad that I wouldn't have to jump at every creak in this old building all night long. "Thanks for coming."

"I came for the map."

"Whatever."

"Tea?" I indicated my cup.

"No thanks."

We talked a while at the kitchen table, poring over the

map, until I could no longer hide my huge yawns. "You go on to bed." He opened his jacket to show the gun in his shoulder holster. "I'll keep a lookout."

"Okay," I said, all joviality gone. "Good night." I touched his arm as I arose, a simple gesture of thanks.

At least that's what it was supposed to be. His scent drifted to my nose. Something masculine and incredibly attractive. He looked up at me, his expression acute. The tension between us grew so thick, I had no doubt we were both experiencing the same emotion. I liked this man, and he liked me. The night suddenly became a lot more interesting.

But Jake's warning about Ethan filled my head before I could do anything I might regret later. I lifted my hand and stepped back.

"Good night," Ethan said, his voice gravelly. His eyes followed me to the door.

In my own room, I locked the door, shed my outer clothing, and fell into bed. Sleep settled over me, and the last thing I thought about wasn't Jake's comforting arms or Ethan's intense stare but Inclar's eye rolling uncontrollably in his head. And the key that was sitting inside the envelope on my coffee table.

In all the excitement with the map, I'd completely forgotten the key.

Chapter 7

The next morning I awoke with the sun, which can really mess up your day in the winter but is an okay thing to do in mid-June. It was Friday, a work day, but I had time before I needed to open the shop, and if I wasn't there exactly at nine, it really didn't matter because Jake would open for both of us. I stretched in my bed under a quilt I'd tied when I was thirteen with a little help from Winter. I felt snug and warm.

Then I remembered Ethan and sat up straight. Was he still here? I pulled on last night's clothes, ran a hand through my short hair, unlocked my bedroom door, and went out into the living room.

Ethan was there, all right. He'd dragged Winter's comfy chair near the door, not an easy feat as it had been made in the days when furniture was built to last more than three years. He lay back in it sound asleep, his hair tousled even more than yesterday and his mouth partially open. He looked like a little boy, and I smiled at the image. Until my eyes fell to the gun in his hand. He'd obviously been worried that Inclar might return. Though it was sweet to put himself in the line of fire, I doubted I was in immediate danger. This was dramatic overkill. Asleep holding the gun, he looked a parody of the courageous private investigator at my sister's dinner table the night before.

I laughed softly, but Ethan didn't stir. I wondered how long he'd stayed up studying the map. No doubt he was anxious to get on the road to see if anything was really there.

Why would Inclar give me a map and then try to kill me? There didn't seem to be an answer, and I hated wasting time playing "what if," though normally I was a master at the game.

What if Summer had survived the cancer? What if I hadn't let Winter go with me to shop for antiques that last day? Or what if we hadn't driven over the Hawthorne Bridge?

I grabbed low-rise camouflage pants and a dark brown shirt from my room and hurried to the bathroom. I showered, humming to myself and feeling more alive than I had in a long time. Only a slight huskiness remained when I tried out my voice, and my throat felt much better.

My smile died when I looked in the mirror and saw two thumbprint bruises in the middle of my throat. Everything came rushing back. My heart thumped and then hammered in my chest as last night's terror flashed into my mind. My stomach churned so hard I felt sick. I gripped the sink until the memory passed.

I should have called the police. But what would that mean for the map and the key?

I gave my hair two minutes with the blow dryer, using a little gel to add body to the red-dyed hair on top. A generous helping of makeup gave me back my color, which I sometimes thought had been leached from my face when my car plunged into the Willamette River.

I opened the door to find Ethan was no longer snoring in the chair, which had been put back in its place. Nor was he anywhere else in my apartment. Both my map and Inclar's were gone, but the envelope holding the key lay untouched on the coffee table next to my marble figurines. Unable to make myself touch it again, I folded it up in the envelope and slipped it into my handbag. I'd have to find some way to take it to the commune undetected.

Before I could get annoyed about Ethan's desertion, I heard a sound at the door, not quite a knock, and I went to see who it was—Ethan, back from wherever he'd gone. I unlocked the door and let him in. He'd combed his hair, probably with his fingers, and it had regained its normal look that skirted the border between professional and messy.

"Sorry, hands are full." He hefted two bags that looked suspiciously like doughnuts and coffee.

Caffeine and trans fat. Processed flour and sugars. I stifled a sigh. "I don't drink coffee," I said. No use in delaying the inevitable confession.

He couldn't have been more surprised if I'd told him I had supernatural powers, which, it could be argued, I do, so I know the look. "What about doughnuts?" he asked.

"I definitely eat doughnuts, just not that kind. Look, forget about them. Come on in, and I'll make us a breakfast that will knock our socks off."

His eyes went to my bare feet. "That'd be pretty hard to do, seeing as you're not wearing any."

"You have a problem with my feet?"

"I think you have beautiful feet."

"Oh." No one had ever said that to me before. The delicious tension of the night before reappeared in that instant.

"Your eyes are beautiful too. In fact, all of you looks amazing. Especially after what you went through yesterday."

That reminded me of someone saying, "She looks great for her age." Qualifiers significantly lessened the impact of a compliment, but I'd try to overlook the additional words this time. He was a man, after all.

"Thanks."

I made him real hot cocoa and fresh whole wheat doughnuts fried in palm fruit oil, along with fresh organic eggs and bacon.

"This really is good." Ethan stared at me with something near admiration. The old saying that you can reach a man's heart through his stomach seemed to be true.

Everything was going great until Jake arrived.

I was washing a pan when he rang, and by the time I'd dried my hands and made it to the door, he was knocking and calling my name. "Oh, you're here," he said.

"I'm eating breakfast." I ran my tongue over my lower lip to check for any stray bacon grease.

"I see." Jake looked great this morning in cargo jeans and an off-white shirt with buttons and long sleeves turned up at the cuffs. The light shirt set off the dark color of his skin and eyes. Eyes that narrowed with suspicion when Ethan appeared behind me in the kitchen doorway. "Am I interrupting something?"

"No, we're just having breakfast. There was a little excitement last night, and Ethan came over to—"

"He stayed the night?"

"Well. Sort of. Not really stayed. It was more of standing guard in case the man came back. And he wanted to see the map, of course."

"What man? What map? What's going on here?" Jake's dark eyes were flashing now, and I recognized anger, which made me angry too.

"Nothing. Or nothing that's any of your business, if that's the way you're going to act."

"I came over here to see if we could compromise on this cult issue, but you've gone right ahead and—"

"She was attacked last night," Ethan interrupted in a somewhat superior air. "I came to make sure she was safe."

Jake's stare went from me to Ethan and back again. "You didn't call me? What were you thinking? We're friends." Not like this guy, his words implied.

I sighed. "Look, why don't you stay here with Ethan and he'll tell you what we found out, okay? Since you're obviously not going to be around to open your store, or the connecting doors to mine, I'd better get there myself. I seem to remember that you usually have a bit of a morning rush." I grabbed my handbag and fled.

For a woman with as many antiques as I had in my apartment, you'd think I'd have more care about locking up. But I always figured that if someone really needed my things worse than I did, they were welcome to them. Besides, a lot of antiques—my favorites, in fact—looked a lot like old junk. Especially crammed in with all the years' worth of things Winter and I couldn't bear to throw away.

Jake had a key anyway, a fact he was probably showing off to Ethan right now. What was wrong with him? The possibility of Jake's harboring secret romantic feelings for me was beyond my ability to entertain at the moment. I was too annoyed.

The morning was chilly for June, but the sun in the east showed every sign that it would burn away the clouds. I looked around, letting the calm of the new day ease my turmoil. I smiled and waved at neighbors as they passed.

My mood was destroyed for the second time that morning when my car didn't start. Great. What now? It sounded like the battery had run down, but I'd replaced it only two months ago. Now I'd have to find someone to let me use their car to jump start it, which I was an old pro at by now, or ask Jake for a ride.

I definitely wasn't going to ask Jake.

Jake and Ethan emerged from my building, Jake jumping on his bike and roaring away without even looking at me. Ethan sauntered in my direction. I opened my door. "Can you give me a jump start? I have cables."

A private eye should know how to jump start a car, but would a math teacher? Probably. Engines worked logically, right? Not like imprints. Though maybe I could find a science behind those if I did more research.

"Aren't you late already? Why don't I give you a ride? We can take care of this later. I'd like to take you to lunch, if you're free. I mean, after you talk to the Harmony Farms people, of course."

Right. I still had to sign up for recruitment. "Sure, but I pick the place, okay?" I never passed up free food, as long as I could get it somewhere I trusted. "There's a restaurant across from my store that you'll love." I slammed my car door shut.

"Aren't you going to lock it?"

"It's not going anywhere. The radio doesn't work, either, so there's not much attraction to thieves." I locked it anyway. Jake had told me a million times that I should be more careful about my car. I'd told him that worrying about locking the store and my apartment was trouble enough.

"You'd be surprised at what I've seen."

"As a private eye?"

"No, on campus. College students are more desperate than criminals these days. The only difference is that the students cannibalize their own cars for parts to sell instead of the cars of others."

I laughed. The man had a sense of humor. Maybe I could learn to like math as long as he didn't try to force me to wear shoes.

Ethan's car was a red BMW, which floored me. Normally I wouldn't notice the make, but this was remarkable. "I didn't know teachers drove cars like this. Maybe I should become a teacher."

He laughed. "This didn't come from teaching. I do other work on the side." His smile faded. "Well, I did until Marcie disappeared. I've been occupied since then."

"I'm really sorry." I touched his arm, feeling the warmth of him through the thin material of his shirt. Before I could draw away, he laid a hand over mine, pinning it in place. My heart thumped a little harder.

"Look," he said, "I'm sorry for the way I treated you at your shop yesterday. Part of me wanted to believe what Mrs. Fullmer said about you, but it's just, well, you run into a lot of people willing to take advantage when someone's vulnerable."

I laughed. "You were easier to convince than most. Believe me. There's a detective down at the police station who probably still suspects I was in league with a kidnapper I helped them catch. Fortunately, I was in Kansas with Tawnia visiting her parents when the little girl went missing."

"That's good." He released my hand and started the engine. "I take it you and your sister are close?"

"Very. There's a strong connection between us. It's hard to

explain." I pushed a button to roll down the window a few inches. I don't know if it was Ethan's presence or my memories, but I was feeling warm.

"What time will you go to the river?" he asked. My apartment was close to my shop, and already we had turned onto the right street.

"Before noon. Maybe eleven-thirty. I'd like to catch them before lunchtime. A lot of people are buying stuff from them then."

"I'll drive you there."

"Better not. If they see you, the game's over."

He made a face. "I guess that's true, but don't take any chances. Don't get into any cars with them. We'll need to get you outfitted with all the recent technology first. That's what I'll work on this morning—getting all that ready."

I nodded, my hand going to the door handle as he came to a stop.

"Autumn," he said.

I looked at him.

"I think we have a connection, too."

What do you say to that? I mean, there was a certain level of attraction between us, but until you experienced the sort of connection I felt with Tawnia or had felt with Winter and Summer—well, it wasn't the same thing at all. But that didn't mean a connection couldn't happen.

I smiled. "I'd like to get to know you better."

"I look forward to it."

"Good." My tone was probably a little too flippant, but in that moment I felt confident and hopeful for the future. Maybe it was time to get over Jake.

I scooted out of the car, the cold cement of the sidewalk a

momentary shock on the soles of my feet. I waved at Ethan, turning before he drove away. Jake had already opened the Herb Shoppe and disarmed the alarms in both stores. All I had to do was open my outer door. No one was in my shop, but Jake was at his checkout desk helping a burly man with a tattoo on his huge upper arm. Jake glanced up at me as I passed the open double doors connecting our stores. I kept my expression steady. I didn't know whether to laugh or cry where he was concerned.

He came to find me when the burly man had gone. I was in my back room filling my teapot with water. "Autumn?"

I turned. "Yes?"

"I'm sorry."

"I'm sorry too."

He hugged me, spilling some of the water from my pot down his sleeve. I set down the teapot, still hugging him, letting myself breathe in his familiarity. He felt so good. I wished the moment would never end.

He held me back from him so he could look into my face, his gaze darkening as it dropped to the bruises on my throat. "You should have called me. I would have come."

"I wasn't trying to have anyone come over. I'm a big girl."

His eyes wandered over my face, down to my bare toes and back again. "I'm aware of that."

Zing! That's the only word I knew to describe the funny way my heart reacted to his statement. *Are you really?* I wanted to ask him. *Look into my eyes and tell me what you see.*

I didn't say any of that, which was odd for me because I'd spoken my mind all my life. Regardless, Jake did continue to look at me, his gaze working to penetrate the walls I'd been building to keep my feelings out of his sight.

Not good. I dropped my eyes.

He sighed and shook his head. "Please call me if anything like this ever happens again, okay?"

I nodded and backed away, tossing him a hand towel so he could blot the water from his sleeve. Normally, I'd have helped him, and we'd have laughed together about our clumsiness, but sometimes a woman has to protect her heart. I busied myself putting the teapot on the stove. "Want some?"

He shook his head. "Maybe you ought to stay with Tawnia for a while. Until they catch this guy."

I shook my head. "It's too tiny there now that she and Bret are married."

"Then stay with me."

Right. That was exactly what I needed. In the old days I wouldn't have thought twice about bunking on his couch, but the way I felt now made it a lousy idea. "I'll be fine, really. He's just a nutcase. I think he actually wanted to help, giving me the map and the key."

"Key?"

"There was a key too." I pulled it from my purse and opened the envelope to show him. He took it out, hefted it, and started to hand it back. I gestured toward the envelope. "It's got weird imprints. Like the confessional booth."

"You mean the one where you fainted?"

Of course that was the one. The only one. I was a fast learner. I'd gone to the church to thank the priest for coming to Winter's home funeral at my apartment. He'd offered a few words to the friends who had gathered to show their last respects. He even joined in writing messages on the cardboard coffin, sang a few old hippy songs, and ate homemade organic food to celebrate Winter Rain's passing. It was the second home funeral I'd had for a parent, and it was no easier at thirty-two years of age than it had been at eleven. The priest's words had comforted me.

I wanted him to know what his presence had meant, but when I arrived at the church, he was occupied with a parishioner. During my wait I'd entered the booth out of curiosity, leaving the door open behind me to stave off the claustrophobia I often felt in tight spaces. The moment I entered, images assailed my senses, horrific and comforting, repulsive and beckoning, inflexible and tender, mocking and sincere, shameful and innocent and it was all I could do to stagger out the door and collapse onto the floor. That was where the priest had found me, passed out on the hard marble, a lump forming on the back of my head. I didn't tell him what had happened. That had been in the early stages of discovering my ability, when I hadn't even admitted it to myself.

"Autumn?" Jake studied me with concern.

What had we been talking about? "Yeah. The one where I fainted."

"The police will need to question him about the key. Did you tell them about it?"

"I didn't call the police. Didn't Ethan tell you? Besides, I don't want to tell the police about the key. If they take it into evidence, I might not be able to free Marcie or whoever might be locked up. The police don't need the key unless they're going to raid the commune."

Jake considered that a moment. "Maybe you're right, but you still have to call the police. You should have called them last night. I would have."

"Maybe that's why I didn't call you." I wished I could take the words back, but it was too late.

Hurt filled his face a moment before it hardened. "Maybe we'd better call Tawnia and ask her opinion."

I threw up my hands. "Okay. I'll call the police. *After* I've had my tea."

"Good." Jake handed me the key, and even through the envelope I could feel the call of the imprints. Hurriedly, I pushed it back inside my bag. Jake turned and left without another word—and not because he'd heard the jingling from the bells tied to his shop door. He'd already ignored that jingling twice during our conversation.

I sighed and picked up my tea.

Jake was right. Regardless of Inclar's original purpose in going to my apartment, he could have killed me.

Or maybe killing me had been his intention all along. Maybe he wasn't responsible for leaving the key. But who else knew where I lived?

Everyone, apparently. Inclar and Ethan had certainly found me without trouble. I was probably in the phone book under Women Who Live Alone. Maybe I should rethink Tawnia's offer to stay in her spare bedroom once they moved into their new house.

No. That was out of the question. I wouldn't allow fear to eliminate my independence. That was no way to live. Still, I wasn't looking forward to talking to the police. The way my luck was going, I'd end up in jail for stalking Inclar.

Sighing, I picked up the phone.

Chapter 8

While other officers in Portland might have heard of me after the bicycle case, Detective Shannon Martin was the only one who really seemed to have it out for me. So of course he was the one who showed up at my shop, less than half an hour after I called. Didn't he have anything better to do? Maybe he just sat at his desk, waiting for me to call.

He walked through the door, his confident bearing immediately attracting the attention of my three customers. Shannon wasn't tall for a man—only a few inches taller than I was. He had rugged features, as though he spent a lot of time outdoors, the sun prematurely crinkling the skin around his eyes and giving him a healthy, wholesome glow. He was sturdily built and compact, each movement efficient and undeniably graceful. His hair was that color between brown and blond, with naturally lighter streaks from his time in the sun. It was slightly longer than when I'd spent so much time with him in May, showing a bit of curl at the ends that surprised me. He was clean-shaven now, a complete contrast to the rugged, sleepless, grouchy look he'd fostered when we worked together on the missing girl and bicycle case. Back then he hadn't made it home in three days to shave or rest.

I didn't want to think about the case now, or about little Alice, whose last moments had been so frightening. It still made me utterly and desperately sad.

Shannon wasn't in uniform, and for that I was glad. I didn't want him to run off my customers. One woman was ready to be rung up, so I helped her while the detective watched and waited. Not impatiently but intently.

His eyes weren't like other men's. There was something about them, something perhaps in their green-blue color that illuminated his face. Or maybe it was the heavy frame of light brown lashes that made them so compelling. I didn't know, really, except that his were the most beautiful eyes I'd ever seen in a man. It was almost unsettling.

There was something else different about Shannon, something besides his girly name, bestowed upon him because of a man who'd saved his grandfather's life: Shannon was attracted to me. He didn't approve of me as a person, but he couldn't help that he was fascinated by me. Whether because of my so-called good looks, my strange eyes, my often sarcastic personality, or my cursed talent, I couldn't say. Because his suspicions ran so deep, he hated his attraction, but he felt it all the same. At times when we'd work together on the bicycle case, I'd caught him staring at me, or for a moment he'd forget to add that cool, unconcerned note in his voice. If he ever allowed himself to shake my hand, he either dropped it quickly or held on a tad too long.

I'd never gone out of my way to encourage Shannon's fascination. Quite the opposite. Early in our relationship, I'd spotted his disdain for me under that placid exterior, flashes of disbelief and anger that he tried to hide. Repulsion. How you could be attracted to someone you suspected of a scam was beyond my understanding. Perhaps if we'd met under other circumstances, things might have been different, but because he couldn't seem to give up his convictions, and I couldn't like anyone who suspected me, none of that mattered.

I thanked my customer and turned casually in Shannon's direction. "Slow morning? Or did you drop everything to come and harass me again?"

"We always take it seriously when someone claims to be attacked." He gave me a smile that didn't match those eyes. "Let's have the story."

Before I could begin, the shop door opened again and a woman entered, looking trim and professional in a navy skirt suit and heels. She was in her mid-twenties, with straight blond hair that looked as if it had been ironed. I was glad that at least her makeup was sensible and she looked sturdy enough to do okay in a fight, despite the snug skirt. Every cop deserved decent backup, even ones as annoying as Shannon.

"Your partner?" I asked.

An almost imperceptible nod. "She was parking the car. She's new."

Definitely an attractive woman—if you liked boring and predictable, which I was sure Shannon did. I knew without his saying that he was training her. She seemed young for a detective, but she'd probably been on the force for five years, or more if I'd misjudged her age. Maybe she came from a family of policemen.

We waited until she reached us. "Autumn, this is Detective Paige Duncan," Shannon said.

"I'm so pleased to finally meet you." Paige offered me

her hand. "Everyone's been talking about what you did last month." We shook hands, and I found myself warming toward her. Unlike Shannon, who would rather pull out all his fingernails than ask me out, she hadn't come thinking of me as a fraud.

Shannon frowned. "We were going over what happened last night."

Paige nodded. "Go ahead."

I briefly recounted the events of the previous day, avoiding mention of Harmony Farms, except to say that I'd seen Inclar earlier when I'd been talking to the group by the river. Shannon's skepticism turned to annoyance when I admitted to calling the police only at Jake's insistence.

"Can you give me a description of this guy?"

Easy enough. "Short, skinny. Graying brown hair. His right eye has something wrong with it. It sort of rolls around in his head. Not all the time, though. Sometimes it looks okay."

"Age?"

"Around thirty, I think. But he looks older, wrinkled. You know, kind of falling in on himself."

"Small and skinny, you say, and he attacked you?" Shannon's voice dripped sarcasm.

I touched my throat. "He did this." Several heartbeats passed as he focused on the marks that by my thinking he should have already noticed.

"I thought he was going to kill me," I added, unable to stop the tremor in my voice or the sudden difficulty I had in swallowing. No matter how I'd shoved the emotions aside in the light of day, last night during the attack I'd been terrified.

A flash of concern chased across Shannon's face, breaking through his stern professionalism. "We'll need to get a picture of that." He nodded to Paige, who I hadn't noticed was carrying a camera case over her shoulder.

At least I was wearing clean clothes. But after a couple of head shots, Paige focused up close on the bruises, so it hardly made a difference.

"You said he pushed you against the wall?" Shannon asked. "Did you hit your head?" His voice was gentle now, and it threw me off balance.

I felt my skull where a large knot had formed in the back. "Maybe that's why I have a headache."

He smiled—the first he'd given me today.

"It's huge. Want to feel?" Too late, I realized that wasn't something you asked an officer who both liked and suspected you. He'd have to reject the offer for propriety's sake, and besides, it wasn't as though he had medical training.

To my surprise, he reached out and placed his hands on either side of my head, his palms over my ears as his fingers gently explored the area on the back of my head. I could feel the warmth of his flesh, the rough patches of calluses that scattered over his palms. Were those from working on the acre of land I'd heard he owned on the outskirts of Portland?

I was beginning to feel decidedly uncomfortable when he pulled away, his face unchanged. "Good inch and a half long," he said to Paige. "And still raised at least a half inch. Remember that for the report." To me, he added, "You say he left a map? Can I see it?"

"Ethan has it. He's the private eye I was telling you about."

He gave me a look that was both reproachful and questioning. "The guy you called when you should have called me."

He and Jake should get together, have a party, and talk about what I should do the next time I was attacked by a madman. "Don't complain," I said. "You were better off sleeping."

"We'll need to dust the envelope and map for prints," Shannon said, ignoring my comment.

"I have the envelope in my bag, and Ethan will be here with the map at lunchtime."

"I'd rather call him and see if he can drop by the station before then. Do you have his number?"

"That's also in my bag."

He hesitated. "Is there anything else you can tell me?"

"No, but you might want to visit the attacker's house. I doubt he's there now, but you might find a reason for what he did. Or some other evidence." Hopefully something incriminating on Harmony Farms.

Paige gaped at me. "You know where he lives?"

Oops. "I guess I forgot to tell you that part. I know his name too, but I think it's a fake one. I'm pretty sure his wife was called Sarah."

Shannon gave me a long-suffering glare. "Why don't you tell us again? From the start. This time don't leave anything out."

"Okay, but you're not going to like it." I bit my bottom lip.

"And why is that?"

"Because I was reading some objects for a couple. The Fullmers. Their daughter disappeared, and I was trying to help them get an idea of where she went."

Paige leaned forward eagerly, awaiting more, but Shannon stared for several seconds before asking, "Did you find her?" His words mocked me.

I sighed. This was going to be a long morning.

I told them everything. Well, everything except my plans to join the Harmony Farms commune and about the key. The minute I heard they were going to raid the farm, I would turn it over, but for now I might need it worse than they did. I wondered idly if I could soak the key in anything to remove the imprints. It was worth some thought. Baking soda and vinegar, my most common cleaning agents, wouldn't likely do the job.

"Do you have a death wish?" Shannon asked after I told him how I'd followed Inclar. But was that a glimmer of admiration behind the disapproval?

I shook my head. "I was curious why he'd left the commune, but I really didn't want to get involved. I wanted to help from a distance."

Now, thanks to Ethan and his sister and Tawnia's new ability, I was heading in even deeper. Maybe that explained how alive I felt. It wasn't a bad trade-off. Focusing on Victoria and Marcie had given me purpose, a destination. Some way to concretely help others. Maybe I wasn't that different from Shannon after all.

"With you as an eyewitness," Shannon was saying, "we'll have all the testimony we need, once we pick him up. Even so, I'd like to see if we can get his prints outside your apartment or on your door. That would seal it. We'll need to get inside the lobby."

In other words, my testimony meant nothing to him. My motives were still suspect.

I'd already given Shannon the envelope—minus the key—and Ethan's cell phone number, but now I fished in my bag for my keys, removing the house set that were on a separate ring from the others. "The big one is to the lobby door. The little one is to my apartment in case you need to go in. Main floor on the left. There's iced tea in the fridge."

Shannon stared at me as if I'd given him access to my bank account.

"What?" I said.

He sighed. "Never mind. I'll return these to you later."

"No hurry. I have another set." I kept several around and had given others to my neighbors and friends. It saved me from getting locked out when I misplaced my keys.

Paige was smiling at me, an almost vulpine eagerness in her expression. "I know you probably get this all the time, but I'd really like to see you read something."

I eased away from the counter, subtly putting space between us. "Sure, any time." I didn't mean it. I didn't want to read anything for a while. A long while. Except the comforting imprints from my parents and my antiques.

"Let's go," Shannon said sharply, his voice a clear reproof.

I smiled at him perhaps a little too gratefully. His eyes met mine, and for that instant, for once in our brief relationship, we were in complete agreement. Giving a curt nod, he turned away.

Paige waved at me as the door shut, calculation in her eyes, and I wondered how long it would be before she brought me a piece of evidence to read. Maybe disbelief and mistrust were better than having my ability accepted outright. Obviously, there was more to Paige than I'd realized.

My legs gave out, and I pushed myself up on the tall stool. Underneath the pounding of my head, I felt a sadness I couldn't name. I didn't even know what caused it. I stared toward the windows facing the street, for a moment blissfully seeing and feeling nothing. My customers were gone, one having taken an antique to Jake's store to tally up with her herbs. She would be long on her way by now.

"I'm sorry," Jake said in a low voice.

I focused on him. He'd passed in front of me to come around the desk, but I must have been too distracted to notice. "Didn't we just do this?" I said.

"Yeah, but I'm sorry again. Well, not about making you call the police but about arguing with you."

"You didn't *make* me do anything, Jake. I knew I should call. That man tried to kill me."

Jake's jaw hardened, but the anger wasn't directed toward me this time. "You are not going home tonight."

I was about to retort that what I did was none of his business, but then he said, "Please. It would really make me feel better if we could figure something else out. I won't be able to sleep at all, if you're alone. In fact, I'll have to come and stand guard outside your door."

He'd do it, too. This was part of why I was so helplessly in love with him. "Okay," I said, my melancholy vanishing. "We'll talk about it later."

He nodded and added briskly, "First things first. I brought a comfrey salve for those bruises."

I hugged him then, and he hugged me back. Whatever else happened in my life, at least I knew I could depend on Jake.

"Let's hurry then," I said. "I think it's time for me to head down to the river."

Chapter 9

The people from Harmony Farms were at the river again. I didn't know if I should be glad or afraid. Director Korin was dressed in the same brown pants and white shirt with the long, old-fashioned cuffs, his broad face accentuated by the ponytail. He recognized me immediately and waved a handful of flyers in greeting. After finishing his conversation with a potbellied man in a suit, he strode in my direction, smiling. I couldn't help thinking how different he was from his scrawny brother. He was tall and strong and healthy, even a little too fleshy. I wondered what he would say if I told him his brother had tried to kill me last night.

"You've come back to buy something?"

I shook my head. "I don't eat anything unless I know how it's made. I'm a little bit of a fanatic, I guess you'd say."

That didn't seem to faze him. "I understand completely. We use all natural ingredients that we grow ourselves, or for the things we can't grow—like bananas—we buy from respected organic providers. The only exceptions are the muffins made with white flour. Those I can't vouch for, but all the others, I can personally attest to the nutritional value."

"You use milk from grass-fed cows? Eggs from free-range chickens?"

"Yep. And no preservatives."

If that was true, joining the commune, however temporarily, might end up being a vacation for me. Especially if, as I hoped, Korin and his followers were what they seemed to be.

Of course, Tawnia's drawing of Marcie seemed to indicate something was terribly wrong, though there might even be a way to explain that. Maybe Marcie had been ill. Maybe the dark solitude had been her wish. Maybe Tawnia didn't have a gift but an overactive, hormonal imagination.

I pulled a few dollar bills from my pocket. "Okay, I'll have a wheat muffin. It's three dollars, right?" A steal for the size if they were really organic.

"I think you'll particularly enjoy the banana nut ones. Or the oatmeal raisin." Korin motioned to one of the youths in the royal blue T-shirts. A young man this time, homely looking, with black hair and crooked teeth.

I gave him my money and bit into an oatmeal raisin muffin. "Wonderful," I said with real admiration. "It took me six months to learn how to make anything this good."

"You cook?"

"Oh, yes. I love cooking."

He seemed pleased with that so I added, "I grow herbs, too. Well, not a lot. My father had an herb store, but he's gone now, so I do the best I can."

If anything, Korin's gaze became more interested, but was it because I knew herbs or because my father was dead?

"I grew up working in his shop," I continued. "But it belongs to someone else now."

"I'm so sorry. That had to be hard, losing it after losing your father. I suppose he left it to you?"

I knew what he was after. "I sold it to pay the bills. But the new owner is nice."

"You still work there then?"

"Only when they really need someone. He has two other employees, and they can mostly handle the business." The truth meant less fabrication to remember.

"I'm sure your sales experience must come in handy in your new job."

I had no intention of mentioning my antiques store. Not only did I want to appear to have nothing holding me to Portland, but according to Ethan, the organization would want everything I owned upon joining, and my shop was not on the bargaining table.

"It's been difficult to work since my dad died," I said instead, shrugging. "I'm sort of drifting right now. I do need work, though."

Let him read what he wanted into that, hopefully coming to the conclusion that I was hurting financially. Maybe they wouldn't expect much from me. But would they trust me to give up my assets on my own, or would they expect to delve into my financial matters themselves?

Korin had asked another question. "Excuse me?" I said.

"I asked if you still knew any health remedies."

"Are you kidding? I could prescribe herbs before I was eight."

"What about headaches? One of our members suffers from them."

"There are a lot of things to take for that." In fact, I'd just treated myself a few hours earlier. "Feverfew, skullcap, ginkgo biloba, melatonin, cayenne, and even peppermint oil. Not to mention magnesium and B vitamins. It really depends on what kind of headache you have—tension, migraine, or whatever. You sometimes have to experiment to find what works for an individual."

"That's amazing," Korin said. "I'll have to get you to write all that down."

I laughed. "Most people think I'm weird."

"Not me. We grow a lot of herbs to sell to different companies, but we haven't been very successful at using them for our own people. That's a real gift."

I tried not to feel good, knowing his intention was to flatter me, to make me feel useful. "I'd love to have a bigger place to grow herbs. Right now I have a frame I built that stands in front of the kitchen window. It's kind of tiny, but it works."

"I bet your mother and your other relatives appreciate your ability," Korin said.

"Actually, my mother died when I was eleven. I'm an only child. Adopted. I don't have extended family." No family now, in fact, except Tawnia and our birth mother's family, whom we hadn't been able to trace.

"I see." Korin smiled benevolently at me, the line between his eyes deepening. If I hadn't suspected him, I would see his expression as concern not calculation. I knew better. In a matter of a few minutes, he'd flattered me, pinpointed my useful talents, learned I had no relatives, and had probed my economic situation. Not bad.

Now it was my turn to lay the groundwork for joining them. "I think it must be nice to live in a group like yours. My parents sort of raised me that way, you know. They were hippies, I guess you'd say. I miss them a lot."

Korin reached out to lay a hand on my shoulder. "It's hard to lose those you love. But you are not alone."

I let my eyes fill with tears I hadn't known were so close. *Fake tears,* I assured myself.

"You are welcome to join us tonight for a meeting," Korin continued. "I can introduce you to all our friends."

My heart thumped. This was the invitation I'd been expecting. "I wouldn't want to intrude."

"No intrusion at all. We love having visitors. The meeting is actually to explain to people what we do. It's open to everyone."

"Well, in that case, I might come."

Korin shuffled through the flyers in his hand. "Here's our flyer. The address is right there."

"Thanks." I gave him a smile as I took the paper.

"I really hope to see you tonight." Again, he touched me on the shoulder with his free hand. I wondered if that was supposed to make me swoon or something because, if so, he was utterly failing. For all his interest in herbs and organic food, he wasn't my type. Maybe this casual clasp was supposed to express brotherhood and make me feel as though I might belong. I was still smiling, after all.

His smile faltered, and I had the urge to whirl around to look for the cause, but he was staring at my throat. "Did you, uh, hurt yourself?" he asked.

Thinking fast, I said, "Just a guy I know. He got a little upset. Still don't know why. It's not like we're dating or anything." Again, close enough to the truth.

"Come tonight," Korin said softly. "You'll be safe there. Among friends."

I nodded, and his hand dropped from my shoulder as I backed away. Several blocks later, I found a bench and sat down for a moment to see if I was being followed. At least that's what I told myself. In truth, I was shaking from the strain of the encounter. I'd never been good at lying or hiding my emotions, and I didn't like it one bit.

I was also worried about going home that night. Whatever I had told Jake, I was afraid of Inclar. I'd have to toughen up if I was going to investigate more cases. *I can do that,* I told myself. I'd taken a couple years of taekwondo lessons as a teen from one of the men who'd stayed with our family, and maybe it was time to pick them up again.

My phone buzzed in the pocket of my pants, so I pulled it out. Tawnia. "Hello?"

"Is everything okay?" Tawnia blurted. "I've been having weird images in my head all morning. When I tried to draw a face for the character in the underwear ad, this really ugly, skinny guy came out. Then I drew that annoying detective who has the hots for you, the one whose picture you showed me in the newspaper."

My mood lightened. "His name is Shannon Martin, but since you've never met him, maybe you could go ahead and use him in the ad." That Shannon would hate it only made the idea more amusing.

"And risk a lawsuit from a police detective? I'm not crazy. I put my team on the ad instead. So what's going on?"

I debated exactly what to tell her. If she knew I'd been attacked she'd worry, but if I kept it from her, she'd kill me when she found out. Besides, with my great experience at fabrication, she'd see right through me.

So I outlined Inclar's attack as quickly and succinctly as possible. "Shannon's checking out where he lives now, and my place. Jake refuses to let me stay at the apartment alone, so—"

"You'll come here."

"Actually, I was thinking of a hotel. They have a really inexpensive one near here where the commune people are staying and—"

"You're not still going through with that!"

"I have to, Tawnia. If you could talk to them, you'd see they aren't all bad. There might be something funny going on, but there's a good chance they're on the up and up. If there is something weird going on, it might be limited to one or two people who are taking advantage of the rest. If I can help Marcie and Victoria, or even just give their families peace of mind, then I want to do it."

"Okay, okay, but did you tell the police this crazy idea? I'd feel better knowing they were in on it."

"No. But Ethan has all sorts of equipment. I'll be okay."

Tawnia gave a sigh. "You know, this is the real difference between us. Your parents raised you to trust people you don't know, to expect them to be their best, while mine taught me to mistrust everyone until they prove themselves. That might not have been the best way, but some people don't deserve to be trusted."

"I know that." I'd learned it only too well after the bridge bombing. But completely mistrusting others, believing they'll always let you down, wasn't my idea of a life. "I made you a promise not to take chances, and I won't. Trust me. Look, I've got to get going. Ethan's taking me out to lunch."

"That sounds promising."

"It's just business."

"No, it's not. I can tell from your voice. You like him." She laughed. "Anyway, don't leave with those weirdos before we talk again, okay?"

"Of course not. I'm going to hear their spiel tonight. I'll call you later and let you know how it goes."

I hung up with relief. I loved having a sister, but I wasn't accustomed to justifying my decisions.

"I'm still nailing down additional equipment from some guys I know," Ethan said, waving his fork in a strangely appealing way. Of course, everything about him was appealing. It helped that we were at Smokey's across from my shop, and I'd just finished one of their incredible organic meat pies, a glass of fresh lemonade, and a huge piece of cocoa cake. The price tag was steep, but the fact that I wasn't paying put me in a good mood.

"I want to be ready by tomorrow morning, just in case," Ethan was saying. "I have no idea when they'll take their next bunch of recruits, but they've been in Portland for three weeks, as near as I can tell, and usually that's all the time they stay in one area."

"Do they market their stuff on Sundays?" Belatedly, I realized they weren't a religion, so they probably didn't care about the Sabbath.

"Yes. It's probably a big day for them, actually."

"Then they won't leave until that night."

"They may not leave at all, or only some of them might leave to get new supplies. Maybe you can find out."

"I'll do what I can."

After he'd paid our bill, we walked across the street where he'd parked his BMW. He opened the door. "We forgot to fix your car."

Oh, yeah. The dead battery.

"How about tonight I drive you to within a couple blocks of the hotel for your meeting?" he said. "Then you can call me when you're finished, and I'll pick you up. We can deal with the car afterward."

As long as he was my chauffeur, I wasn't in any hurry. "Fine by me."

"Well, thanks for coming to lunch with me and for doing all this. For the first time in a long time, I feel hopeful."

"I haven't done anything yet." But it was fun, both the mystery and spending time with Ethan. I wonder what would happen between us once this was all over.

He slid into his seat, his smile turning to a grimace. Reaching under him, he pulled out a rather large prescription bottle. "Oops."

"What's that?" I hoped it wasn't anything serious. It'd be just my luck to finally meet a great guy, only to have him dying of some rare disease.

"Some old medication of Marcie's." He held it up briefly, and I barely had time to read the word *phenelzine* on the label before he tossed the bottle into the glove compartment. I heard the clink of the pills inside.

"Was Marcie ill when she left?" I asked. Maybe that explained why she was in pain in Tawnia's picture.

"No. I think the pills were to help her sleep," he said.

I could imagine why she'd want that. Nights had been the hardest for me after the death of each of my parents. But I'd still had Winter after Summer died, and I had Tawnia by the time Winter's body was discovered in the river. I was glad Marcie had Ethan. At least she hadn't been completely alone.

I was also happy that Ethan didn't think to offer me the pill bottle to read, but he couldn't know that most people had powerful feelings about their medication and often the imprints left on the bottles were startlingly clear. I doubted it would add anything to what I'd already discovered, but maybe when I was feeling up to it, I'd ask to read the bottle.

"Well, I'll see you tonight." He stood up again and gave me a quick, unexpected kiss on the cheek that sent a little jolt to my heart. Definitely something there.

I watched him drive away before walking into my store. As I reached for the door, I glimpsed Jake through the window of the Herb Shoppe. Had he seen the kiss? I told myself I didn't care.

Inside, Thera was waiting for me so she could leave. Since she would likely be working overtime next week while I was out of town, she was going to spend the weekend with her daughter and grandchild.

I put on an apron and disposable gloves in the back and began cleaning the two silver metal side chairs I'd found earlier in the week at an estate sale. They were Anglo-Indian style, twentieth century, with ram heads curving inward on the top of the back as though to embrace their occupants. Both could use reupholstering, but the five hundred bucks for the pair had been a steal. Once I'd carefully cleaned the silver without removing the patina, I would double or triple my profit. That is, if I didn't fall too much in love with them myself.

I was reading a book on upholstering to see if maybe I could attempt changing the fabric on my own instead of taking them to one of my contacts, but I had to be very careful. Like most antiques dealers, I often walked a fine line between making things appealing to customers and destroying the value.

After more than two hours, I threw down my rag and pulled off my rubber gloves, tossing them into the garbage can under the table. Back in the shop, I pushed myself up onto my stool and leaned against the counter. No sign of a single customer.

My computer was on, and I moved the mouse to bring up my browser. What had the name of that drug been? Phensomething. I was pretty sure it had ended in a zine. In a few minutes I had it on the screen: phenelzine, an antidepressant drug. Not sleeping pills, as Ethan thought.

"Ah," I said, though the information wasn't surprising. Marcie had been a woman in severe distress—I'd seen that from the little ring. Reading further on the page, I learned that an abrupt cessation of an antidepressant could cause serious side effects. That might explain Tawnia's picture.

Next, I typed in Ethan's name and Willamette University. His name came up on a dozen different sites, highlighted in the browser listings. I nodded. *See, Jake. He is who he says he is.*

I didn't click on any of the pages because I didn't see the point. Besides, Jake was coming through our adjoining doorway, so I quickly exited the browser.

"Pretty dead, huh?" Jake said.

"You busy? Need my help?" I craned my neck to see if there were customers in the Herb Shoppe.

"No." He ran a finger over a small section of desk. "Randa's got it."

I waited some more, wondering what he'd come to say.

"About Ethan," he began.

Ah, of course. "I did some checking," I said. "He is at Willamette University. But don't worry. I'm just helping him out. That's all."

"It looked more serious than that a few hours ago."

There, it was out. What he'd come to say.

I forced a laugh. "If I had a dollar for every guy who tried to kiss me over the years, I'd be on the beach in Hawaii all winter. It didn't mean anything." At least not yet.

He rolled his eyes. "Nothing wrong with your ego, I see."

"You wouldn't understand my fatal attraction. Since we're friends, I mean. But believe me, I'm a magnet for men." I bent down to retrieve my handbag, mostly so I wouldn't have to see his reaction, or lack of one. Because it certainly hadn't been true in the past year.

"You know what?" I added. "It's so slow today that I'm going home to get ready for the meeting with the commune people tonight." I'd told him about that before going to lunch, and had been relieved that he hadn't protested like Tawnia. "Maybe I'll take a nap. I'm a little tired, and I don't know how long those things last. Do you want me to leave the connecting doors open? Or should I shut them? I don't mind closing early if it's too much inconvenience. There's only an hour left."

"You're going to your apartment? Alone?" He leaned forward, his elbows on my counter, his dark hands coming to rest near my paler ones. "And what about your car?"

That's right. I'd forgotten. I'd have a bit of a walk.

"Didn't we decide it's not a good idea for you to be there alone? I'll take you. No, don't protest. Randa can take care of things here. I doubt it's going to pick up. Friday afternoons are always slow."

I didn't protest, not because I wanted him to take control but because I was the tiniest bit afraid that Inclar would return to finish the job—whatever that had been.

"Okay, great. Let's go."

Ten minutes later when we drove up to the apartment building, all the nearby parking stalls were taken, two by police cars and another by a white, unmarked vehicle similar to the one I'd seen Shannon Martin drive. Sure enough, I spotted him coming from my building.

"Over there," I directed Jake. "There's a spot."

He pulled his bike into it. "Wonder why so many police are here."

"Guess we're going to find out."

Shannon watched us approach without expression, but his aqua eyes were as compelling as always. He must get a lot of mileage from them at the police station. Even I wanted to confess everything to him—the key, the meeting tonight, my plans to join the Harmony commune to find Marcie and Victoria.

"What's wrong?" I asked, injecting annoyance into my voice to cover up my guilt at withholding information. "Did he come back?"

He shook his head. "No. We're just finishing up the prints. There appear to be some nice ones on the door, larger than your own. We'll let you know."

"Did you pick up Inclar? Or whatever his name is." If they had, I'd sleep better tonight.

"His real name is Daniel Foster. Went by Danny when he actually used the name. He's going by Sam Armistead at the moment. But no, we didn't find him. His place has been cleared out. Landlady said he owed a month's rent."

"So he could be anywhere." I felt a chill and instinctively leaned toward Jake.

Shannon's eyes followed my movement, narrowing slightly. He'd once accused Jake of encouraging me to exploit people, so they held no love for each other. "We'll be out here watching the building tonight."

"You think he's coming back?" I hoped this was only Shannon taking his obsession with criminals a little too far.

"There's more. Mr. Foster's wife is dead, like you said, but it wasn't from natural causes."

"She was murdered?" I exchange a horrified look with Jake.

Shannon nodded. "Strangled with a silver chain in her own bed less than a year ago. Supposedly, her husband was out of town at the time, but they could never find him for questioning, and he hasn't turned up since. There were no fingerprints on the chain and no solid evidence leading anywhere."

Jake put a comforting arm around my shoulders. "You think he did it?"

"He could have. There doesn't appear to be anyone else with a motive. Maybe he fled to Harmony Farms after he murdered his wife. The neighbors claim she'd recently moved into the building by herself. No one knew her very well."

"Maybe she'd left him," I said.

"Can't say for sure. We're tracing her now, seeing where she lived before that. We'll find out more soon."

I rubbed my hands over my tired eyes, trying to think. Now that my initial shock was fading, I saw holes in Shannon's hypotheses. "This was a year ago, right?"

"Yes."

"Inclar didn't leave Harmony Farms until January, and I had the impression he'd been there a long time. He could have already been a member when she died. He might not be involved at all."

Shannon's lips pursed. "Or maybe he joined to have an alibi."

"No. He believes in Harmony Farms—or at least the concept. Besides, he loved Sarah."

"How do you know all this?" Shannon's expression changed to suspicion. "You didn't mention talking to him about his wife. Or did you know her, too?"

"Of course I didn't know her." I hesitated before adding, "I felt the imprint from a watch he gave his brother."

Shannon let out an impatient sigh. "Look, you'll be safe tonight. We'll be out here in case Danny Foster returns."

"Fine. Just don't expect me to bring you coffee and dough-nuts." I didn't know why, but the detective brought out this snippy side of me more than anyone else.

"You don't need to stay here for Autumn's sake," Jake said dismissively. "I'm looking out for her."

Shannon's eyes bore holes in Jake. "Sorry. Now that this is related to a cold case murder and two missing women, I've been officially assigned to the case. If either of you see Foster, contact me immediately."

We didn't respond, but Jake's arm tightened around me as we started toward the building.

I could feel Shannon's eyes digging into my back. I wanted to turn and flip him off, but my parents raised me better.

"You can let go of me, Jake," I said when we were finally inside, out of Shannon's view.

Jake looked at me blankly, and for a moment I saw some-thing unreadable in his eyes. This wasn't the Jake I knew. There was something . . . different about him.

"Huh? Oh, yeah," he said finally. His arm dropped from my shoulder, and the moment was over.

But with the murder, everything had changed, and suddenly I wasn't so sure about going to Harmony Farms.

Chapter 10

I was surprised to see that the small hotel had any type of conference room, much less one that looked as if it could seat a hundred people. The room was already filled with several dozen youths, most wearing the royal blue T-shirt proclaiming *Love Is the Only Thing That Matters*. There were a few white shirts too, the kind with the blue lettering both Marcie and Victoria had been more familiar with: *Only Love Can Overcome Hate*. But I didn't recognize anyone from either Victoria or Marcie's imprints.

A few people present obviously didn't yet belong to the commune. Some stood out—three blue-haired teens with multiple piercings, a large woman with a dour expression, an unshaven man in an ill-fitting suit, a good-looking man with a serious limp. Others could have been anyone off the street: a young woman with a toddler, four young men in jeans, two young girls who looked decidedly underage, a handsome older man with white hair, and a woman wearing a blue nursing uniform. I wondered which category I fit into.

One young man was talking with a disciple, his tones bitter. Something about his old man. I wanted to slap him and say that at least he had a father. But perhaps his old man beat him.

Settling into a seat, I thought of Jake, whom I'd finally convinced to leave me to nap in my apartment since Shannon and his police buddies were staking out the place. Jake had left with an expression on his face that approximated a glare, and I was glad he'd gone because he wouldn't have been happy seeing Ethan show up at my door to drive me to the hotel.

The man Victoria had known had disappeared into the crowd, so I settled into a seat to watch for him. I wasn't left alone long. One after another of the young disciples came over to smile, ask polite questions, and then eventually drift away. They asked nothing difficult and didn't seem to expect anything of me. Crazy as it seemed, I felt a part of this odd group. How much more inviting had it seemed to Marcie and Victoria, both of whom had been dealing with great pressure?

The young mother was glowing with the attention. A knot of women disciples had formed around her, oohing and aahing over her child. *A little boy,* I thought. *Why is she here?* From a distance, she seemed like any contented mother. Her dark blond hair was drawn back into a casual ponytail revealing a nice facial structure. Healthy, if a little on the thin side. Her dress pants were too large, as was the turtleneck shirt she wore, the neck loose and drooping down as if the cloth was old and tired, and her brown walking shoes were scuffed. By contrast, the little boy wore stiff new jeans, a crisp blue and white shirt with a baseball over the left breast, and blue tennis shoes that looked completely unused—at least from this distance.

A stack of paper with a song printed on it was making the rounds. I took a copy. Apparently, we were going to sing. I didn't recognize the words or the melody, but I didn't have much musical talent, not like Jake, who'd recently picked up the guitar.

"Ah, you're here." I looked up from the paper to see Korin, still in the same brown pants and old-fashioned white shirt. There was embroidery on the cuffs, I noticed, and I wondered who had done that. This evening his long hair wasn't in a ponytail but hanging free.

"Hi," I said, but my eyes had gone past him to his companion. I hoped my stare wasn't too obvious.

"I'd like to introduce my new friend," Korin said gesturing. "This is Jake."

Jake. *My* Jake. The terribly good-looking, muscular mulatto man I'd kicked out of my apartment two hours ago.

"Jake, this is, uh . . . Oh, dear, I never learned your name."

"You can call me Autumn." I had already decided to give my real first name but to make up my last if they inquired further, apparently a decision I shared with Jake. So far last names hadn't been encouraged.

Jake shook my hand as if we didn't know each other at all. "Nice to meet you, Autumn."

"You too, Jake," I said lightly, but I narrowed my eyes to show him I was not in the least amused with his checking up on me.

"Jake works construction," Korin continued, "but he also has an interest in nutrition. I thought you two might have a lot in common."

"Sure," I said, eyeing Jake's stained white T-shirt and holey jeans. He never wore those jeans unless he was deep cleaning the Herb Shoppe.

Jake smiled at me like an angel. I grimaced back. As soon as I got him alone, we were going to have words.

In the end, we weren't allowed to sit together. As Korin began asking everyone to be seated, his disciples slid between every newcomer. *Nicely done,* I thought. Isolation would eliminate whispered conversations of doubt.

A girl led us in an interesting song about human responsibility to tend the earth before it was too late, and afterward, Korin began to preach. It was not a religious sermon, but he spoke with fervor about love toward all men, kindness, forgiveness, and service to nature. He was a powerful orator, even without a microphone, and the whole crowd was in his grip. Jake appeared to be listening intently along with everyone else, but it was Korin's very skill that had me doubting his sincerity. I would have preferred to see him make a few mistakes, to stumble on his words or gaze off into the distance to collect his thoughts. Then again, he'd probably given this same spiel hundreds of times. No wonder he'd been promoted by the farm's founder: he was mesmerizing.

Yet whether this group was a positive or negative force remained to be seen. I would reserve judgment for now.

Korin began talking about the farm where the commune members lived together in peace and unity. I wondered if my parents had explored such places. I seemed to remember one of their friends mentioning a commune they had lived in before opening the Herb Shoppe. Why had they left? Had they simply outgrown it? As a child, I'd never been interested in their lives before I had entered the picture; now I craved every bit of knowledge.

I pulled my mind back to Korin, who was explaining that upon joining Harmony Farms, people were required to turn over worldly assets in exchange for fellowship with the commune. There would always be food to eat, clothes to wear, and extended family support. Love. All members worked hard for the good of everyone. There was no want or fear. The way he explained it made me want to sell my shop and donate my tiny retirement fund. To someone who had nothing to lose, I'm sure the spiel made a far larger impact.

Then it was time for the bad news. The group would be leaving for Salem to hawk their wares, so potential members would need to either join now, travel to Salem to investigate further, or wait until the commune members returned to Portland.

"There's no hurry," Korin assured us in his fluid voice. "We should be back in a few months."

With those simple words, Korin had glibly added an urgency that would encourage people to join immediately or to follow the members to the next city. I recognized it because I used the same method in the store when a customer hesitated too long over buying an antique. I knew if they left without the piece, they often wouldn't find the time to come back, even if they loved it, so I made sure they understood it would likely be gone, and though I might find something similar down the road, it wouldn't be exactly the same. This always helped them decide one way or the other, and usually they'd buy the piece.

However, there was a huge difference between me and Korin. I had a two-week return policy in writing, whereas Korin, if Ethan was right about the group, had no such safety net for his customers.

Or did he?

I raised my hand and waited until Korin pointed at me. "What if I join and then change my mind?"

Korin smiled. "You are free to leave whenever you wish.

Harmony Farms does not believe in forcing anyone to do anything they don't want to do. Unless it's their turn to wash dishes, of course." Everyone laughed.

So there was at least a verbal return policy, though there was no way to determine if it was upheld in practice.

"And our assets?" asked the man in the ill-fitting suit.

"Held for several months until you make your final decision."

"Is there any kind of initiation we have to go through?" asked one of the blue-haired teens.

"Nothing like that, though we do hold a three-day fast when new members join, a symbolic cleansing from the outside world."

"No food for three whole days?" This came from the woman with the toddler.

"Don't worry. That doesn't include the children," Korin explained. "Those under twelve don't fast, and the twelve to fifteen age group do it for only one day. And water and juices are permitted, if you find it too difficult. But remember you are not alone. Every able member takes the journey with you. For lack of a better word, it's quite spiritual."

Three whole days? An occasional fast was good for the body, but three days seemed excessive. At the same time, I'd have been surprised if they didn't require it at all because fasting was a primary tool of psychological control. I wondered if these fasts were held only when new members joined or also at the whim of the leaders—perhaps when people became too energetic or restless.

Korin went on about the fast, waxing poetic, if the faces around me were to be believed, but I tuned him out as I pondered what food I should smuggle inside my suitcase.

When Korin sat down, a few disciples arose and talked about how their lives had been without meaning or purpose before joining the commune and how they loved their lives now and had many friends. One young man said he hoped to marry another Harmony Farms resident and raise a dozen children within the loving arms of the society.

That was over the top for me, but the young mother's round face shone with hope. When had I become such a cynic?

"I'm in," called the boy who'd been complaining about his father. One of the other young men echoed his statement, but the others looked down at their hands and said nothing. The large woman and the old man got up and left.

After the meeting ended, there were refreshments—homemade muffins with juice. To my surprise, the young mother approached me. Up close I could see an ugly bruise on her neck peeking from underneath her sagging turtleneck, and the green of a nearly healed bruise covered one side of her face from cheek to jawbone.

"Isn't this wonderful?" she asked, balancing her son on her hip. "Harmony Farms is going to keep us safe." She included me in her "us," and I knew she'd spotted the marks Inclar had left on my neck.

"So you're joining," I said.

She nodded. "I met them at Christmastime last year, but it took a while to get the courage to change my life, you know? A few weeks ago, I learned they were back, and I've been at these meetings ever since. Being with them makes me happy and gives me hope. I'm staying here tonight, and tomorrow I'll be going to the farm. You could come too."

"Okay," I said.

"Really? Oh, good!" She bounced the toddler in her excitement. Beneath the bruises and the frightened expression, her fine-boned face was ripe with the beauty of youth. She probably wasn't more than twenty, and I was sorry she felt she had no other options in her life. "I was a little nervous going alone. Well, it looks like some of those boys are going, but that's not the same thing as a woman. You understand."

Before I could reply, she was waving Korin over. "She wants to come with us tomorrow!"

Korin's gaze fell on me as he approached. "Is that right?"

"You were very convincing," I said, hoping my skepticism didn't show.

His smile was self-deprecating. "It's a little too smooth, I know. But it's all true. Three years ago, I gave my life to this wonderful cause, and I've never regretted it a single day. Of course, you know everyone has to work hard on the farm."

I shrugged. "I'm not afraid of work."

"Well, we can certainly use someone to teach us about herbs. We don't have a doctor."

"I have a few books about herbal remedies I can bring." I tried to sound as eager as the young mother without overdoing it.

"Wonderful," Korin said. "We would be glad to have you. But are you sure you can leave so quickly? Won't you need more time to take care of everything for an extended, perhaps permanent absence?"

"I don't really have any reason to wait." Now was when I had to be careful not to show too much eagerness. Perhaps give them a reason to believe I would be a sincere follower, and Inclar had given me that. I touched the bruises on my neck until both their eyes were drawn to them. "I'd rather not go back to—" I broke off and looked down at my hands, hoping they were buying it. In case they weren't, I added, "I do have some money in the bank that I'd like to get out. It's not a lot, but it's my life savings. The bank's open tomorrow morning, so I can get it then."

"Do you need some place to stay tonight?" Korin asked gently.

Guilt wormed into my mind, but this was for Victoria and Marcie. "No. There's another place I can go, but I won't have many clothes to bring."

"You won't need them anyway. We have a dress code at the farm, and we make most of our own clothes."

Now this I was interested to see. I was pretty handy with a needle myself.

I felt eyes staring at me, and I looked up to see Jake across the room practically digging a hole in my face with his eyes. I could sense the concern as if he were shouting it. I looked away before Korin noticed.

The young mother squeezed my hand. "I'm so happy you're coming."

I didn't even know her name. "By the way, I'm Autumn," I said.

She squealed. "Oh, you've already chosen a new name! Then I want to be Summer or maybe Spring."

"Spring," I said. "That's more unusual, and it suits you."

"Well chosen," Korin said. "Founder Gabe will have the final say, of course, because we don't want to have too many repeats, but I can't imagine him refusing."

The statement chilled me. How could this Gabe have so much power over these people? Neither Spring nor Korin seemed to think that odd.

"I can't wait to see him," Spring said a little breathlessly.

Korin laughed, an infectious, booming sound. "You won't have to. He'll be here tomorrow before we leave. He's coming in with the new supplies and to oversee the move to Salem while I take you and the others back to the farm."

I don't know why that relieved me, but I preferred to be in and out of the farm before its founder ever returned.

"Will he speak to us tomorrow before we leave?" Spring asked. To me, she added, "He's incredible. I had the privilege of hearing him speak last December."

"We do hope to have him speak. Just make sure you're here a little before we leave at two." Korin smiled at us and drifted away.

I was glad he left because I was burning with questions. I'd just connected something Spring had said earlier about being around the Harmony group at Christmastime. Had she known Victoria Fullmer? Victoria had first met the commune members at Willamette University in Salem, but she'd come home to Portland before she left with them, so it was possible she'd missed her final exams to follow the commune members. She might have run into Spring at some of the meetings.

"I had a friend once," I began, "who was attending these meetings. Victoria. I wonder if you might have—"

"Brenda!" a voice roared.

My gaze shot to the doorway, where a short, husky man stood with his fists clenched at his sides, his face red with fury. "You come over here this instant," he commanded.

Spring had given a little gasp, and now she moaned. "Jimmy. He found me."

The room was utterly still. I didn't have time to look around to see what everyone else might be doing because I was too busy being horrified that Spring had taken two steps forward.

"No!" I grabbed her wrist.

She looked at me. "I'll come back later, or in a few months if I can't get away now."

"You don't have to go with him. We're not going to let him hurt you. None of us. You just have to say no."

"Oh." It was a tiny sound coming with a puff of air from her small mouth.

Jimmy hadn't held still. He was striding toward us purposefully, like a man filled with righteous indignation. He moved fast, too fast. My thoughts couldn't catch up. In a moment, he'd grab Spring and leave. I did the only thing I could do.

I stepped in front of her.

"Out of my way!" he growled.

"She's not going with you. Leave, or we'll call the police."

"She's *my* wife!" This he yelled in my face. He wasn't much taller than I was, but decidedly stockier and insane with rage. I wished I'd thought to grab Spring and run out a back door, but here we were.

"These crazies have no right messing with my family! They're coming with me now. Brenda, let's go!" A stream of curses followed.

He made to go around me, but I put out an arm. "You don't have to go anywhere," I told Spring. "He doesn't own you."

Spring made a frightened noise in her throat, but she didn't obey his command.

He brought up a fist, hurling it at me. Pain exploded in my cheek, and I was knocked sideways to the ground. Spring screamed. I curled, arms going up to protect my head as I wondered what would come next. Nothing did. I risked a peek to see that Jake had knocked Jimmy to the floor. From where

Jake had been across the room, he must have started moving the second the man came through the door.

Jake leapt on top of Jimmy and was poised for another strike when Korin's voice thundered, "That's enough!"

Jake's jaw worked with anger, and I knew that if he hadn't been playing a role for Korin, he'd probably have given Spring's husband the thorough thrashing he deserved. With effort, he lowered his hand and climbed to his feet, his eyes still wary. I'd known Jake was strong, but I hadn't suspected he could fell a husky man like that with one blow.

Male disciples now flanked Korin, and their combined bulk made a solid wall between Spring and Jimmy. Someone helped me to my feet, and I stood a little unsteadily next to Spring. Her son had buried his face in her shoulder, whimpering softly.

"You will leave now," Korin told the man firmly.

"She's my wife!" Jimmy insisted. "You can't hold her against her will."

Korin turned to Spring. "Do you want to go with this man?"

For the long space of several heartbeats, Spring didn't speak while Jimmy glared at her, a cruel confidence seeping into his expression. I felt heartsick at what I knew would happen. I reached out to her, squeezing her arm in encouragement.

"No," Spring said at last. "I don't want to ever see him again." My breath whooshed out in relief, and I wasn't the only one.

"Would you like me to call the police?" This question Korin directed to both of us.

I glanced at Spring, whose head gave a tiny jerk to indicate no. "I guess not," I said reluctantly. My cheek was already swelling, and when I touched it gingerly, I could feel my skin slick with blood.

"You need to leave now," Korin said to Jimmy.

The man's upper lip curled. "This isn't over!"

Korin folded his arms. "Yes, it is."

"I'll come after you!" Jimmy yelled. "I'll get the boy!" With another snarl, he was seen to the door by two of the larger male followers.

I put an arm around Spring. "Good for you."

"What if he really does get little Jim?" She was shaking now and clinging to her son as tightly as he was clinging to her.

"He won't." Korin put a hand on her shoulder. "He'll never find either of you."

Spring smiled tentatively, the tension running out of her body. "Thank you so much," she whispered.

But Korin's promise seemed ominous to me. How could he promise such a thing unless he did have a way of making people disappear?

Jake had wedged his way between the bodies to get to me. "Are you okay?" he whispered in my ear.

I nodded. "I think it's time to go."

"I'll take you."

I didn't protest because at that moment I wanted nothing more than to be with Jake. I would explain to Ethan later why I hadn't called him to pick me up. As for fixing my car, well, it looked as though I wasn't going to need it for a while. Besides, I could always call a mechanic.

Korin's thoughtful gaze had settled on us, though I didn't think he'd overheard our conversation.

"I'll meet you outside," I said in an undertone, smiling at Jake as though thanking a total stranger for his help.

"I'm on the bike." This a little apologetically.

"That's okay." In fact, it was perfect. I could hold onto him and pretend my cheek didn't feel like raw hamburger.

While I bade farewell to Spring, Jake went outside to wait for me. I glanced at Korin to see if he noticed me leaving, but he was caught up talking to a group of young men. I went outside and climbed on the back of Jake's bike, resting my good right cheek on his back. He was wearing his leather jacket, and I breathed in the smell of leather. Neither of us spoke.

We went straight to my apartment, and I didn't notice or care if Shannon and his partner or whoever was still watching. Jake washed his hands in my bathroom and then doctored my cheek with comfrey salve.

"You need to learn to duck." His finger rose slightly, rubbing over the preexisting scar under my left eye, one I'd gained in the Hawthorne Bridge bombing. His touch felt good, even though it brought back terrible memories.

"I've decided to take up martial arts again," I said.

"Good."

After his doctoring, I sipped herbal tea on the couch, wrapped in Summer's afghan, her comforting imprints washing over me.

"You can't join them," Jake said. "Look at you."

"This has nothing to do with Harmony Farms. That girl's husband is nuts, that's what."

He snorted. "They're all nuts!"

I laughed. "That's what everyone said about Winter, and half your clients are considered crazy as well."

His face relaxed, and despite himself, he grinned. "Okay, okay. *We're* all nuts. But don't you think this is a little beyond crazy?"

"I feel I owe it to those women. I can't explain it exactly, but it's like I'm finally coming to terms with this ability or whatever it is. Maybe I'm not supposed to help people only by sitting in my store reading imprints. Maybe it's time I did more."

The doorbell prevented me from having to explain further. Jake strode toward the door with the gait of a young man looking for a fight. He hadn't liked what I'd said, and I bet he was actually hoping Inclar was outside the door so he could direct his anger elsewhere.

The back of the couch was to the door, so I had to turn to see him open it to Detective Shannon Martin. I groaned and held the afghan up over my cheek. "What are you doing here?"

He crossed the room in four large strides. "Got a call from the suits outside. Said it looked like you'd been attacked again." He stared pointedly at the afghan.

I dropped the pretense and the afghan. "It's nothing. I stepped into the middle of a domestic dispute, that's all. Wrong place at the wrong time."

His eyes narrowed. "Are you sure this has nothing to do with Danny Foster?"

"Huh? No. Of course it doesn't."

"I was with her," Jake said. "She's telling the truth."

Shannon's eyes dug into him. "You sure *you* didn't do this?"

"Oh, yes, I have the habit of hitting my best friends." Jake held up a fist. "Do you have a problem with me? Maybe we should take care of that right now!"

"I could always arrest you."

I stood and faced them, hands on my hips. "Get out of here, both of you!"

"I'm not leaving," Jake said stubbornly. He turned to Shannon. "But don't let the door hit you on the way out."

It wasn't really in Jake's character to be rude, but Shannon seemed to bring it out in him, much as he brought out the sarcasm in me.

Shannon stood his ground.

I threw up my hands. "Fine. You two do what you want. I'm going to bed." I looked at Jake. "If my sister calls, not a word of this to her. Got it?" It'd be just like Tawnia to come running over here and spend the rest of the night trying to talk me out of my plan. "I'll tell her myself later."

"But—" Jake began.

"But what?" Except I knew what he'd meant. I knew it as if he'd spoken it. We were that attuned to each other, at least with some things. What he meant was, if it hadn't been for Shannon, Jake and I would have sat close together on the couch until very late, perhaps watching television or an old video. Perhaps I would have fallen asleep with my cheek on his arm. Feeling safe.

I forced my bitterness aside and gave him a smile. "Thanks for being here." To Shannon, I added, "I have no comment, detective."

They were quiet for a moment, but as I went into my room, I heard Shannon ask, "She has a sister?"

I smiled to myself. Everyone thought he was such a great detective, but he hadn't been able to find out even that much about me. I wanted to laugh, but it made me sad instead.

I didn't stay long in my room because I really needed to use the bathroom, and the men didn't seem to be in a hurry to go anywhere. So much for my grand exit. I should have forced them both to leave, but I'd been raised in a household that had welcomed everyone, friend and stranger alike.

As I made my dash to the bathroom, I saw the men standing

by the fireplace, Shannon holding a picture in his hands. I recognized it as the one Tawnia and I had taken the year before, shortly after we first met, the time when we'd cut her hair like mine. My face was slightly thinner, even then, but aside from that we were completely identical in the photo. Shannon's eyes met mine as I firmly shut the door. Let him wonder. Or let Jake explain the miracle. I didn't care.

Jake had left his keys on the bathroom sink, and later after I washed my hands, I picked them up and stood staring into the mirror.

I felt the lack of something huge, something I couldn't name. It wasn't my sister, it wasn't my friends or my job, it wasn't even God. It was an emptiness, an itch I couldn't scratch, a hunger I couldn't feed. It was watching TV at night alone. Eating everything in the cupboard without sating the urge to consume. It was climbing and never reaching the top. Of needing something but not knowing what.

I stared down in my hand and saw the flat metal silhouette of a woman that hung on the key ring: Jake's mother. His grandmother had it made shortly after his mother died, and he always carried it with him. Imprints. I'd been reading his imprints.

I squeezed the keys tightly. I had no idea Jake felt this way. Nor did I know how to go about asking him about it or trying to help without betraying what I'd done. Regardless of how close we were, I simply couldn't do that. These feelings were far too personal.

I set the keys back on the sink and left the bathroom.

Chapter 11

I had it all—nickel-sized earrings with mini transmitters, a two-way radio transceiver, and a tiny phone with email capability. Plus, Ethan had the map. There was no way he could lose me, but just in case, he promised to follow Korin's car to the hidden compound and then place another phone or transceiver at the base of the tallest tree he could find near the buildings in case I might need it.

Of course there was a lot we didn't know, such as whether the farm was patrolled or encircled by an electric fence, so we had backup plans. The phone could be buried at the base of a pole holding up the fence directly west of the entrance, or thrown over at midnight by the closest gate on the second night there. Or had I turned those last two around?

Well, it didn't matter because I wouldn't need any of it. "How do I look?" I asked Tawnia, who'd come with Bret to the shop so she could say goodbye. I'd left off my makeup and worn a flowered, sleeveless broomstick dress.

"I thought they wore those T-shirts. Didn't you say they gave you one?"

"I packed it with the other clothes I don't mind losing to their dress code. But I'm going to arrive in style at least."

"You look wonderful."

"I'd better enjoy it while I can," I said dryly. "For all I know, Harmony Farms has a law prohibiting dressing up. Come on." We walked toward Jake and Ethan.

I felt a tiny bit of satisfaction at the frustration on Jake's face. Neither he nor Shannon had been at my apartment when I awoke, though I felt their presence in the breakfast dishes drying on the counter and the pair of officers outside the building in a police car.

Jake had tried again to talk me out of my plan after I'd arrived at the shop that morning, but I remained firm in my decision to help Ethan find Marcie and Victoria. If everything went well, I'd be back to work by Monday or Tuesday. Meanwhile, Jake, Thera, and Randa would take care of my store.

I hugged Tawnia. "I'll call you," I said brightly. "Don't have that baby while I'm gone." She rolled her eyes, and that made it easier to walk toward the door.

When I tried to hug Jake goodbye, he shook his head. "Forget it. I'm going with you."

"What?" Ethan and I said together.

I frowned at him. No wonder he was still wearing those torn jeans. "Don't be ridiculous. One of us has to stay here."

"I'm not letting you walk into this alone, and that's final." Jake folded his arms across his chest.

Tawnia grinned. "I think it's a great idea. You look the part." I knew she was referring to his locs, which she insisted on calling "dreads," but what she and many other people failed to understand was that far from being a mess of tangled, unkempt hair, his locs required a tedious process of careful washing and twirling with special products. I mean, I loved Jake's look, but he probably spent more time on his hair than I did on mine. Of course, most days I left home with my short hair wet, but still.

"You can't leave your store," I protested.

"Why not? You're leaving. Randa and Thera are perfectly capable."

"I promise I'll come by after work every day to make sure everything is running smoothly," Tawnia volunteered. She looked happier than she had all morning, and I knew that was because Jake would be able to keep an eye on me.

"What about your class?" I asked Jake.

"I'll miss it," he said tightly. "If we're there that long."

I looked at Ethan for support, but he shrugged helplessly.

"Okay. Fine. Let's just go." I wasn't as annoyed as I pretended. It was touching Jake felt he had to drop everything and come along, and if things turned ugly, he'd proven to have a fantastic right hook. On the other hand, I'd hoped to get to know Ethan better. I'd especially enjoyed imagining sneaking away from the farm to share at least one romantic rendezvous under the pretense of discussing options. With Jake there, that possibility significantly decreased.

Outside, I climbed into the front seat of a blue, fifteen-passenger van Ethan had found somewhere. Jake ended up in the back with our luggage, but he had to sit on the floor since all the seats had been removed. "I borrowed this from a friend," Ethan said when he saw me looking at the monitors and other electronic equipment that lined the windowless walls of the van.

"You have nice friends."

"You know," Jake said from the back, "my bike would fit in here. Might come in handy to have something else to drive besides this van, especially if we need a quick getaway."

Ethan liked the idea immediately, but I wasn't so sure. "Isn't it too heavy?"

Both men disagreed, and soon they had managed to put in the bike and stabilize it by tying a web of ropes to every available surface. Jake packed boxes on each side to further protect his baby.

"You know they'll put you to work building something, right?" I said to Jake when we were finally on our way.

"Yeah. Korin says they're expanding."

"But you haven't worked construction in ten years. Or more." Since his first attempt at college, to be exact.

He shrugged. "It's the sort of thing you don't forget."

I thought he might change his mind after a few days of heavy labor. "We'd better hurry," I urged Ethan. "I'm supposed to be there by now."

He nodded and stepped on the gas. It was then I noticed the prescription bottles lying in the plastic compartment between the two seats—the bottle that looked like the one I'd seen before, and two thinner ones.

"Are these all Marcie's?" I asked.

He nodded. "When you find her I don't know what condition she'll be in. She may need them."

"It's dangerous to stop medicine cold turkey," I said. It was also dangerous to combine certain medications. From my research on the Internet the day before, I was pretty sure two of the bottles were antidepressants. Perhaps one hadn't worked, and the doctor had switched her over. Marcie would know which to take. But why keep the pills that hadn't worked? "You want me to stuff them in my bag?" I started reaching for them, preparing myself for the unwelcome flood of imprints.

Ethan intercepted my hand. "No," he said. "They have her

name on them, and they might be discovered. I'll keep them here until you find out where she is and what's happening." He released my hand and put his own back on the steering wheel. "Besides, it's been a whole year. Probably have to take her to the doctor first."

He was right, of course. Yet I felt the perverse desire to reach out and take the bottles, to see what mysteries they might hold. I might even be able to tell which one Marcie had been taking. Instead, I clasped my hands in my lap, realizing the imprints might be worse than those on the tiny gold ring. I needed to be sharp today, so they would have to wait.

"When we get her back," I said, "I bet Jake and I could find something that would help her. Something herbal, I mean."

Ethan glanced over at me briefly and then back to the road. "I'd appreciate that."

"Uh," Jake said from the back, "we're close enough. You should probably stop here."

Ethan pulled over to the curb a half block from the hotel. He jumped out to grab my bag and then gave me a hug. "Good luck," he whispered in my ear. His freckles stood out in the brightness of the afternoon sun, which filtered through his thick curls.

"Thanks." All too aware that Jake was watching us, I hefted my single battered suitcase and started walking.

Jake somewhat reluctantly handed over his bike keys to Ethan and grabbed his own duffel. I hurried to put space between us so we wouldn't arrive at the same time. As I turned into the hotel parking lot, I saw the blue van moving to a better vantage point nearby.

The meeting room from the night before was filled with the same people, minus most of the visitors. From across the room,

Spring waved at me. I was relieved to see her, worried that she might have followed the angry Jimmy home after all. I dropped my bag near the door and went to sit by her. Or as near as I could get. She had young women from Harmony Farms on either side of her.

"I thought you'd changed your mind," she whispered, leaning over the girl between us. "One of those young guys who said he was going hasn't shown up."

"I had some trouble getting here. Are you okay?"

"Great."

"He's here," said the girl between us. She had straight brown hair, no makeup, and a smooth complexion I would have envied as a teenager.

"Who?" I asked.

"Founder Gabe."

Oh, that's right. Their leader. I sat down lower in my seat, hoping not to be noticed, though with my battered face it was unlikely I'd remain undetected for long. This morning a dark bruise had appeared under the skin, spreading upward from the wound to the space under my eye.

Founder Gabe was a nice-looking man with black, slightly gray-flecked hair parted on the side. It fell rakishly to his cheekbone in the front and was long enough to reach his collar in the back. As Victoria's and Marcie's imprints had shown, he was older than Korin, but I put him in his mid-fifties, even older than Marcie had guessed. He had an average build without any extra flesh and moved with confidence. On his way to the front of the room, he stopped often to shake hands or hug members of the commune.

"Thank you for the warm welcome," he said when he'd reached his destination. "It's wonderful to be reunited with all of you. I bring you love from your brothers and sisters at the farm, who are eagerly awaiting your return. Most of you will be staying on with me, and I thank you for your continued service here. I'm confident as we move to the next city that we will be as diligent and hardworking as always. We also have some new members here today, I'm told, and I look forward to getting to know you individually when I return to the farm in several weeks. Until then, Director Korin will take good care of you."

I stifled a yawn. He was handsome, sincere, and even charismatic, but he had none of the hypnotic appeal that Korin exuded when he spoke. Could this simple man be hiding evil behind his honest blue eyes?

I was nodding off by the time Gabe had finished. My slumber hadn't been exactly peaceful last night, and my cheek throbbed despite the comfrey salve. At least I hadn't needed stitches.

"Autumn!" Spring whispered urgently, waking me. Korin, once again wearing his hair pulled back in an elastic band, was coming toward us with Founder Gabe in tow. He looked more content than I had ever seen him.

"Spring, Autumn, I want you to meet Founder Gabe. He's the father of our great organization. This is the man who literally changed my life." To my surprise tears came to Korin's eyes. He had been so sure of himself each time I'd met him, so serene, but now he was like a little boy in the presence of a sports hero, and I felt awkward watching the man's emotions.

Smiling, Gabe put a hand on the shoulder of the larger man and squeezed briefly before turning to us. "I'm so pleased to meet you both." Gabe took Spring's hand in his and stared into her eyes. "You have chosen your name well." He released her and touched Spring's son on the cheek. "Handsome little guy, isn't he? What's his name?"

"Silverstar, if that's okay."

"Of course it's okay, but you know he may want to change it when he's fourteen. We allow them that."

Spring nodded happily. "I just want him to be happy."

"Exactly." Gabe beamed at her as though she were a student who had earned an A grade.

Then it was my turn. Gabe reached toward me. Instinctively, I checked his hands. He wore a plain, thin wedding band. I always noticed rings these days, and not just because I was single. I'd become careful touching frequently-worn objects belonging to others, especially on a day like this when I wasn't wearing any of my antique rings for comfort. I didn't want to know their secrets. I didn't want to know their agonies, especially if they were self-wrought and I could do nothing to help them—which was true in most cases.

But learning about Founder Gabe was part of the reason I was here. Bracing myself, I extended my hand, hoping the contact would be brief, but he held on as long as he had with Spring. His eyes met mine, a nice, clear, forceful blue that could have belonged to any confident man. I could see him taking my measure and noticing my heterochromia, though he didn't ask about it. Then all I could feel was the warmth of the gold band against my skin.

He/I watched an older woman with long black hair, white skin, a babe in arms. She was laughing, and the love he/I felt for her was powerful. Another scene of the same woman, younger this time, about my age. *A white dress flowed around her, and a ring of flowers circled her head. The love in my heart made tears come to my eyes.*

Whatever this man was, he loved his wife with an intensity I could only envy.

He had spoken to me, but so powerful were the imprints, I hadn't heard. "I'm sorry?" I said. "I didn't catch that. I'm a little sleep deprived."

The founder smiled, which made his face vibrant. "Korin told me what happened here last night. You will be safe with us. Both of you." He extended his gaze to include Spring before moving on to meet the young man who was angry at his father and the other man who was still wearing his ill-fitting suit.

Jake appeared at my side, his dark eyes worried. "You okay?"

I was feeling energized by the positive imprints, despite the tears filling my eyes. "He had a ring," I said in an undertone.

"And?"

I shrugged. How could I say, "He loves her in the way I wished you loved me?" Instead, I said loud enough for Spring to hear, "He seems very sincere. I like him."

"I knew you would." Spring's gaze was on me. "Hey, your eyes. Do you wear different colored contacts or something?"

"No, I was born this way."

"Wow. That's so cool." Her attention shifted to Jake. "Are you coming to the farm with us?"

He nodded. "I thought I'd give it a try."

"I'm glad." She shifted the weight of her son to her other hip. The boy reached up to rub the old green bruise on her face, as though trying to remove a spot of dirt.

"I never thanked you for last night," Spring continued. "I really appreciate what both of you did for me. Jimmy wasn't always like this, but it's getting worse, and since little Jim came—I mean Silverstar—I knew I had to do something. I don't want my son growing up like that."

"It was nothing," Jake said.

I couldn't say the same thing—my cheek was aching too badly for that—but I was happy Spring and her son would be safe. I hoped the farm was what she needed, if only for a short time.

"Have you told them you're going?" I asked Jake.

His attention was elsewhere. I followed his gaze and saw Detective Shannon Martin striding toward where Korin and Gabe stood talking with the angry young man and several disciples. With Shannon was his partner Paige Duncan, dressed immaculately in a navy pantsuit.

"Uh-oh," I muttered.

"What's wrong?" Spring asked. "Oh. Who are they?"

I was too busy worrying to answer. Looking the part of a detective, Shannon wore dark pants and a black blazer with flecks of green and blue. He had a blue shirt underneath, open at the neck, and black shoes. His hair was combed back, and even from where I stood across the room, I could see his eyes demanding answers.

Time to make an exit. Jake was sidling to the far door where a knot of youths were chatting animatedly, and I started after him.

I was too late.

"Hey! What are you doing here?" Shannon waved imperiously, and I knew if I didn't respond, he'd come after me. He was that kind of man.

He was going to ruin everything.

"You know him?" Spring asked.

"He's a police detective." I made the words sound like a curse. I couldn't help myself. I'd come so far, and to have him stick his nose once again in my business when I was close to discovering the truth about Marcie and Victoria was too much to endure.

My feet dragged as I made my way over to where Shannon stood with Korin and Gabe.

"You can be sure we will do anything we can to help," Gabe was saying. "We had no idea that Inclar had become so unstable since leaving us. If we hear from him, you may be sure I'll contact you."

"Thank you." Shannon's demanding gaze shifted to Korin. The detective seemed so involved with his questions that I began to hope I could escape after all. Yet as I began inching away, he pinned me in place with his eyes.

"My brother was very upset at his wife's death," Korin said. "I can't believe he'd hurt anyone, much less Sarah. Yes, they had separated, but we all believed it was only temporary. He adored her."

"Well, the attack might indicate that he was responsible for his wife's death." Shannon glanced at me, as though for confirmation, but I held rigidly still.

"We can't know that for sure," Korin said. "Was the woman he supposedly attacked known to him or a complete stranger?"

I waited for Shannon to blow my cover, but he said, "Someone he'd apparently met once." I stifled a sigh of relief, but already Shannon's gaze turned to me. "So," he drawled, "I should have guessed you'd be here."

"I don't know what you mean, detective," I said coolly.

"Well, you people tend to stick together, don't you?" He looked pointedly at my bare feet, his action directing the other men to look down as well.

A smile played on Gabe's lips. "I'm sure I don't know what you mean, though we are happy to say that Autumn is joining our brotherhood."

"You're *what*?" Shannon glared at me, his face darkening a shade.

"How do you know each other anyway?" Korin words were mild, but his brown eyes narrowed and his strong body tensed.

There was no way around discovery, except pure bluffing. "I don't know him, not really," I said quickly. "A little girl went missing some time back, and this detective interviewed everyone in the area."

"I see," Korin said, looking from me to Shannon.

"Did they find the girl?" Gabe asked.

I felt suddenly faint. *I saw the man, standing in front of the bicycle, forcing me to stop. So afraid! Mommy, help!*

A flashback of the girl's imprint, which had apparently imprinted upon my mind as it had upon the bicycle. It was one of the biggest drawbacks to reading imprints; they forever became a part of my memory as if I'd live them. And like real memories, they could return unbidden.

In a blur of movement, Shannon reached to support my elbow. I was glad he didn't wear a ring because I really didn't want to know anything more about him.

"Are you all right?" His hand was firm, his skin smooth except for those rough patches on his palm.

"Fine." I shook him off.

"Your face doesn't look fine," he said.

I was glad I'd given him only vague details of what had happened last night, though he hadn't been too happy at my evasiveness. If he knew the damage to my cheek was connected to Harmony Farms and Spring, he might not stop until he'd delved to the bottom of everything, and then Korin would know I was the woman Inclar had attacked and that I was joining them under false pretenses.

Yet wouldn't it be better for Spring to press charges against her husband? I doubted she would be content to hide out at Harmony Farms forever, and that meant dealing with Jimmy at some point. Maybe I could testify to the injury later.

The ache in my cheek had become a pounding in my head. I desperately needed rest. I gave Shannon a blank look, silently begging him to let it drop. He didn't.

"I'm sure you gentlemen will be happy to use Autumn's ability in your business," he said.

"We've been hoping to find an herbalist." Gabe smiled again easily, and Korin nodded.

Please, oh please, I thought.

"I didn't mean that ability." Shannon feigned surprise. He was a good actor and so compelling that everyone nearby was riveted. "What? Don't tell me you haven't heard."

"It's none of your business," I said in a low, dark tone. I wondered if my hands would fit around his neck.

"Autumn can sense emotions on certain objects," Shannon continued. "Yep," he added when he saw Korin and Gabe's puzzled stares. "Or so she says. That girl she was talking about? Well, she touched her bike and saw what the girl had last seen—her killer." Shannon gave me a self-satisfied smile.

"Is this true?" Gabe asked.

"I, uh, sometimes feel something when I touch certain objects," I admitted reluctantly. "Not always."

Shannon arched a brow. "Oh, come on. You're being far too modest. Unless you're admitting to fraud."

I wished he were dead. "I don't know what you're talking

about. If you need to talk to me, I'll be outside." I left quickly, grabbing my suitcase near the door. I wondered what Shannon was telling them now. When I dared a peek, Korin's face was flushed and his large hands clenched into fists at his side. He had a good two inches on Shannon and probably forty pounds, but the gun I knew Shannon carried and his badge evened things up quite nicely. Even without the weapon, I wouldn't put it past Shannon to have a few tricks up his sleeve.

As I watched, Korin relaxed and smiled, as though his anxiety had been in my imagination. Gabe was nodding gravely, and he reached out to take Shannon's card. I stepped away from the door so I couldn't be seen. Where was Jake? I looked around the parking lot, but he was nowhere, which probably meant he was still trapped inside. At least Shannon hadn't singled him out. I lifted my bruised face to the afternoon sun and tried not to worry.

A few minutes later, Shannon paused as he emerged from the building, his young partner in tow. "What are you really doing here?" he demanded in an undertone.

"I'm hanging out with *my* kind of people."

"You don't belong here."

"You don't know anything about me." To prove my point, I added, "You didn't even know I had a sister. Are you this careless with all your suspects?"

"You aren't a suspect."

"To you, I am."

We glared at each other for a long minute, and I had to admit that it was kind of fun hating him. He relented first, a hint of a smile briefly tugging at the corners of his mouth.

"Be careful with these guys. I don't like that man."

I shrugged. Maybe he was right about Gabe. I didn't know him well enough to be sure. Even an evil man could love his wife.

"That PI you gave the map to doesn't seem to be answering his phone," Shannon added. "I've left him messages. I need to see that map."

"Maybe he's busy. Look, it's not the same thing exactly, but I emailed myself a copy of the area. The X on the map pushed under my door was right in the middle of that green splotch in the middle of the Internet map. More or less."

"Very scientific."

I ignored him. "If you stop by my shop, my sister can get it for you."

Shannon's eyes fell to my suitcase. "Are you really joining them?"

"Just visiting for the weekend."

"Are you taking your phone? How can I reach you?"

I shook my head. "I'm sure it can wait until I get back. Unless you have any more missing people you need me to find." I tried to say this with a touch of disdain, but I'm not sure I pulled it off. At least it shut him up. Paige Duncan grinned with enjoyment at our exchange.

Korin was coming toward the door. "Please go," I whispered urgently.

"You don't have some crazy idea of playing detective, do you?" Shannon hissed. "Is that what this is all about? We can't protect you if Foster shows up there."

I ignored him because Korin and Gabe were bearing down on us. Gabe had a determined look in his eyes that didn't bode well for me. Probably coming to rescind my invitation to join Harmony Farms.

I glared at Shannon. "Just go!" To my great relief, Paige tugged at his elbow and Shannon left.

Forcing my mouth into a smile, I turned to face Korin and Gabe.

"Interesting character," Korin said, staring after Shannon's sedan as they pulled from the parking lot.

"With a name like Shannon, he has to be conflicted," I muttered with what I knew was very bad grace. Winter and Summer would have warned me about attracting negative vibes from the universe if I continued in that vein.

"Pardon?" Korin said, though I thought I saw a trace of amusement in his face.

"Nothing important," I assured him.

"Autumn, are you sure you want to join us at Harmony Farms?" Gabe was studying me again, his eyes narrowed. "It's apparent this detective has some sort of fascination for you and this ability of yours, and we have a lot of members who like their privacy. We don't want to invite the law into our business. I'm sure you understand."

That was funny, seeing as Spring was joining them solely to get away from her abuser. Then again, maybe Gabe had something to hide from the law but not from a man who might easily be made to disappear. Regardless, this had likely been Shannon's plan when he'd spilled my secret. No one wanted to be spied on, especially if they were hiding something, so if there was any chance I did have an ability, they'd cut me off sooner rather than later.

"It's not like I seek him out," I said. "I'd be happy if I never saw him again."

"Did you really do that?" Korin asked. "Find the girl by

touching her bike?" His tone was casual but compelling. Gabe blinked, as surprised as I was by the sudden question.

Once again, the dark imprint pushed at my mind, but I held it back. "I'm not a psychic. I didn't tell them where to find the girl. I identified her kidnapper. Working with a police sketch artist, that is." I'd also told them where the abduction had taken place—which hadn't been where they'd found the bike. But Korin and Gabe didn't need to know all that.

"I see," Korin said.

They probably thought I was either crazy or a scam artist. "Look, if it makes you uncomfortable, I can leave." I regretted the words the second they came from my lips. If I didn't go to the farm, I wouldn't be able to locate either Victoria or Marcie.

Gabe turned to Korin, a question in his eyes. Korin let long seconds pass without speaking. Then his hand shot out to my elbow. He had a strong commanding grip, as forceful as his speaking voice. "You will stay," he said calmly. It was almost an order. To Gabe, he added, "I think we have a duty to offer Autumn a place with us. She'll be safe at the farm, and I'll take complete responsibility."

"Very well." Gabe smiled at me. "Welcome to our family, Autumn."

Just like that I was back in his good graces. Even so, I felt a difference in the way Gabe studied me as I loaded my suitcase into one of their white vans. I told myself it didn't matter. He was staying here, and I would be gone from the farm before he returned. That would have been a comfort if I hadn't already learned that nothing ever turned out the way I expected.

Chapter 12

The van was a white, fifteen-passenger vehicle that was, according to Jake, prone to rollovers. The back seat had been folded down to accommodate our luggage, and I sat next to Jake in the middle of the remaining three rows of seats. Spring and her son were strapped in behind us.

In front of us sat the angry young man, whose name I'd barely learned was Ronald before he announced that he was changing it to Blade. I thought that a little violent, but Korin smiled benignly and said something about the blades of grass growing long and verdant at the farm.

Blade looked taken aback, but Jake said, "A double meaning. I like it."

Blade grinned. I thought the name fit his nature, if not his looks, which, from his muddy brown hair to his light brown eyes were rather ordinary. He was slighter than Jake and shorter, and when he wasn't scowling or griping about his father, he was quite pleasant.

On the same row sat the man in the ill-fitting suit. He had black hair and sunken cheeks and was slow of speech, stuttering occasionally, but his sad green eyes were alive with intelligence. He was taller than he looked because of the way his shoulders slumped and his body pulled inward, as though he was afraid of the world. I felt sorry for him, and I wondered who had broken his spirit. Or maybe his heart. He kept a briefcase on the empty seat between him and Blade. He called himself Menashe, which Jake later told me means "to cause forgetfulness" in Hebrew. I didn't ask how he knew that because Jake was always coming up with interesting bits of information. He had cousins from the Caucasian side of his family who were Jewish, so maybe he'd picked it up from them.

In the two front bucket seats sat Korin and one of his disciples, this one blond and scrawny with blotches of freckles, which had probably given him his name: Patches. He looked as though a wind might knock him over. Like many of the commune members, he had crooked teeth, which I knew shouldn't matter, but ever since I'd paid for my own braces in my early twenties, I noticed things like that.

We were a silent bunch, though we did sing a few camp songs in the beginning, led by Spring and Patches, who had a surprisingly beautiful voice, though not as rich and deep as Jake's and Korin's. Blade couldn't carry a note, and Menashe didn't even try. I stopped after the first two songs because my cheek hurt when I sang. That was when I curled up on my seat and the empty one beside me and went to sleep. I would have preferred to lay my head on Jake's lap, but he was to my left, on the side of my hurt cheek, so I had to be content to pillow my head on my arm. Besides, that might look a little too cozy since we were still trying to pretend we didn't know each other.

We got out once at a gas station to use the bathroom, eat, and stretch our legs. I looked around to see if I could spy

Ethan's blue van, but only when we were pulling out did I see him drive into the station. I caught Jake's eye and nodded.

Then it was back into our van, where I slipped off the tracking earrings because they were bulky enough to hurt my ears. I knew from television that tracking devices could be minuscule these days, and I wondered if Ethan had bought or had borrowed ancient equipment. Maybe that's just what happens when a math teacher turns PI.

I ended up sleeping the rest of the way to the farm. Occasionally, I would wake enough to feel Jake's hand on my back through the leather jacket he'd laid over me.

"Autumn, we're here." Jake's voice brought me gently to wakefulness. I looked around me, the dim light in the van bright enough to make me squint. I heard Silverstar whimper and Spring hush him. By the disarray of Spring's hair, I knew she'd also made good use of her empty seat.

"Come on," Korin boomed. "Let's meet the gang."

Darkness and trees filled my vision everywhere I looked, except for directly in front of us where a long, low-slung house extended the length of two or three normal houses. A few feet of neatly-tended grass stretched across the front of the house, bordered by a circular gravel drive. Music came from some-where, stuff that sounded like what I remembered from square dancing in fifth grade.

Leaving our luggage in the van, we followed Korin toward the house.

"Did you see a fence?" I whispered to Jake, sticking my earrings back into their holes. "When we came in, I mean."

He nodded. "About a mile back. I'd guess eight feet high but not chain link. Some thinner stuff tied to posts. Didn't look very strong."

"Electrified?"

"I don't think so. It was kind of hard to see through the trees, but I think it was more the kind to keep animals in, not people."

"Good." I relaxed slightly.

"Heard them say this place is three hundred acres," Jake added. "It's somewhere beyond Rome, though they seem to have property in the town as well. We stopped for a few minutes at a building there while you were sleeping. Smelled really good, like a bakery."

Korin climbed the stairs to the rough porch that ran the entire length of the house, his ponytail bouncing. Instead of heading toward the door, though, he turned along the porch and went around to the back of the house. I took care where I placed my feet because the boards of the porch were so rough that even my callused feet were in danger of splinters. Small, unlit windows periodically dotted the walls of the house, reminding me of a college dorm.

The porch continued the entire way around the house, where two similar structures sat at right angles to the first, forming three sides of a square with space for the porches in between, as well as a bit of grass that led through to the square. On what would have been the forth side, rows of vegetables stretched out into the darkness. Trees in the dark forest on either side of the second and third houses loomed tall and protective.

In the center of the square behind the house was a large patch of pavement where electric lights blazed on top of poles set at regular intervals. Near the bases of these poles, wood fires burned in metal barrels. The moon shed her light like a blessing upon the crowd that filled the square, dancing to the music or talking with their friends. Most were in their twenties, but dozens scattered over other decades, including at least six babes in arms and two grannies in rockers. Laughter sounded above the music. There was a hoop for basketball, not currently in use, poles for a volleyball net, and a spacious sandbox in one corner. Women were carrying platters to two long tables already crammed with food. Apparently, they knew how to eat—and I was suddenly ravenous.

"At least they have electricity," I whispered to Jake when I saw the lights.

"There were windmills on a hill a few miles away," he told me. "Korin said they belonged to Harmony Farms. Anyway, it looks like a family reunion."

He should know. Though his parents were dead, he and his sister had a grandmother and more cousins than I would ever know what to do with.

"Much more friendly than some families I've seen," I commented. Everyone was smiling and apparently having a good time.

Korin gave a signal, and the music cut off abruptly. "Hello, everyone!" he boomed from our elevated position on the back porch. "Sorry about stopping the music, but I knew you'd want to meet our newest members."

Cheers met his proposal.

He introduced us each by name and indicated that we should descend the stairs to meet our new family. As I stood at the bottom of the stairs, people came toward me, waving their arms and lifting their voices in greeting. Some hugged me or kissed my undamaged cheek. Blade was already well into the crowd, taking advantage of his newbie status by firmly planting kisses on any willing girl in sight. To one side, Spring was almost surrounded by women holding babies.

Menashe, on the other hand, stayed motionless on the middle stair, looking horribly uncomfortable. For no reason I could explain, I found myself moving in front of him, intercepting well-wishers as they approached. Jake stood beside me, smiling and nodding with a professional storekeeper smile. Until that moment, I hadn't realized he had a fake smile in his repertoire; he'd always treated his customers like friends. This was different. These people weren't long-time customers or new acquaintances. They had an obvious eagerness to please that was painfully noticeable, almost an invitation to be taken advantage of. They didn't know us, and yet I had the distinct feeling they would give me the last bit of food or their only shirt off their back if I asked for it, all the while praising Founder Gabe for the opportunity to serve. For me, it was similar to walking into a room full of people like my adoptive parents. If I felt unbalanced by it, no wonder Jake and Menashe were uneasy.

Korin descended two steps, reaching out a hand to rest on my shoulder. "Don't worry. You'll get used to having so much family." He gave both Jake and me a little push forward.

The music began again, and we were drawn into the crowd. We danced, everyone twirling around without a care for specific partners. I started to loosen up, feeling pretty in my broomstick dress and not at all cold despite the night air. Most of the other women wore dresses too, made of bright material, though of a more simple cut. Not old-fashioned exactly, but modest, with sleeves of various lengths. They wore no jewelry except the inexpensive beads I'd seen them selling at the riverfront. Most of the men and boys wore rough brown pants or jeans and dress shirts, mostly white or blue. A few of the younger children wore the commune T-shirts with their jeans.

Jake was gazing around distractedly as he danced. I realized he was examining faces to see if Marcie and Victoria were here, and I began doing the same. If we found them tonight, everything would be resolved and we could go home.

After twenty minutes, Jake caught up with me and put his arm around my waist, bending to whisper in my ear. "See them?"

"Not yet." Was it wrong to hope we didn't find anything for a few days? Though I didn't know how that would be possible because everyone seemed so open and friendly. If Victoria and Marcie were here, we'd run into them soon. "Maybe we should ask around."

Jake shook his head. "We'd better wait to get the feel of things."

I looked for Menashe and saw that he was at the food table. My own stomach growled. "I'm going to see what they're eating."

"Better eat a lot," Jake said. "Fasting begins tomorrow."

I groaned, having completely forgotten to smuggle in snacks.

"Didn't you listen to the spiel? Everyone in the community feasts and then fasts for three days after new people arrive." He gave me a mocking look. "You really should do more research on the cults you join. Or at least listen during the meetings. You should be grateful they allow liquids."

I hit him hard. "Let's eat."

Before Jake could reply, he was swept into the crowd by a few giggling pubescent girls, one reaching up to tug at his locs. I grinned and made my way alone to the tables of food.

I chugged down a delicious drink that tasted faintly of peaches and apples. Nonalcoholic, which was a good thing, because the children were also drinking the mixture. There were banana muffins, pumpkin cookies, pies, meat dishes, salads, fruits, vegetables, all set out in beautiful homemade pottery dishes. I knew they probably didn't eat like this every day, but I was still impressed they could put on a spread like this in what was practically the wilderness.

I ate. A lot. I vaguely wished Tawnia could be here to experience it all. Everything tasted as if it came straight from the garden or the fields, without any vitamin-depleting processing. At the moment my heart was softened toward Harmony Farms.

I ate more. After all, there were those three days of fasting to consider. Though Winter had sworn that an occasional weeklong liquid fast was cleansing, I'd never gone for more than two days without solids. And I'd regretted that.

The trees above the houses danced a little in the evening breeze, scattering shadows over the tops of the roofs of both side houses. It would have been a little frightening to be out here alone, but with all the company and the music and the food, it was a slice of paradise.

Which meant I needed to be careful not to grow too relaxed. I still hadn't seen either Marcie or Victoria—and what did that mean? Either some people hadn't chosen to attend the dance, or they couldn't. Or maybe they had changed so much I couldn't identify them among the more than a hundred faces.

My gaze ran over the square again. Nothing out of the ordinary, except a long shadow near the far end of one of the side houses, as though a light was coming from outside the square and falling on something solid. But what? The shape of the shadow was tall enough to be human.

Hoping no one noticed me, I slid in that direction, passing Menashe, who nodded and quickly looked away. He seemed relaxed now that no one was pestering him.

The light faded quickly toward the end of the side houses, the shadow I'd seen nothing more than a darker splash on another shadow. Probably a pole of some sort, highlighted by a light someone left on in a window facing the garden. Yet as I approached, the shadow moved. My chest tightened in momentary alarm, but when the shadow disappeared altogether, I knew whatever had made it must have moved around the houses and into the forest.

The night had grown chilly, or maybe I was too far away from the burning barrels to feel the heat. I rubbed my bare arms as I debated following the shadow, but I'd watched enough TV to know what happens to nosy heroines. No, I wasn't going tramping anywhere until I knew more about what I was up against.

I eased back into the party. Jake was at the food table talking with Menashe. Blade and Spring were laughing and dancing. Korin was nowhere to be seen. Had he been the person behind the house? And so what if he had? He probably had a lot to check on now that he was back.

Like a prisoner in a darkened room?

Then I saw his broad figure. He was standing by one of the heating barrels near the back porch of the front house, toasting bread on a stick and laughing with a woman who had long, straight black hair and pale skin. She seemed familiar to me, though I'd never seen her before, at least not with my natural eyes.

Gabe's wife, I realized. His much younger wife. She was clearly attractive but not nearly as beautiful as in the imprint on his ring, the way he saw her. Her pale face was devoid of makeup, her skin smooth and translucent, and her laughing dark eyes were framed with long black lashes that were better than any store-bought paint. She had a face models craved—all but her nose, which was slightly too large for her oval face, and the noticeable scar that ran parallel to her jaw on the left side. Her figure was lithe and supple but not overly thin. In fact, she had nice curves, with hips a tad too wide for modern tastes, but for her they were just right. She was the picture of womanhood, childbearing, and motherhood. Earthy and comforting. But also mischievous. I could see that in her dark eyes. Something else that hadn't been in her husband's image of her. Even as I thought this, she reached out and tugged on Korin's ponytail. He flicked it away from her as they both laughed.

Korin caught my eye and beckoned. I went toward him, curious about this woman who had elicited so much feeling in a man, as though by watching her I could uncover the secret of making a man fall in love with me. Not just any man, of course, but the right man.

I wondered if she loved Gabe as much as he loved her.

"Autumn, this is Harmony."

Of course she was Harmony. Not only did the name fit her perfectly, but now I knew how the commune had found its name. "Nice to meet you," I said. No last names were used here, but like her husband, she wore a thin band of gold. Not plain like his but with facets cut across the surface so it caught and reflected the light.

"Welcome to the farm." She took my fingers and squeezed them as a friend might, and her skin was dry and cool against mine. Her ring didn't make contact.

"I actually thought it'd be more farm-like," I said.

Her laugh was bright, like a child's. "You can't see the two barns from here. Or much of the fields. We've cleared nearly a hundred acres. Most of it we use for grazing, but we grow all our own food. Gabe wanted to have our main barn closer than it is, but I convinced him to leave these trees and build it way out there." She waved in the direction of the side house opposite our position. "Good thing, too, or you'd smell it." We laughed with her.

"What about the bathrooms?" I asked. "Do you have indoor plumbing?"

"We have water piped to the kitchens and the bathing rooms indoors, but toilets are still outside for now." She pulled a flashlight from a pocket of her dress. "They're in the trees behind us, if you need them, not too far past this house."

I nodded, thinking the location of the bathrooms might explain the shadow I'd seen. It made sense that someone dancing at the end of the square near the garden would go that way around the long side house instead of walking the length of the square to go around the other side.

"Would you like me to show you?" Harmony asked.

"Please." My bladder was suffering from all the punch. It wasn't every day I had anything remotely healthy offered to me in drink form, and I'd overdone it.

She smiled at Korin. "Excuse us, then."

He nodded, and I wondered if it was my imagination that he let her go with reluctance. They were probably close friends and they'd have a lot to catch up on. As Korin was Gabe's second-in-command, his friendship with Gabe's wife was only natural. Still, it made me uncomfortable that I hadn't yet spotted Marcie or Victoria. With every second they were missing, the greater the likelihood that something suspicious was going on in this paradise.

Behind the house Harmony clicked on the flashlight, the beam casting otherworldly shadows on the tree trunks and shrubbery. My hand glided over the rough bark of a tall tree, and I experienced something I was at a loss to describe. Not imprints or emotions, but something ancient and wise and benevolent. I wondered if my imagination was working overtime again.

"I bet the children love to play here."

"They adore it. That's part of why I insisted Korin design the houses this way. Not enough forest left here to get lost in or to attract the biggest wild animals, but enough to have a good game of hide and seek and chase a rabbit or two."

"And hide the bathrooms."

Her laugh trilled out a little too loudly. "Exactly."

We were quiet a moment, following a dirt and pine needle path that was wide enough to allow us to walk side by side. She moved like a dancer, graceful and aware of her body.

"Korin likes you," she said after a few moments of quiet. "Or at least it seems that way to me. He was watching you."

Thanks to Shannon, I wasn't surprised. I had that effect on almost everyone who knew about my strange ability. It had nothing to do with romance. For my part, I hadn't once thought of Korin as anything other than a particularly eloquent kook, who had a kindly tendency toward his misshapen brother. I had judged and dismissed him quickly, placing him in a box labeled "Not my type." Now I wondered what kind of man he was inside. If it had cost him personally to stay behind when his brother had left the farm. If he had known his sister-in-law well before her death. If he'd ever been married.

I didn't know what to say to Harmony, so I shrugged. "I think he's watching everyone. His brother's missing, and he's probably concerned about him showing up here."

"Oh?" Yet something in the way she said it made me feel she already knew about Inclar.

"There was some trouble with his brother back in Portland. A detective came to the hotel. I thought someone might have called to let you know."

"There's no phone here."

I hadn't considered that.

"We do sometimes get messages from our business in Rome," she added, pulling back a branch overhanging the path and holding it so I could pass. "That's closer for messages, but no one came from there today except you guys."

"I don't know much else."

"Ah." She didn't seem concerned.

"Did you know his brother?"

She nodded. "And his wife."

"She was here?" This surprised me.

"For a little while. But she left, and then she died. Inclar—that's Korin's brother—didn't like staying here because of the memories."

"I see." I remembered from the imprint on Korin's watch that he had let Inclar out of a locked room. Why had he been locked up? "Do a lot of people leave here?"

"A few." She laughed. "Not many. Most choose to stay."

"Do you and Gabe have children?"

She didn't seem to think it odd that I should know she was married to the commune's leader. Apparently, there weren't many members named Harmony. "We have one little girl. Five years old. Flower. Oh, I know"—she laughed self-consciously—"it's a silly name, but she is like a beautiful flower to me. She'll change it when she's fourteen, I'm sure, but for now it serves her well."

"She was born here?"

She nodded. "We'd just completed the houses. Took us four years and a lot of work."

"I'll bet."

"Gabe and I wanted more children, but I was already thirty-five when I had Flower, and it just hasn't happened." She hesitated before adding cheerfully, "We feel fortunate to have so many other children here to love."

"So how many members are there?"

"Almost two hundred now."

"Are all of them here tonight?" I didn't think there'd been that many at the dance.

"Twenty or so are at the bakery in Rome, and another twenty are with Gabe in the city. Some are watching the animals, and a few are sick in bed."

"So everyone lives in those three houses?"

"Yes. We'll give you a tour tomorrow, but basically the house we passed coming out here is divided in half for the single men and the women. The house opposite is for families. The main house has the kitchen, laundry facilities, a meeting room, and the leaders' quarters."

I wondered if the leader's quarters were any better than anyone else's, but I didn't say that aloud. As Gabe's wife, she wouldn't take that well.

"So how many are married?" I asked.

She laughed again. "That's important, isn't it? Don't worry.

We have more unmarried men than married men. Gabe encourages marriages, but no one is ever forced. You can date anyone you'd like."

"I guess that's good," I said in a tone that told her I wasn't interested.

We walked along in silence. "What, no more questions?" she asked at last.

When I didn't respond, she gave another short burst of laughter, and I didn't know whether to be offended or not.

"It's just all so new," I offered.

Her hand touched my shoulder with a fleeting movement, a butterfly kiss. "Please, don't be offended. I forget what it is to be new. I'm afraid we are too blunt and rough here sometimes, but I'm glad you're here, and I hope you'll be happy."

Before I could respond, her light shone on a building with rustic wood siding. "Here we are. This side is for the girls. The other is for the boys. It's not bad. We installed flush toilets last year, and there's electricity." She opened the wooden door and flipped on a switch.

The place didn't even smell. "Thank you," I said.

"Do you think you can find your way back? We have a horse about to foal in the barn just beyond those trees, and I'd like to peek in on her. I'll leave you the flashlight."

"I just follow the path?"

"Yes. The wide one. It goes straight back."

"What about you?"

Her laugh tinkled like warm drops of rain on a pond. "Oh, I don't need light. The moon is out. But I'll take a lantern just to be sure. We keep a few extra out here because the children like to play pranks and leave each other in the dark."

The image made me laugh.

She opened a narrow door next to the bathroom entrance, revealing a closet filled with cleaning supplies and lanterns. After taking a lantern but not lighting it, she extended the red flashlight to me, deceptively small for such a bright light. "I'd like to have it back later," she said. "It's one of the few battery-operated ones we have left. I use it a lot."

"Sure." I took the light without thinking and watched her go. I was glad she didn't look back because strong images from the flashlight were shifting in my mind, and she might have been concerned at my expression. This was no ordinary flashlight, one people had used uneventfully, and I had none of my antique rings to soften the mental explosion.

Of the three missing people connected with Harmony Farms, the one in this imprint wasn't one I'd been hoping to find.

Chapter 13

"Why are you here?" I said.

Or rather Harmony said, as it was clearly her voice in the imprint. She was speaking to Inclar, who had appeared in the circle of her flashlight.

Trees loomed all around in the darkness, and I was horribly afraid.

"Is he here? I don't want him to know I came."

"Is who here?" I kept my voice gentle, forcing myself to approach Inclar. Slowly so he wouldn't be startled.

"I had a key. I came to tell him."

"Come back to the house with me."

"No!" Inclar's crazy eye rolled wildly. "She's crying. I can't. He can't know. Not about the key."

"Who can't know? Inclar, you're making no sense. Come in and have some food." My voice was unsteady now.

"I'm so tired." Inclar slumped against a tree.

"Then come with me."

"He'll never let me leave again."

"You won't have to."

"I did a bad thing."

That feeling I could relate with only too well. "Everyone does bad things sometimes. Look, I'm sure if you talk to Gabe and Korin, everything will be okay. Just come with me to the house."

Inclar's right eye stopped rolling, and for a moment he stared at me intently.

My breath went in and out and in again. My heart thundered in my chest.

"He will never leave you," he whispered, "but he will not be here." All at once he brushed past me, knocking me down in the brush near the path. I screamed. My fingers lost their grip on the light, and the scene went abruptly dark.

Instantly, the imprint was replaced by older, more pleasant ones. A colt taking its first steps in a darkened barn three years earlier. A view of stars from a hilltop where a woman I knew was Harmony lay curled in a man's arms, his face hidden by the dark, a private tenderness between them. This last scene repeated itself, slight variations stretching over at least several years. Strong but so intertwined that the images changed before I could get a decent lock on them. Though joyful, they did nothing to erase or even calm the fear the first imprint had left.

The images faded, and I was able to uncurl my own fingers long enough to drop the flashlight. It thudded to the cement walkway near the outhouse and went dark. I took a long, slow breath, feeling shaky. The terrifying imprint of Inclar had occurred not more than twenty-four hours earlier, and Harmony's fear of him mingled with my own. Was he around still? Perhaps waiting to finish the job he'd started in the lobby of my apartment? Detective Martin had warned me that he couldn't protect me here, and now I wish I'd heeded his advice.

I held my breath and listened. Music still came from the

dance, but that was far off. There was no other sound. The outhouses had been built in a small clearing in the forest, or the trees had been cleared for the purpose, and I saw that Harmony had been right about the moon. It was bright enough for me to see the path, even without the dim light coming from inside the bathrooms.

Leaving the flashlight where it lay, I went inside to relieve my strained bladder. The walls were made of cinder blocks and painted a shade of pale yellow. A line of sinks stood opposite a row of toilet stalls. A space at the end that had once been a communal shower had been fitted with more sinks and stalls, so apparently the bathing facilities had been moved to the houses when they'd pumped in the water. I was glad for that. The bathroom was remarkably clean, though there were a few dead bugs under the corner sink and cobwebs near one of the small, high windows that were fitted with privacy glass. A bar of soap lay at each sink, and there were real hand towels that were so clean I knew they must be changed daily. No mirrors. Apparently, primping wasn't encouraged here. A wall hanging with neat, even embroidery stitches reminded people to shut the door when they left in order to keep out the critters.

I turned on the faucet gingerly, but no imprint reared to assault me. *What now?* I thought as I dried my hands.

I wished it were already the next day so I could take a tour and figure out the most likely places for someone to be hidden. I wanted to be introduced to those who weren't around tonight. While I was still determined to believe there was an explanation for Marcie and Victoria's absence, I had a sinking feeling in my stomach that coming here hadn't been such a wise idea. Meeting Harmony had only underscored this feeling. Something about her made me uneasy.

Why had Inclar come here? Had he told someone about the key that was even at this moment tucked into a torn patch of lining in my suitcase? I hadn't dared touch it again, but I hadn't wanted to carry it openly to the farm, either.

Well, one thing was certain, I wasn't getting anywhere standing in this bathroom looking at the painted wall. My nerves felt jangly, disconnected from reading the imprint about Inclar. I needed something to steady me.

Patting my dress to find my pocket, another reason I'd chosen this outfit, I brought out the tiny phone Ethan had given me. No service. I'd seen that one coming. But the two-way radio was working, which meant Ethan must be in range. I felt relieved.

I shoved it into my pocket as giggling warned me someone was approaching. Two barefooted girls burst into the bathroom, the taller one carrying a lantern. Both had blond hair past their shoulders, and the older one had the beginnings of an overbite, but that was the only thing that distinguished them in the dimness of the bathroom. They stopped when they saw me, their eyes opening wide.

"Hi," said the older one softly. She ducked her head. The younger girl gave me a shy smile and disappeared into a stall.

"Hi," I replied and sauntered toward the door.

Freed from further politeness, the older girl darted into a stall, clicking the door shut more firmly than necessary.

Outside I picked up the flashlight with one of the hand towels I'd taken from the bathroom. No need to see the image of Inclar again; it'd been clear enough. But the flashlight wouldn't go on, no matter how I fiddled with it. I hoped Harmony had extra bulbs.

I was torn between hurrying back to the square and finding

a secluded place out here where I could contact Ethan with the radio. I wasn't scheduled to contact him until tomorrow night, unless there was an emergency, but Inclar's showing up here seemed emergency enough. Maybe Ethan could contact Shannon and let him know. Was Inclar important enough for Shannon to call in favors from whatever police jurisdiction was responsible for this area, or would he come here himself? I couldn't exactly depend on his fascination with me or the case extending that far.

The woods appeared deserted except for traffic to the bathrooms, so I decided to find a place to contact Ethan. As long as I didn't go too far away, I should be able to find my way back or at least scream loud enough for someone to find me.

As I pondered which way to go, the girls came from the bathroom and tripped past me, running with sure feet down the dim path. The light from their lantern hit the trees more than the path, but that didn't seem to stop them. Their giggles drifted back to me. No doubt they'd tell their friends they'd seen me here, looking blank and stupid. They might even come back with a few of those friends and an adult or two to see what was taking me so long.

To the left then, away from where I'd seen the shadow disappear behind the house, though I was already some distance from there. I wasn't afraid exactly. I was sure it had only been someone heading to the outhouse. Well, almost sure. Now that I knew Inclar had been here, it could have been him.

I'd have to stay alert.

Off the path, walking was a little more difficult because of the undergrowth. It was darker because the trees were thicker, but I felt more secure, as though the darkness caressed and protected me. I'd always enjoyed the darkness, even as a child.

Perhaps that's because Winter and Summer had taken me with them wherever they went regardless of the time of night. The darkness was my friend, and this night I felt embraced by the shadows.

For all that I was barefoot and the occasional stick poked my foot, most of the forest floor was soft and loamy, with much more give than I expected. It was colder, though, but walking kept the night chill at bay.

I walked until I was sure I was out of hearing range of the bathrooms. The trees continued to stretch out before me with no sign of an end, and that surprised me. Harmony's assurances that the children wouldn't get lost or be in any danger had made me envision something much smaller.

At last I spied a fallen log and settled on it, listening to the night sounds—the chirp of a cricket, the rustle of a rodent, the hoo-hoo of an owl. The air was fresh here, breathable and sweet, but now that I wasn't walking, my arms felt cold. The elevation wasn't much different from that of Portland, but it felt much cooler here. Perhaps because of all the vegetation. I'd give a lot for Jake's leather jacket, but all I had was the hand towel. I set down the flashlight and shook out the towel. It was slightly larger than my hand towel back home but a far cry from bath-size. At least it covered my neck and capped my shoulders.

Everything was quiet around me, and after waiting a few more minutes to be certain I was alone, I turned on the radio and called Ethan. Since he'd probably realized by now that our phones didn't work here, he should have his radio on. He had plenty of batteries, so it was his responsibility to be ready in case I contacted him.

"Ethan, it's me. Are you there?" I released the call button

to a light flurry of static and waited, hoping he was in range. I might have to move closer to the fence if he didn't respond, though in what direction that was, I was no longer sure.

Louder static and then Ethan's voice, "I'm here."

I blew out a relieved sigh. His reply had been a little noisy for the quiet night, so I turned down my volume and put the receiver up to my ear.

"Is everything okay?" he added. "Did you find Marcie?"

"No. Sorry. I haven't seen her or Victoria. They're having a party here, but not all their members came."

He didn't reply, perhaps too polite to ask me why I was contacting him early if I hadn't found his sister.

"I'm calling because Inclar was here," I rushed on. "I think you should tell the police."

"Is he still there?"

"He could be, but I haven't seen him."

"Are you worried he'll attack you again?"

"I'm worried he'll recognize me." But I was worried about the other too. After someone tries to choke the life from your body, you can't feel comfortable knowing they might be lurking nearby. "How far away are you?" I was wondering if it would be possible to meet him. Not now, of course, when they would be expecting me back, but maybe tomorrow after I'd had a chance to look around.

"I'm quite close actually. That is, if you're still wearing the earrings."

"I am."

"Then I'm point six miles away from your location. I hid the van off the road, and I've been checking out their fence. Eight feet high. Not very secure. A pain to climb but easy to cut through. But you'll need to be careful because men are patrolling the area. They come around every fifteen minutes or so, at least along this stretch."

That seemed odd because the compound was so secret, and farm animals certainly weren't going anywhere with that eight-foot fence in the way. That meant the patrols were there for another reason. "Maybe it's because of Inclar."

"Or to keep people from leaving." There was a stubbornness in his voice that I found unappealing.

"They said I could leave any time."

"Yeah, but I've been thinking. If that's true, why can't I find anyone who knows where this place is? Anyone who would talk, that is. There are no ex-members. Not a single one."

"There's Inclar."

"You said his brother unlocked a door to release him. Against the leader's will."

"Maybe he was crazy even then."

"Anyway, Inclar's wanted for questioning in his wife's murder. Not exactly a cult success story."

"Which means we should definitely tell Detective Martin that Inclar came here."

"Yeah, you're right." His voice was tentative. "Except what if Martin comes blazing in and blows your cover before you find Marcie?"

"He didn't blow it at the hotel. At least about Inclar." Belatedly, I realized Ethan didn't know about that, so I quickly outlined my encounter with Shannon and Harmony's founder. I was still irritated at Shannon for telling Korin and Gabe about my ability, but I'd let him know that myself when I saw him again.

More static, and then Ethan said, "If the police think Gabe and Korin are hiding Inclar, and they come and actually find him here, you'll be needed to identify him. They'd have no choice but to blow your cover."

I thought this over for a moment, not liking the idea or the fact that Ethan had pointed it out.

Ethan's voice came through again. "Look, if you feel you're in danger, we should call the police right away."

I made a quick decision, one I hoped I wouldn't regret. "Let's give it another night or so. He's probably gone now, anyway. I'll ask around." Or at least I'd touch things. If Inclar's appearance had caused such a poignant imprint on the flashlight, there's no telling what other imprints might exist because of him.

"If you're sure." His voice changed, becoming deeper and slightly gravelly. "Your safety is the most important thing." The words were a caress that sent a warm shiver to my stomach. I could picture him at that moment, blond curls ruffled by a worried hand, blue eyes drawn with concern. It was easy to forget my irritation when I thought of him that way.

"I'm fine," I said. "But I've got to get back now. They'll be sending out a search party soon."

"You'll contact me tomorrow?"

"Like we planned." I didn't wait to see if he broke through the static again but shut the radio off quickly. It was a comfort to know that at least one of our contact methods worked. Two if you counted the tracking device in my earrings, which now felt like a weight dragging me down. A distinct ache matching the one in my wounded cheek had begun in the lower region of my earlobes. I took the earrings off for the second time that day and put them in the pocket of my dress with the useless cell phone.

Picking up the flashlight with the hand towel, I began

walking carefully in the direction of where I thought the houses should be. I hadn't come all that far, maybe a half mile, and I was a strong walker, even though my toes were now officially cold. The smell of the earth and the trees and rotting and growing things was intoxicating, and I wanted nothing more than to find the hilltop in Harmony's peaceful rendezvous and sleep under the stars. With a warm blanket or two. It was a beautiful night to be alive.

My euphoria dimmed sometime later as even my tough soles began to feel the pressure of the stabbing twigs and the occasional rock or rotting splinter of wood. Surely I had been walking much longer than necessary to get back to the outhouse path. At this rate I'd end up in the fields or the pastures. There seemed to be only slivers of moonlight seeping through the branches above, as though I'd gone deeper into the forest instead of retracing my steps. Swallowing hard, I forced myself to stop and face the fact that I had no idea where I was. I heaved a sigh, disgusted at myself for being so directionally challenged.

Wait, wasn't that the music? I could hear it faintly but coming from behind me and slightly to the left. Apparently, I'd overshot the outhouses and was nearer the end of the side house where I'd seen the shadow, though deeper in the woods or I would have seen the bathrooms as I passed. Well, that was no problem. I'd angle back to the house, following the music, and find one of those lovely burning barrels and get warm. Happier now, I moved with purpose, using my free hand to steady myself against the trees.

That's when my foot landed on something both bulky and soft. Something that didn't belong with the rest of the forest floor. Some animal that had escaped the pasture? A bag of grain abandoned on the way to wherever they were stored? I stepped backward, my eyes dropping, straining to make sense of the longish lump before me. I leaned closer to get a better look.

Horror rose in my throat as I registered the sightless eyes, one of them staring up into the trees, clearly lit by a shaft of light stabbing through a break in the overhead leaves, the other rolled upwards at an odd angle.

I'd found Inclar, aka Danny Foster, and he was dead.

Chapter 14

*P*anic welled in my chest. The darkness was no longer friendly but pregnant with malice. I knew from the imprint on the flashlight that Inclar had been alive the night before, and the corpse didn't smell, so he hadn't been here long. I saw no blood or visible signs of what had killed him. No trickle of red down his face, no crusted bullet hole or knife protruding from his stomach. But he wasn't at peace. His mouth was stretched into a grimace, and his loose right eye was rolled up as if recoiling in terror.

That was all my mind registered in one great information dump, and then I was backing away, circling the lump of lifeless flesh and running. Running. Heedless of the debris piercing my feet, of the brush that clutched at the skirt of my dress as I passed, as though trying to hold me back. I struggled on, the broken flashlight wrapped in the hand towel brandished like a weapon.

Someone had murdered Inclar, and that meant I needed to get as far away from that spot as soon as possible. Except I was hopelessly lost in these cursed trees that seemed to stretch with no end across the face of the entire earth. I panted loudly in the quiet, and my heart clanged inside my chest like a dozen kids banging on pans with their mothers' metal spoons.

I hit a tree, tripped over an exposed root, and collapsed to the earth. Hugging my knees to my chest, I gulped in deep, heaving breaths, trying not to sob with my terror. Slowly sanity returned.

Inclar was dead, but that didn't mean I was in immediate danger. No one was hunting me, or they would have found me already, alerted by my wild, panicked flight through the forest. I took out my two-way radio.

"Ethan," I said urgently into it. "Ethan, are you there? Hurry, pick up."

Three agonizing seconds passed before the comforting burst of static that signaled his response. "Autumn? What's wrong?"

"Inclar. He's dead. I just found him."

He made a noise of disbelief. "What killed him?"

"I don't know. I stumbled over him on the way back. He's just lying here in the woods. I didn't wait around to check how he died. We have to get to Rome and call the police." Detective Martin, to be exact. He'd mock me for not trusting him, but I was willing to endure that and more to get out of here.

"What about my sister? I don't want her hurt if there's a confrontation."

"I'm sure the police will be careful. Think of it this way— with Inclar dead, they'll turn this place upside down in search of her."

He should be happy about that. As for me, I felt a keen disappointment that Gabe and possibly Korin were running a scam after all. The people I'd met tonight were so happy and content with their simple lives. Everything would change for them now.

There was a long pause. Too long for my shot nerves.

"Ethan?" I whispered frantically, imagining Harmony Farms lookouts taking him into custody. I scooted closer to the huge tree I'd run into, feeling the ancient comfort that was completely oblivious to my short-lived human struggles.

"I'm here. Don't worry." He sounded a bit out of breath. "Just checking the tracking monitor. I can give you directions to my location using the earrings. But what about Jake? Are you bringing him too? Or are we leaving him there?"

Jake. In my terror, I'd completely forgotten him.

"I'll go back for him, and then we'll meet you."

"Are you sure? He shouldn't be in too much danger if—"

"I'm not leaving him!" I ground out. "He's only here because of me."

"Okay. Okay." Another static-filled pause before he said, "Autumn, you have to be even more careful now. You can't rouse their suspicions. If there's been one murder, there might be others. You have to be careful."

My irritation faded.

Static. "What I'm saying is, if you go back for Jake, you might have to stay the night." Ethan's voice was calm, but it did nothing to stay the frightened pounding in my chest.

I wanted to protest, but he was right about the need for caution. I'd been away from the dance far too long as it was, and with these new, higher stakes, I couldn't risk being caught and questioned. "We'll be careful. If we see it won't work tonight, we'll stay."

"So I'll wait to hear from you, either way." His voice was loud again, too loud.

I reached for the volume, but before I could twist the knob, a hand fell on my shoulder. I jerked my face upward, trying to see who had me, a scream rising in my throat.

"Shhh, it's just me. Ethan."

Choking down the scream, I twisted my body to better see his face. "You idiot!" I hissed.

"Sorry." He made a sympathetic noise as he released the hold on my shoulder, drawing me to my feet and encircling me with one arm. He felt warm and inviting. Unlike me, he was dressed warmly in jeans and a sweatshirt jacket. By the illumination of the flashlight he carried, I could see his face was flushed from his quick jaunt through the trees.

I leaned against him, soaking in his warmth and his presence. "You shouldn't be here. They'll recognize you."

"When I saw on the tracking monitor how close you'd come to the fence, I thought it was worth the risk. I wanted to make sure you were okay."

"I'm fine."

"You're like ice." He clicked off his flashlight and pulled me closer, rubbing his hand up and down my arms to warm me. I wondered what I would do if he tried to kiss me. We hadn't known each other long, however handsome he was, and I'd never seen him in his own environment. I didn't know if he had friends, or if he liked the outdoors. I didn't even know how he felt about preservatives or microwaves.

Besides, there was a dead body sharing our forest. That thought put a decided damper on things. That and my feelings for Jake.

I took a tiny step back, breaking contact. My trembling from the cold had stopped. In fact, warmth was now rushing through my veins at his closeness.

"I guess you need to get back to find Jake," Ethan said.

"Yeah."

"I won't let anything happen to you. I promise."

If it had been Jake or anyone else, I would have retorted that I could take care of myself, but it felt good having Ethan worry about me. "And I'll do my best to find Marcie."

He frowned. "They own three hundred acres. What if they've stashed her somewhere no one will ever look?"

I thought of the key Inclar had given me. "It's possible, but we know she was here, so we won't let the police give up until they've gone over every foot of ground."

"I wish you could have looked around more, that's all. Before the police alert them to our suspicions. But I guess that's out now, if you and Jake manage to sneak away tonight."

"The police should surprise them. They won't have time to cover much."

He nodded, but I could see the misery in his eyes. "Just keep in mind what I said about getting caught."

I shuddered at the possibility. "If we don't contact you in two hours, maybe you should go to Rome and talk to the police without us."

"It's a tiny place. They may not have a police station or the personnel to conduct a raid."

"You'll have phone service. You can get things in motion and then come back to wait for us to sneak out."

He considered this for a time. "You know, even if you can get out tonight, maybe it would be safer if I went for the police now and you waited until they arrive in force before you try to leave."

He wanted me to stay? In my mind the suggestion was tantamount to betrayal. Inclar was dead, but before he died, he might have told someone he'd given me the key—the key that made me sick and woozy with the images imprinted on it. If he had, I'd be in danger. The cold of the night seeped into my heart.

"Wait a minute," I protested, giving him an icy glare. "Weren't you the one worried about Marcie getting hurt in a police shootout? I don't want to be in the middle of something like that, either, especially if they somehow suspect that I'm involved with Inclar."

"And you were the one who said the police would be careful," Ethan countered. "Besides, I'd tell them you were inside to make sure they didn't do anything stupid. If I went into town right now or as far as it takes for my phone to work, instead of waiting to see if you guys can sneak out, the police would be able to get here that much sooner and you wouldn't have to risk getting caught."

I said nothing as I pondered the idea. Was keeping Jake and me inside a way for Ethan to ensure that the police wouldn't burn everyone out or shoot people on sight, thus protecting Marcie? Or did he really believe I'd be safer waiting? Every instinct urged me to run fast and far from both the farm and Inclar's lifeless body, but the more I thought about it, the more logical Ethan's plan sounded.

"Believe me," Ethan said into the silence that had fallen between us, "I'd rather take you with me right now, but since you won't leave Jake, staying and playing the part might be safer than if you try to sneak away tonight. Your danger of getting caught is too great. One man's dead, so we know they aren't joking around. Whatever they're hiding is big enough to murder for. They'll be stepping up their fence patrols, I bet. It won't be as easy for you to get out as it was for me to get in."

Despite my sense of betrayal, what he said made sense.

With Inclar dead, there was no telling what the commune might do to protect their secrets. The smart thing to do would be to go with Ethan now, but I wouldn't leave Jake behind. Already I had an itchy feeling as though I needed to hurry back to him, to make sure he was all right.

This meant the shock of seeing Inclar's body was fading. Funny how you adjust to such things. I'd been close to a lot of dead bodies in my lifetime, what with Winter and Summer having died and also their friends' propensity for home funerals. Inclar's remains had frightened me more than any other corpse, even Winter's, which had been in the river for a week and whose flesh had been swollen and rotting. Maybe it was the location. Inclar's aloneness. The unsolved mystery of what had happened to Marcie and Victoria. Yet somehow I had already moved on.

"Okay," I said with a sigh. "We'll wait until the police come—but you have to get them here as quickly as possible."

"I will. Meanwhile, keep your eyes open and radio immediately if you need me. I hope I won't be out of range more than an hour or so while I'm contacting them." He leaned his face close to mine. "Be careful," he whispered.

His lips brushed mine, warm and compelling, but the moment was over almost before it started. Mostly my fault because I started thinking about Jake and wondering if he was worried about me. As far as kisses went it was rather boring. I'd bet even Detective Martin could do better. Maybe Ethan was as grossed out about sharing the forest with Inclar's body as I was.

I could still hear the music faintly, but it was hard to tell where it came from. I gave Ethan a wry smile. "If you'll just point me in the right direction, I'll be on my way. The music is coming from over there—I think."

Ethan gave a low chuckle. "I'll take you closer. Until we can see the lights at least. As long as you're around people and they don't know you found Inclar, you'll be fine."

"Even if they knew I found him, it's not connected to me." Unless he'd told them he'd given me the key, of course. Even if Inclar had talked about the key in connection with a woman he'd met, they might think him crazy enough not to worry about pursuing it.

"Let's hurry," I added. The itch to find Jake had become a growing hole, deep and wide and gaping. I leaned over to pick up the towel-wrapped light.

Ethan glanced at it curiously. "What's with the towel?"

I shivered a little, remembering Harmony's fear. "A memory of Inclar is imprinted on the flashlight. That's how I knew he was here—before I found him. I don't want to feel it again."

"Ah. I see." He shrugged off his jacket and placed it around my shoulders before switching on his own flashlight. The setting was dim, not something that would call attention to us, but helped immensely to illuminate our path through the brush. He took my hand, and we moved in silence toward the music.

"How accurate is your timing of imprints?" he whispered after a moment. "Are you sure Inclar was alive last night?"

"Pretty sure. Besides, he didn't look like he'd been there long."

"Was he stiff? That could pinpoint the time of death a little."

"I didn't exactly touch him. Well, I did step on him. I don't think he felt stiff, but I can't be sure."

Ethan nodded. "So he was killed sometime after the imprint and before you found him. That doesn't narrow it down much."

"A coroner should be able to pinpoint it better."

"I wonder who killed him." This he said idly, not really expecting a reply.

I answered anyway. "My bet is on Gabe. He could have done it last night or early this morning before he left for Portland."

"And leave him in the woods all day for someone to find?"

"He could have wounded Inclar and locked him up. Maybe he got loose and died trying to leave."

"I guess." Ethan's face was lit up momentarily by a patch of moonlight, and his features were drawn and anxious. I liked knowing that he wasn't as calm as he seemed.

At the same time we both noticed a faint light coming in our direction. Or sort of in our direction. A bit off to the right. "You go ahead," Ethan whispered, snapping off his light. "Maybe they're looking for you. I'll stay here behind this tree. Shout if you need me."

If it was the killer, he meant, but we both avoided saying that. I moved on ahead, more carefully now without the light. My feet were frozen, but at least I still had Ethan's jacket.

Oops. Ethan's jacket. Too late to give it back. I wondered what excuse I could give for somehow ending up with a man's jacket in the middle of the woods.

My body tensed as the light in front of me grew larger. A lantern, I saw now, swinging from someone's hand. I squinted, trying to make out the person carrying it.

Please don't be the killer, I thought.

"Autumn? Is that you?" Someone rushing toward me, and in the next second I was being hugged to Jake's chest so tightly I couldn't breathe. He must have been looking for me for some time and with ample concern, because worry was imprinted on his jacket. Faintly, but enough for me to feel uncomfortable so close to him. I drew away, as he held up the lantern, looking me over. His forehead was deeply furrowed, and his locs were in disarray, as though tree branches had pulled at them during his search.

His smile died as he took note of the sweatshirt jacket I wore. "You were out here with Ethan, weren't you?"

"He came to make sure I was all right."

Anger flared in his eyes. "Why would you risk being discovered? People noticed you were missing. What happened to contacting him tomorrow night?"

Ethan stepped into the light of Jake's lantern. "That was before she found a dead body."

"What?" Jake scowled at him before turning back to me.

"It was Inclar," I said. "I learned that he'd been here, and I radioed Ethan so he could tell the police, but on the way back to the houses, I stumbled over Inclar's body in the trees."

"You're sure it was Inclar?"

I nodded. As I envisioned the corpse, the shakiness in my stomach returned. I knew the memory of that sightless eye rolled up in Inclar's motionless head would cause me many sleepless nights.

"How did you find out that he was here? Who told—" Jake broke off as he spied the way I held Harmony's useless red flashlight in the towel. He understood at once what it meant because he set down his lantern and gently took it from me, hand towel and all, placing it in the pocket of his jacket. "That bad, huh?"

Ethan looked thoughtfully from one of us to the other, and I felt a rush of irritation at Jake for knowing me so well. "Thanks," I muttered with ill grace.

I shrugged off Ethan's jacket and passed it to him. "You'd

better get going," I told him. To Jake, I added, "He's driving into town to notify the police about Inclar."

"Isn't that going to throw off our plans?" Jake said. "I mean, if the police show up?"

"A man is *dead!*" I reminded him. "We have to report it. They might cover it up if we don't. In fact, now that you're here, we should both go with Ethan. The police will have to look into it now."

Jake's body tensed. "You're right. You should definitely go with Ethan. But I can't leave yet. I'm going to look around, starting tonight when everyone's sleeping. That's what I came for."

I gave him a stubborn glare. "I thought you came because of me."

"Well, that too. But now there's another reason." He hesitated a heartbeat before adding, "I saw her."

Ethan's face became animated. "My sister?"

"No, a girl who looks like Victoria Fullmer. If it is her, she's gained a lot of weight, and she's a bit out of it. Vacant, dreamy. She was with a few other women who brought food out to the tables. I didn't have the chance to talk to her."

"Then we can't leave yet," I decided. "And no"—I held up a hand to silence the words I knew Jake would speak—"I'm not leaving without you. That's final."

I waited for Ethan to insist on everyone leaving, but he only nodded. "Okay, but be careful." He looked at Jake. "Can you find your way back?"

"No problem."

"As long as you keep an eye on each other, you should be okay."

Jake nodded. "We'll be fine."

We all seemed to be adjusting to the fact that there was a dead body in the forest not far from us, some adjusting better than others. Of course, I was the only one who had actually seen the corpse, so it was only natural that I'd feel the most creeped out.

Ethan reached over and squeezed my shoulder. "I'll see you soon." It was a promise, no doubt an attempt to make his intentions toward me clear to Jake.

"Okay," I said. Jake's face was impassive.

"Bye," Ethan muttered and turned away. I watched as the darkness swallowed him.

"Show me where the body is." Jake retrieved his lantern.

I made a face. "I'm not sure I can find it again. It was somewhere past the bathrooms near the end of that side house. But farther out in the woods. I think."

"If I get you close, do you think you could find the place?"

"Maybe."

Jake slipped off his jacket and pulled it over my bare arms, ignoring my feeble protests. I relented because already his worry had faded from his jacket. Most clothing imprints are like that—fleeting. If the jacket hadn't been leather and Jake's emotion so strong, it probably wouldn't have held the imprint in the first place.

"We'll have to hurry," Jake said. "Korin will be looking for us."

"You told him I was gone?"

"No, but I heard him ask a woman where you were, and she said she'd left you out here with a flashlight. Of course I couldn't tell them about your lack of a sense of direction."

"The light broke."

He nodded. "When you dropped it because of the imprint. I figured that much. Anyway, since I was going to the outhouse myself, I volunteered to look for you."

"You found it by yourself?"

"No. They gave me this lantern and sent a boy to show me the way. Once we got there I told him I could manage."

We tromped through the woods in silence for a few minutes. The music was louder now, and with the movement my feet felt warmer. I flexed my toes into the dirt of the forest floor and felt strangely comforted.

"Okay," Jake said. "There's the outhouse."

"This looks almost right. Maybe farther into the forest."

After a minute more of walking, my flesh became alive with goose bumps. Not anything to do with my talent but because the area looked familiar. "Around that tree," I panted. I remembered vividly the shock of seeing Inclar lying in the dirt, and my stomach grew taut as I anticipated the body.

It was gone.

"Are you sure this is the place?" Jake asked.

"It was right here. I swear!" There was the tree beneath where Inclar had lain, the gap in the leaves where light had flickered down to his sightless good eye. "See, there's an impression." But the light from the lantern was too weak to show details.

Jake studied the spot doubtfully, moving the lantern slowly over the spot. He was probably remembering how terrible I was with directions, but I was sure we'd found the right place. It *felt* right.

"Are you sure he was dead?" Jake asked.

"I'm sure."

"Did he have any wounds? Maybe he was just passed out."

"He. Was. Dead," I insisted, punctuating every word.

With a shaky hand, I reached out and touched the tree, feeling nothing except the ancient calm feeling that pervaded the entire forest. I fell to my knees and scrabbled in the dirt, searching for something, anything, that might have retained an imprint of Inclar's final moments.

"It's got to be here. Something's got to be here. He was dead. I saw it!" Even I recognized the frantic note in my voice. Had I been imagining all of it? Had Inclar even been here at all?

Jake grabbed my hands and held them. "I believe you."

The words calmed me, and after a minute, he began brushing the dirt and decaying plant matter from my hands. The smell of the mixture was sweet and foresty; his touch was gentle and hypnotic.

After a moment, he pulled me to my feet and picked up his lantern. "Let's get back."

"What will I say about how long I was gone?"

"How about you saw a squirrel or something and followed it. Then you tripped and your light broke and you got lost. I found you when you called out."

"I guess." I was too mentally and physically exhausted to come up with an alternate scenario of my saving him, as I might have on another day.

We'd gone only a few yards when a light flickered in the distance, from the direction I thought might be the outhouse.

"Then again," Jake said nearly under his breath, "we've both been out here a long time. And if a dead body really was here, we might need something more convincing to cover our tracks." With a smooth motion, he stopped and pulled me into his arms.

And kissed me.

The kiss was warm and exciting and promising all at once. I felt as if I were on a roller coaster plunging down a vertical incline and yet cradled in a hot tub full of bubbling water. Not at all a casual kiss between friends. Not simply pleasant, but filled with mind-tingling, heart-pounding passion. The kind of passion that made a woman forget everything else. I opened my mouth to his, tasting him. Pushing myself closer.

I hadn't expected this, but it was everything I'd thought it could be. Did he feel it too? Because, friendship or no, I wanted more than anything for this kiss to be real.

Chapter 15

"There you two are." Korin loomed from behind the trees, looking large in the dancing shadows cast by his lantern, a bear of a man. "We were beginning to worry."

Jake gave his spiel about finding me, and Korin put a comforting hand on my back as if I were an old friend. "I'm glad Jake found you. You're probably freezing. Poor thing."

"It's better now with Jake's jacket."

Not to mention the kiss, but Korin didn't comment on that, though he didn't seem surprised, either. I remembered Harmony's comment about Korin liking me. His calm reaction to Jake's and my supposed closeness didn't seem to validate her idea. Unless I'd taken her meaning wrong.

"Let's get something warm into you. And on you." Korin gently propelled me in the direction of the houses, or at least what I hoped was in that direction. "It gets quite cold out here at night even in the summer. We should have fixed you up better before sending you out into the wilderness like this. We'll change all that tonight before you go to bed." He gave a hearty chuckle.

I craned my neck, trying to see Jake's face, but he was behind us now. No chance of glimpsing how he'd felt about our encounter.

The party was winding down when we returned, and Korin deposited me near a fire barrel before going off to find someone to assign me a bed. Jake had his hands shoved deep into the pocket of his torn jeans and didn't meet my gaze. He looked almost like a stranger at that moment in his old clothes, his locs askew, but when I examined his brown face it was all Jake.

"What?" he asked, finally lifting his eyes.

"What was that all about?" I had to bluff my way through the question because it was what I would have done if it hadn't meant anything to me.

"Making it look real, that's all." His dark eyes skidded past mine.

"It sure felt real."

He dragged his eyes back to me. For a moment neither of us spoke. At last he opened his mouth, but I would never know what he was going to say because at that moment Korin returned with a large woman wearing a bright red dress.

"This is Scarlet," Korin said. "She's in charge of housing and clothing, so if you ever need anything in that respect, see her. She'll get you both fixed up with clothes and a bed."

She was big and beautiful and black, and I knew her instantly from the woman in one of Tawnia's drawings, the time she'd been trying to sketch Victoria. All doubts that my sister was sketching scenes from real life were put to rest once and for all.

Scarlet placed her warm brown arms around me. "Ah, child. I heard you got lost." I detected a slight southern accent in her honeyed voice. She was about my height and easily six times my width, but she wore her mass with a confidence that didn't need excusing. Her face was round, and her eyes large and expressive. She was cuddly, for lack of a better word, and I loved her instantly.

I found myself leaning against Scarlet, letting her whisk me away from Jake to a bathing room inside the women's side of the singles' house where she already had water boiling on a big black stove. Apparently the indoor piping Harmony had talked of didn't include hot water, but there was plenty of wood stacked by the stove and more where that came from, according to Scarlet.

"My, don't you have the prettiest eyes," she said as she poured water into a metal bathtub in a corner of the room.

"Thank you." Pretty was a far sight better than weird.

"Would you like a cup of hot tea?"

"Yes, please."

"Why don't you get into the water, child, and I'll bring it to you."

I shed Jake's jacket and my dress, sighing with pleasure as I edged into the hot water. A few minutes later, Scarlet gave me a humongous cup of herbal tea and left me alone to soak. Was it safe to drink? Well, nothing I'd eaten here so far had done any damage.

Sipping, I surveyed the room from the big tub, noticing the triple line of tiny cubbies full of toothbrushes, hairbrushes, and accessories. Next to that was the largest sink I'd ever seen, and a wide mirror.

I used a bit of shampoo from a large communal bottle on the nearby table, smelling the sweet scent of chamomile. The bottle had no label, and I suspected it was Harmony Farms's own brand. The lump on the back of my head wasn't nearly as bad as it had been Friday morning, and as I gently washed the area, I remembered Shannon's measuring it. Had he learned any more about the case? I wished I could tell him about finding Inclar.

Scarlet returned shortly with a stack of towels and a flannel nightgown that was long and billowy and comfortable. She clucked over a scrape on my big toe, bandaged it with deft hands, pulled socks over the bandaged foot and over the good foot, too, and finally toweled my short hair until it was almost dry.

"There now," she said. "I bet that feels a darn sight better. You just brush your teeth right here, and then it's off to bed. I took the liberty of movin' some of your personal objects here earlier. We use this toothpaste. It's biodegradable."

I reached for the toothbrush in the indicated cubby and saw that it was indeed mine, complete with its yellow plastic cover. Somehow it didn't feel awkward, her going through my things, though a part of my brain said that it should. I didn't even mind sharing toothpaste with strangers. My sister would be appalled.

When I was finished, Scarlet put another arm around my shoulders and led me down a narrow hall to a small room with two wooden bunk beds and the same cheap linoleum floor as in the hallway.

"I've already put your things in the dresser," she said, "except for what you won't be needin'. And there's more, includin' a jacket and shoes, if you want them. We can't have you catchin' your death of cold. It may be summer, but nights are still cool here till August."

I spied my suitcase on one of the lower bunks, a small pile of rejected T-shirts and Jake's jacket lying nearby. My stomach tightened as I opened the case and saw that it was empty except for the wad of cash Ethan had given me, the useless cell phone, and the two-way radio that had been in the pocket of my dress.

My heart sank. At least Inclar's key hiding under the lining still seemed to be safe. Maybe.

"I'm washin' your dress," Scarlet drawled. "Hope that's okay. There was dirt on it. I'll bring it back later. It's a pretty thing for dances."

Was she going to let me keep the radio too? Ethan had been careful to choose one that resembled a regular radio, but anyone who looked closely might understand its real function.

Korin appeared in the doorway. "Everything all set?"

Scarlet motioned to the suitcase. "I think Autumn here has brought us some things."

Korin smiled as he scooped up the eight hundred dollars and the electronics from my suitcase. "Won't need these. This phone is useless out here. The radio too. But we can sell them, and it will help support the cause."

I wanted to ask what would happen if I didn't stay.

He extended a paper on a clipboard. "This is the asset transfer paper. You'll see that it's conditional for the first year. Just fill in the blank with your legal name and sign it."

Scanning the document, I saw the complicated wording did appear to be conditional, but it was confusing enough that it might actually be binding from day one. I signed the name Sandra Bernard with a hand that definitely didn't resemble my own.

"We're very happy you're with us, Autumn." Korin took the paper, glancing briefly at it. "I hope you will be content here."

"Oh, I think she'll fit in right well," Scarlet said. She picked up Jake's jacket. "You might want to return this to that young fellow."

"Wait!" I reached for it. "Harmony's flashlight is in the pocket. I dropped it and it broke. Will you tell her I'm sorry? I hope it can be fixed." I uncovered half the flashlight, holding it with the jacket.

Korin didn't take it. "Harmony lent you her flashlight?"

"Yes."

He still didn't take it but studied me. "You felt something when you touched it, didn't you? What did you feel?" His voice was comforting and compelling, and I wanted to tell him everything. About his brother's attack, Inclar's conversation with Harmony, and his body lying in the forest. Korin had arrived with us, so it was unlikely that he was responsible for his brother's death. Besides, I'd seen him give Inclar money, so there had to be love or some kind of connection between the two brothers.

Korin waited, but before I could spill everything, Scarlet took the flashlight and pushed it into Korin's hand. "Hush, now. Stop grillin' the child. Some rest is what she needs, and she ain't going to get much of that if she don't get to bed. Now get on with you." To my relief, she shooed him out the door and partway down the hall.

He slapped at her hands as he left and said with a light note, "Scarlet, I don't know how I'd run this place without you."

"You just keep rememberin' that," she said.

When she came back to me, I was studying the bunk beds. I hadn't expected so many beds in such a small room.

"Everyone shares in the beginnin'," Scarlet said. "That's part of the fun. Later you have a choice, though most of us still choose the bigger room and the company."

This was a bigger room? Well, it was large enough for three feet between the two bunk beds and contained four narrow dressers, a small electric heater, and a built-in closet, so I guess that was their idea of luxury. I'd hate to see what the small rooms looked like. As for sharing, I didn't mind since I needed to ask questions. I only hoped my roommates were willing to talk.

"So this half of the house has rooms for the single women?" I asked, wondering about Jake.

"That's right. There's a separate entrance to the men's side. But we're buildin' a new house for families back through the trees on the other side of the square, so we women are gonna move over to the old married building soon and give this whole place over to the men. Then we'll all have a bit more space. The men are sleepin' on triple bunks right now." She hugged me to her rounded bosom. "I'm so glad you're here, child. You just let me know if you need anythin'."

"Thank you."

She released me, gathering up my suitcase and the clothes she'd marked for discarding. I sighed at losing my Hard Rock Café T-shirt from Las Vegas, but it was time for a new one anyway.

"I can't keep my suitcase?" I asked, wanting to check for the key.

"Don't worry. It just goes in a closet out there in the hall. Not enough room to store it in here. Come on, I'll show you. Oh, but you can keep these." She set down the suitcase and took my earrings out of her pocket. "We normally sell the gold and gem jewelry. But these are plastic, so you should keep them. We make prettier ones here if you'd like to learn how."

I was glad to have them back. At least Ethan could still

track me, even if I put the uncomfortable things in the pocket of my jeans instead of in my ears.

When Scarlet started to reach for the suitcase again, I beat her to it. "I'll carry it," I said. "You have the clothes. What do you do with those anyway?"

"We make them into rags. We don't throw much away."

I followed her from the room, awkwardly unzipping the case a little to check for the bulge of the key. Still there. I stifled a sigh of relief.

The closet was two doors down and stuffed with other cases, linens, cleaning supplies, and odd furniture. "This way if anyone ever needs to go anywhere," Scarlet explained, "they have a case to use. We share them. I hope that's okay."

I doubted I had a choice, so I nodded. At least there was no lock on the door, which meant I could get Inclar's key whenever I needed. It was safer in the case than in my room.

The outer door opened, and women began to stream in, talking and laughing, though in a more subdued manner than I'd expected from this college dorm setup. They greeted me as they passed, smiling and nodding.

"Autumn!" Spring came through the doorway and launched herself at me. "I heard you were lost. I'm so glad you're back! Are you okay?"

"She was just a little cold and dirty," Scarlet assured her. "But we fixed that right up. Now where's that angel child of yours?"

"Oh, one of the women has him. He fell asleep, so she let me lay him down in the kitchen by the stove." To me, she added, "They keep a bed there for babies to sleep in while they cook. She said she'd bring him as soon as the dishes were done."

"He's in good hands, then. We're all family here." Scarlet

turned back inside the closet and grabbed the frame of a wooden toddler bed, standing on end. "Think this'll be big enough for your boy?"

"Oh, he'll sleep with me."

Scarlet released the bed. "Okay, but if you change your mind, it's right here. Those little ones grow awful fast and wiggle a lot. A woman needs her sleep. Especially around here. Lots of work to do." She clapped her hands. "To bed now, everyone. The mornin' comes early, even on fast days."

The women were already filing to their rooms. I guessed everyone had already used the outhouse, but I wondered what Spring would do with her son. Or maybe he was still in diapers.

Scarlet led Spring to the room across the hall from mine. "We're not together?" Spring frowned, her eyes troubled.

"No, child, you're in with me." Scarlet placed her big brown arm around Spring's thin shoulders. "At least until a private room opens up. I wanted to be sure to help with that little boy of yours. Been a long time since we had one that cute 'round here." She winked at me, and I was glad to see Spring smiling again.

"I'm just across the hall," I told her.

She hugged me. "Everyone is so nice. I feel so safe here. It's exactly what I thought it would be."

I wondered if she'd still feel the same after three days of fasting, and I also wondered if all the other women and men might be a little resentful at having to fast because of us, though I hadn't seen anything from them that showed such emotion. Maybe they were accustomed to fasting often.

Back in my room, a girl with dark hair and slanted eyes was already in one of the lower bunk beds, wearing pajamas made from the same flannel as my gown. Her face was sharp, pointed, delicate, reminding me of the classic renditions of pixies or fairies.

"I'm Autumn," I said. "I saw you earlier, but I don't know your name."

"I'm Essence," she replied in a soft, childlike voice.

"Nice."

She laughed. "I may change it again. I feel different sometimes."

"Does anyone use their real names?"

"I never ask." She gazed through me as she spoke, almost as though I wasn't there at all.

"Are we the only ones who sleep in here?" I pressed.

"There's another girl, too."

"What's her name?"

"Misty. She works in the kitchens."

"No one else? There's four beds."

She had to think hard about that. "There was another woman, but she moved to a private room last fall when there was an opening."

"An opening. Someone got married, huh?"

"No."

"Then what happened?"

"It was a woman, and she got sick. I haven't seen her, so I think she left."

"Do a lot leave?"

She shrugged. "I don't know."

"What do you do here?"

"I tend the herbs in the greenhouse."

Ah, so that explained why I was her roommate. "I'm interested in herbs, too. I brought some herbal remedy books."

"That's nice." Essence closed her eyes, ending any hope of

extracting more information. "Turn out the light when you're ready, okay?"

I sat on my own bed, feeling suddenly restless. Now that the fear and cold were at bay, my body was raring to go, the sleep I'd had in the van enough to last me a few more hours. Did I dare sneak out and take a peek around?

I stood and started for the door but found I wasn't brave enough to leave the room. Inclar's corpse being missing was even more frightening than my knowing where it had been. Could someone have come across it as I had and moved it to protect the children? Surely they would call the police in that case.

Of course, that didn't really matter because Ethan was already on his way to talk to the police. I hoped he didn't try to call me on the radio, though, now that Korin had it. Ethan wasn't supposed to call, but he might in an emergency.

I crossed to the narrow dresser where Scarlet had put the belongings she'd considered acceptable. My underclothes were all there, as well as my face cleanser, moisturizer, and Jake's comfrey salve. In the second drawer I found a half-dozen T-shirts with the commune logos. The next drawer held the two pairs of jeans I'd brought and a pair of the sturdy homemade work pants I'd seen both the men and the women wearing here. The bottom drawer held socks in good condition but obviously not new.

The small closet, I found, was divided into four slots. One was empty, two had five or six hanging items, and one held a dress and skirt near my size. Like the socks, they were in good condition but had obviously been washed before. Below these were a pair of sturdy oxfords, which I could tell right away were too large. I bent to touch them, but the imprints were so faint

I couldn't tell who they might have belonged to. At least they weren't negative. My feet weren't as sensitive at feeling imprints as my hands, and normally people didn't feel anything strongly enough at foot level to leave much of an imprint, but wearing strongly imprinted shoes could be as severe a problem for me as stepping barefooted into that confessional had been.

I cast a glance at Essence, but she didn't move and her eyes were still shut. I ran my hands across the clothes in the closet, unsurprised when nothing of interest jumped out at me. Above the sparse clothing were small shelves, one for each person. Mine held my two herb texts and my parents' poetry book, one was empty, and the other two held a scattering of paper and pens, bead jewelry, a lovely clay vase, a bottle of lotion without a label, and a faceless religious figurine with a cross on its chest. Nothing more.

I was amazed at the simplicity of the way these people lived. I had never been one to care much about clothing or new things, but my antiques meant something to me. Touching them, seeing them, caring for them. It had nothing to do with the value of the object, but the beauty of the items themselves, the care given them by their original makers or owners, the feeling of connection and continuity. My two roommates had nothing like that. They had tossed off their past lives like so much refuse and hadn't filled them with any substitutes that I could see. No journal, no needlework, no pictures, nothing that gave a hint of who they had become.

I wondered what kind of pain they were in to live this way and what kind of people they had left behind.

I felt compelled to touch the few objects that had either been kept by or given to the women in this shared room. Taking a deep breath, I rested my finger tentatively on the stack of paper and felt nothing strong enough to evoke a scene. The pen was the same, as though my ability had deserted me.

I could only be so lucky.

The tiny, pretty vase was different. It carried a decidedly contented feeling, and I could clearly see the face of the young man who'd made this for one of my roommates. He had a shy expression, the reddest hair I'd ever seen, and a myriad of freckles on his boyish face. No words accompanied what I saw, and I felt almost as though I were peering through a haze because nothing except the boy's face was clear. Odd.

When I touched the religious figurine, swirling images leapt to life, leaving me sickened and weak. Evil images of darkness. *Horror. Fear. Hurry . . . they're coming. "Take this. It's all I have left." I pressed the figurine into another woman's hand. Tears leaked down my face. Pain. Soon there would be more screaming.*

That was all. I couldn't see either of the woman's faces. I didn't know if that was because of my reaction or because the skewed perception belonged to the woman who had owned the object. But the imprints were beginning to replay. Why couldn't I put the figurine down? I didn't want to experience the imprints again, but the figurine remained in my hand as if glued there.

A sound came from the door behind me, and as I whirled to face whoever had entered the room, my fingers lost their hold on the figurine. I bent, grappling to save it, but it shattered on the floor. All there was to do was to look at the broken pieces while I hugged myself, trying not to be sick. I wondered if my roommates would harbor resentment toward me now.

I glanced at Essence, lying on her bed, but beyond cracking an eye for a brief instant, she didn't acknowledge the newcomer or my error. My eyes slid back to the plump young woman standing before me. "I'm sorry. I didn't mean to break it. I shouldn't have touched it."

"It's okay," the woman assured me. "Don't look so upset. It was just an old thing someone gave me. I never liked it, but I didn't know what to do with it. You can touch anything of mine you want any time. I don't mind."

She smiled, and in that instant recognition came to me. This was the young woman I'd seen in the mirror imprint left on her hairbrush, the time when she'd been so angry at her father that she'd wanted to throw it at him.

I'd found Victoria Fullmer.

Chapter 16

I shouldn't have been surprised to see Victoria, given that I knew she'd joined Harmony Farms and Jake had said he thought he'd spotted her. It wasn't even unusual that we were rooming together, as she was one of the more recent residents. But I was surprised—and saddened—at her appearance. The nineteen-year-old had aged dreadfully, the sudden weight gain doing most of the damage. But there was also a fearfulness in her that I hadn't felt in her imprints, a fear I hadn't noticed in the other disciples. Or hadn't wanted to notice. Victoria's weight wasn't a matter of genes or part of the process of aging but a protective covering. I saw that as clearly as if she'd told me herself. Unlike with Scarlet, the weight didn't sit at all naturally on Victoria's small frame. The Fullmers would be horrified to see their daughter now.

Victoria—called Misty, now—helped me clean up the broken bits of the figurine before slipping out of her shoes, exchanging her skirt and blouse for pajamas, and climbing rather laboriously to the top half of my bunk and stretching out. Even her toes were swollen, reminding me of cute, chubby baby feet, except that her toenails were in desperate need of a trim.

"I moved up here when I heard you were coming," she said, her breathing strained.

"If you'd rather have the bottom bunk, we can trade."

"It's okay. I don't mind at all."

Minutes later she was asleep. I'd lived at home during my brief stint in college, so I didn't know for sure how dorms were, but these roommates didn't fit into my idea of sisterly bonding. I'd chatted more with complete strangers I'd never see again. If I'd actually joined Harmony Farms, I'd be having second thoughts about now.

I was being selfish, of course. Neither of my roommates had any idea that I'd been lost in the woods and had discovered a dead body. They didn't know I could read imprints. Of all possible gifts, why did I have this particular one? I could have personally gotten more out of, say, premonition. Winning a lottery would give me an opportunity to help a lot of people.

I started to set my earrings on the dresser but changed my mind at the last moment and nestled them inside my extra underclothes. Once the light was off and I was in bed, I felt even more sorry for myself. I bitterly missed Tawnia and Jake and Bret. Was Tawnia drawing now? Had she seen me in the trees with Inclar's body? I hoped not. She'd be freaking out even without the pregnancy hormones.

I wasn't in the least tired. Every nerve felt alive, perhaps because of all the honey I'd taken in my hot tea. Come to think of it, I might be feeling restless because drinking so much tea had made my bladder stretch tight again. But no way was I going to tromp through those dark woods alone to the outhouse, not with a murderer loose.

Or was there really a murderer? I'd started to doubt myself, thinking maybe Inclar had been sleeping or passed out. I'd never been one for flights of fancy, but this place was getting to me. Or maybe Ethan's worry was getting to me. I'd met Victoria—at least I could report that to her family. Now I only had to find Marcie. If she was here in the singles' dorm, she would have to be one of the women who came back late, like Victoria. Or perhaps she was among the families. After a year she might have remarried and was maybe even expecting another child.

I didn't believe it. Tawnia's picture hadn't shown a happy woman but someone who'd desperately needed help, and after seeing Scarlet, I believed in Tawnia's newfound talent as I'd been forced to believe in mine. Had our birth mother also been gifted in some odd way? Or maybe another relative? Since our birth mother and the doctor who'd delivered us were both dead and no other blood relatives were in sight, it was possible we would never know.

Wherever my ability came from, I felt good about helping Ethan find Marcie and hopefully talking Victoria into coming with me when I left.

Aside from my stretched bladder, I was warm and comfortable. Except now that I was alone in the dark, accompanied only by the soft snores of my two companions, my mind went inevitably to the day's events and particularly the two kisses. One too brief to really savor, and Jake's, the kiss that hadn't felt like friendship. Even thinking about it made my heart feel funny. Not funny ha-ha but funny as though I might pass out.

Or was that my bladder?

I pushed myself to my feet. Well, while I was awake, I could at least investigate the women's dorm. On stockinged feet, I crept slowly to the door. The wooden floor creaked, but neither of my companions stirred. Our door was one of the few closed, and it squeaked as I opened it. I guess I should have thought to bring oil. Shannon would get a kick out of that idea, if he ever found out. He and his fellow detectives probably carried a can around in their pocket whenever they planned to sneak around.

Or did detectives always get a warrant first? Probably.

I felt my way down the hallway, lit only by the moonlight filtering through the sheer curtains over the single windows between each set of bunks. In each room everyone seemed profoundly asleep, as though exhaustion had irrevocably claimed them. Shadows reared up in the corners of the room and seemed to flit and dance as I passed, but the movement was only in my imagination.

It was weird. Subdued. Otherworldly. There was no reading with a flashlight or giggling in the dark. Were the women drugged, or just plain overworked?

I didn't think I'd find the answer here, but I was determined to check every room. My heart thumped furiously as I opened the few closed doors, not a lock in sight, but those rooms were tiny and had only a single bed with a sleeping woman. Most of them were older. One gray-haired granny had her mouth wide open under her hooked nose, snoring loud enough to wake her neighbors. No wonder she slept by herself.

Besides the closet and the bathing room, there was nothing else to see. Every bed was occupied, except the one in my room and another in the room next door. Thus, the reason for Jake and his supposed building skills.

I saw no one who remotely resembled Marcie, though I might have been mistaken in the dark. Had she left the commune? If so, why hadn't she contacted her brother? Or was she somewhere else? Perhaps in that dark room where Tawnia had drawn her.

An urgency I couldn't explain fell over me. I needed to find Marcie.

I was hungry, too, despite the dinner I'd eaten. Ravenous, in fact. Only Tawnia would understand how that could be true. I wondered if I could find my way to the kitchen for a snack. I mean, it wasn't as if the fasting day had begun, and I didn't intend to follow it anyway. I'd fast for a good cause but not for joining a commune. I also thought about emptying my bladder somehow in the bathing room, but I remembered Harmony saying the refuse water went to the fields. That was why they only used biodegradable soaps, toothpastes, and shampoos, so using an inside drain was out of the question.

But I really, really did not want to go to the woods. Maybe they had a port-a-potty somewhere.

The outside door to the women's dorms didn't have a lock, either, so I went out onto the long porch overlooking the deserted square. The lights atop the poles were still on but dimmer now, with only the bottom half of the crystal glass gleaming as though there might be two bulbs inside, one for regular use and one to act as a nightlight. The brightness of the moon overhead did a far better job at illuminating the square than the dim light. The tables were gone, and there was no litter anywhere to be seen. Several lights filtered through curtained windows in the married dorm, but even as I watched, they winked out.

The porch moaned horribly as I crossed it, and the outside air was cool, though I was well protected in my long-sleeved flannel nightgown. I edged down the stairs, my feet feeling confined and almost clumsy inside their stockings. It was amazing how the thin covering insulated my feet from the usual sensations.

Only the smallest sound gave warning, and then an arm went around me and another over my mouth. I experienced a sense of déjà-vu, though I realized how unlikely it would be that Ethan could have sneaked back so quickly. That left the person who had killed Inclar. My heart pounded in my chest. I readied my elbow for attack.

"It's me," Jake whispered before I launched the jab. When he was sure I understood, he started to release me.

I avoided my first reaction to sag with relief and slapped his hands away.

"Sorry. I didn't want you to scream."

I certainly was jumpy enough to have screamed, but I wouldn't give him the satisfaction of knowing that.

He was looking at me oddly, and I realized it was because of my gown. "I didn't pack pajamas," I said defensively. Another small point of contention between me and my sister. She believed in pajamas, three fresh pair a week. I, on the other hand, didn't see any harm in sleeping in underclothes or a T-shirt as long as it was fairly clean.

"Looks like something my grandma wears."

Great. Just the image I wanted him to have of me. "I saw Victoria," I said to distract him. "No Marcie, though. Unless she's in the married housing."

"I don't think so. I watched them pretty carefully as they went inside tonight. I did some looking around, too, and there are no hidden rooms that I can find."

"You've been in there?" I jerked my head toward the front house.

He nodded. "Kitchen, big work room, laundry, offices, and rooms for Korin and Gabe. No basement."

"Do you think Marcie left? Maybe we could ask around."

He shook his head. "We'll have to be careful. I mentioned the possibility of leaving to one of the men, and he wouldn't even look at me after that."

"There have to be work places here," I said, thinking of Tawnia's picture. "Where they make the soaps and things. Maybe she's there."

"The kitchen's big enough for that. And the meeting room has tables that probably double as work stations for some of those crafts they sell."

"Well, they have barns and a henhouse."

"Two barns from what I've been able to learn, a big one out behind the married housing and a smaller one beyond the outhouses."

"Oh, and a greenhouse," I added, remembering my new roommate and her herbs. "They raise their own food, so they could have a lot more buildings we don't know about. Any of them could have a secret room."

"Let's go look for them."

I glanced reluctantly toward the woods, but I wasn't quite so afraid now that Jake was with me. Besides, the police would be here soon. "I need a pit stop first," I confessed.

"I want to get another look at where you saw Inclar's body, anyway. Look what I brought." This time instead of the borrowed lantern, he held up a chunky blue flashlight, the one he used at the store back in Portland during blackouts. It had the most powerful beam I'd ever seen.

"They let you keep it? They took Ethan's phone and the radio he gave me."

"Didn't seem to bother them. They did say something about the batteries running out eventually. Apparently, they don't restock batteries often."

"Probably because they're more expensive than whatever's in those smelly lanterns. Plus, they're hard to recycle. Not good for Mother Earth." I caught his smile. "Hey, I can't help it if I happen to agree with some of their beliefs. Humans can be terrible for the environment. I think I'd give up my cell phone altogether if it weren't for Tawnia."

"Thank heavens for Tawnia then. Don't you remember how many times you've had to call me when your car has broken down?"

"Maybe I should give up driving." Winter and Summer had never owned cars.

His grin was mocking. "Maybe. But you won't."

He was right. I needed my car to search for antiques. I was a terrible hypocrite. "Come on." I tugged on his arm. "Let's go."

We walked into the woods a short distance before he turned on the flashlight. It wasn't exactly like walking in broad daylight, but the path was completely illuminated, the dark shadows pushed back to a safe distance.

"Here." He shoved something into my hand. An organic blueberry muffin.

Instantly, I forgave him everything. Even for the kiss, which I was thinking about way too much now that we were together and alone, but not for a million muffins would I admit it.

I gobbled my muffin on the way to the bathroom, where Jake waited for me. Then he led me back to the place where I'd seen Inclar's body. With my wonderful sense of direction, I wasn't sure it was the right place until we were actually upon it, but Jake's steps were sure.

With the flashlight it was easier to see the indentation in the sparse shrubbery at the base of the tree where Inclar's head might have been. Something that looked like dragging marks curved off to the left, vanishing into a stretch of undergrowth.

"Wait. Is this blood?" Jake held the light closer to the indentation. A patch of darkness marred the dirt between the greenery, as though someone had poured a cup of used oil there. Except it wasn't glistening like oil. Tiny bits flaked off one of the leaves when Jake moved it aside.

Dried blood.

I was both relieved and frightened at the same time.

"He didn't drag himself away," Jake said.

"No."

"Let's follow it. If they have a hidden place, you can bet that's where they'll put him—at least temporarily."

It took a while to locate a trail, but once we did, it was a matter of following the bits of dried blood and depressed vegetation. Whoever had moved Inclar was either too slight to carry him or hadn't wanted to get blood on his own clothing.

"This isn't going anywhere except toward the dirt road we came in on," Jake said after awhile.

I grunted. I'd thought we'd been going in the direction of the fields.

"We'd better be careful, then," I said. "Because of the guards."

"Guards?" Jake stared at me.

"Ethan said he saw some."

"Did they have guns?"

I shrugged. "I don't know."

Jake switched his light to a lower setting, and we crept along. When we reached the road, the signs of dragging and blood vanished altogether. Jake indicated the hard-packed dirt. "Must have loaded him into something."

"Did they go out or in past the house?" Earlier I'd noticed another dirt road skirting the married housing, presumably the way to the barns or fields.

"They could hide him anywhere. There's nothing for miles. Three hundred acres, plus all the land between here and Rome." Jake scrubbed a hand across his face, which for some reason made me stare at his lips.

He caught my eye. "Uh, Autumn, about before."

"You mean when you kissed me?" The words fell from my lips before I could bite them back.

"I hope it was okay. We're still friends, right?"

Friends. I hated that word. "Don't be ridiculous. It'd take more than a kiss to drive me away." I spoke jokingly, but instead of my words reassuring him, an annoyed glint came to his eyes. Obviously, he wasn't prepared to joke about it.

"Let's follow the road to the larger barn," he said coolly. "It'll be easier than going through the woods, and we won't need the light out here on the road. No use in announcing our presence."

We'd gone about fifty yards when we heard a shout behind us. "Uh-oh," I said.

Jake pulled me off the road, and we began running. I stubbed my bandaged toe painfully on an exposed root.

"Must be a guard," I panted, looking around to see if the man had a gun.

Not one but two men were behind us, though they didn't seem to be carrying anything except flashlights. I hoped I wasn't wrong.

"Split up!" I yelled at Jake. I thought I might be able to outrun them, but the darkness was making speed difficult.

"No!"

Ignoring him, I curved away and sprinted for a large tree. If I could reach it before they caught up to me, I could use the tree to change my direction without being seen. Behind me a light bobbed between the trees. I wondered if our pursuers could make out the details of our faces.

I darted around the tree and changed direction. I was mentally congratulating myself when I slammed into a solid figure. Without hesitation, I jerked my foot upward at his flashlight, hitting it with the ball of my foot and knocking it away. It was a move I'd practiced as a teen in my taekwondo class, and I didn't have time to be amazed that it actually worked.

With a grunt he lunged for me. His fist caught the left side of my face, the side Spring's husband had bloodied, making me cry out with pain. The momentum from his punch hurled me backward into a bush, and everything went black for an instant. Then he was coming toward me, his round, flat face lit eerily by the moonlight.

I jabbed at him with my feet, catching him in the chest by surprise. He cried out as he fell. Leaping from the bush, I started to run, but the world spun around me. I forced myself to take a step. I was too slow. A hand closed over my ankle, and for the first time in my life I wished I were wearing heels. Sharp spiky heels that I could use as a weapon.

Down I went, face splatting on the narrow path. It was softer here, not packed like the trail to the bathrooms, but pain reverberated through my left cheek. I had the impression of a fist coming down on the back of my head, and at the last minute, I turned over, limbs flailing. He was on top of me in an instant. I desperately reached for something to use against him. Finding only a handful of dirt, I threw it into his eyes. He bellowed in rage as he rubbed at his face. I dug my elbows into the ground, trying to pull myself out from under him.

He laughed, a mean sound that sent shivers up my spine. He was enjoying this! That knowledge gave me strength, and I managed to move myself a few inches. His body leaned forward, his hands reaching for my neck.

What now? More dirt? Would it even stop him? There was no chance of curling my feet up to use against him as I had done against Inclar. This man was simply too big and heavy. Maybe if I surrendered, I could convince him that I'd gotten lost looking for the outhouse.

I pushed at him, trying to find air. My hand touched his belt buckle, a huge piece of engraved metal at his waist. Images shot through me—terrifying images of rape, torture, of blood welling from a wound. Screams echoed in my ears until I didn't know if the events had happened or were happening now. Maybe I was the one screaming. I saw Inclar's rolling eye. A flash of Gabe's face drawn in anger. And Marcie. Thin to the point of death, her expression one of agony.

Gasping, I pulled my hand away as though I'd touched an open flame. "No," I protested feebly, my last strength drained by the imprint. He laughed again.

Then my scrambling right hand felt a rock, one heavy enough to give me trouble moving it. I hefted it, the jagged edges digging into my skin. With a loud grunt of effort, I brought it up and slammed it into his head.

He crumpled. Unfortunately, he crumpled on top of me, and he was so large that it took more strength to move him than I could coax from my wounded body. My right hand that had wielded the rock felt like it was broken, and the other arm pulsed pain with each heartbeat. That meant I must be bleeding there. Hopefully, not too badly. I made a mental note to ask Shannon to recommend a place for self-defense lessons. I'd need more training if I was going to stay in this line of work.

That's when I knew I was delusional. I was an antiques dealer, nothing more. Coming here had been a huge mistake, and I was going to leave the first chance I got—dragging Victoria with me, if I could.

Provided, of course, that I could get this guy off me before he woke up and finished the job he'd started.

The pain in my arm and wrist were fading a bit, so I pushed at the man's body. It took me three tries before I managed to get enough momentum to roll him off. With relief, I lay next to my unconscious attacker, gulping in air.

When I closed my eyes to rest, the memories of the imprints were still there, a revolving mass of confusion and terror. It was impossible to block out the scenes. I shook uncontrollably. I couldn't place the mishmash of imprints at any exact time, but those of Marcie and Inclar were recent. Very recent.

I don't know how long I lay next to the guard, shuddering and feeling the terror that wasn't mine—and mine had been strong enough to begin with. My skin felt hot and flushed, and my stomach threatened to disgorge the muffin Jake had given me. I was totally and completely exposed.

Sometime later I heard footsteps and felt the gentle touch of Jake's hands. "Autumn, you okay? I've been searching everywhere for you."

I couldn't answer. Tears slid from my eyes and into my hair.

"Autumn, talk to me. Where does it hurt?" When I didn't respond, Jake lifted me so I was sitting. "What did you see?"

This time I was glad he understood what had happened, but I still couldn't talk. "It's going to be okay," Jake murmured, as though to a frightened child. "I'm right here with you." He dropped his flashlight in my lap and pulled me into his arms, cradling me to his chest like an infant.

My hands inadvertently touched his flashlight. I didn't expect an imprint, but suddenly I was looking at myself—a half transparent figure that signaled a fading imprint. One left by Jake.

Autumn was illuminated by the flashlight, her antiques all around her. "Let's have a picnic," she said. "It's almost closing time. Besides, with the snowstorm and the power outage, most people will be heading home."

I/Jake followed Autumn to the back room, where we ate whole wheat crackers and cheese from a grass-fed cow, washing it down with cold herbal tea from the mini fridge. The lack of power was already making itself felt in the store, and I spread a Mexican blanket over Autumn's shoulders to ward off the cold. We were close. I wanted to be closer.

Jake wanted to be closer?

I remembered that day. Jake and I alone in the store at not quite six o'clock, the winter street already dark. I'd thought he was trying to jolt me out of one of my sad moods that day, but now I wasn't so sure. Could he really have felt strongly enough to leave even this faint imprint? Or did I only wish it to be so?

"Autumn?" Jake whispered.

"You hate cold tea." My voice was scarcely a whisper.

"What?"

"This flashlight. We used it the day of the power outage. We drank iced tea, but you hate it cold. I never knew."

"Because we normally drink it hot. The company was good, though, if it left an imprint." There was caution in his voice now, as though he worried what I might make of that.

He didn't need to worry. The imprint was faint, and I really couldn't say that I wasn't imagining it.

"Look, can you move?" Jake asked. "Is anything broken?"

I wanted to smooth away the concern on his forehead, but my hand wouldn't obey the silent order, though I felt much better already. "I'm okay." I blew out a soft, unsteady sigh. "But Marcie's here. Or was a day or so ago. She's somewhere in the dark. They take her food." I had no doubt now that my key opened her door, but finding that door would be difficult. "She's not the only one who's been there. It's what they do to the people who want to leave." Inclar had talked about screaming, and now I knew that the room Marcie was in was somehow connected.

"You could be right," he agreed. "If people started leaving, they'd want their assets back. Imagine the lawsuits, the negative press."

"I'm thinking Marcie had fifty thousand dollars disappear with her, not to mention the proceeds from her furniture. We need to talk to Detective Martin. He'll know how to follow the money trail. I bet Gabe's rolling in fat Swiss bank accounts."

"It could be for the power. For some people, power is everything."

That image didn't go with the one I'd seen of Gabe, but then what did I know of evil masterminds?

Jake took hold of my elbow. "We need to get back to our rooms before these guys wake up."

"You knocked yours out too?"

"Two of them." There was a hint of amusement in his voice. "But even together they weren't as big as this one."

"Girl's gotta do her share."

He chuckled. "Think you can walk? I could carry you."

"I'm okay. But my wrist hurts, and I think my arm is bleeding."

He lowered the setting on the flashlight and ran it over the left sleeve of my nightgown. Sure enough, blood seeped through, but not nearly as much as I'd feared. Jake couldn't get the sleeve of my granny gown up high enough to examine it, but I finally convinced him I wouldn't bleed to death.

I looked down on the face of the unconscious man. "Will they recognize us?"

"Mine won't."

"I don't think this one will. But I can't be sure." I hesitated. "He isn't dead, is he?" Despite the horrific images I'd seen imprinted on his buckle, I didn't want to be the instrument of his death.

"No. He's bleeding a lot, but head wounds tend to do that. It doesn't look like too much swelling. Aside from a headache, I think he'll be fine when he wakes up." Jake's dark tone told me he wished otherwise.

"Don't worry. The police will be here soon. He'll get what he deserves."

"If he doesn't run off first."

There was that. But neither Jake nor I were in a position to do anything to stop him. We couldn't exactly tie him to a tree for the rest of Harmony Farms to discover in the morning.

Jake helped me to my feet and kept his arm around me as we picked our way through the trees. Somehow, I'd run back toward the gate instead of toward the houses, but Jake's internal sense of direction turned us the right way. "This time we go through the trees."

I agreed.

Sudden lights behind us brought a sinking feeling to my

stomach. *Not again!* Seconds later the roar of an engine came within hearing range. "Let's go see who it is," I whispered. "Maybe it's the police."

"Already?"

I shrugged. "Depends on how fast Ethan rode your motorbike. I'm guessing he took that and not the van. Or maybe he found a place to call Detective Martin." I was eager to see even Shannon at this point.

Jake shook his head. "Even if Ethan found service, Portland's too far for Detective Martin to be here so soon."

He had a point. Well, I'd settle for any officer who would take us safely away from here.

Jake and I slipped back toward the gates, under cover of the trees. We went as close as we dared and peered around a large tree. "Uh-oh," Jake said.

There was a rushing sound in my ears. The last time one of us said that, we'd been jumped by the guards. "What is it?" I craned my neck.

"Looks like their leader."

Sure enough, Gabe jumped out of a green sedan and began opening the gate. His face wore an angry, determined look.

Fear crawled down my spine.

Chapter 17

Jake half dragged, half carried me most of the way back to the houses. Instead of appreciating his closeness, I was too busy worrying why Gabe had shown up so early. It was entirely possible that someone else had also discovered Inclar's body and reported it. Regardless of who had killed Inclar, I didn't understand why the corpse had been left where it could be so easily discovered. Unless it hadn't been a corpse at the time it had fallen—there was always that, I suppose.

Was Harmony somehow involved?

I ran over the sequence of events in my mind, but the only thing I knew for sure was that Inclar was dead now and that he hadn't been dead Friday night. I would be interested to know if Korin was aware of his brother's death and what would happen to his belief in Gabe if he did know. Maybe telling Korin what I'd seen would help me discover the truth. He might be on our side.

Another thought occurred to me, stupefying me with its possibility. What if Gabe had driven back now because he'd discovered I was the woman Inclar had attacked? Maybe he knew Inclar had told me things, had given me the key. Maybe he wanted to get rid of me before the police came sniffing around.

Whatever happened, I needed to find Marcie and get her to Ethan. I could imagine how happy their reunion would be. "He never gave up on you," I'd tell her. "He's the reason I came." Because that was true. After it was all over, Ethan and I would date and see what might happen. There was nothing complicated or mixed up about my feelings for him like there was with Jake.

Gabe's sedan had arrived at the houses before we did. Lights glowed in the main house, signaling his presence.

"Can you walk now?" Jake whispered.

"Yes."

He set me down, and I switched off his flashlight that I'd been carrying. We approached the side of the main house, opting for the cool grass instead of the squeaky porch. Before we rounded it completely, Jake's arm shot out and stopped me, putting a finger to his lips.

"He was just gone," a woman was saying urgently. I recognized Harmony's slightly husky tone, though she wasn't laughing now. "He left right after you did."

"Who'd you tell about him?" Gabe's voice was controlled but without the gentleness I'd heard him use with the youth in Portland.

"Just Korin when he arrived."

"Then where is he?"

"I already told you—I don't know."

Presumably they were talking about Inclar. Or his body. But aside from the fact that Gabe had lied to Shannon about knowing where Inclar was, it didn't mean much. Anyone on the farm could have killed him, though my bet was still on

Gabe since he was likely responsible for placing the perimeter guards who'd attacked us. You didn't put guards at a place like this unless you had something to hide.

"I have to be sure this isn't going to cause problems."

"Yes." Harmony's voice was scarcely a whisper.

"You aren't hiding something from me, are you?" A tiny sliver of the gentleness was back in Gabe's voice.

"No. I promise. Come to bed, Gabe. We can worry about this in the morning."

I peeked around the corner and caught a glimpse of them in each other's arms before Jake yanked me back. I tried to reconcile this submissive Harmony with the confident woman who had been teasing Korin earlier. The change of attitude was too noticeable to be a coincidence.

Or maybe she was a good actress.

Could she be involved with Korin? Maybe the two of them were plotting together. No, I couldn't see that. Korin had been too deferential to Gabe. I couldn't forget the tears in his eyes back at the hotel in Portland.

I felt a stab of frustration. We had a dead body that had disappeared, a missing woman in a locked room we couldn't find, and no solid evidence.

Silence had crept over the square, signaling Gabe and Harmony's departure, but only after the lights in the main house winked out did Jake let me head back to the women's dorms. He hugged me tightly before we parted in the square and whispered, "Be careful."

"I will."

I wondered what time it was. We'd been gone for hours, I was sure. Maybe longer. We hadn't started sneaking around until after one, and given that sunrise came near five-thirty, and the sky started getting light sometime before that, we might not have much time before everyone woke up. After all, there were cows to be milked, eggs to gather, pigs to slop, horses to feed. In fact, I was pretty sure the sky was getting lighter already.

As I opened the door to go inside, my worry turned to horror when I caught sight of my nightgown, now streaked with dirt and torn in two places. Not to mention the blood drying on the sleeve. I'd have to stash this some place and wear a T-shirt from now on, taking care to dress after everyone else was in bed so they wouldn't ask what had happened to the gown.

It doesn't matter, I reminded myself. *The police are coming, and by tomorrow night I'll be back in my own bed wearing whatever I want.*

I did need to look at my arm, however, and maybe find something to wrap around my right wrist. Thankfully, I'd seen where Scarlet kept the first aid kit when she bandaged my toe earlier. I felt my way to the bathing room and closed the door behind me, at last flipping on a light that had me blinking at its brightness.

Retrieving the first aid kit above the rows of cubbies, I pulled down the elastic neck of my granny gown to get a look at the wound. I had to manipulate my arm just right to see a nasty puncture from whatever I'd fallen on. Hopefully nothing that would cause an infection. They had a little antibiotic cream in the first aid kit, but I would really have preferred to use a little comfrey and goldenseal. Since I hadn't brought anything but Jake's comfrey salve for my bruised face, I'd have to familiarize myself with their stock of herbs to make a good poultice.

Not that I'd have much time since Ethan should be back soon with the police.

I hummed as I wet a rag and wiped the drying blood from my arm, thinking of Ethan and going home. Tawnia and I would laugh about all this someday—after she stopped being angry at me for not leaving the farm sooner.

I tried not to think of the guard I'd left unconscious in the woods, knowing that he'd come to or be found soon. Instead of worrying about him, I'd be better off using my time praying he wouldn't recognize me.

Soft steps came down the hall, the floor boards squeaking softly. Would they pass by or come inside? I scanned the room for a place to hide. But all I could see was the metal tub where I'd bathed, and its position didn't afford much protection. Better to bluff my way through than to be discovered trying to hide. I held my breath. For a few blessed seconds, it seemed as if the steps would go on past, but as my muscles began to relax, the door cracked open.

"Who's here?" Victoria stood in the doorway, blinking at the sudden light. "Autumn? Is that you?" Pause and then a little gasp as her eyes adjusted. "Oh, my goodness, what happened to you?"

"Nothing. I'm fine. I—uh—I had to go the bathroom. It was dark. I fell."

"Oh, you poor thing!" Closing the door behind her, she moved quickly over the space between us. "You should have woken me. I would have taken you."

"I didn't want to be any trouble."

"No trouble. I can never sleep past four-thirty even on fast days. I'm too used to being in the kitchen making sure the men have breakfast when they come in from milking. I thought since I was up, I'd start boiling water for baths. We don't have water heaters here. Yet. They have one at the main house. One of those electric ones that heats water right when you use it. We'll be getting one here soon."

She had taken over cleaning and bandaging my arm. "In the winter we keep a port-a-potty in here for emergencies. It gets really cold, even with our electric heaters. Wow, that must have been some fall," she added, eyeing my face. "I mean, you had a cut and bruise before, little bit of a black eye, but now it's much worse. What happened anyway? The first time, I mean."

"Spring's husband was trying to make her go home with him, and I got in the way."

"You mean that new girl with the cute baby? I watched him last night while he was sleeping in the kitchen. Darling boy. Her husband wanted her to stay?" She sounded almost envious.

"He wasn't finished beating her."

"Oh." Victoria swallowed noisily. "Anyway, you should do something about your face." She finished the bandage on my arm and pulled me over to the mirror. I stared. The cut on my cheek had ripped open again, there was a spreading bruise on my jaw, and a slew of new scratches. The older bruise under my eye had a new, darker one over it, and purple marks stood out on my throat, deeper than the ones Inclar had left me. I hadn't remembered any of this during the struggle, but now that I saw it, exhaustion leaked through me, stealing what remained of my energy.

I turned to her urgently. "Do you have any makeup? I mean, it would cover a little of this at least. I know you don't wear it now, but you used to, right? Did you bring some with you? Or know someone who did?"

She nodded. "I'll show you what we have. We don't use it much. Well, one of the girls who is sweet on a boy might if she has a pimple or something. Someone always buys a bottle when they go to town." She reached for a small basket next to a table that held a sewing machine. Inside were a half-dozen used bottles of base and cover-up in differing shades.

"Thanks, Victoria."

She froze, the basket stretched between us. "What did you call me?" Her eyes were anxious, looking small in her bloated face.

With a sinking feeling, I realized what I'd done.

"You didn't fall, did you?" she asked.

I shook my head. "One of the guards—"

"No." She held up a hand to stop the words. "I don't want to hear."

"I'm leaving here soon. I want you to come with me."

All the color drained from her face. "I can't," she whispered, her eyes darting to the door and back again. "Please don't let them hear you say that."

"They said I could leave any time."

Her head shook rapidly, but with so little back and forth movement, I couldn't tell if she was saying no or if she was having a seizure.

"Victoria, what's wrong?"

"Misty," she corrected. "And please don't talk that way." Her breath came faster now, her ample chest heaving. She was frightened, horribly frightened.

"Look. I know your name because I talked to your parents. You're why I'm here."

"They sent you?" A new expression flitted over her face, one I almost didn't recognize as hope. But that's what it was. Alive one second and gone the next.

"They've never stopped looking for you."

Tears filled her eyes. "I—I—" She glanced again toward the door.

"We're also looking for a woman named Marcie. She lost her husband and her baby before coming here."

If anything, her fear cranked up a notch, becoming pure terror.

"What is it? Tell me!" I touched her arm, but she pulled away.

"I have to go." She started quickly for the door but stopped before she reached it.

"Please," I begged. "Talk to me."

Without responding, she hurried to a huge armoire next to an old washing machine and pulled out a clean nightgown in the same material as my dirtied one. She threw it in my direction.

The gown fell at my feet. "I can help you," I told her.

"No," she said, "you can't. Stay away from me!" With that, she whirled away.

I stared after her, uncomprehending. If I hadn't already known something was up, her reaction would have cemented any suspicion. She wanted to leave here, maybe had even tried to escape in the past, but something or someone prevented her from trying again.

Who? Only Gabe and Korin and Harmony could wield such power here. Or Scarlet. And maybe some of the guards.

With Victoria knowing my true reason for being here, I now had a new worry. If she told someone, I could be in serious danger. My only hope was that her fear would keep her from doing anything rash until the police arrived.

First things first—I needed to get cleaned up. If Victoria had awakened, others wouldn't be far behind. I pulled off the nightgown as quickly as I could and pulled on the clean one. Then I washed my face, blotted it with a towel hanging on a hook, and dabbed on a bit of cover-up. When I was finished, I could tell I had on makeup, but except for the healthy bruise on my jaw, my face didn't look much different from the day before. Or wouldn't once the cheek scabbed over again. I'd have to remember to put vitamin E on it every day so it would heal more quickly.

I used towels to clean the dirt from my legs, silently grateful for the black socks that had protected the bandage on my big toe. The bit of dust and dirt that had crept through the socks was nothing compared to the dust and dirt on the rest of me. I threw the towel in a basket near the sink and left the room, flipping off the light. Feeling my way in the dark, I found the storage closet and stashed my nightgown behind a suitcase on a top shelf. By the time Scarlet discovered it, I'd be long gone. Maybe everyone would be gone.

Three more creaky boards and I was in my room. Victoria had left the door open, and I was relieved to see her bunk occupied. I'd been worried she'd run outside and blunder into a guard or, worse, go straight to Gabe and Harmony.

I didn't realize until I stopped moving how much my body ached, especially my wrist, which I'd wrapped in a rag, twisting it up and around my thumb to immobilize it as best I could.

Everything at the moment depended on how fast Ethan brought the police and whether or not the guard recognized me.

"Victoria?" I whispered.

No answer.

"I know it might be hard to believe," I told her, "but somehow I'm going to make sure everything is okay—for both of us."

Chapter 18

It felt as though I'd no sooner closed my eyes than the world exploded into light and movement. Footsteps pounded down the hall, and people called out to one another. Scarlet and someone else were talking loudly outside our open door. I pried open one eye. Essence was still in bed on the other bottom bunk, but even from below, I could see the top one was made, the corners tucked in neatly under the mattress above the slats that held it. My head ached fiercely, but that was nothing a little tea couldn't help—providing I could find the right herbs.

"It's about time you woke up," Spring said, coming inside the room with her son perched on her hip. She looked better today, though her greenish bruises were still visible. "You must have been tired. Oh, look at your face! It's even worse today."

"Yeah, when I got lost in the forest last night, I fell down pretty hard."

Spring nodded. "Things like this always look worse the next day." Spoken by someone who had reason to know.

Scarlet had followed her in, her large brown eyes soaking up everything about me. "Child, what's wrong with your wrist?"

"Must have happened last night too."

Scarlet clucked her sympathy. "You should have told me. I have somethin' better than that old rag. I keep elastic bandages in a drawer. Come along, now." Her southern accent was deeper this morning, as though she'd been steeped in southern dreams. I wondered where she came from and how she'd ended up here.

"Where's, uh . . . Misty?" I said, forgetting for a moment Victoria's new name. At least I didn't call her Victoria, which was an improvement over last night.

"She's getting breakfast for the little ones. They don't fast, of course."

My stomach rumbled at the notion of food. After pulling on some jeans and a commune T-shirt, and slipping Jake's comfrey salve into my pocket, I left my unmade bed and let Scarlet lead me back to the bathing room, where she wrapped my wrist. The pain wasn't as bad as when I'd first injured it, but the joint felt stiff. When she finished, I rubbed salve into the scratches on my face and touched up the makeup as Spring watched with interest. I offered her some for her own bruises, and she accepted with a smile. She looked young and carefree this morning, the fear gone or at least laid to rest temporarily. I hoped nothing I did at the farm would change that for her.

"About the fast," I said to Scarlet, my stomach driving me to distraction, "we can drink, right?"

"If you want, though many choose not to the first day."

"It's just my headache. I could use some herbs."

"Come over to the kitchen. I'll show you where we keep them."

"I'll come along," Spring said. "I need to feed Silverstar." She kissed the boy's face exuberantly.

The back door to the main house opened to a large entryway that would have been more usually found in the front of most houses. But then this door was, for all intents and purposes, the main entrance. Across from the entrance I glimpsed a door to a large room with several women inside, but Scarlet turned left down the hall and then veered left again into the huge kitchen. Delicious smells preceded our arrival, making my stomach eager with its protests.

Two long tables filled much of the available space in the kitchen, their scarred wooden tops showing they were well used—and for more than just eating. A handful of children sat devouring a breakfast of bacon, eggs, and hash browns—all of which, Scarlet informed me, were grown or raised right here on the farm. Cups of foamy milk sat before the children, and I wondered if it was still warm from the morning's milking. A few vacant places showed where other children had already eaten, their empty plates awaiting removal. A pile of bacon was growing on a plate near Victoria, who stood cooking before an industrial-sized wood stove.

Light poured in through large windows that faced the back porch and the square. The curtains were open, and I could see men and boys outside, walking around purposefully. A few young girls emerged from the direction of the outhouses. Only two women were tending the smaller children in the square, and I wondered where the rest were and what they were doing.

My eyes riveted once again on the pile of bacon. I sighed a little too loudly. Victoria glanced at me and then away again.

"Right here's the herbs," Scarlet said, showing me to a row of wooden boxes with a knob on the top of each lid. "They're all marked. Feel free to use whatever you want. We always have a pot of water boilin' here for tea." She turned to Spring. "Would this boy like some oatmeal? There's a pot here, all cooked and ready to go."

"I'm sure he would," Spring said.

I made myself some feverfew and raspberry tea, and while it was steeping, I made up a comfrey poultice using olive oil as a base and put it on my left arm, rebandaging it. I saved a bit in the bottom of the cup to put on when I changed the bandage again later. Though the police should arrive soon, there would be a long drive back to Portland, and I wanted a head start on healing before Tawnia saw me.

I was relieved that there were no imprints on the dishes or utensils I used, or on the herb containers, though I hadn't really expected any. These were mundane objects no one really cared about. I could almost pretend to be normal and that I was at Harmony Farms because I wanted to be.

Scarlet paused in gathering used dishes from the table. "That's a great talent you have."

For a crazy moment I stiffened, thinking she meant reading imprints, but she was only referring to the herbal remedies, which to me could hardly be called a talent. I'd mixed my own herbs with Summer from my earliest childhood.

"I could do better steeping it a few weeks and then mixing it with beeswax and a little lavender," I told Scarlet. "I make all my own salves, poultices, and lip glosses that way."

"I can't wait for you to show us how. Now we mostly just wash and package herbs to sell. We'd have to buy the beeswax, though. That's one thing we haven't gotten into yet. We usually trade for our honey."

I nodded, my eyes drifting to the pile of bacon Victoria was bringing to the table. What I wouldn't do for a piece—or ten.

Scarlet laughed. "It's mind over body, child. Don't you worry. We'll keep you busy. You'll be proud of yourself once you're finished."

I was pretty sure the only thing I'd be was hungry. I felt as weak as a kitten.

Classic cult tactics, I thought. *Starve the people, work them hard, wear them down. Makes them pliable.*

"Open your mouth, Silverstar," Spring crooned to her son. "Look, there's raisins and honey. Yum."

Besides Victoria, Scarlet, Spring, a few remaining children, and the teenager washing dishes, we were alone in the large kitchen. "Where is everyone else?" I asked.

"Working," Scarlet answered. "We make quilts and clothes on Sundays. Or the women do. We take a break from the fields and crafts, but if we don't do the sewing, we won't have clothes to wear. We enjoy talking to each other."

"And the men?"

"Out with the animals and taking care of other odd jobs. We'll have a meeting later on, all together."

Spring's face glowed. "Did you hear? Founder Gabe's back. We learned about it this morning while you were still sleeping. Aren't we lucky?"

At the stove, Victoria's fork clattered to the floor. She tried to catch it but instead bumped the large frying pan and splashed hot bacon grease over the top of the stove.

"Ow!" she cried, shaking burned fingers.

"Gracious me!" Scarlet hurried to help her stick her hands under cold water, which at least was plentiful. I made myself stand and help clean up the black stove. It was really hot, and I wondered how much wood it used—not that it mattered, since they had more old and dying trees in the woods than they could ever use. The children gathered around Victoria until Scarlet shooed them away.

"Do you know a remedy for this burn?" Scarlet asked me.

I stopped my cleaning and walked over to the sink to examine Victoria's fingers. Red but no blisters. "First degree. Not too serious. But it's going to hurt for a while. Best thing right now is that water to stop it from burning anymore. After the pain is bearable, I can make up a comfrey poultice to aid in healing. Vitamin E can help later, if you have some."

Victoria didn't look at my face as I spoke, and I could feel her curling away from me. Scarlet frowned at her reaction but said nothing. I picked up a thick rag and went back to cleaning the stove, careful not to burn myself.

"You keep those fingers under that water," Scarlet said to Victoria. "I'll go get some bandages." I knew she meant the cloth ones like Victoria had used for my arm when she'd discovered me in the bathing room, and that was the best thing for her burn, so I kept silent.

Victoria shook her head, darting another frightened glance at me as I approached to rinse out my rag. "I'll go with you. There's water there too. And I don't want a poultice."

Scarlet shrugged. "Okay, child, whatever makes you feel best." But she raised her eyebrows at me as if to say, "Kids these days. Don't know what's good for them."

Victoria and Scarlet left, followed shortly by the teenager, who'd finished the dishes, even those left on the table by the children. No lack of work ethic here, not even in the young. Spring finished feeding Silverstar and washed her own dish. "I'm going to see what they're all doing. You coming?"

"I'd better put this food away so Victoria and Scarlet won't have to." I knew just the place to put it—in my stomach.

Spring glanced down at what remained on the serving plates. The gaze wasn't in the least covetous, and I gained a new respect for her. "Want help?"

"No. Won't take long. I'll catch up to you."

As she left, I quickly dried my hands, already imagining the taste of the bacon. I grabbed three pieces and shoved one into my mouth.

"Oh, yeah?" Harmony's voice drifted in from the hallway. "Well, I'm not too sure about that." By the sound of her voice, she was heading this way.

I wondered what they did with people who didn't follow the rules. Without thinking, I yanked open the rather odd handle of the walk-in pantry and dived inside, pulling the door nearly closed after me. The door seemed to have some sort of spring, so I had to put my foot at the bottom to make sure it didn't close all the way.

"Did he say why he came back so early?" another voice said. Korin.

"He missed me, I'm sure." Harmony laughed. "Look, no one's here. The children must be finished. Someone needs to put away this food."

I put my eye up to the crack in the door. She looked bright and rested, despite her late night.

"It's Misty's duty this morning," Korin said. "I wonder where she is?"

"Oh, she's not gone far, I'm sure," Harmony said.

Looking around me, I became aware of two things: one, I was cold, and two, I wasn't in a pantry. It was a large refrigerator, with dozens of long, bed-sized racks, the top ones very close together. Many of the lower ones were filled with metal milk jugs and plastic food containers, but the upper ones were completely empty except for what looked like several clear bags full of fresh herbs. That explained the strange outer handle, but at least there seemed to be one in here, too, so I wouldn't get locked in even if they noticed the open door.

Harmony reached out for a slice of bacon and popped it into her mouth. "Oh, goodness," she said with fake brightness. "I forgot it's fast day."

Korin blinked several times. "Harmony, what if they see you?" One hand reached out to touch her, but she skirted out of range.

"Fasting's a dumb idea. We aren't a religion. We're people working together and enjoying life the way we like it. When did that change?" Anger tinted her voice now.

"Fasting bonds people. Helps us focus on what's really important. You know that."

Harmony reached for another piece of bacon, chewing it with deliberate enjoyment. Korin watched her, and I understood in that instant I'd been right about him. He was hopelessly taken with her. She could eat a full seven-course meal on fast day and his feelings wouldn't change. I couldn't tell how she felt about him.

"You won't tell," she said. "And it wouldn't matter if you did. I was here first. This is my home. I built it."

"I like you being here," he said mildly.

Harmony was unsurprised by his words. "Well, I'd better go find our newest members. Give them the tour I promised. I'm particularly interested in the new girl, Autumn. If what you say about her is true, we might have a new line of sales. Herbal remedies should go for more than the herbs alone."

I expected Korin to say something else about my ability to read imprints, but he remained silent. I was glad.

"I'd better put away this milk first." Harmony's hands went for the pitcher on the table.

Clutching my remaining two pieces of bacon, I willed her not to go to the fridge. For something else to happen. Anything. I prepared to jump away from the door, maybe to pretend I was rearranging the contents of the fridge. Of course the moment I moved away, the door would shut, giving away my spying.

"Oh, I'll get that, Harmony." It was Victoria, back to the work, even with her burned hand.

Harmony's brow creased. "What happened to your hand?"

"Just a little burn. It's nothing really. I'm fine. I'll get this stuff put away."

"If you're sure."

Victoria smiled at Harmony, a real smile of genuine affection. "I'm sure."

"Well, if you need me . . ." Harmony gave her a little hug, avoiding the injured hand, and left the room without giving Korin another look. He was watching her, though. So was Victoria, but her tenseness returned now that Harmony was gone.

Korin nodded at her. "Is everything okay?"

"Yes." Her voice was scarcely a whisper.

"Let me know if you hear of anything strange," he said. "We're worried that someone might have come into the farm last night. Some of our patrollers were attacked."

"Attacked?"

"Yes. So it's important I hear about anything that's odd or out of place."

Would she tell how she'd found me in the middle of the night? But Victoria only nodded, her voice apparently gone.

Korin smiled at her. "I'm very happy with you, Misty. You've come a long way, haven't you?"

Again the nod. She was looking not at him but down at the chipped linoleum. Did she like this man? Or was she terrified of him? I didn't know her well enough to judge.

Korin left and Victoria relaxed. That is, until she opened up the refrigerator and found me busily reorganizing a shelf, two pieces of rolled up bacon having taken the place of my foot to keep the door open. The bacon fell out between us, uncoiling.

Victoria stared at me, but neither of us spoke. I smiled sweetly, bending to pick up the bacon, tossing it into the garbage can on my way out of the kitchen. Fortunately, my appetite was gone.

I emerged from the kitchen in time to see Korin's ponytail vanish into what looked like an office at the far end of the long corridor. I went the other way, not wanting to run into him just yet, though I wanted to talk to him soon. He hadn't given me away to Harmony, and that meant I might be able to trust him. Besides, he had a right to know his brother had been here and that someone had killed him.

I moved down the hall, the wood floor under my bare feet smoothed by many people before me. No splinters here or imprints, just smooth wood and some kind of waxy build-up. Voices caught my attention, and I followed my curiosity past the outer doors on my right to the room opposite them that I'd glimpsed on the way in. This room was larger even than the kitchen and held a dozen long tables, half of which were folded and pushed to the side to make room for three quilting frames that were in various stages of setup. There was also a large loom and several other machines I didn't recognize.

They weren't kidding when they said they made their own clothes and blankets.

The work on the quilts had been abandoned, and the women, old and young, gathered around Harmony, talking with her and basking in her light, and I realized something at that moment. Gabe might be the charismatic figurehead for Harmony Farms, and Korin's compelling speeches might attract many new converts, but Harmony was the reason it all worked at the core. That the women loved her was apparent, and she seemed to care about them too.

Where did that connect with the murder of Inclar and Victoria's fear? With Marcie's disappearance? Harmony could be exactly what she seemed, or she could be something far, far worse.

The voices in the room fell silent, and eyes wandered to where I stood in the hallway looking in. With the new damage to my face, I wasn't surprised my presence had such an impact. Harmony smiled and drifted toward me, followed by some of the others, including Spring and her son.

"Good morning, Autumn." Harmony dipped her head, but her eyes slid past my face, going to someone behind me.

I turned and saw Gabe emerging from a door farther down the hallway. His handsome face was drawn, and he looked older than I remembered, but when he came into the room, he greeted everyone with a smile and gentle words, turning on the charisma like a switch. He might not be as good a speaker as Korin or as vibrant as his wife, but he knew how to work people, especially those starved for emotional nurturing.

Harmony took her husband's arm. "I'm just about to give our new members a tour, Gabe. Would you like to come along?"

"I really shouldn't." Gabe rubbed his fingers over her hand. "I need to discuss some things with the boys here."

That's when I noticed the three men, who must have come in the wide back entryway after I'd passed and were now awaiting Gabe. Not just any men. One was the guard I'd bested by pure luck. He had a white bandage around his head, but besides that he looked healthy. From the cuts and bruises on the other men's faces, I guessed they had been Jake's attackers. I ducked my chin and didn't meet the guard's eyes, turning to Spring and her son. A baby was always an excuse to tune out any conversation, and I was thankful Silverstar let me take him from his mother's arms. I made sure to keep the bruised side of my face away from the men.

"Okay, then," Harmony said to Gabe. "Go take care of your business. We'll miss you." On tiptoes, she gave him a quick kiss on the lips, and for a brief instant, his tension eased.

"Have fun," he said.

Harmony laughed. "We will."

I dared a peek at the men and was relieved to see that no one was interested in me. Even so, I held my breath. An instant of recognition, and I might be rotting in the same hole as Marcie.

Harmony motioned us to come with her, and I followed quickly, leaving Spring to take up the rear. "Is he too heavy for you with your hurt wrist?" Spring asked, running to catch up.

"No, not at all."

"I think he weighs a ton. Sixteen months, and he's as tall as most two-year-olds."

"We could leave him with someone here," Harmony suggested.

"No, it's okay. If Autumn gets tired, I'll carry him." Spring was wearing a Harmony Farms T-shirt today, like I was, and except for the fading bruises that told of a hard life, she looked too youthful and carefree to be the mother of the boy I carried.

Harmony stopped a child and asked him to round up the rest of the newcomers, but Jake and the other two recruits were nowhere to be found. I began to feel a little uneasy. Where was Jake?

"Looks like it's just us," Harmony said with her customary laugh. "More fun that way," she added conspiratorially.

"We could wait," I suggested.

"No. Gabe or Korin can take them around later. I really want to show you our herbs right away. See what you think."

"Would it be okay if I took something to my room first?" I asked. "It's a poultice I made earlier." I also wanted to get the tracking earrings Ethan had given me. With those guards lurking around, I needed a way he could find me in case I mysteriously disappeared.

"Sure." Her gaze deepened as she took in the colors of my eyes for the first time in the sunlight. Like her husband, she didn't bring it up, and I was grateful.

I handed Silverstar to Spring and went back inside to the kitchen, hoping no one had cleaned the mug. No one had. In fact, the kitchen was exactly as I'd left it, and Victoria was nowhere in sight. I rummaged through the many drawers until I found a tiny container that would hold my mixture and spooned it in, placing the dirty mug and spoon in the sink. They contrasted with the mounds of clean, drying dishes on the long countertop. So many mouths to feed and not a dishwasher in sight. If that didn't give a new meaning to the word tedium, I didn't know what did. Sighing, I hurriedly washed the mug and spoon.

My appetite was back. I couldn't resist gulping down another piece of bacon, which was delicious despite being cold. I swallowed quickly. There, a little strength to tide me over.

In the hallway, a movement caught my eye. I glanced and saw Victoria emerging from what I'd thought was Korin's office at the far end. She blinked once at me, her round face chalky, then put her head down and scurried back to the kitchen. Frowning, I made my way out onto the back porch.

"Look who we found," Harmony sang out from the cast iron chairs on the porch where she and Spring had settled to watch a group of children playing basketball while they waited for me.

To my relief it was Jake, lounging against the railing next to them. "Hi," I said.

"I hear we're going on a tour."

"Just have to put this in my room." I showed him the herbs.

"I'll walk you there."

"Men aren't allowed inside," Harmony called after him.

Jake nodded at her, all charm, tipping an imaginary hat. "I'll wait outside, then."

"Except for Korin," I muttered to Jake as we started across the square. "He comes inside. At least he did to take away my money and my radio. And make me sign that contract."

"What have you been eating?" Jake asked.

"Eating?" I feigned innocence. The sun was high enough that it was shining down on his face now, newly shaven. I wondered when he'd had the time to do that.

"You have grease on your lips."

"Can't be. We're fasting for three days, remember?" I ran my tongue over my lips.

Amusement danced on his face. "I smelled bacon cooking when they hauled me up before dawn to milk the cows. Leave it to you to find it."

"Hey, I went through a lot last night." He, I noticed, didn't have a mark on him.

"I know." His expression sobered. "Your face looks bad."

"Gee, thanks."

"I mean, like it hurts." There was tenderness in the words, and perhaps—perhaps—just a little bit more.

"Looks worse than it is." Truthfully, my muscles and the cut on my arm that he couldn't see hurt far more. At least the wrist was feeling better. "It'll just take me a moment," I said outside the singles' quarters. For some reason, I felt reluctant to meet his eyes. Maybe I was afraid I wouldn't see what I hoped to find there.

I hesitated when I passed the supply closet, remembering the key in my suitcase. We might need it today, if not on our tour, then later. Or maybe when the police arrived. But if I was going to carry it, I wanted something to wrap it in, even if it would be in the pocket of my jeans. A bit of homespun cloth from the first-aid kit would do the trick.

I looked both ways before slipping into the bathing room and then into the supply closet, wrapping the key carefully several times. At the last moment, I stuck it inside my bra instead of my pocket, close to my underarm, hoping the imprints wouldn't leak through too much. If things turned bad, I didn't want anyone finding the key on me.

A woman was in the hall when I stepped from the closet, but I smiled at her as if I had every right to be there, and she nodded back. Once in my room, I saw that someone had made my bed. Shaking my head, I opened the top drawer of my dresser to put in the herbs.

I froze. Something wasn't right, though it took me a minute to figure out exactly what. When I did, my heart skipped a beat. The tracking earrings Ethan had given me were no longer in the drawer.

Chapter 19

"Who could have taken them?" I whispered to Jake as we walked a few steps behind the others on our way to what Harmony lovingly referred to as the cow barn. He didn't know, of course, and had already said as much, but I was on edge since discovering the loss.

After I'd returned from my room, Harmony had taken us back inside the main house and shown us the common rooms, including the kitchen Jake supposedly hadn't seen yet, and the big laundry facilities across the hall from the huge room where the women worked on their quilts. Then we'd toured the married housing, consisting of separate bathing areas for the men and women and rooms slightly larger than those in the singles' house, each with a smaller attached room for the children. In neither building had we seen any sign of a false wall or hidden room.

Jake frowned. "Where'd you put them? Could someone just have moved them?"

"I put them in my top drawer last night after my bath. Inside my underwear. They aren't anywhere in the drawer or in the closet. Whoever took them—it was deliberate."

I didn't tell him about Victoria coming out of Korin's office. The two weren't really connected, were they? She would have no reason to turn over my earrings. It's not as though she knew something was odd about them. Still, they were missing, and that meant someone suspected me. A shiver crawled up my spine, as if unseen eyes followed us through the trees.

"We have to hurry and find Marcie," I said. "This is getting too weird." I regretted not leaving with Ethan last night. Tawnia was going to kill me—if someone else didn't beat her to it.

"I'm thinking if they have a hidden room, it probably won't be in a high traffic area," Jake said. "Otherwise people would hear them shouting, wouldn't they?"

"Maybe they have and are too scared to care."

But he was right. We certainly hadn't heard shouting or crying during our sneaking around last night.

We'd entered an area where the trees were different. Fruit trees—at least half a dozen varieties.

Harmony paused and waited for us to catch up with her. "This is where we're building the new married housing." Sure enough, the ground next to the trees was broken and already large cinder blocks were in place as a base.

"With flush toilets?" Jake asked.

"Yes, and separate bathing rooms, one for each family."

"Good reason to get married."

Harmony quirked one eyebrow. "I can think of a lot better reasons."

So could I, but after my experience at the outhouse last night, I agreed completely with Jake.

Harmony motioned us onward, picking up the pace. "And through these trees, we have our biggest barn and pasture, and our grain silos. This is where we house all your typical barn animals and milking cows, calves we are raising for beef, and turkeys and goats. You get the idea. There's a chicken coop out back."

"Even room for a spare rat or two?" Jake asked, as the large barn came into sight, resplendent with a recent coat of red paint. The roof was shiny and made of metal, which I thought was rather practical.

Harmony trilled her infectious laugh, tossing her head so the ebony tresses caught the sunlight. "More than that, I'd guess. They eat anything, so they keep the place clean, and the cats keep the number of rats down, so it's a good balance."

Spring sneezed. "Excuse me," she muttered. A gray and white cat came toward us, winding its body between Harmony's legs and heading toward Spring, who backed away. "I'm afraid I'm allergic to cats," she said.

"Oh, sorry." Harmony shooed the animal away. "I'll have to remember that when we give you your work assignment. Have you had any trouble so far? We do have a few cats hanging around here."

"It's not usually a problem if they're kept outside," Spring said. "But I don't make a habit of petting them, just in case."

"Good." Harmony put an arm around her shoulders. "Why don't you wait out here while I show the others inside the barn?"

I'd been in several barns hunting for antiques, and this one was no different. Large loft for storing hay, stalls for the animals, a barrel of grain, tools on hooks, even space for a tractor. Several young men were cleaning and repairing leather items, while three younger boys chased a chicken. If it had a hidden room, I couldn't tell.

"Did you really milk a cow this morning?" I whispered to Jake.

He nodded. "Right there in that stall. Clumsy thing stepped on my foot."

"I'll stay away from her, then."

Harmony led the way outside again. "There's another barn and field for the horses on the other side, behind the closer outbuildings, which we'll see in a while, but if we go through the fields instead of back through the housing area, you can see our greenhouse." Her eyes went to my bare feet, where the white bandage on my toe was already dirty. "It's a bit of a hike. Are you sure you're okay?"

"My feet are tough," I said. "As long as we aren't running, I'll be fine." Running from a crazed killer, that is.

"She never wears shoes," Jake put in. I glared at him, and he added quickly, "At least that's what she claims."

"Why?" Spring asked.

So I went into the whole convoluted explanation about shoes throwing out my back and my parents being hippies and how I'd liked to freak out my schoolteachers. "Mostly, it's a habit," I confessed. "I hate shoes, so I don't wear them."

"I bet you don't make your bed, either," Jake said.

He knew I didn't. "What's the point if you're just going to get back in it?"

Harmony laughed. "You're my kind of person, Autumn." I remembered the bacon she had stolen and had to agree. Of course, she might be involved in a murder, and I most definitely wasn't.

As we passed the barn, we saw two older men in a clearing, their skin wrinkled and brown, working on a tractor. If I could judge by the laughter floating over to us, they were enjoying the company and the sunshine. A few younger men had spread out under a tree, talking, though they jumped to their feet when they spied Harmony.

"Go back to what you were doing," she told them with a laugh and a wave. They didn't, though, grabbing buckets and disappearing into the barn.

We arrived next at a field of herbs, lush and green under the warming sun. Living in a city, I'd never seen so many herbs growing in one spot or so many different herbs growing together. Herbs for healing and cooking—and for selling, of course. I shared a gaze of wonder with Jake, who was even more excited than I was. He walked on the path toward a long, squat greenhouse, mumbling under his breath as we passed different rows, "Comfrey, peppermint, lavender, sweet basil, milk thistle, yarrow, chamomile, feverfew, lemon balm, cayenne." I was glad Harmony was ahead and couldn't hear him. I laughed, feeling the last bits of last night's terror fading away in the sunlight.

"It's beautiful," Jake said with feeling, as we reached the greenhouse. His eyes were on the long drying racks that ran the outside length of the greenhouse, encased in screens that kept the bugs out while the herbs dried naturally in the sun.

"There's more inside." Harmony studied Jake for a long minute, and I wondered what she was thinking. If she was any kind of smart, she'd realize most builders didn't get that excited over herbs.

Inside the greenhouse, I wasn't surprised to see Essence seated on the ground by a bed of seedlings, watering them carefully. Next to her was a slight young man with bright red hair and freckles all over, and I knew him at once for the boyfriend who'd given her the pretty vase in our room.

"Hi," I said.

The boy quickly shoved something into his pocket, his eyes meeting mine and his face arranged in a carefully bland smile. "Hi."

Essence nodded her sharp face in my general direction, but her slanted eyes didn't meet mine.

"Shouldn't you be doing your chores?" Harmony asked the boy, who nodded, jumped to his feet, and shot out the door, his steps a little unsteady.

There was a sweet smell in the greenhouse, one I recognized from my youth. Even hippy parents who didn't believe in smoking pot themselves knew other hippy people who did. It took me only a few minutes to locate Essence's stash in the corner of the greenhouse, growing lush and unchecked.

"Marijuana," I whispered to Jake. He looked closer, his mouth rounded to an O.

"Beautiful plants, aren't they?" Spring gushed. "All this greenery is so inspiring."

Harmony smiled at us, her hands folded across her stomach. I could see in her stance that she was proud of what she and Gabe had built with their followers and also that she had not a clue in the world that Essence was growing pot.

Or was that an act? For all I knew, she and Gabe put drugs in everyone's food at night so they would be willing slaves forever. But I was beginning to like Harmony, and I didn't want to think of her that way.

After leaving the greenhouse, we crossed fields of vegetables and grains used for feeding those on the farm and also for sending to the factory in Rome, where rotating shifts of disciples ground the grain and made most of the muffins and breads they sold in the towns. "We don't use preservatives, so the finished products only last five days without a change in freshness and taste," Harmony said. "But we have a truck that freezes them, so we take out in the morning only those we'll sell that day. When the truck is empty, someone drives it back for more. It works really well, and a few stores order from us quite regularly now."

"So that's what goes on at the factory," I mused. "I heard someone mention it."

"We work in rotating shifts. You're welcome to sign up for a shift in a few months, but we like people to stay close to the farm for the first while. You know, to really get the feel of life here."

And so you're sure they won't run away, I thought.

"And now for the most exciting part," Harmony said. "The horse pasture." She was off again, through a field of grapevines. I followed, feeling strangely content, the dirt warm and crumbly beneath my feet.

The horse pasture also had a barn, small but newer than the one for the other livestock. Harmony was positively glowing as she introduced a beautiful brown horse, whose sides were distended. "Any day now," she said, "and we'll have another foal. Do any of you ride?"

"Never have," I admitted, as Jake and Spring shook their heads.

Once again, Jake and I looked carefully around inside the barn during our tour, but again there seemed to be no hidden door. I trailed my fingers along the door, the walls, but there wasn't a single imprint hinting at a secret room or any emotion at all that I could detect. I shook my head at Jake.

"So, this is the farm," Jake said to Harmony. "Very impressive."

"Have we seen it all, then?" I asked, an idea forming in my mind.

"Yes."

"Oh, because I was wondering where they make the pottery. There were some beautiful pieces in Portland. I was hoping maybe someone could teach me how."

Harmony laughed. "Fox, the red-haired boy we saw in the greenhouse, is the one to talk to. He's our most talented potter, and I'm sure he'd be glad to show you how. Actually, he does most of his work out here on the other side of the horse barn because it's closest to the kiln. In the winter he drags everything inside the main room, though. Makes a terrible mess. Eventually, we're hoping to add on a room for the pottery out here."

She took us around the far side of the horse barn where a carport of sorts had been added to the structure. It had a roof, half a wall, and surprisingly sturdy shelves built into the side. These were filled with vases and pots of all sizes, like those I'd seen the brotherhood selling near the Willamette River. Two throwing wheels sat in the corner where the half wall met the barn, and a thick power cord ran from them into the woods.

"What's in there?" I asked, thumbing toward the trees where the cord vanished.

Harmony smiled. "The bathrooms. We've basically gone in a big circle. We'll cut through there to get back to the houses."

"What'll we do when we get back?" Spring's demeanor was weary now, and she looked as wilted as her son sleeping in her arms.

"You can join the women working on the quilts," Harmony said to her. To me she added, "I imagine you'll want to talk to

Essence about setting up whatever you need for your remedies. We can order any size plastic containers that you'll need. We have some already, but you'll probably need others. Of course, we'll want to start small, test the waters." Her voice was filled with subdued excitement. I was standing on her left side now, and I could see the scar along her jaw line. It looked serious, and I wondered what had happened. Had there been an accident on the farm?

"You'll have to schedule any kitchen time you might need with Scarlet and her staff. And they can assign you people to help if you need them."

"I'd love to help," Spring said.

I didn't know how well that would work with little Silverstar occupying so much of her attention, but as I didn't really plan to stay, I simply nodded and smiled. "Sounds perfect."

"As for you," Harmony told Jake, "they'll be starting on the walls of the new house tomorrow, so you may want to go over the plans." She glanced between us again, a slight smile forming on her lips. "Seeing as how you two have hit it off, you might be needing a place soon, so the faster you can build it, the better."

I wondered if her comment came from her observation of us today, or if Korin had told her about finding us kissing last night.

Jake laughed. "Where are these plans?"

"Let me show you." Harmony took his arm.

"You coming?" Jake looked in my direction.

"Yeah." I wanted to get my bearings back at the compound before I tried to find the greenhouse again. Otherwise, I might end up lost.

Spring fell into step with me, her movements stiff. "Can I carry him for you?" I asked. My body was aching, but she appeared ready to drop. Her eyes were red, and she was sniffing. I looked around for cats, but I didn't see any.

Spring hesitated. "Are you sure?"

"Of course. I should have offered before. Don't worry. My wrist is fine." My face and arm hurt far more at the moment, but she didn't need to know that.

Spring handed him over carefully. Silverstar's head landed on my shoulder, on one of my bruises, to be exact, but I endured the pressure since I didn't want to wake him.

"Jimmy usually carries him when we go for walks," Spring said out of nowhere.

My stomach clenched. "Do you miss him?"

"No." We walked for a few minutes more, the silence broken only by the low hum of voices drifting back to us from Harmony and Jake.

After a while, Spring sighed and began again. "Being around these women, especially Scarlet—well, it reminds me of my mom. They've been so supportive, and I wonder if maybe she would have been too."

"You didn't talk to her about what was happening between you and Jimmy?"

Spring shook her head, her eyes wide and sad. "What could she do? What if he hurt her? That's the first place he'd look for me. Besides, I was thinking maybe she'd tell me 'I told you so,' or maybe that I had to lie in the bed I'd made, but I could have been wrong. She didn't want me to marry Jimmy in the first place, you know. She said he had mean eyes, small and beady, and that she was afraid for me. Of course, I was in love and didn't listen. I mean, lots of people have small eyes and they aren't abusers." She paused, considering. "Now I'm thinking she might have helped me."

"Well, you're away from him now, and it's nice here."

She smiled. "Yeah. But I think I might be allergic to all these animals."

"I hope not. Wouldn't be a good place for you, long term, if you are. They don't seem to be much into medication."

"Maybe I'll get over it. Do you think they would let me go into town and contact my mom? You know, just tell her I'm okay and not to worry?"

She hadn't told her mother she was leaving? Maybe that's what separated youth from maturity. I would never have disappeared without letting those closest to me know. I'd learned the week Winter had been missing that not knowing what happened to a loved one was like a kind of death.

"You could ask," I said. "They should let you. If they don't, maybe you shouldn't be here."

Spring's face creased in a frown. "What do you mean?"

"I'm just saying they should let you." On my shoulder, Silverstar was moving, digging his face into my bruise. I took the opportunity to switch him to the other side. "But if by some chance this place doesn't work out for us, I want you to know that you always have a place to stay with me."

"You have a place?"

I didn't want to say too much. "I know how to make a living. And you're always welcome wherever I go."

Her eyes filled with tears, and she tilted her head toward mine as we walked. I tilted mine too, and since we were about the same height, our heads were touching. "I wish," she said softly, "that I'd met you last year." Then she gave an impatient snort and added, "Well, we're here now—Spring and Autumn. All we need is Winter and Summer."

My parents, I wanted to say. But I didn't. Because Winter, having been the last person found after the bridge collapse, was still fairly well-known in Portland and talking about him might lead to a discussion of who I really was and my reasons for being here. I stayed quiet.

Back in the square, I got directions from Harmony and started out again for the greenhouse. Jake caught up with me before I'd gone far.

"Nothing," he said. "Absolutely no place for a hidden room."

"What do you mean? There's three hundred acres here. It could be anywhere."

"I meant in the main areas. I thought finding it would be easier than this."

"We may have to wait for the police. Once they get interviewing people, someone will talk."

"But don't you see, Autumn? Even if the police come, with no body they only have your word."

"I'll tell them about the guard's buckle."

"Like they'll believe that."

"Detective Martin would," I said, not knowing if it was true. "I already helped him find one murderer."

"Maybe. He still wouldn't like it, and he wouldn't have jurisdiction here."

I heaved a sigh. "Okay, so we keep looking. First, I'm going to talk to Essence. I want to know about those drugs."

Jake nodded. "I'm going to meet with the guys about the building and then sneak off and check out the countryside."

"If you get a chance, go to the gate and see if Ethan left us another radio and try to contact him if he has. It really isn't like him not to have brought the police already."

Jake blew out an irritated breath. "This could be exactly like him. We don't really know the man at all."

"He's okay. You know how long he's been looking for his sister. And I told you already that I checked him out on the Internet. His name came up in connection with the university." Though I hadn't actually looked at the sites, the search page clearly showed he was with the math department.

Jake shrugged. "I'm just saying something isn't adding up here."

"Well, duh, but if there's a radio there, he may be able to tell us something more. For all we know the local police are on the take."

Jake grimaced, but he didn't continue the subject. "I'll check the gate. You just be careful."

"I will." He left, striding across the square with an animal-like grace, sure and powerful. The few women watching the children eyed him as he left, and I felt a little jealousy at their freedom to give him such admiring looks.

Shaking the thoughts away, I started out between the rows of vegetables on the far side of the square. These, Harmony had explained, were the plants most commonly used for consumption at the farm—lettuce, carrots, broccoli, spinach, squash, cucumbers. I passed them all. I should have reached the potatoes and the berry patches, but somehow I ended up near the foundation of the new building, which meant I'd seriously curved to the left when I was only supposed to slightly curve. The good news was that I knew where I was, more or less, and I could cut through the trees here to the right and probably emerge in the fields near the greenhouse.

All the while, my mind was churning with questions. Did Gabe and Harmony know about Essence's drugs? Did the drugs work into the setup here, or were they Essence's secret? Obviously one she at least shared with the red-haired Fox. Hopefully, she would have some answers for me.

A movement beyond the foundation of the new house caught my eye, and instinctively, I ducked behind a tree. Then I felt silly because it was probably Jake taking a look at what they'd done so far. Fortunately, I peeked before I stepped out. Instead of Jake, I saw Gabe and Korin with the guard from last night and two others flanking them some distance away.

My heart flipped into overdrive, making me want to flee, but I held my position because they were coming my way. *Just step out and say hi,* I told myself. My feet wouldn't move.

"Where is he now?" Gabe's voice came into range.

Korin replied, but I couldn't hear his softer voice, which was odd, given that he was so good at projecting during his speeches.

"We have to take care of this immediately," Gabe said. "There's too much at risk."

I still couldn't hear Korin's reply, but it sounded soft and pleading, the way I'd expect a man to sound after learning his brother was dead. Had they found Inclar's body wherever someone had moved it?

Gabe stopped and faced Korin, and now I couldn't hear him clearly, either. " . . . risk we have to take . . . snooping around . . . Harmony . . . nothing to do with us."

Korin was nodding, his demeanor intent and respectful. But when Gabe started walking again, a flash of something else rolled across his face. Courage? Fear? I couldn't say.

"Come on. Let's do this," Gabe said.

They were closer to me now, flanked by the guards, and I hugged the tree, not daring to peek out. I waited until they were past me and then followed. I was quiet on my bare feet, and they were making so much noise I wasn't worried about their hearing me. They seemed to be walking in a direction that would take them nearer the cow barn than the greenhouse.

My heart still pounded in overtime. For no reason at all, I thought of Shannon. Did the detective feel like this when he tracked criminals—tingly, purposeful? Alive? Maybe now I would see where they had hidden both the body and Marcie. I hoped they weren't in the same place because if Tawnia's drawing and the imprints were correct, Marcie was already on the edge of madness.

Their voices had faded, and I began to hurry, afraid of losing them but also afraid they'd discover my presence. I was so involved in worrying and sneaking along that I broke out into the clearing surrounding the main barn before I realized where I was. I stepped back into the trees and scanned the area, finding nothing but packed dirt and two cats lounging in the shade of the barn. Gabe and Korin were nowhere to be seen. They hadn't been far enough ahead of me to get to the barn, but I couldn't see where else they might have gone.

Maybe they were somehow behind me now. Maybe they knew I'd been following them. Suddenly, I felt small and helpless and exposed, despite the trees surrounding me.

Looking over my shoulder, I hurried in the direction of the greenhouse, hoping this time I wasn't the one being followed.

Chapter 20

Nothing happened. No one emerged to confront or accuse me. I didn't see another living thing, except a pair of birds in a tree, who took flight as I passed, sending my heart pounding again.

After a little side trip to a big field of potatoes, I found the herb fields and the greenhouse. Essence was still there, looking rather spaced-out. This time I knew why. I sat down beside her where she was staring off into the distance, apparently having watered all the seedlings that needed daily attention.

The floor of the greenhouse was packed earth, and I was glad for my jeans. Essence herself was wearing some wide-legged culottes made from the same brown material many of the men and women used for pants—the same cloth I'd seen in bolts in the meeting room. These were badly sewn, as though hurriedly, or perhaps the first in a homemade pattern. Her T-shirt was white with the familiar blue lettering, a copy of the one I wore.

I pulled a few mint leaves from a plant and popped them into my mouth, savoring the flavor. Essence glanced at me, actually focusing on my face for a full two seconds, but didn't comment on my breaking the fast.

"Do they know?" I asked into the silence. "About the marijuana?"

She didn't look at me but stared at the ground, like a little child caught in a wrongdoing.

"Come on. I just want to know."

She shrugged. "Maybe they know."

"What do you mean?"

Coming to her feet in a single graceful movement that said a lot about her physical condition, she beckoned me to the corner. "Sometimes when I come in here, some of the leaves have been cut." She pointed to a section. "I don't know who does it."

"Could it be that boy who was in here?"

"Fox?"

"Yeah."

"He might have, but I don't know why he would. I give him all he wants."

I moved closer to her. "Why do you use it, Essence? Is it so bad here?"

"Two years ago I wanted to go home. Now I don't."

I studied her pointed features, her dark hair making her face appear pale and sickly. "Who gave you these plants?" I said the words slowly, deliberately, so she would be sure to understand.

She looked at me again, a sharp, piercing stare that shot a sliver of terror into my heart. Her eyes weren't green, as I'd thought they might be, but a light brown and frighteningly empty. "No one." She turned away.

I followed her. "Someone gave them to you. Who was it? Why won't they let people leave?"

No reply.

"What if you didn't have to stay? What if you could leave now?"

She shook her head. "This is my home. I have a purpose. I love my work. And I love Fox. We're getting married when the new house is finished."

"Will Fox protect you from what's going on here? Not that I know what's going on because none of you will tell me anything."

She whirled on me. "Go away! Go away now! I don't want to talk to you, and I don't want to see you again."

I glared at her. "What are you so afraid of?"

At my words, she crumpled into a heap on the ground, knees to her chest, head tucked, arms curled up to cover her head. Sobs broke through. "I don't want to go back. I don't want to go back. I don't want to go back."

I knelt beside her and patted her back. "Shhh. It's okay." She cringed at my touch but gradually relaxed, her sobs subsiding. "Essence, where don't you want to go back to?"

"To the dark."

I'd suspected she hadn't been talking about civilization, but the words confirmed this. "The dark place," I said. "Where is it?"

She curled tighter and said nothing. Maybe she didn't know. I put my arms around her, but she seemed to have gone into some sort of trance and didn't appear to notice me. Her breathing was shallow and irregular. "Are you okay?" I asked.

No reply.

I'd never felt so helpless in all my life, except at the bank of the river watching the divers search for Winter's body. Fear grew into a tight knot in my chest. If I managed to carry her back to the houses, would they take her to a doctor? I doubted it.

I stayed where I was, holding her, and eventually, after what seemed like forever, I felt her muscles unclench. Her breathing deepened and evened out. "I'm sorry," I whispered. "I won't ask you any more questions. But I will tell you that I'm here to help you. That's why I've come. You are not alone."

So many promises I was making—to Victoria, Spring, and now Essence. Women I didn't even know, not really.

Essence didn't reply, but I hadn't expected her to. I squeezed her one last time before moving away. Whatever I was searching for, Essence wasn't ready to trust me with what she might know.

She had, however, confirmed the existence of a dark place. Where could it be?

I had reached the door when she spoke in a faint whisper. "We grow all our own food, you know. We bottle a lot in the fall. The pantry—have you seen it? It's always full. Of course, it's not big enough for all the bottles and vegetables. They can last all winter if stored right. And not just onions and apples and potatoes. You can store almost anything if you wrap it right."

She'd finally gone over the edge. But at least she was talking again, and that was an improvement. "That's great," I said.

"You never go hungry here. Never. Except on fast days."

I nodded. Her thin face was pinched and desperate, denying her claim. If there was so much food here, why didn't she eat it? That made me wonder again about the drugs, but Essence didn't seem to be avoiding food because of what was in it. Maybe her habit made it so she didn't care to eat.

Her eyes were wild, not really seeing me. Her head drooped. "So much food," she whispered. "Cold."

She wasn't talking about the greenhouse. It was almost stifling in here, and if not for the open doors at either end, it would have been a lot hotter. I took two steps toward her. "Can I do anything for you?"

"Please go," came the muffled request.

So I left. What else could I do?

I wasn't above snacking in the fields as I made my way back to the houses. A little of this and a little of that. I didn't worry about washing the produce because I figured that any fertilizer or pesticides they used here were probably natural and wouldn't stay on the leaves long enough to hurt me. The rows of herbs and vegetables, washed by the rain and nestled in these cleared fields, were a complete opposite to the terror I'd felt with Essence. Part of me wanted to sit in these fields and stay forever, and the other part wanted to run away as fast and as far as I could. Back to my comforting antiques and my sister.

Yet how could I leave Spring and Victoria and Essence? And what about Marcie?

I'd almost made it back to the houses when a thought hit me with the force of a truck. I actually sat down by a row of cabbages to think it through.

Essence hadn't been wandering in her thoughts. She'd been giving me a clue. If the pantry in the kitchen wasn't big enough to store all these vegetables for the winter, where did they store them? Another barn? No, it would have to be somewhere cool, but deep enough not to freeze. A root cellar, maybe. A dark, musty root cellar.

If there was one, maybe it didn't hold just vegetables, especially now when the harvest was months away. With so many people to feed during the winter, there could even be more than one cellar. Maybe we weren't looking for a building at all but a hole in the ground.

The police didn't come.

I was beginning to worry about Ethan. Had the police refused to believe him? Was he waiting outside the gate worrying about me? Wondering about Marcie?

Jake was also missing, but I knew he was scouting the area. I only wished I could tell him about the root cellar so he could look for that too. But what did an entrance to a root cellar look like? A few of Winter's friends who lived in houses instead of apartments had them in their backyards, and they ranged from little hut-like structures that descended immediately into the earth to a flat door that could be hidden by a couple of bales of hay.

We'd have to search the barns more carefully.

Back at the main house, Scarlet trapped me and began grilling me about what I would need for the herb salves and remedies. Then she put me to work on the quilts with the other women. Spring was there, looking decidedly worse with her allergies. I tried to convince her to go lie down, but she would hear none of it. The quilts, I learned as we worked, were sold online from the factory in Rome or sometimes sent to craft fairs. They would each bring in hundreds of dollars.

Where did the money go? Some of it went to supplies, like needles, special threads and the finer materials, but since so much was made here, there would be substantial profit, especially added to the proceeds from the other crafts. The money was likely buying materials for the new house and upgrades for the older housing, but I doubted that took everything. If I could find out where the money went, I might be a long way toward deciding who was behind the fear that lurked here.

Harmony left the women after the first quilt was finished, carrying it in her arms. On the pretense of making more tea, I followed her. I waited until she had opened the door to her room before calling out to her.

"Can I speak to you for a moment?" I walked toward her quickly as I spoke, hoping she wouldn't shut her door and come to meet me in the hall.

She turned, her face smiling. In this dim light, she was even more beautiful, and I wondered at what I had seen imprinted on the flashlight and about her relationship with her husband. He loved her deeply, I knew that, and yet last night she had been almost servile toward him, frightened.

Of him? Or something else? I wished I knew what she felt for him because that would help me know if I could trust her. I knew I didn't trust Gabe.

"What is it?" The shadows under Harmony's eyes were more noticeable here than outside, making her look not frail but human. Needy.

"It's about Spring." I glanced around as though afraid of being heard.

She gestured me into her room. I couldn't have planned it better. During our tour, she'd only indicated the door to her room, but now I'd get to see inside. It was about half again the size of the one I shared with Essence and Victoria, holding a queen-sized bed and a dresser. The worn cherry furniture was better quality than the wooden bunks and had obviously come from a store, though none of it was sumptuous by any standard. I suspected it was the set she'd brought with her when they'd come originally. A door opened to a smaller room, and there I saw part of a wooden bunk bed. Their daughter's room, I assumed.

Harmony watched me, a question in her eyes. "Looks just like the married quarters," I said.

She laughed. "Pretty much. Except we made the bed frames there. In fact, we made all our frames except the few metal ones we have in the singles' rooms."

"Not the mattresses?"

"No."

Somehow I was relieved to hear that Harmony Farms wasn't completely independent of the world.

"Is something wrong with Spring?" Harmony gently reminded me of my purpose.

"I think she's having a problem with allergies or something. She's about had it, but I can't get her to rest, and fasting for three days . . ." I shook my head. "She won't even take tea."

Harmony set the folded quilt on her bed. "Why don't you make her some tea, and I'll talk with her?"

"What about medication? I know some herbal remedies for allergies, but it's going to take a while to find something that works for her."

"Korin will have some over-the-counter medicines. He keeps that sort of thing in his office. A lot of people come here addicted to different things and usually cutting that off cold turkey is best."

"But allergies are different, aren't they?"

Harmony shrugged. "We do have several people who suffer a bit for a month or so out of the year, but nothing too severe. She will adjust."

"I hope so. But what if she doesn't? What then?"

"That will be up to her."

The implication, of course, was that she could leave, and Harmony seemed to be sincere, but I felt a dread in my stomach that didn't bode well for Spring.

"I'll go make the tea," I said, keeping the doubt from my voice.

"Put plenty of honey in it. That will help."

So Spring received the best tea I could make, and if it was slightly on the too-sweet side, she didn't complain but drank it all down with some pills Harmony had given her. Then Harmony sent her to lie down with Silverstar, and I went back to quilting, thinking it would be better to buy a machine for all this hand-stitching than to waste so much time on the needlework. But machines cost money, and handmade quilts would bring a better price.

A few minutes before what would have been dinnertime, if we hadn't been fasting, a bell rang. Soon both men and women began setting up chairs in the square for the meeting I'd heard people talking about all day. Though Harmony Farms wasn't a religion, many of the people joined together on Sundays to discuss ideas. Shortly, Korin began a riveting discourse on the joys of service and the evils of riches.

"He's missed his calling," Jake said in my ear.

I was standing on the square, leaning back against one of the vertical porch railings of the singles' quarters. After sitting in front of the quilt for hours, I wasn't about to sit again. My feet felt warm on the cement of the square. "You mean as a televangelist?"

"He seems sincere."

"Mesmerizing, you mean. Look at everyone staring."

Jake chuckled. "If I were Gabe, I'd be worried."

Gabe was nowhere in sight. Nor was Harmony. I wondered if their disappearance involved a root cellar.

"Did you go to the gate?" I asked.

"Nothing was there."

I didn't like that. Ethan had been searching for Marcie for over a year now, and he wouldn't give up easily. I gave a frustrated sigh.

"What?" Jake asked.

"I heard Gabe and Korin talking about someone today. I thought they were talking about Inclar, that maybe Korin had found his body, but what if they were talking about Ethan? What if they found him?" It was the only explanation for why Ethan hadn't yet brought the police.

"We should try to get back your radio. That way we could contact him."

I regarded Jake with new admiration. "It's probably in Korin's office. The farthest door past the kitchen. Harmony pointed it out, remember?"

"I'll go now."

"What makes you think *you're* going?"

"He may be bigger than me, but I bet I could flatten him."

I scowled. "This has nothing to do with your hormones. If anyone goes, I should. Harmony seems to think he has a thing for me."

"Oh, so now who's talking hormones?"

I rolled my eyes. Big brother Jake playing his protective role again. "I've been thinking we should talk to him anyway. Tell him about Inclar. After all, he gave his brother money. That has to show he cares about him. He could help us nail Gabe."

"What if he's involved?"

I sighed. "I don't know. But we're still no closer to finding Marcie, and with Ethan missing, the police might not be on their way."

We were whispering, but a few of the others were looking at us pointedly, so we edged away from the meeting, walking around the singles' quarters to the front of the main house.

"I should go in now while Korin's speaking," I said.

"I still think I should go."

I shook my head. "I'm the one who saw the body. And in case he catches me, I have to be the one who goes in."

"I'll keep watch outside the door."

"Not so close. If I do get caught, someone needs to stay back and wait for a chance to either get me free or go for the police."

Jake's lower jaw jutted out, and I was sure he'd refuse. He looked sexy and strong and stubborn. "Please," I said.

That was when I did something I hadn't planned on. Something absolutely stupid and irresponsible.

I kissed him.

I couldn't help myself. This might be the last time I saw him before our cover was blown.

He didn't respond for a moment, but then he kissed me back. Passion shuddered between us, setting every inch of me on fire. A delicious, mesmerizing fire that beckoned with promises of much more. When we drew away, we were both out of breath.

"What was that for?" he growled, and I suppose that was his right since I'd started it.

Why do you think? I wanted to shout. "Thanks for everything. You know, just in case things don't go right."

He frowned. "That's how you say thanks? We may only be

friends, but I'm still human. You can't kiss a guy like that unless you mean it."

I'd meant it, but his pointing out that we were only friends made me feel about two inches high. "Forget it," I muttered. I turned away from him, not wanting to see his face again. Ever again. Not until I was good and dead from my embarrassment.

His hand shot out and turned me around. "Autumn."

"What," I said, still not looking at him.

"Be careful."

That was it? But then, what did I expect? I sighed, and all the fight went out of me. "I will."

He held me to him for a long moment, and I rested my head on his shoulder. *You shouldn't hug a girl like this unless you mean it,* I told him silently, but how many times had he held me exactly like this since Winter died? I'd needed him so much.

His hand stroked my hair, his fingertips sinking to caress my scalp. The gesture reminded me of Essence and how I'd tried to comfort her. As a friend.

"There's something else I forgot to tell you," I said with a frustrated sigh. "I think I might know where we should look for Marcie."

As I told him about the possibility of a root cellar, he nodded. "That makes perfect sense. I don't know why we didn't think of it before."

"Uh, because neither of us lives on a farm?"

He smiled. I smiled. We were back to being ourselves again. Friends.

"I'm going now," I said.

"I'll wait in the kitchen. That should be far enough away but close enough to hear you if you call out."

The front entrance to the house led into the large meeting

room where we'd been working on the quilts. Those were finished now, the frames put away for another day, the room dark and empty of people.

I walked through it and out into the hall, turning right. I passed the larger, back entrance on my left and Gabe's office nearly opposite, wending my way down the hall to the kitchen and beyond. I could still hear Korin outside talking. What if his office was locked?

I needn't have worried. Like every other room in the place, there was no lock. I waved to Jake and went inside. The room was equipped with a large oak desk that took up as much space as a bed. There was a computer and shelves that held many books and two opaque plastic containers. A safe stood in the corner, and that was locked. Interesting. I wondered if Gabe had one in his office as well. Two of the desk drawers were also locked, but none had keyholes big enough to fit the key I still had wrapped up in my bra.

I left the light off because it wasn't dark outside yet, and though the light in the room was dim, it was sufficient. The obvious place to begin were the plastic boxes, as I could see electronics poking out of one. On closer inspection, I saw phones, music players of all sorts, car keys, and even a garage door opener. There. My radio. It felt cool in my hand, and I itched more than anything to get out of there and find a place to turn it on.

The glint of a cell phone on Korin's desk kept me from leaving. Why was it there instead of in the boxes with the others? Stuffing the radio in my front pocket—only possible because these old jeans were so loose—I walked over and picked it up. I expected something, an imprint, some slice of information, but there was nothing. Apparently, this phone didn't mean much to the user. Or it was new. I opened it, pressed the red button, and punched in Tawnia's number.

It started ringing.

Harmony had said there was no phone service here. What was going on? Apparently Korin had a plan that did have service. Or Harmony had lied.

"Hello?" Tawnia said.

"Hi. It's me."

"Autumn! I've been so worried. Ethan said he'd call."

"He hasn't?"

"Not once. Is something wrong? I drew that man with the weird eye, the one who attacked you in your apartment. He looked dead! And you were fighting with some big guy. Tell me I'm imagining things. I'm going crazy here."

"Stop talking and listen. I don't know how much time I have."

"What do you mean? What's going on?"

I was about to tell her when the door opened. Korin stood there, his husky body framed by the light coming from the hallway. It had grown darker in the room, whether caused by a cloud in the sky or because I'd spent too long studying the electronics, I didn't know. He flipped on the light switch. There I stood, behind his desk with his phone to my ear.

Caught.

Chapter 21

orin stood with his arms folded across his chest as I blundered on to Tawnia. "Yes, Deedy. I just wanted to make sure that little Shannon was taken care of," I said into the phone. "Cats are pretty independent, I know, but he's declawed and won't last long on the street. If you could find him a home, I'd really appreciate it."

"What are you talking about? Are you and Jake okay? What does a cat have to do with anything? You aren't talking about that detective, are you?"

I pressed the phone tightly to my ear, cupping my hand over it to prevent her voice from carrying. "It's exactly as I expected here. Lovely. You could join if you want. Of course your boyfriend might not want to leave his job. I know he's worked a long time for that veterinarian clinic, but there are a ton of animals here. He'd like that. Hey, gotta go now. Just wanted to make sure Shannon didn't starve." I clicked off the phone and looked up into Korin's blank expression.

"What are you doing in here?" he asked, his voice mild.

Outside I could hear someone else talking. Perhaps Gabe? I

should have realized Korin wouldn't be the only speaker at the meeting.

"I came to talk to you," I said. "And then I saw the phone and thought about this stray cat I've been feeding. I forgot to get someone to take care of him before I left. I came so suddenly. Well, you already know that."

"Why *did* you come to the farm, Autumn?" He shut the door behind him and came toward me, holding out his hand for the phone. I met him around the desk.

"Because it seemed the right thing to do."

"Do you still feel the same?"

I thought of Victoria and Marcie and Essence. Spring. "Yes."

"So you didn't come to tell me you want to leave?"

I shook my head. "I came because yesterday when I lost my way in the woods, I stumbled on a man. I-I think he was dead." I paused as I considered how much to tell him. Should I say that I knew the man was his brother? Maybe not yet. I still didn't know how far I could trust him. "He was a skinny man. Had something odd with one of his eyes. I was frightened so I ran away, but then I started worrying about it, so I went back and he wasn't there. I was afraid to say anything because I didn't want to be any trouble. Maybe I imagined it all."

I was particularly proud of the tremor in my voice on the last sentence. I told myself I was acting, not really scared, and that Tawnia would be proud since normally I couldn't fake anything. I only wished my knees weren't shaking so badly.

Korin's eyes gleamed. "You're sure he was dead?"

"I guess he could have been unconscious. It was dark and I didn't have a light, but it was unnatural, the way he was lying there. I'm pretty sure he was dead. There was blood in the brush, and it looked like he'd been dragged away."

"I was afraid of this." He sat down heavily in one of the chairs in front of the desk.

"What do you mean?"

"The man you describe might be my brother. He used to be a disciple here, but he left. I helped him leave. But some people weren't happy about it." Korin's voice was distant and unemotional, as though he either didn't really care or was repressing great emotion.

"I thought anyone could leave when they wanted."

"That's the way it's supposed to be. But some here do not feel the same way."

"Founder Gabe?"

He shrugged. "I don't see how anything could go on here without his knowing about it. I'm having a difficult time coming to terms with what I've discovered in the past few days. I'm not sure what to do."

I sat in the chair across from him. "What do you mean?"

Korin didn't respond but occupied himself in turning the phone around in his hand. "I got this satellite phone when we were in Portland last week in case I needed it. I guess I felt even then that something might be wrong." He fell silent for a moment but then shook himself. "Maybe you can help me."

"Me?" I didn't like the sound of this.

Korin went around the desk, reaching in his pocket for a key. From inside the top drawer, he pulled out a man's thick silver bracelet and offered it to me. "You said you feel things sometimes. What do you feel on this?"

I took it hesitantly because Korin obviously thought it was

important. The instant the metal touched my palm I felt the anger. White hot anger that consumed.

"Why did you let him go?" I/Gabe said. "Don't you know what you've done? The police will be investigating the murder. They could track him back here."

Korin's face, crumpling with fear before my fury. "He's my brother. I had no choice. Please, forgive me."

There were earlier imprints associated with the bracelet, quiet, peaceful ones that had been all but obliterated by this confrontation.

"What have you done?" I sneered again as the first imprint began to replay,

I let the links slide between my fingers and fall onto the desk. "Your brother," I said. "The man was your brother. Gabe was angry at you for letting him leave."

"At the time I thought it was because my brother was unbalanced after his wife deserted him, and Gabe wanted to make sure he was okay before he left. But now I'm beginning to think Gabe had no intention of ever letting him go, and that makes me wonder about the others who've wanted to leave here. Maybe they're not really leaving. They don't take anything with them when they go." Korin shut the drawer without relocking it and came around the desk.

"Come with me. There's something I want to show you. Maybe you can pick up some impressions there. It's the place where my brother was held before I let him out."

"What if that's where someone's hidden his body?" And Marcie? Would we finally stumble on her?

Korin's hand was on my shoulder, his fingers digging into my bruise with a little too much pressure.

"Uh, you're hurting me," I said.

"Sorry." He eased up on my shoulder. "I'm having a hard time thinking of my brother being dead. If it really is my brother."

"What are you going to do?"

Tears glistened in his eyes. "I don't know."

"Shouldn't you call the police?"

"We aren't in any city. Gabe is the law here."

That made me shiver. Marcie had trusted Gabe and look where it had gotten her.

As we passed the kitchen, I glanced in and saw Jake talking to Scarlet. He didn't react, but his eyes met mine. I knew he'd be following me shortly.

The meeting was disbanding as we walked out onto the back porch. Gabe and Harmony were there, casually talking with others. Gabe spotted Korin and motioned him over with an imperious wave.

"I'd better go," Korin whispered. "I don't want to make him suspicious. I'll show you the place later."

Jake came from the house, still talking with Scarlet. Without so much as looking my way, he went into the square and started playing basketball with a group of boys.

That's when I saw Victoria staring at me from the square, her round face a mask of indifference. No, not quite indifference, because there was fear in every line of her body as her gaze slipped to where Korin was conversing with Gabe. I felt sick because all at once I realized that her chubbiness in the shapeless dress that she wore wasn't due to overeating at her job.

Victoria was going to have a baby.

But who was the father? I had no way to determine if her

pregnancy had driven her here five and a half months ago, or if it had begun later. I wanted to go to her and throw my arms around her, but I knew she wouldn't welcome it.

When Korin returned to my side, both Gabe and Harmony were with him. Korin's face was tense, his eyes darting back and forth, but when he spoke, he sounded normal. "Gabe would like to come along on our little walk," he said to me.

"And me too." Harmony firmly took my arm, and we stepped off the porch together.

I didn't like the way things were going. Turning my head, I caught Korin's eye, but he shrugged. Apparently, he was as afraid of Gabe as I was. Gabe's face was black as death, and he looked much older and more frightening. Couldn't anyone see the change?

Harmony did. She released me and took Gabe's arm. He didn't appear to notice.

Korin drifted to my side. "It's okay," he whispered. "Just come along."

"Where are we going?" Surely Korin wouldn't take me to examine the hidden room now.

"To the body."

To the body? "He knows where your brother is?"

"He claims Inclar was found earlier today in the woods by one of the boys. So Gabe had him moved to the place I was going to show you. Once we're there, touch things. See if there's any proof about who did it."

"But are we safe with him?"

"I think so. He'll blame the murder on someone else. An outsider maybe. Perhaps whoever attacked our men last night. As long as we don't openly accuse him of anything, we should be fine."

We walked in silence, the world seeming darker once we'd entered the woods, though it wasn't yet dusk. I hoped Jake had seen me leave and was following. We were heading in what I thought was the direction of the new house. I didn't want to go along, but I was curious despite myself.

I also wondered about Ethan. I was almost sure Gabe had him stashed somewhere. I opened my mouth to ask Korin if Ethan was the man he and Gabe had been talking about earlier, but caution stopped me. Something about this whole situation didn't feel right. If Gabe was connected with Inclar's death, why would he show us the evidence instead of getting rid of it?

Perhaps his rule here was so absolute that he had no fear of being caught.

In front of us, Gabe's figure could have been carved from granite. Harmony kept looking back at us every so often and then at her husband's face, the motion almost calculated rather than worried.

We passed the new housing site and walked in the direction of the main barn, but Gabe stopped at the edge of the clearing near a large boulder I'd passed a few times that day. He nodded to Korin, and together they grabbed the rock and rolled it to one side, revealing a metal door.

"Are you sure this is the right place?" Gabe asked Korin. "I don't know who could put him in here. There was nothing here earlier when we checked. It'd take at least two men to do it."

Fear shot through me. Gabe's words told me two things. One, that this was where he, Korin, and the guards had disappeared today; and two, that he hadn't been the one who had hidden Inclar's body. Had I misunderstood Korin?

"How did you get into the root cellar to find him?"

Harmony asked me. "You would have needed help to find it, much less get inside." She sounded amused, but there was a careful note in her voice that belied her joviality. "Or did you just put your hand on the rock and feel that he was in there?"

My gaze whipped to Korin, and I saw him smiling. Not the easy, friendly smile he'd used before, but a predatory, triumphant grin. I started backing away, but I thumped into something immoveable behind me. The guard from last night.

I dived to the side, trying to get away, but the guard was ready for me. His fingers tightened around my arms, making me gasp with pain. Worse, two more men materialized from the trees to stand behind Gabe and Harmony.

A trap, I thought. And not just for me, but for Gabe as well. Was Harmony a part of it?

"Would someone like to tell me what's going on here?" Gabe's fists clenched at his side. "Did or did not this young lady use her ability to determine there was a corpse in here? Korin? Can you please explain?"

Korin gave him an easy grin. "Oh, I can explain. When I learned about Autumn's unique gift, I suspected she wasn't your ordinary needy disciple. That's why I convinced you to let her join even after that policeman showed up. Today when Misty told me Autumn had been sent from her parents, that only confirmed the matter."

"So?" Gabe's brow furrowed. "We'll take Misty back to the city, if that's what she wants. We'll take both of them back. We have nothing to hide."

"Oh, but we do." Korin shoved his hands into the pockets of his brown pants, as though talking about the weather. "You see, I realized Autumn might use her nasty little talent to trace my sister-in-law's death to me."

Harmony gasped. "You killed Sarah? Why?"

"She was going to hire a lawyer to get back her share of the money Inclar had given us from the sale of their house."

"You told me you thought Inclar had killed her," Gabe said. "He'd left by then."

"No, he hadn't. He was here." Korin motioned toward the metal door. "He was in conditioning."

"Conditioning?" Horror filled Gabe's expression, one that reminded me of Essence's terror. Like me, Gabe must guess at the meaning.

"But you let him go," I said.

Korin's jaw worked. "He wasn't going to tell anyone. Or so I thought." He glared at me as if I was responsible, which I guess in a way I was. "I would have taken care of everything, but then Gabe had to come rushing back from the city because after we left, he learned from the detective that you were the woman Inclar attacked. Gabe knew Inclar was here because he'd seen him and let him stay in my room Friday night. Gabe was actually worried Inclar might try to hurt you again. He didn't know I'd already made sure it was too late for Inclar to do anything to anyone."

"You killed your own brother?" I shouldn't have been surprised but somehow I was.

Korin snorted. "I did him a favor. He was miserable without Sarah—and more than half crazy." In a flurry of steps, he crossed the space between us, grasped both my arms, and shook me. "What did Inclar tell you?"

"Nothing! I don't know anything about a murder. I just wanted to make sure Victoria—Misty—was okay, that's all."

Korin's calm returned. "She wanted to leave, but she won't now. None of you will."

"Come on, Korin, this is ridiculous." Gabe took a step toward him. "Let's sit down and talk this out."

Korin snorted. "What's ridiculous is watching you think you run this place when it's Harmony and I who run everything." He glanced at Harmony, but the shadows were growing darker, and I couldn't see her expression.

"Enough." Gabe reached for Harmony as though preparing to leave, but Korin put his hand in his pocket and drew out a small pistol.

"You're not going anywhere except down there." He nodded to one of the guards, who opened the apparently heavy steel door with a grunt, revealing a steep set of stairs that disappeared into total darkness.

"Korin," Gabe pleaded.

"Shut up. I've decided what I'm going to do about Autumn because she may be useful, but I haven't decided what happens to you yet. That may depend on your dear wife."

He turned to Harmony. We all did. She was the unknown factor in all of this. Korin extended a hand to her. "You know how I feel about you. I think you feel the same about me. Come with me. We can have it all."

She took a step forward, and now I could see her better, though her eyes were black and fathomless in the gathering darkness. My heart was pounding because I had no idea how I wanted this to go. If she loved Korin, then Gabe and I were doomed. But if she didn't love Korin and could pretend to until she got help, that would be better. I wished my talent was stopping time so we could discuss the options.

Harmony's chin came up. "You've been a good friend, but Gabe is my husband, and my heart belongs to him." She stepped sideways toward Gabe, clasping his hand. Korin stumbled backward at her words, his eyes going wide, mouth slightly ajar.

Gabe met Harmony's glance for a brief, telling moment, and I realized the whole of their world began and ended with each other. They might have a child and separate goals and different friendships, but they existed for one another. Living with them so long, Korin had been blind and stupid to think anything else.

Korin recovered his shock. "Then you share his fate," he sneered, his words becoming twisted and ugly. He reached out to shove Harmony down the stairs, but Gabe pulled her out of the way, taking the blow himself. He fell into the hole and disappeared, soundlessly except for the soft thumps of his body hitting the stairs.

Harmony hurtled herself carelessly after him, calling his name. "Gabe, Gabe, are you okay? Oh, Gabe!"

For a moment Korin's expression was that of an abandoned little boy, but the next instant it hardened. "You next," he ordered, waving the gun at me.

The guard released me, and I stumbled toward the cellar, calculating my chances of escape. I figured they were near zero. I didn't want to discard my life so carelessly, but once I was in the hole, my chances would slip to the negative side.

I faked a left and then darted right, charging behind one of the men. At any second, I expected a bullet to slam into my back. Or perhaps my head.

"Get her!" screamed Korin.

I ran.

I reached the nearest tree before I went down, the guard's weight heavy upon me. A cracking sensation in my chest was followed by a terrible, shooting pain through my left side. My head hit the ground next, bouncing up and slamming back down again. I lay there too stunned to do more than gasp for each painful breath.

After a moment, the guard's weight lifted, and I was rolled forcefully over. Korin towered above me with the pistol pointed directly in my face.

"You're lucky," he said, calm again, "that Shannon is not a common name for any male, even a cat. It is, however, the name of that detective in Portland. Small world? I don't think so. That's where your luck comes in. The only reason I don't kill you now is to assess what damage that phone call did. I don't even care any more about exploiting your ability. Don't try to get away again. I'm not a patient man, and there are three hundred acres here, plenty of space to make a skinny little thing like you disappear."

Chapter 22

I'd like to say that I miraculously overcame my four attackers despite my aching ribs and many bruises, but, no, I went docilely and gingerly into the hole in the ground that I knew Korin meant for my imprisonment, if not for my burial. To the darkness Essence so feared.

Korin seemed impatient for me to descend and was already motioning to one of his men to start closing the door, though my head wasn't yet clear.

"Wait!" I said. "What about Marcie? Is she down here? Her brother's been looking for her, and he won't stop. He's a PI now. He's already talked to you. He knows I'm here. A lot of people do. The best thing for you is to leave before he brings the police."

"Don't worry about Marcie. As I told her brother, she left us a long time ago. It's not my fault she doesn't contact him. I don't think she likes him much." Korin laughed. "And now the best thing for *you* is to get down there before this door knocks you down."

I hurried, hunching to protect my head, half afraid I would stumble over Gabe's broken body. The dirt wall to my left was covered with chicken wire, and I used that to help me keep my balance as I hurried down the stairs.

At least Korin hadn't mentioned having Ethan in custody. I clung to the thought—and to the hope that he wouldn't harm Jake.

The door above clanged shut, and the pin slid in. Then the scrape of the rock. I hoped there was enough air to survive. Did a root cellar need air, or was that the point?

The stale, musty smell of dampness assaulted me as I went down the last few stairs, which were surprisingly solid, though I couldn't see their construction. The blackness felt heavy all around me, and claustrophobia kicked in, making my stomach churn and my heart race.

"Harmony?" I called.

"Down here. Be careful." Her voice came from farther down and to the right.

"Is Gabe okay?"

"I think so."

"I'm all right," came his faint assertion.

A light went on, and I could see Harmony kneeling beside Gabe, but the light didn't travel much beyond that. When the stairs ended, I almost ran into the wall in front of me, lined completely with what looked like two-by-fours. I turned and moved slowly toward the others, trying not to jar my tortured ribs.

The space was compact, with shelves and crates and bins, all mostly empty except for several large crates of potatoes in one corner. Shrunken onions were braided together and hanging in a dozen bunches from the ceiling. Gabe's recumbent form took up most of the floor space, but I crowded in and squatted next to them, rubbing my arms to stave off the cold that permeated everything this deep in the earth. My feet were the only things that were relatively comfortable, accustomed as they were to exposure.

Though small, the cellar wasn't as cramped as I'd expected, and with Harmony's flashlight, apparently now repaired, the compression feeling of my claustrophobia eased. As long as I breathed easily, had a bit of light, and kept my thoughts from running wild, I'd be okay.

"What now?" I asked, holding a hand over the throbbing in my left side.

Harmony shook her head. "I don't know."

"He can't leave us here," Gabe said. "The others will look for us. They'll know something's wrong."

"Yeah, but will they look in here? I mean, right away?"

Both Harmony and Gabe were silent. "Maybe not for a while," Harmony said finally. "Not until fall. They'll fill the other cellars first."

"How many cellars are there?" I asked.

"Three," Harmony said. "There's one out between the square and the garden, and another by the greenhouse. They were Korin's idea, and they've worked really well. We always had a lot of spoiled food before. They're mostly empty this time of year. Like this one."

Which left plenty of space to imprison anyone who objected to Korin's policies. I didn't say it aloud, but I didn't have to. Harmony gave an expression of dismay, while Gabe closed his eyes tightly, as though to shut out the knowledge.

"Fortunately," I said, "they were too busy getting me down here to check my pockets." I pulled out my radio to show them. "Korin took it when I arrived, but I stole it back before he found me a little while ago in his office."

"What is it?" Harmony eyed the radio doubtfully.

"A two-way radio. A friend of mine is on the other side." Or had been. I didn't want to jinx anything by adding that.

"Does it still work?" Harmony turned her face heavenward. "Oh, please let it work!"

"It was working when I had it last." They watched as I flipped the dials, but no static greeted my efforts. Turning it over, I worked off the lid to the battery compartment. It was empty.

Disappointment flooded me. So much for that.

"Will these batteries in here work?" Harmony held up the flashlight. "They're double A. There's four inside."

I grinned. "I think so! I mean, it came with a rechargeable battery pack, but my friend said he wanted to make sure regular batteries could work in a pinch. Shine the light here before you take them out so I can see how they go in." After some scrabbling around in the dark, I got three of the batteries in, and the unit turned on. Static had never sounded so beautiful.

I pressed the transmit button. "Ethan, are you there?" I asked. Nothing. I tried several more times with no better luck. I even climbed back up to the top of the stairs and tried it there. Still nothing. I was too upset to cry.

"The radio seems to be working fine," I said. "But I don't know about the range or if being under the earth is affecting it. Or even if my friend is still out there." For all I knew, Korin had him in another pit somewhere.

I returned the batteries to Harmony, and when she turned the flashlight back on, I could see the glimmer of tears in her eyes. "We'll think of something," I said. Picking up a potato from the crate, I rubbed it against my jeans before taking a bite.

"At least we won't starve right away. Water might be a problem, though."

Harmony stared at me, something changing in her face. "What Korin said . . . and the radio—you didn't come to join us, did you?"

"No. And even if I did, I don't believe in fasting unless it's for religion or a body cleanse."

She giggled a little crazily. "Neither do I."

Gabe shrugged. "There are fewer complaints when we're fasting."

"People were always fine before," Harmony countered.

I shifted my weight to see if that would ease the pain in my ribs. "So is that new, then? Don't tell me—I bet it was Korin's idea."

"We didn't intend that sort of control." Gabe struggled to a sitting position, his hand to his head as though it hurt. Blood oozed from underneath his fingers. "That's not what we started out doing."

"Well, it's what it's become. Some of your people are very, very afraid, and that's been going on for a least a year, probably two or three."

Gabe hung his head. "When Korin joined us, I thought I could travel more, help more people. He's so competent."

"What about the money?" I asked. "Who takes care of that?"

"There isn't any money. Not after supplies, the land payment, and—" He stopped because we all knew the truth. "Korin," he said. "I turned it over to him."

I wanted to tell him how stupid he was, but there was no point. He was as much an innocent as Winter had been.

So rooted in the present and in doing good that he couldn't fathom the idea of anyone taking advantage of him.

"I caught him smoking marijuana with one of the younger women when you were away last month," Harmony said into the silence. "She didn't even know what it was and was quite out of it when I found them. I was furious. He promised never to do it again if I let it drop, and I've been watching him carefully since, but I can't be everywhere. I don't know where he got it."

I did. What's more, I bet Korin had been the one to give Essence the plant in the first place.

Gabe sighed. "You should have told me."

"You depend on him so much. And he seemed sincerely embarrassed."

That was the problem. Korin was a master at deception.

"Someone will come," I assured them. "I have friends who know I'm here, and they won't abandon me. Meanwhile, we have to think. Make a plan."

"But what if no one comes?" Harmony whispered, panic growing in her voice. "Even if they do, they might never find us. It's so far down. We could scream for hours and no one would hear. Oh, this is all my fault!"

Gabe put his arm around her, drawing her close. "It's okay, honey. It's okay." His voice calmed her, but I didn't know for how long. She would begin worrying about her child soon, if she wasn't already. At least there were plenty of women here who would step in and care for Flower. But as safe as the girl might be for the moment, I knew that wouldn't last. She would be used as a weapon against her parents, who would eventually give everything to Korin to save her life.

We had to get out of here. "How strong are these cellars?"

I asked, eyeing the walls that seemed to be made up of chicken wire stapled to heavy wood beams set at regular intervals. The chicken wire might not hold us back, but the endless packed dirt beyond would pose a real problem. "Is there any way we could force our way out? Maybe through the ceiling?" Though the ceiling wasn't high, the light didn't extend far enough for me to see what held it up.

Gabe shrugged. "I don't really know. Korin had complete charge of the construction. I do remember a lot of wooden support beams over the top and both plywood and metal sheets over the whole thing. Not sure we could get through that without tools. He said he wanted them to last. I inspected the cellars after they were finished, but I haven't been back since."

"Except for today," I said.

He grimaced. "We were searching for Inclar. I told Korin it was time to turn him over to the police, if he was still around, or at least tell them he'd been here. It was too dangerous having him scaring people and possibly attacking you again. But of course Korin didn't like the idea of the police snooping around. He wanted to make sure Inclar was gone and then forget it."

"Guess we know why," I muttered.

No one replied. "Look," I said, fishing the key out of my bra. "Inclar put this under my door in Portland. Hold out your hand. I don't want to touch it after it's unwrapped."

Harmony held out her hand. "Then it's true what Korin said about you being able to see things from certain objects. No wonder he was so interested in you."

Her tone implied a strange sort of satisfaction that Korin still loved her best, and only my talent had attracted him. I supposed every woman had some level of vanity, even a woman like Harmony, who had given her whole heart to her husband.

I set the small bundle on her hand and pulled the end of the cloth until we could see the key. Harmony shook her head. "We don't have any locks here, except the safes, and it's the wrong size for those."

"Unless . . ." Gabe trailed off and began looking around. "This cellar seems smaller than I remember. Normally you only want cellars just big enough for all the food because it keeps better that way. But we have a lot of vegetables, and we needed room for the canned fruit, so we planned to make them larger. This cellar is near the orchard, and we thought we might also use it for apples. Or maybe even have a place to hide things in case of natural disaster. Or war. We all agreed it'd be good to be prepared. Maybe it's the shelving that makes it look small in here, but there isn't enough room here for the barrels of apples we harvest."

"Are you saying there might be more to this place than we're seeing?" I scanned the walls, but the darkness revealed nothing to me except the glint of Harmony's light off the chicken wire.

"I don't know for sure. It just seems smaller now. Add that to the fact that I've been over the entire immediate area of the farm on foot today, including all the cellars, and I've been out on horseback searching further. Inclar was nowhere to be seen. If he's dead, as you say he is, I don't know where else he could be."

I saw where he was going. "Except in a hidden room somewhere. Maybe one down here."

Gabe met my gaze without confirming or denying the statement.

"But you own hundreds of acres," I said. "Korin could have taken Inclar anywhere."

Harmony shook her head. "Korin hasn't disappeared for

any long stretches since he arrived yesterday. In fact, he's been hanging around constantly. I thought it was because he knew I was worried about Inclar, but maybe he was afraid I'd find something out."

"Probably just trying to hit on you," Gabe muttered.

"Don't be angry." Harmony leaned against him. "You're the only man I've ever loved or ever will love." Her voice was solicitous, the age-old tones of a woman reassuring her man. Yet there was an underlying note that gave me pause, though I didn't know for sure what it was. They were in their own world again. Gabe lifted his hand to her face and rubbed his fingers the length of her scar.

"It's okay," she murmured. "My father's long gone. He can't hurt me now. Thanks to you." They hugged as I tried to ignore how uneasy the words made me. Gabe might not have killed Inclar, but that didn't mean he was incapable of murder.

"Korin could have had one of his men dispose of the body," I said. "But let's assume he didn't. Let's assume he kept Inclar close to make sure no one found him. Harmony, can I use your flashlight?"

Harmony started, as though she'd forgotten I was there. She extended the flashlight to me, and I noticed it was the same one I'd broken the previous night. Apparently she had a supply of bulbs. "What are you thinking?" she asked.

Retrieving the cloth that had been around the key, I wrapped it over the handle of the flashlight before taking it from her, not wanting to relive the scene with Inclar or the romantic moments she'd shared with the man I now knew must have been Gabe.

"I'm thinking what if this cellar really was bigger at one time?" I started running the flashlight slowly along the walls.

"What if Korin uses it to hide things? Or people? He could even have hiding places in all the cellars."

Harmony sucked in a breath, but she didn't say anything. She and Gabe watched the trail of light over the walls. Nothing but the chicken wire and boards and dirt. Closer to the ceiling were more wood beams, and the ceiling itself was a maze of them. Standing on the shelves, I ran the light over the beams near the ceiling, but there was nothing unusual, so I jumped down and worked my way along the walls to the base of the stairs, where a two-foot section of the wall was entirely made of wood. No chicken wire. When I banged on the boards, they echoed hollowly, instead of with the thump of a solid wall. "Hello," I said.

"What is it?" Gabe asked. Harmony jumped to her feet and came over.

"Look." I showed her the keyhole in the door. It was at hip level, low enough not to be noticeable unless you were really looking.

Gabe limped over to us. "Try the key."

Harmony started to hand the key back to me, but I shook my head. "You do it." I couldn't hold both the key and the flashlight without more cloth, and I couldn't touch that key with my bare hand unless I wanted to risk passing out.

"Are you okay?" she asked. "Why are you holding your side?"

"I tried to get away. I think they broke a rib or two."

She murmured dark words under her breath that I was too tired to decipher, but it had something to do with how Korin would suffer if she ever laid hands on him. Her hand trembled as she inserted the key. "It goes in but it won't turn."

"Might be rusted. Let me take a look." Gabe jiggled it this

way and that, finally turning it with obvious effort. He pushed the wooden section inward to reveal a damp space so dark it was impossible to get a sense of its size from where I stood.

I angled the flashlight around. "Bigger than out here," I said. The room smelled like an outhouse.

"Oh, no," Harmony said softly.

The light had fallen on a thin figure under several tattered blankets. Next to the figure was a blue forty-gallon water barrel, a large basket, and what looked like an unlit lantern. At first I thought the figure was Inclar, because it was about the same size, but then I recognized the scene from my sister's drawing.

"Marcie!" In seconds I was kneeling beside her, wincing as the movement sent agony through my ribs. Was she dead? No, she was moving now, sitting up, her eyes squinting against the light. A putrid stench wafted up from her wasted body. In her arms she clutched a rolled up blanket like a baby.

"I don't want to leave the farm. Really, I don't. Can we come out now? I promise I'll be good. Please. I'll do whatever you want. I just want to take care of my baby."

"Are you Marcie?" I asked.

She blinked. "Who are you?"

"I'm a friend of Ethan's. Your brother."

"No," she murmured faintly. "Don't bring him here!" Her eyes went past my face, trying to see who was with me. I flashed the light toward Gabe and Harmony.

"Rubin!" Marcie cried, one hand reaching out toward Gabe, the other hugging the bundle to her slight chest. "I've been praying you'd come for me. Kayla has missed you, and so have I!"

Rubin and Kayla, I remembered, were Marcie's dead husband

and baby daughter, which indicated how far she'd gone from reality.

Harmony gave her husband a little shove, and he knelt beside me, taking Marcie's hand. "It's going to be okay," he murmured. To me he added, "I had no idea she was still on the farm. Korin told me she changed her mind and went home."

"How long ago was that?"

Gabe looked to Harmony for verification. "A month, I think. But she was different before that. In January she disappeared for two weeks."

"She was probably here."

"From how hard it was to get in," Harmony added in a fragile voice, "she isn't visited very often."

I bit my lip. "Korin must have another key, though. Inclar left here months ago with this one."

Marcie cried while we watched helplessly, a soft, heart-wrenching sound. I wished there was something more I could do for her, but even breathing hurt my chest. Finally, Harmony moved around to Marcie's other side and gathered the woman in her arms. "Shush, now. It's okay. It's okay."

Things weren't exactly okay, but what else could we say?

The basket near Marcie was filled with dried meats, shriveled fruit, and rotting vegetables, though from the looks of Marcie's thin frame, she wasn't much interested in food anymore. The water barrel had a spigot near the bottom and several quart-sized glass jars to drink from. They were empty, and I wondered if she'd grown too weak to turn the spigot.

Gabe picked up the lantern near Marcie. Unlike the others I'd seen at the farm, this one was battery operated with two thin fluorescent light bulbs, but it gave out only a dim glow when he turned it on. My hatred for Korin increased tenfold.

How could he treat someone this way? No wonder Essence had taken refuge in drugs.

We sat without moving or speaking for several long, silent moments. I had no idea what the others were thinking, but I was contemplating pulling off the chicken wire and trying to dig our way out with pieces of wood from the potato crate. If we started at chest level and worked up, we might eventually get out—if Korin didn't come back and kill us first.

"You're not Rubin." Marcie's eyes were open and staring. "You're Founder Gabe." She gave a desperate cry. "I'm not dead, then. I'm still here, and he's going to come back."

"Korin will not hurt you again," Gabe said, standing. He made a forbidding figure in the dim light. "I promise."

I didn't know how he could promise that, short of killing either Korin or Marcie, and I didn't bet on his chances for the former.

"Help is coming," I told Marcie. "Your brother's been looking for you. That's why I'm here. I came to find you."

"Ethan?" She gazed at me, but we'd already lost her again. Her eyes were wide with terror, and her body shook uncontrollably. If there had been a baby in the blanket, it would have smothered by now. Harmony stroked her hair and murmured comforting words in a low voice. She seemed unmindful of Marcie's stench or the dirty blankets that held who knew what kinds of small critters.

I moved slowly and carefully to my feet. "We have to get out of here," I whispered to Gabe. "Let's look around. See if we can find something to help us pull off the wire so we can dig. This flashlight isn't going to last long. Once we start digging, we'll have to turn it off to save the battery—even if that means digging in the dark."

Gabe stared at me for a moment, perhaps surprised at my initiative. "Good idea," he said finally, his voice low. For my ears only. "I think neither of us can pretend that Korin will ever let us out of here alive." His gaze went from his wife to the unseeing Marcie, his expression dark with poorly concealed fury, as though he could already imagine Harmony degenerating to Marcie's condition.

In silence we walked to the wall and began searching for a likely place. At one point, Gabe picked up a piece of broken two-by-four from the ground. "Better than fingers for digging."

I was glad he wasn't afraid of hard work. "Look, more blankets," I said. "Probably more than one person was down here at a time." Had Victoria been here at one point? Or had Korin only showed her what might happen to her if he was denied his will?

We hadn't found a place for waste yet, though there had to be one because of the ever-increasing smell in this direction. Maybe covering it with a blanket would help.

What I found next was worse than any latrine. The light fell on a scuffed slip-on shoe, and I followed it up a thin, short leg to the torso and at last to the narrow face I recognized only too well. The loose right eye was still rolled up in terror, perhaps in realization that his beloved brother had killed his wife and was about to murder him.

We'd found Inclar.

Chapter 23

Inclar's body looked decidedly worse for wear. I jiggled his leg with my foot and found it stiff with rigor mortis, but that's as far as I was willing to go to check out his condition. Luckily, the latrine was just beyond him, because three seconds later I lost the potato I'd eaten and all the vegetables from the field. Heaving over the pit, I tried not to pass out from the pain in my ribs.

"Marcie," Gabe said, once my heaving had ceased. "What happened to Inclar? Do you know?" He took a few steps toward her and Harmony.

For a moment, Marcie didn't answer, her chin tucked near her chest as she lay in Harmony's arms. Finally she gave herself a little shake and began speaking. "Inclar was out there." She sounded lucid again, and her high, thin voice carried easily in the small space. "He called to me through the door. Said he wanted to let me out, but he'd given someone else the key, and he'd have to come back. I was afraid to answer at first, but then I did. After that Korin came, and they were arguing."

"About what?" Harmony asked.

"About me, about what really happened to Inclar's wife.

Inclar was going to turn himself in, lead the police here, ask some psychic to read the chain that strangled Sarah. He ran away, and Korin went after him. They brought him back a few hours later. At first I thought he was unconscious, but he wasn't breathing."

That meant she'd spent the night and day alone in a tomb-like pit with a dead man. Marcie was quiet again, clutching her blanket baby and turning to push her face into Harmony's shoulder like a frightened child. Harmony rocked her gently.

Gabe walked back to Inclar and squatted down, gently turning Inclar's head with the two-by-four. "I think he died from a blow to the back of the head."

That fit with what I'd seen in the woods. "I guess Korin didn't have time to move him right when it happened."

Gabe stood after his perusal of the dead man, his face tight. "Look here." He pointed to a place where the chicken wire had run out along the wall and the builders had instead tied wires to span the gap between the beams. "Some of these will be easy to undo, and we can stretch out the others with this two-by-four. We'll have to move the body first to get to it."

The body. It was sad to see a man so reduced to such a description. What a waste! Inclar should be with his beloved Sarah, both alive and in good health, and Marcie should be in the comforting arms of her brother. Inclar was beyond any help, but I'd darn well make sure Marcie had a chance.

A noise from the other room shattered the sudden silence. We froze for a precious half-second before we scrambled to the other room. Marcie moaned as we left, but we had to see what was happening.

Maybe Korin had come back to finish us off. "We may have to jump him," I murmured.

Someone was already coming down the stairs, and my heart lightened when I saw by the thin light filtering in from several flashlights above, that it was a woman. Spring, in fact.

We were saved!

She crouched suddenly, and the door behind her slammed shut, leaving us again in total darkness. "Autumn?" Spring called with a sob.

"I'm here," I said. "Just come to the bottom. Carefully." I directed the beam of the flashlight over the stairs and us so Spring could see where we were.

"I was trying to find you, and I couldn't, and then I went to talk to Korin and he said you'd left. I couldn't believe it. You wouldn't have left without telling me."

"Of course not."

"I told him I was going to leave for a little while to see a doctor about my allergies and talk to my mom. He said I couldn't and that if I tried, he'd take Little Jim and hand him over to his father, and I'd never see him again." She was crying in earnest now, and I had to go up a few steps to help her down.

Spring latched onto me tightly, and I gasped with pain, but she was too upset to notice. "How could he take my baby?"

"Where's Little Jim now?" We'd dropped the pretense of calling him Silverstar. Those days were over.

"He gave him to Misty, the girl from the kitchen."

"Then he'll be fine," Harmony said. "Misty loves children. She'll take good care of him. Now, let Autumn go before you break another of her ribs. We've got a plan. We're going to dig our way out."

"Maybe we should try the radio again," I said, returning Harmony's flashlight. "My friend might have just been gone for a while." Harmony eagerly opened the flashlight and handed over the batteries, but there was no answer.

"I don't think the signal's getting through," Gabe said.

"We dig then." Biting back bitter disappointment, I followed the others back to Marcie's prison. Spring gasped to see her and began to worry again about Little Jim. Ignoring everyone, Gabe grabbed hold of Inclar's feet and moved him to the other side of the latrine. I was glad he didn't ask for help. I didn't think I could bring myself to touch the rigid corpse.

From Marcie's supply basket, I removed one of the glass jars that had held water, hoping to use it to dig. The imprints came suddenly and unexpectedly—bright, terrible flashes of aching thirst and helplessness that seared me. Terror, need, want, loneliness. Oh, the soul-killing loneliness! With a cry, I let the bottle fall to the ground, where it clinked against another bottle, knocking it over and breaking it.

"What is it?" Harmony's flashlight blinded me for an instant.

I shook my head, blinking back tears. "Maybe one of you can use the bottle. I can't."

Thankfully, Harmony didn't question me but picked up an intact bottle and a large, knifelike piece of the broken one and strode toward the wall.

"We have to do this tonight while they're sleeping at the farm," Gabe said. "In the morning it might be too late."

I wondered where Jake was and hoped he had the good sense to stay away from Korin. What if he hadn't? What if Korin had killed Jake, as he'd killed his own brother?

I had to warn him. But to do that, we had to get free. I went to find a piece of wood.

Long minutes of digging turned into torturous hours. I sat

down to rest near Marcie for a moment, my body drenched in sweat, and my ribs so numb with pain that I no longer felt them. I imagined a rib piercing a lung and killing me, the idea almost a welcome alternative to being entombed alive. My hands were raw and bleeding from the tedious digging, my injured wrist throbbing and swollen, and I had numerous cuts up my arms. But staying busy kept the fear away. Fear of the cramped space, of the dark. Of Korin.

Gabe, Harmony, and Spring were equally bad off. Spring was taking a turn carving out the dirt, having managed to break a pointed piece of wood off one of the potato crates, and she worked with all the fierceness of a mother separated from her child.

Harmony had begun worrying aloud about her daughter as well, but each time Gabe comforted her. "It's night. She's in bed asleep. Probably with her friends. She's fine."

"What if we never get free?"

Harmony had voiced all our fears. If Korin continued as the leader of Harmony Farms, he would use the people and discard them when he was finished. The children would be raised in strict obedience and worship of that evil man, brainwashed to do whatever he required of them. Memories of suicide pacts other cults had made haunted me, and I couldn't stop thinking of poor Victoria/Misty, her longing for home, and the baby that swelled within her. The face of a victim.

"We'll get out of here," I said. "Sooner or later. My sister knows where I am, and her husband. And Jake."

My words felt empty. No one had to say that we might not live long enough to see the farm freed of its tyrant.

Gabe picked up his piece of two-by-four to help Spring while Harmony came to check on the sleeping Marcie. We were using Marcie's dim lantern now to save our flashlight, which meant we worked almost completely in the dark.

"Marcie has a fever," Harmony told me. "She needs a doctor."

"Her brother's nearby somewhere. As soon as we're out of here, he'll take care of her."

Harmony sighed. "I didn't get to know her very well. I regret that now." Her voice lowered to a soft whisper. "It was because she was so taken with Gabe, you know. I've been used to some of the men falling for me, and I knew that sometimes bugged Gabe. That and the silly things I sometimes do to tease him. But this was the first time I'd ever felt jealous of another woman. I was actually glad when Korin told me she'd left."

"You don't have to be jealous of Gabe," I said. "He adores you."

"Things could change."

"I don't think so. When I first met him and he shook my hand, I felt an imprint from his ring. If you could see yourself as he does, you'd have no doubts."

She looked down, veiling her thoughts with her lashes. "Sometimes I worry that he'll wake up and realize I'm not what he bargained for."

"Oh, he's probably already realized that, but he doesn't care. He loves you just the way you are."

Harmony's face glowed. "Thank you for telling me." She was quiet a moment as she smoothed Marcie's hair. "I do seem to remember Marcie saying she and her family weren't on good terms. That she joined us to get away."

"Her husband and child died. Her brother thought she was okay, but apparently she wasn't. He's been trying to find her for the past year."

"That's sweet."

"It is. I'm a little worried about him, though. He should have brought the police by now."

"Hey," Gabe called before Harmony could respond. "We've reached some sand. It's just pouring down. Come help us clear it away."

Spring was kneeling inside the hole we'd begun, hunched over, her small body barely fitting, and she was shoving sand through the small space between her legs. We cleared with our hands as fast as she could get it out. When the vein of sand ended, we were back to digging, but Spring was able to kneel without crouching in the hole now.

Harmony shook her head when I offered to take another turn digging. "I'll do it now. We're close. No use in damaging your ribs or your wrist further."

"Try to go straight up," Gabe directed her. "As soon as you clear out a little more, I'll be able to fit in there." He'd actually done most of the digging, his farm muscles more developed for the task, but lying half in and half out of the small hole hadn't been easy.

After what seemed like an eternity, Harmony yelped as dirt began falling around her. She dived from the hole into her husband's arms.

Spring and I didn't even wait for the dust to settle before we were clearing out the hole, Spring crouching half way inside the opening and me standing on a potato crate.

"I can stand up," Spring said, doing just that. "I think I see a crack. We did it!"

"Shhh," I cautioned. "Korin might have left a guard."

"Let me try now." Gabe traded places with Spring. It was a tight squeeze for him, so he jumped out and worked vigorously on the sides for a while before climbing back in. We all watched eagerly, except for the sleeping Marcie, as he scraped at the dirt above him, trying to widen the crack to freedom above.

"I need something to stand on," he said. "Can't get any leverage this way."

Spring and I hefted up a crate. Standing on it, he dug for a while longer and then said, "I can see stars."

Finally, he threw down the two-by-four and jumped up. All we could see of him were the tips of his shoes as he dangled in the crevasse we had excavated.

He was back in less than a minute. "I can't see anyone out there. This part is in the clearing, though, so we'll have to hurry. No way anyone will miss the hole as they head for the barn in the morning."

Sore and bleeding, we emerged from the pit. Spring went first, and then Gabe lifted me up while Spring helped me through. My throat constricted in fear at the tight squeeze, but that discomfort was overridden by the pain flaring in my ribs. Blackness threatened, but I managed to get through without passing out. Then Spring and I grabbed Marcie as she came hesitantly through the hole, supported entirely by Gabe from the other side. Harmony followed her, bringing the smelly blankets to protect Marcie from the night chill. Gabe climbed through last.

"Quick! Into the trees," I urged.

Gabe carried Marcie, while the rest of us darted glances at the shadows.

"What do we do now?" Spring asked. "I want to get Little Jim."

"We will," I said. "But first let's try the radio. My friend may have already contacted the police."

I put in Harmony's batteries again and turned on the radio. "Ethan, are you there?" I let the button go.

At her brother's name, Marcie moaned, but she was burning with fever, and I wasn't sure if she understood that she was almost saved.

Almost being the key word.

Harmony gestured for her husband to lay Marcie down on the ground with her head on Harmony's lap. Spring crouched next to her.

"Ethan, come in, please," I said.

Nothing. My mind rapidly turned over the possibilities. Korin was armed, and we were far from civilization. Too far to walk anywhere. So unless we could steal a vehicle, we would be forced to deal with Korin ourselves.

"Ethan, so help me, I'm going to kill you!" I growled into the radio. Where could he be? Worry made me angry.

A crackle from the radio and then, "Autumn?"

"Yes!" He sounded odd to me. "Where have you been? Have you called the police?"

"Ethan's not here. There's no sign of him. This is Jake."

Relief poured over me, turning my muscles weak. "Are you okay?"

"I'm fine. I've been looking for you all over. I followed when you left the square, but someone jumped me from behind, hitting me with a club or something. I was out for a good while. What happened to you? Where'd you go?"

"Korin locked us in a cellar. Gabe and Harmony are with me. Spring is too."

"Everyone okay?"

"Yes. Well, mostly. We found Marcie. She needs a hospital. Any idea where Ethan might be?"

"Everything looks like it's here in his van, but he's gone, and so are all the keys. I'm trying to hot-wire my bike, but it's harder than it looks. Plus, the muffler looks damaged. I guess he tried riding it. I just hope it still works."

Even if we got Jake's motorcycle working, we'd have to hide Marcie in a safe place until the police arrived. She was in no condition to ride on the bike.

"Do you know where Korin is now?" I asked.

"Last I knew he was in the office with some of his men. I don't know if they brought anyone else inside because I couldn't watch both sides of the house. So I came looking for Ethan."

"Something's happened to him. He wouldn't have up and left everything."

"For once we're in agreement. Look, I think we just about have this solved. Where are you?"

I let static fill the air as I looked at the others.

"Tell him we'll meet him in the barn," Harmony said. "It's the closest shelter, and we need to make Marcie comfortable."

I conveyed the message to Jake, and then we waited among the trees while Gabe went to make sure no one was in the barn.

"You realize it's dangerous to stay there," I said.

Harmony shrugged. "What else can we do?"

"I'm going to get my son." Spring stood, looking determined, and I knew I wouldn't be able to change her mind.

"Wait," I said. "Let Jake and me go with you. Besides, we need to figure out where Korin is. Maybe we can steal his phone or a car."

"Maybe he's already taken off." Spring squatted back down near me.

"No way," Harmony said. "He means to kill us all." She was rubbing the scar on her jaw again.

"Your father did that?" I asked.

She took her hand away. "He was drunk. Gabe found me bleeding in the street, and we've been together ever since."

"What happened to your father?"

"I never saw him again."

"And Gabe?"

"What do you mean?"

"Did he ever see your father again?"

She stiffened. "Gabe didn't do anything wrong. Now or then, if that's what you're implying. We didn't intend for any of this to happen." Though I couldn't see her expression, there was anger in her voice.

"I believe that," I said. "But both you and Gabe have to share some responsibility." I tried to keep my tone neutral, but it came out harsher than it might have had I not been beaten and thrown into a hole in the ground and left to die. I was exhausted both physically and mentally, my wrist ached, and my ribs burned fire so that every breath was a challenge. "Korin would never have been able to do any of this if your people had more say in running this place. If family visits were encouraged, if everyone received proper medical care and vacation time. If they didn't have to work from sunup to sundown or fast just because someone new joins. That may help with crowd control, but I'm not sure it's at all what you intended when you built this place."

Her anger ignited. "We give them a home! We love them and take care of them. We give them everything they need."

"Only if they stay forever, and that makes it no choice at all." I set my hand on her shoulder. "Imagine—if people kept what was theirs before they joined. If they actually owned part of the farm or received some kind of wage for their work. You're good at leading, you and Gabe both, and part of what you have created here is wonderful, but even in a family there has to be some recompense and agency."

Harmony's anger died as suddenly as it had come. "We do have a problem," she admitted. "I know that. But you have to understand that it wasn't always like this. Korin changed things. Slowly, so we didn't realize how far we'd gone."

The story of humanity, walking closer and closer to the edge until we don't even realize when we fall.

Spring had been following the conversation, watching our faces intently, wiping her watery eyes on her sleeve. "I really loved it here," she said softly, "but thinking that I was never going to see my mom again . . ." She didn't finish.

Gabe was coming toward us now across the clearing, running. "It's clear," he said when he reached us.

He carried Marcie to the barn, and with effort we got her up the stairs to the hayloft. The loft was long and empty-looking, with only a few dozen bales of hay remaining. These stood to the left of double outward-opening doors at the far side of the barn loft, where I'd learned the men used winches to pull up the hay from a cart outside. The few bales must mean the farm was nearly ready to harvest another crop of alfalfa. It also meant not enough coverage for a proper hiding place, but we settled Marcie behind them anyway, still wrapped in her smelly blankets and clutching her pretend baby.

All the time, I kept wondering where Jake was. If he had hot-wired the motorcycle, he should have been here by now.

"Harmony," Gabe said, "I think you should stay with Marcie. She shouldn't be alone."

Harmony nodded reluctantly. "What will you do?"

"We'll check out the house and see what our options are.

He can't be everywhere at once. Don't worry—we'll be careful."
Gabe caught my eye. "We'd better go. Maybe your friend will
meet us out in the trees. If not, Harmony can tell him where
we went."

As Spring and I climbed down the ladder, Harmony clung
to Gabe, and he clung right back. "Be safe," she whispered.
"Please come back to me." Caught up in a world all their own,
they hugged and kissed.

Averting my gaze, I turned my mind back to the problem
at hand. If Jake ever showed up, the wisest thing would be for
him to drive the motorcycle into town. Well, a phone would be
better, but unless Korin was a complete idiot, he was protecting
his new satellite phone.

Unfortunately, there were a lot of variables in my plan.
Rome might not have a proper police force, or they might be
under Korin's control. If Jake had to drive to yet another city,
that would leave Marcie and the rest of us at risk for far too
long.

Besides, what about Spring and Gabe? Spring wasn't about
to leave her child behind, even to hide temporarily in the
woods, and Gabe's eyes shone with a vengeful glint I didn't
trust.

I joined Spring outside the barn, the clearing lit by the
moon. The earth here was soft against my bare feet and still
warm from the earlier sun, unlike under the trees where the
earth had been cooler. My feet were the only part of me that
was warm, though Spring, also in short sleeves, didn't seem
much bothered by the night air.

Where are you, Jake? I thought. I was really beginning to
worry now. If anything happened to him, I'd never forgive
myself. I took as deep a breath as I could, my ribs aching.

"You okay?" Spring asked.

"I don't know."

She took a step toward me, reaching out her hand. Gently, she probed the area beneath my left breast. When I winced, she nodded and moved to the next rib. "I think only two are damaged," she said at last. "Cracked, but not completely through. It'll take four to six weeks to heal, and there's really nothing you can do about it except try not to hurt it again."

"How do you know?"

She frowned, a forceful thing that seemed to be in lieu of tears. "I broke two ribs once."

"You mean Jim broke them."

She looked down and nodded. At that moment, I wanted nothing more than to break all of Jim's ribs.

"You'd make a good nurse or doctor," I said. "You have a gentle touch."

She smiled and opened her mouth to speak, but our attention was distracted by a moving light at the edge of the trees. Someone was standing there. Was it Korin? Fear shot through me, tingling to the tips of my fingers. I wanted to run back inside the barn and out one of the stall doors. Run forever so I could be safe. I reached out and grabbed Spring's hand. I heard Gabe inside the barn, nearly to the door. I'd need to warn him before he was seen.

The figure stepped out and began running toward us. Immediately, I recognized Jake's easy lope, and the fear turned to joy. I ran to meet him, stifling a cry of greeting in case our voices carried. He grasped me tightly, lifting me up in his arms, and all the happiness of seeing him turned into white-hot pain.

"Put me down, Jake," I said, gasping.

"What's wrong. Are you hurt?"

"I'm fine."

"We think she has a cracked rib or two." Spring came up behind us with Gabe.

Jake scowled at me. "Why didn't you tell me?" Trust him to spoil the moment.

"I didn't know you were going to—" My voice choked and tears threatened. "Never mind." But I didn't need to say more. He shoved his flashlight in my hands and once again the comforting memories of that night at the store appeared in my head, fainter than before but still present. Not my imagination. I smiled at him gratefully.

"What took you so long?" I said, regaining my voice. "Where's the bike?"

"Had to cut the motor before I reached the main house. Ethan really did a number on the muffler when he rode it, and now it's too loud. I ended up pushing it to those trees right in front of the house and left it there." Under his breath he added, "Should have known a math teacher wouldn't know jack about riding a motorcycle."

"Come on," Gabe said. "We shouldn't stay here." Yet as we hurried across the clearing toward the trees, he glanced back at the barn, as though he could see Harmony kneeling by Marcie in the loft. I knew where he really wanted to be, and the fact that he could leave her because of the responsibility he felt for the others at the farm made my opinion of him soar. On the other hand, given that glint in his eyes, he could simply be thirsty for revenge.

"So what's the plan?" I asked no one in particular.

"You and I will go for help," Jake said. "The others should hide somewhere."

"I want my son." Spring's voice was tense with stress.

"You go," I told Jake. "I promised to help her."

"I'm not leaving without you. Gabe can go with Spring."

Gabe shook his head. "I'm going to find Korin. These are my people, and I have to protect them."

Jake stopped moving, blocking our path. "Are you guys nuts? That madman tried to kill you! He still might."

"I don't care." Spring pushed past him and strode into the forest.

Another thought occurred to me. "Jake, on the radio you said Korin's in his office, maybe he's got Ethan there. If so, we have to save him."

"Isn't that what the police are for?"

"Korin's got a gun," I reminded him as Gabe hurried after Spring.

"My point exactly." Jake glared at me, his face barely discernible in the darkness under the trees. I wanted to put my arms around him and hold on with my eyes closed, forgetting any of this ever happened. First I had to keep my promise to Spring. And maybe stop Gabe from doing anything he'd later regret.

"We have to help them." My teeth clicked together as I spoke because I was seriously cold now, though the temperature didn't seem as low as the night before.

Jake muttered something unintelligible as he peeled off his jacket and helped me into it. Then, avoiding my wrapped wrist, he put his hand under my elbow, and we hurried on through the trees. Jake picked the easiest path, careful of my ribs and my bare feet, though the pain in my ribs far outweighed any other discomfort. The warmth from his jacket had made my shivering stop, and I felt grateful for that. It was easier to think now.

We caught up to Gabe and Spring at the married housing, where they were peering around the corner. No one was in the square, but lights were coming from somewhere inside the main house, though not brightly enough to be coming directly from any of the rooms whose windows faced the square. That meant perhaps the hallway or the main room or one of the offices. We couldn't be sure exactly where.

"There's a window to Korin's office," Gabe said. "We can go around and look in."

"What good's it going to do if we find him?" Jake said. "He's got a gun, remember?"

"If I can get inside my office, I'll have a gun too."

Jake started moving. "Okay. You women stay here. Keep an eye out."

Spring shook her head. "I'm going after my son." Before any of us could stop her, she was darting across the square. I started to go after her, but Jake grabbed my arm.

"Someone's coming!" he gritted as I struggled to free myself.

Sure enough, the light on the back porch had come on.

Chapter 24

Spring hesitated when the light flipped on but then picked up speed. She reached the stairs to the women's side of the singles' house, vaulting up them in one leap. She didn't even look back as she opened the door and flung herself inside.

I waited for the bang of the door, but she had the presence of mind to put her hand out behind her and it closed without a sound reaching us.

Meanwhile, the back door to the main house opened, and Korin and two of his goons emerged. No sign of Ethan. I held my breath to see if they'd notice the door to the women's dorm closing, but they were too involved in their own conversation. They weren't attempting to be covert, and the murmur of their voices carried to us, though we couldn't make out the words.

They were coming our way, so we had no choice but to circle around to the far side of the married house to stay away from them. With Jake's arm against mine, I crouched at the end of the structure in the dark and waited for them to disappear into the trees. Everything about Jake was on alert, from his taut muscles to the grim expression on his face. I had no doubt that if I was safely back in Portland he'd be following Korin, awaiting his chance to attack.

"If they're going to the cellar, they'll soon find out we aren't there." Gabe's face showed his age and more. Something new had come alive in his expression, a burning ugliness that I felt echoed in my own heart.

"Then we'd better get Spring and get out of here," Jake mumbled.

"There's enough time to check the office," I said.

Gabe nodded. "And for me to get my gun."

Frustration gleamed in Jake's eyes. "Fine. Let's do it. But I don't like the way that porch is lit up."

"We'll go around to the front." Gabe started forward, slowly at first to be sure Korin was gone.

We sprinted to the front of the main house. It seemed to take far longer than I expected. My ribs burned horribly, but I had no choice except to continue on. Ethan was in danger—I just knew it. Once in the front, we took the time to check Korin's window. Light streamed around the edges of the blinds, but we couldn't see inside.

"Follow me," Gabe whispered, heading to the door. He went in first, his shoes clunking on the wood floor. I went next, soundless on my bare feet, and Jake followed almost as quietly.

Beyond the main room, the hall light was on, and every few steps we took the floorboards creaked. "Better use cushioning in your next building," Jake muttered.

"Shhh," I said.

"Be careful," Gabe whispered. "Korin had a third man with him earlier." He slipped into his own darkened office, while we continued down the hall to Korin's. Gabe came out again before we reached the door, his face pale and his hands empty except for a carved wooden statue. He shook his head, and I knew that meant Korin had found his gun. Of course he would have planned ahead.

That's when I noticed Jake had also picked up a short, sturdy branch from outside. Not much of a weapon against a gun but it was something.

Jake put a hand on the doorknob to Korin's office. "One, two, three," he mouthed, and sprang forward. Gabe followed him, statue raised. I was on his heels, numb with dread.

Inside the office, Ethan sat in a chair in front of the desk, the chair angled so his side was toward us. Ropes secured both hands and feet to the chair. I'd scarcely had time to notice Korin's third man, surprise etched on his face, before Jake launched himself toward the man, knocking him to the floor. His fist drew back and pounded. Once, twice. A sickening crunch and the struggle was over.

"Autumn." Surprise registered on Ethan's face. "You're okay!"

"What happened?" I asked. "Why didn't you get the police?"

He looked down at the ropes. "Well, I've been a bit tied up."

"You weren't here earlier," Jake said. "Where were you?"

"Those men found me right after I left you last night. I tried to radio you, but there wasn't an answer."

"Your radio was back at the van," Jake said.

"Well, yeah. They followed me back, and I put it down before they got me. They actually kept me tied in the van until just a few hours ago. But I swear I didn't tell them anything about you two."

I was working at the ropes on Ethan's hands, but his fingers grabbed mine. "What happened to you? Are you okay? What about Marcie?"

His fingers felt warm and strong. "She's alive—barely. We need to get her to a hospital or she won't survive."

"Then we need to hurry." He rubbed his wrists, but they didn't look too sore. He was lucky they hadn't cinched the ropes more tightly—or thrown him into a dark pit.

While Jake tied up the unconscious man on the floor, Gabe untied Ethan's feet. "Where did Korin go?" Gabe asked Ethan.

Ethan came to his feet. "I don't know. I tried to convince him that I'd pay to have my sister back, but he didn't even confirm that she's here. I don't know where he went."

"She's been in a root cellar for at least a month," My eyes went to Korin's desk where the three prescription bottles sat, the same ones I'd seen in Ethan's van. "You brought her medication? I thought you said it wouldn't be safe to give them to her." I reached out for the bottles, but he caught my hand in his, staring at the cuts on my dirt-stained fingers.

"I know she has to see a doctor first, but I thought the pills might convince them to let me see her, so I asked Korin's men to bring them along. Look, is she really okay? Did you tell her I was coming? Did she say anything?" Sadness filled his face. "I just hope she forgives me for all my mistakes."

"She was too far gone to tell us much." I rubbed my hand up and down his arm, a show of sympathy, and he took the opportunity to step closer.

His fingers touched my cheek near the cut. "This looks a lot worse than the last time I saw you. Something else happened, didn't it?"

"Sorry to interrupt this tender reunion," Jake growled before I could respond, "but we really need to get out of here."

Ethan put his hand on my arm, where I imagined I could feel the heat of him through Jake's jacket. "Where's my sister?" he asked me.

"In their big barn. That's out to the left beyond the trees, if you're looking at the house straight on."

"I know where it is. I did a little reconnaissance before you called me last night." He smiled, and I felt more at ease. We had evened the odds a little. Four to three now. Five if we counted Spring.

"Come on," Jake urged. "We have to move."

We were walking down the hall on our way out the front when we heard steps on the stairs. My heart shifted into high gear, a heavy thumping in my chest.

"Great," Jake muttered. Shoving me into the dark confines of Gabe's office nearly opposite the back entryway, he jumped across to the other side of the hallway and stood poised to attack. Gabe and Ethan waited on the side closer to where I hid in the dark office.

I considered my options. Even if I dared make noise trying to get out the window, I wasn't willing to leave Jake and Ethan. I stood with my back against the wall, steeling myself for the confrontation to come. I kept seeing the little pistol in Korin's hand and that froze me in place. Would I be able to move when the time came?

An odd sound came from outside the half-open window. A thrumming sound. Something else Korin had in store for us? Or was it just my heart?

With a burst of shouts, the fighting began. The cries and grunting compelled me into the hall. Gabe was down on the ground, apparently unconscious, and near him Ethan wrestled with the big man who'd attacked me last night, the one whose belt buckle testified of the terrible things he'd done to others. Jake was on the far side, struggling with the other guard, a blur of punches and maneuvering. I couldn't see Korin, which made me even more nervous. Had he found Marcie and Harmony?

Ethan cried out as the big man landed a punch to his stomach. For a man who'd supposedly trained in martial arts, he wasn't making much headway. I scooped up Gabe's fallen statue, and with all the strength I could muster, smashed it at the base of the man's skull. To my surprise, his eyes rolled up and he collapsed.

"Thanks," Ethan wheezed.

"No problem." I touched my right wrist gingerly, wondering if this time I'd broken a bone with the impact.

Jake was standing over the other man. "We need to get some rope." But even as he spoke, he was turning to new movement at the back door.

Korin stood there, his customary ponytail partly loose from its elastic and framing his wide face with wisps of stringy hair. He wasn't alone. Spring was with him, her arms around her sleeping child, her eyes bright with terror. Korin's pistol pointed at her head.

"Nobody move," he ordered in a deceptively calm voice, as though he'd asked us if we'd like bacon with our eggs.

"Okay, now, we're just going into my office and wait for my friends here to wake up and then we'll take care of you." His eyes flicked over me, took in Jake's presence, paused on Gabe's still form, and finally came to rest on Ethan. "Your sister, it seems, has flown the coop."

"I guess our deal's off, then. If you can't deliver, I won't pay."

Korin shrugged. "That's okay. Something tells me she might bring me more than you were willing to pay—once I find her. Certain things she said are beginning to make sense now." Underneath the anticipation, Korin's voice was beginning to show strain.

The tendons in Ethan's neck bulged. "When I get my hands on you—"

"Put your muscle where your mouth is," Jake blurted suddenly. "You're all talk, but I suspect there's a lot you aren't telling us, Mr. Math-Teacher-Turned-PI."

Ethan blinked at this sudden attack, but I knew Jake was only trying to distract Korin. "You're just upset because Ethan likes me," I yelled at Jake. Two could play at the distraction game. "Well, I'll tell you something—I don't need a brother. At least Ethan doesn't treat me like a baby sister."

Jake's nostrils flared. "He's using you!"

"Says you!" I shouted more loudly. "At least when he kisses me he doesn't give me any of that fake crap you dish out!"

His voice rose to meet mine. "You're the one who's always saying how grateful you were for my support after your father's death. I won't use that to make you feel obligated to me!"

"I don't feel obligated to you or to anyone! ANYONE! And I'm not your little sister, so stop treating me that way!"

Jake blinked as words eluded him. I understood. We weren't faking this scene. Not a bit of it.

In the next instant, Jake's muscles tensed. I knew what he planned. He lunged toward Korin at the same moment I slammed into Spring and her son, knocking them to the side. She cried out as they fell near the door. The loud crack of the pistol reverberated through the house, ricocheting at least once before finding its target.

Please, not Jake, I thought, turning frantically, ignoring the agony of my ribs.

Jake and Korin were struggling for the gun, both very much alive. It was Ethan who had his hand over his arm, staunching the flow of blood beneath. Nothing life-threatening, I saw.

"Run!" Jake yelled at us. Spring leapt immediately for the door with her son, but I started toward Jake. Ethan let go of his wounded arm and grabbed me.

"Get her out of here!" Jake gasped.

"No!" I tried to shake off Ethan. "We have to help him!"

Jake and Korin were still fighting for the gun. Pulling myself from Ethan's hand, I dived for the wooden statue.

A rough arm closed around my neck, bringing me up short. The big guard had regained consciousness—and he was insane with fury.

Now I understood why Jake had wanted me to run. I choked as the arm tightened.

"Help her!" Jake ordered Ethan.

Ethan looked back and forth between me and Jake several times before sprinting to the door and out into the night.

"He'll bring help," I rasped. The guard tightened his grip.

Truth was, I didn't really have much hope of help. If Jake didn't best Korin in the next few seconds, we'd both end up dead, and then Korin would find and kill Ethan and do whatever he pleased with Spring and her son. And Gabe and Harmony and Marcie and everyone else.

I was ready to give in to the tempting blackness when I felt her presence.

My sister.

Clawing at my captor's arm, I screamed, "No, Tawnia! Get out of here!"

That distracted Korin. There was a loud *crack!* as Jake knocked his forehead against Korin's face, sending him reeling. Jake ripped the gun from his hand. The air to my lungs was completely cut off now, and the blackness was encroaching. I thought I saw shadowy figures coming into the room, but I didn't know if they were friend or foe.

"Step away from her," came a deadly voice.

The big man abruptly let me go, and the next moment I was falling. I didn't care. I just wanted air. I sucked it in, not minding in the least the torment in my throat and ribs.

I never hit the floor.

When I could see again, I found myself supported in Detective Shannon Martin's arms—arms that felt safe and strong and better than anything I'd ever experienced.

Until I remembered Jake.

Frantically, I turned my head, wilting as I saw Jake was okay. He met my gaze for a long, telling moment. He was also surprised and relieved that we'd survived. That I'd survived.

Then he knelt by Gabe's unconscious form, and the moment was over.

"What, no sarcastic comment?" Shannon's voice sounded strangely gruff.

I dragged my eyes to his. Emotions swirled in his face, but I couldn't identify any of them. "Now that you mention it," I croaked, "you did cut it a bit late."

"You're still alive, aren't you?" His eyes wandered over me as though making sure.

"No thanks to you."

"Should I leave?"

I wanted to roll my eyes, but I couldn't. I hurt everywhere. If he hadn't been holding me, I'd probably fall to the ground and lie there in a puddle of pain. "And waste this opportunity to question me? If only I could be so lucky."

"I do have a lot of questions."

I sagged away from him. "Help me sit." The sooner I sat, the sooner he could be free from me, and me from him. He eased my sore body down to the floor in the hallway and squatted next to me.

"Where's Tawnia?" I asked. Behind Shannon, I could see another officer cuffing Korin and his men. Jake was still trying to wake Gabe.

"She and her husband are in the chopper with my partner."

Ah, a helicopter. That explained the odd thrumming sound I'd heard earlier. "No, she's not." Every word hurt my throat. "She's close." But she wasn't as close as my fear had first made me believe. The main thing was that Tawnia was okay, and the knowledge made me want to cry with relief.

He sighed. "Should have known she wouldn't stay put."

"How?" I asked.

Shannon's eyes narrowed. "You mean, how did we find you?" When I nodded, he continued, "After your call, your sister contacted me because of your talk about a cat that didn't exist. She'd also drawn frightening pictures of you, and she was pretty much hysterical. Fortunately, I got that map you'd saved on your email, since that math teacher you told me about never returned my calls, and we were able to pinpoint this location." He shrugged. "I broke a few rules."

I smirked with more than a little difficulty. "See? I'm a good influence on you."

"You still owe me one."

And I was sure he'd make me pay. Probably on his next missing-person case.

Gabe's eyes were open now. He stared, uncomprehending, until Jake began explaining what had happened. As Gabe struggled to sit up, Shannon's partner came into the hallway, dressed in another navy pantsuit, her gun drawn. I wondered if Paige Duncan ever wore anything but navy, but at least the pants afforded more movement than the skirt she'd had on the first time we met.

"Is it clear?" she asked. Her ironed hair was a bit mussed, as though she'd run through the woods.

Shannon sighed. "Let her come in."

"I tried to make her wait in the chopper, but not even her husband could get her to do that. Short of shooting her—"

He waved aside her explanation. "It's okay. Go get them."

Seconds later, Tawnia was there, crying and holding me. One minute she was asking if I was okay, and the next she was scolding me for not keeping my promise to get out at the first sign of danger. "I'm never letting you do anything this stupid ever again!"

"That goes for me too," Jake agreed.

I smiled, or tried to. My muscles weren't obeying, and at the moment I was content to sit slumped there in the hall against the wall. Shannon was watching both me and Tawnia, and I knew he was comparing us. Everyone did.

"Did you see Ethan?" I asked Tawnia. I was wondering if he had gone for help or had only saved himself.

"I saw him outside. They're bandaging his arm."

Near Jake, I saw Gabe trying to get to his feet. "Rest a minute," Jake told him. "We'll send the officers out to get Harmony and Marcie." Gabe didn't respond, his attention focused on the floor near his leg.

Paige Duncan poked her head back in the door. "Uh,

there's a lot of folks waking up over here. I could use some help from someone in charge."

"I'm in charge," Korin said arrogantly. "They won't listen to anyone else."

Paige laughed. "I don't think so. They're asking for Founder Gabe, and unless I miss my mark, he isn't you."

"I'll get free," Korin sneered at her. "You won't be able to make the charges stick. Not one of them will testify against me. You'll see."

"I will," I said, the words more a croak than human speech.

Korin let off a stream of curses, but everyone ignored him. Except Gabe, who started moving in his direction, his face set in rigid lines. Something glittered in his hands.

"The gun!" I shouted.

I was too late. The shiny little pistol was already firing.

Korin's body tensed momentarily, a look of surprise on his face. Then he slumped against the wall where he stood, red welling from his chest. A second later, his body collapsed against the wall and slid to the floor, leaving the wall behind him spattered with gore.

Tawnia screamed, her hands going instinctively to protect her unborn baby. Bret stepped in front of her.

The pistol fell from Gabe's fingers. "My people are finally safe," he said, "and he'll never be able to hurt Harmony."

"Don't we know anything about securing a crime scene?" Shannon shouted at his partner and the other officer." Look, you two get out there and calm those people while I get this bozo locked up somewhere. Before we have a riot on our hands."

Shannon took Gabe to his office, where he handcuffed him to his chair. "Stay here," he ordered, "or I'll shoot you myself."

"You can go outside," Jake said. "I'll look after him. I don't think he'll give us any trouble."

"No, I'll watch him," Bret volunteered. "You go with the detective. Those people might listen to you better than any of us. They know you at least a little."

One look at Gabe's pale, defeated face, shaking hands, and absent expression was all Shannon needed to make him agree to Bret's suggestion, but not before he went over the office for weapons and cuffed Gabe's other wrist to the opposite armrest for good measure.

"I'll send in one of my officers as soon as I'm outside," Shannon told Bret. "If you'll give me a hand, Jake, we'll find something to cover our dead guy in the hallway before we go outside."

As Jake and Shannon left, Tawnia put her arm around my shoulders. "Are you hungry?

"I don't believe this," Bret said, a note of humor in his voice. "After all that's happened, you're talking food?"

"Don't listen to him," Tawnia said. "He has no idea."

My stomach was growling, and I was weak from lack of eating anything but herbs and a raw potato all day, which I'd lost in the pit after finding Inclar's body, but the truth was I didn't know if I'd be able to get my mouth to work right or my throat to swallow.

I leaned on my sister. "I could use some water."

"Just a drink? Nonsense. What you need is something solid. You know you'll feel better."

I didn't protest, knowing that finding food would give her something to do.

"Wow, look at this fridge," Tawnia said, once we'd gone to

the kitchen and she'd settled me at the table. "It's huge. Maybe we should get one like it installed in our house."

I actually smiled.

Now that the danger was over, I began thinking about what Jake and I had said when we were yelling to distract Korin. How much of what he'd said was real and how much did I simply want to believe? I hadn't come to any decision when Spring entered the kitchen with Victoria and Essence. Spring was still carrying her son, who was rubbing his eyes, his face red from crying.

"Are you okay?" I asked, glad Shannon had let them come inside.

Spring sat across the table from me, rocking back and forth to calm her son. "Thanks to you and Jake."

"You'd have done the same for us."

Essence sat next to Spring, but Victoria remained standing awkwardly next to the table. For a few seconds, all we heard was Tawnia moving things around inside the fridge and making the occasional exclamation of discovery.

"I want to tell you I'm sorry," Victoria said finally. "I told Korin what you said about leaving, about my parents sending you." Tears leaked down her round cheek. "I didn't want to, but I thought maybe he was setting me up. You know, testing me to see if I was loyal. I was afraid, especially for the baby." Her hand went to her stomach. "I didn't think I'd be able to . . ." Her words drained away.

"Survive in that cellar, you mean." I reached for her hand. "I don't blame you one little bit. You don't have to worry anymore. Korin isn't going to hurt you or anyone ever again."

"Thanks to Founder Gabe," Essence put in, and we nodded

in troubled silence. We were all glad Korin was gone, but murder was still murder.

"Do you think my parents would still want me to come home, even with the baby?" Victoria asked in a soft voice.

"Of course." I wanted to ask if the baby was Korin's, but I already knew the answer. Victoria's fear spoke for her.

"Then I want to go home."

"I do too," Essence said. For the first time since I'd met her, she was alert. "Fox and I both want to leave." One of her hands disappeared beneath the table, and she brought out my earrings. "I'm sorry for taking these. It's been so long since I had anything different."

"You can have them," I said. "Really, I don't mind. They make my ears hurt." Ethan would just have to repay whoever he borrowed them from.

Tawnia emerged from the fridge, her hands full. Victoria rushed to help her. "We're having something to eat," Tawnia announced. "Anyone want a bite?"

Essence and Victoria shook their heads, looking pale at the very thought. But Spring grinned. "Are you kidding? I'm starving. I'll eat anything at this point."

A loud shout from outside drew our attention. "What's going on out there, anyway?" I asked.

"Some of the men are demanding to talk to Gabe," Victoria said. "The policemen don't seem to be able to control everyone. That's why we came inside. If Harmony was here, she'd put an end to it, but we can't find her. I sent someone to get Scarlet, so maybe she'll calm everyone down."

"Harmony's in the barn," I said. "Did they send someone there?"

Spring shook her head. "Not that we heard. But there are

too many people out there asking questions to hear much of anything."

"What about Ethan?" Tawnia turned from where she was slicing thick slabs of homemade wheat bread. "Strange that he didn't come in to see how you were."

Cold fingers shuddered down my spine at her words. Ethan had run when we'd most needed him. Maybe I shouldn't be surprised he hadn't come inside after the crisis was over.

"He must have gone to the barn to find his sister after they bandaged his arm," Spring said. "Flesh wound, I think they said. Bleeding a lot, but not too serious."

"You didn't see him out there just now?" I asked.

Spring shook her head. "No."

"And he didn't ask any of the officers to go with him?"

"I don't think so. Is that a problem?"

"Maybe not." But suspicion curled through my gut. I lurched to my feet and hurried to the kitchen door as fast as my sore body would allow.

"Where are you going?" Tawnia dropped her knife.

"Down the hall to Korin's office."

"It's natural that Ethan would want to see his sister," Tawnia said, hurrying after me.

"I think he should have taken someone to help her, that's all. It seems strange to go alone." He might be too crazy with worry to wait, I supposed, but something still felt wrong.

The man who had guarded Ethan was gone, but the medicine bottles were where I had last seen them on Korin's desk. This was the piece of the puzzle that didn't fit—two simultaneous prescriptions for anti-depression medicine. And the way Ethan had carted them around, always intercepting my hand before I could touch them.

I gritted my teeth as my fingers closed around the bottles, steeling myself against the truth. As expected, the imprints came easily.

I reached out to give the tablets to Marcie, standing over her until she put them in her mouth. "Just take these, and the pain will be over soon," I said kindly.

I recognized Ethan's voice, so that had to be his hand proffering the medicine.

Marcie reluctantly downed the pills, falling quickly asleep.

"It's your mother's fault for leaving the money to us equally," I said, my/Ethan's voice becoming dark and hard. *"It belonged to my father, not yours, and you will never have it. After a few more weeks of preparation, an unfortunate overdose will correct everything. It won't matter that I spent my own share or that my tenure has been ripped from me. No one will be able to prove I did anything wrong. You, my dear half sister, will cease to be a problem."*

Ethan had planned to murder her. No wonder the imprints were so strong.

I dropped the bottles, which clunked onto the wood floor. Blood whooshed through my veins.

"What is it, Autumn?" Tawnia stood beside me. Spring was behind her, Little Jim on her hip.

"Ethan didn't come to save Marcie," I said. "He came to kill her—and maybe Harmony, too, if she's in the way. Hurry! We have to help them."

Chapter 25

I pushed past them and started down the hall. "We have to tell Jake and the others."

"What's going on?" Bret said, as we passed Gabe's office.

I repeated what I'd told Tawnia and Spring, hardly slowing my pace

"If that's true, you have to free me!" Gabe cried, his gaze no longer absent. "I have to get to Harmony before he does."

I didn't answer. There was no time, and I didn't have much voice left anyway. I fled toward the door, averting my eyes from the blanket-covered mound and the bloody gore staining the wall. At least Korin's body was covered, unlike his poor, betrayed brother in the dark, musty cellar.

Outside, chaos reigned. Instead of men arguing for the freedom of their leader as I'd expected, everyone milled about in confusion, staring with horror as fire devoured the singles' house, the men's side almost completely engulfed in flames. A dozen or so of the men were running with buckets of water toward the burning house. Jake, Shannon, and the other two officers were nowhere in sight. Screams sounded from inside the burning house. I couldn't tell if they came from the men's or the women's side.

"Make a line to the well!" Scarlet bellowed, striding across the square. "We have to get this fire out before it takes everything!" She pushed people into place as her bulk hurtled toward the well at the far side of the square. Menashe, Blade, and several others ran after her with buckets.

More screams. Two women emerged, coughing, from the women's side of the house.

Where was Jake? I hoped he was helping put out the fire and not inside playing hero.

I turned to Spring and Tawnia, who'd followed me out of the house. "You two find Jake and Shannon and get them to the barn. Have Bret and Essence help you look."

"What are you going to do?" Tawnia's fingers dug into my shoulders.

"I'm going to help Marcie."

"No!" Looking at her was like gazing into a mirror; my terror was written plainly on her face.

"If I don't go, two women are going to die. I have to warn them. What else can we do?"

Several long seconds passed, and then her jaw set. "Go." I knew how much it cost her to say that.

"Okay. But you be careful too." I reached out and laid a hand on her stomach, taut with the baby inside. Our eyes met, and we both nodded, the connection between us so strong that our wills were indistinguishable.

"You'll never get there in time," Spring said. "He was gone before I came inside."

"I've got to try. Just make sure you find Shannon and Jake."

I ran back into the house, through the meeting room, and

out the front door to the trees. The motorcycle Jake had stashed was there, not hard to find at all if you knew what to look for. The wires he'd used to bypass the key system were exposed and ready to rejoin. It started on the first try.

Now if I could remember how to drive the contraption.

Riding a motorcycle is a lot like driving a car, except for the balancing thing. Worse, shifting the gears using the spiked pedals on a bike can be very painful in bare feet. Too late now. I gritted my teeth and shifted to second, third, fourth, my foot protesting numbly at the abuse. I almost wiped out twice before I got to the moonlit dirt road that led past the houses, through the trees, and to the main barn. The route was much faster than walking, but unless Ethan had returned to his van first, he had a good head start.

The unmuffled roar of the bike would warn Ethan of my approach. I wanted to believe my presence would make a difference to what he was planning, but the truth was that Ethan had played me from the start. I thought now of all the instances where he had urged me on in this search, backing off only as I fell into step with his will. His fake concern was all too apparent now, and I felt like an idiot for falling into his trap.

I wished I'd listened to Marcie more carefully when she had protested the mention of Ethan's name in the cellar, instead of chalking it up to her insanity. One thing was certain: I didn't save Marcie once to let her fall into his hands now.

Would I be in time? Or was he at this moment strangling the poor woman? Or would he use the big gun he'd shown us at Tawnia's?

I was going so fast that when I came upon a dip in the dark road, I nearly wrecked the bike. My ribs screamed with pain at the jolt, but I held my seat. Barely.

The barn was in sight. I should have cut the power and run the rest of the way, but I suspected Ethan had already heard me if he was there, and I wasn't in shape for running. So I drove all the way up to the door of the barn and cut the engine. The sudden silence was deafening.

I took a painful breath that brought tears to my eyes as I limped the few steps to the open door, pushing myself to go faster. The lights inside the barn were on as they hadn't been earlier. Ethan was here. I had to do something quick and loud.

I jogged across the short space to the ladder leading to the hayloft and started climbing. "Harmony?" I called hoarsely, hoping to interrupt whatever might be going on above me. "The police are here, and we're going to get Marcie to the hospital. You won't believe everything that's hap—"

A figure loomed at the top of the ladder. Ethan. Too late, I realized I should have kept my mouth shut and tried to sneak up behind him.

Innocence was my best defense. "Oh, there you are. Everyone's looking all over for you. They'll be here in a minute to help us with Marcie."

"You touched the bottles, didn't you?" he asked without expression.

I stopped climbing. "What are you talking about?" My voice held a hateful little quiver at the end, one I didn't think he'd attribute to my being choked.

"If there's one thing I've learned from teaching math, it's logic. I think you touched the bottles and you learned something you shouldn't have. Everyone was busy with the fire, so you came yourself. Now get up here."

I took a step down the ladder.

"Up!" His hand pointed down at me, and I saw the glint of a gun barrel.

"You weren't being held in the van all this time, were you?" I said, stalling for time. "You didn't even try to contact the police."

"Bingo! I was waiting for an opportunity to catch Korin alone—which I did shortly before you showed up."

"Why?"

"To offer him money to make sure Marcie never left here, of course. The idiot would have followed through if you hadn't ruined things."

"But you were tied up."

"Only until he brought me proof of her death and I could pay him. Shut up now and start climbing."

I considered diving off the ladder, tucking and rolling out of his range. Even the idea made my ribs ache.

"Don't even think about it." He pushed the gun a few more inches in my direction. "I've had a whole year to practice. I'm really good. Better than I ever was at teaching math."

"Why did you lose tenure at the college?" Certainly not because he was looking for Marcie.

"I was fired. That's what happens when you date coeds and come to work after staying out all night." His shoulder lifted in a half shrug. "I hated that job, anyway. I shouldn't have had to work at all."

"You mean if Marcie hadn't taken your money."

"If you don't get up here in two seconds, I *will* shoot you."

So I climbed up the rest of the ladder, but as slowly as I dared. His hand closed over my sore right wrist, yanking me the last few inches.

"Ow," I said. The bandage on his own arm had a bright

spot of red leaking through, but he didn't seem fazed by the wound.

He stepped closer, his eyes hard. "If I'd had any idea one of the leaders here was a crook, I'd have bribed him a long time ago and you wouldn't have been necessary." He pushed me in the direction of the bales of hay where I knew Marcie was hidden. I felt sick. Had he already killed them? The bare wood of the nearly empty loft reminded me somehow of a huge coffin.

We rounded the bales, and I saw Harmony first, her body curled face down on the thin layer of hay on the floor. Blood oozed from the back of her head, dripping around to the front of her face and then pooling on the floor. But she was breathing.

Behind her Marcie was awake and half sitting, propped awkwardly up against a bale of hay. The ragged bundle of pretend baby was no longer in her arms. "Please, Ethan," she said. "Why are you doing this? I left you everything. Wasn't that enough?"

"You gave these people money."

"That was mine and Rubin's. I didn't take the money that had belonged to your father."

"I can't get at it. Not unless you're dead or you sign it over to me."

"I'll sign it over. I don't want the money!"

"Sorry. You won't be leaving here, dear sister." He barked a strangled laugh. "And I've made sure the cult won't collect on any contract you might have signed."

He'd talked about the fire before, but only now did things click into place. "You started the fire?" I asked.

He smiled. "It'll spread to all the buildings. They're so close."

I tried not to think about Tawnia. Surely she and Bret would get to safety.

"Please, Ethan," Marcie begged. "I'll do anything."

"Even if I believed you, it's too late."

"It won't work," I said. "The others know I came here and why."

"It'll be my firsthand account against their conjectures." Ethan nearly spat the words. "Because in the end, I'll be honored for trying to find you, for trying to stop Harmony from killing you after you discovered that she had killed Marcie to protect her secret lover, Korin, from going to prison, not knowing that her estranged husband had already killed him."

A gasp came from Harmony, who was turning over on the floor, wiping the blood from her eyes. "Is Gabe okay?"

"What does it matter?" Ethan jeered.

He'd obviously crossed over the line of sanity, perhaps never to return. He'd be discovered and go to jail, but that wouldn't do any of us any good if we were dead.

With a grunt, Ethan pushed me toward the other women. I tripped over Harmony's feet and fell to the floor with a force that made my ribs burn.

Ethan brought up the gun with a steady hand. His face was no longer handsome but contorted with greed and hatred. His fingers began to contract.

I dived forward and to the side, and the bullet slammed into the floor where I'd been. Harmony's scream sounded like the grating of metal on wood. On hands and knees, I scrambled away, drenched in agony that emanated from my rib cage. I'd cleared the hay bales, which left Ethan behind me, but I didn't see how I could make it to the ladder and down before he finished with the others and came after me. Darkness from the pain in my ribs was already beginning to fill my vision.

No, that was one of the doors at the end of the loft. The

door now gaped halfway open, revealing the dark night outside. Gabe climbed through the gap, grabbing onto a bit of rope hanging from a winch to pull himself up the rest of the way. Almost before I registered his presence, he was hurtling toward me, rounding the bales of hay, and leaping at Ethan, who had the gun pointed at Harmony. Gabe still had handcuffs on both wrists, and dangling from one was a piece of broken chair.

The men struggled for the gun, falling down to the wooden floor with a loud crash. Over and over they rolled. I crawled toward them, wondering what I could do to help Gabe.

"No, Gabe," Harmony moaned.

I pulled myself to my feet. One step, then another. What could I use against Ethan? Desperately, I searched, finding nothing but bales of hay that I couldn't lift on a good day, much less in my weakened condition.

The gun went off. This time there was no sound of the bullet hitting the ground. I stood frozen, Harmony's sobs the only sound in the sudden stillness.

Ethan climbed to his feet, leaving Gabe sprawled on the floor, hands over his chest, blood spreading under his fingers. Harmony crawled toward him. Ethan aimed again at Harmony's head.

I hurled myself at him, my sight momentarily blanking with pain. He fell backward under my impact but didn't lose his grip on the gun. His fingers latched onto my hair, forcing my head back. I felt the coldness of the gun barrel between us, digging into the soft flesh under my chin. He wrenched me off him onto the floor, the gun still against my throat. I couldn't move for the fire in my chest. Couldn't breathe. All my chances were gone.

A shot rang out. I closed my eyes and stopped breathing. Ethan's body went limp over me. I took another breath.

"Autumn?" Shannon's voice, coming from the direction of the hayloft ladder. In seconds he was there, rolling Ethan off me. "Are you okay?" His voice was scarcely a whisper. Fingers pressed up against my throat as he checked for a pulse.

I forced my eyes open. His face was streaked with soot, and he smelled like fire. His eyes reminded me of the green-blue of the ocean on a cloudy day. I'd never been so happy to see anyone.

"A cloudy day, not a clear one," I murmured. His face was moving, the features whirling together. I wondered if I was going to throw up.

"Is she hurt?" It was Jake's anxious voice moving rapidly toward us.

I turned in his direction with a small cry. He was safe! He was here! He knelt next to Shannon, and after a few moments, my eyes managed to focus on his face. Like the detective, Jake had been fighting the fire, and his already dark face was blackened with soot. Worry lined his brow, the deep furrows broken by an oozing gash that would likely need stitches. No doubt he'd been playing hero at the burning house.

"Pulse is strong, but she's incoherent," Shannon said. "She might be in shock." The space of a few heartbeats passed before Shannon arose, conceding his place to Jake. "Try to keep her warm." Without a backward glance, he crossed to help Harmony staunch the flow of Gabe's blood.

"Are you hurt?" Jake asked, kneeling over me. "Did he shoot you?" His fear was palpable.

I managed a tiny smile. "Do you mean Shannon or Ethan? Because I'm pretty sure they both fired at me tonight."

Jake gave a disgusted grunt and began peeling back the leather jacket, searching for signs of injury. I groaned and slapped his hands away. "Nothing hurts too bad—except my ribs. Don't touch them."

He gathered me gingerly in his arms, the soot on his face running with tears and blood from his cut. For a long moment he simply held me. I wanted to look into his eyes, to see what secrets they might tell, but exhaustion took me. I closed my eyes and drifted for a moment. As long as I didn't move or breathe too deeply, I could stay here forever.

"How did Gabe get away?" I asked finally, forcing my eyes open. It hurt worse than before to speak.

"Tawnia and Spring broke his chair and let him go after they sent Bret to search for me. They were afraid they wouldn't find me in time."

"Gabe saved us."

"We were still almost too late."

"But you weren't." Or Shannon hadn't been. I'd probably have to thank him someday.

He nodded and stroked my cheek with his finger.

Several yards away, Harmony's sobs grew louder, becoming violent, choking sounds. "Oh, Gabe. No! You can't die! Please, don't leave me. Please!"

But he was already gone.

Still on his knees, Shannon set a hand on her shoulder as she wept over her husband. Nothing more, just that hand on her shoulder to let her know someone was there. I bit my bottom lip and clung to Jake for a long time until the first fingers of dawn began trickling through the hayloft door.

Life had changed irrevocably for all of us.

The next few hours were busy getting Marcie treated and onto the chopper, the bodies cleared away, and the last of the fire put out. Ethan had been wrong about the fire taking all of the compound. Under Scarlet's competent direction, the residents of the farm managed to save the other two houses and were already planning to rebuild the one they'd lost.

Another chopper was coming, and this one would carry Tawnia, Bret, Jake, and me back to Portland, where I'd been ordered by Shannon to check into a hospital. Later a bus would arrive at the farm for anyone else who wanted to leave.

Tawnia had fixed me a breakfast of bacon and eggs and milk, and I'd made her happy by eating all of it, even though the eggs were slightly burned.

Spring appeared in the kitchen, sliding into the seat next to me. "I came to say goodbye."

"Aren't you going back to Portland?" I was reduced to whispering now, and deep bruises were appearing on my throat.

She shook her head. "I've decided to stay, at least for now. Harmony needs help, and with Victoria leaving, Scarlet could use someone in the kitchen." She smiled and lowered her voice. "Besides, Harmony promised to pay an attorney to help me settle things with Jimmy."

"You sure?"

She hesitated. "I can't leave her. She's lost so much, and no one really understands what she's going through. Not really."

I knew what she meant. Harmony's soul had been entwined with that of her husband. Her terrible grief was etched on her face, aging it by ten years. Every trace of playfulness was gone. Even so, she had risen to the occasion, walking among her people, bestowing a touch, a kind word, letting them know the farm—their home—would go on for as long as they wanted.

"Harmony is renaming the place Harmony Farming Co-op," Spring said. "They'll need a nurse, and I've been thinking that as long as I can get my allergies under control, I might get some training and see what happens. I'm also going to talk to my mother. I'll keep in touch, though."

I blinked back tears. "You'd better." We hugged, careful of my ribs. Little Jim, ever in his mother's arms, gave my hair a parting yank.

As Spring left, Jake strode into the kitchen. He'd washed his face and his forehead had been bandaged. He needed a good shave, but he looked great. "The helicopter's here."

"Finally! I'll go get Bret." Tawnia disappeared into the hall.

"Do you want me to carry you?" Jake asked, helping me to my feet.

I'd been able to walk from the barn to the farm's van, but my injuries had been fresher and less painful then. Now every inch of me throbbed with hurt. If Scarlet hadn't wrapped a clean stretch of cloth around my chest, I would probably need a stretcher. "Might be a good idea."

His arms went around me, careful but sure, and it was worth admitting to the weakness to enjoy his closeness. Without thinking, I brought my good hand up and rubbed it over the roughness of his jaw.

"Autumn?" His voice was tight.

"I don't feel obligated," I whispered.

"Well, I don't feel anything for you that I feel for my sister." He shook his head. "That came out wrong. I mean—"

"Shut up and kiss me."

So he did.

Not long or with passion, which was good, because I was close to passing out. But I planned to demand better after I healed. Much better.

Meanwhile, I was going to ask Shannon about those taekwondo lessons. For next time. Somewhere out there more people needed my unique kind of help, and I would be ready.

TEYLA BRANTON has worked in publishing for over twenty years. She loves writing women's fiction and traveling, and she hopes to write and travel a lot more. As a mother of seven, it's not easy to find time to write, but the semi-ordered chaos gives her a constant source of writing material. She's been known to wear pajamas all day when working on a deadline, and is often distracted enough to burn dinner. (Okay, pretty much 90% of the time.) A sign on her office door reads: Danger. Enter at Your Own Risk. Writer at Work.

Under the name Teyla Branton, she writes urban fantasy, paranormal romance, and science fiction. She also writes romance, romantic suspense, and women's fiction under the name Rachel Branton. For more information or to sign up to hear about new releases, please visit www.TeylaBranton.com.

Made in the USA
Middletown, DE
24 August 2018